THE GOLDEN KEY

Adela had to save herself with the only weapon she had as prisoner of Marshal Yuan. That weapon was her own incredible beauty. Night after night she gave Yuan the pleasure he demanded, and now she was putting the final pieces of her survival plan in place with Chen, the young and handsome soldier who guarded her. He had become her golden key to fulfillment—and to escape.

And as Chen held her in his powerful arms, his hands and lips rousing her to wild hunger, his magnificent manhood satisfying her again and again, she knew she had never before experienced such ecstasy.

"You are the most beautiful woman I have ever been with, but you are as far above me as the sun and moon."

"Not so, Chen," she said. "I am flesh and blood, heart and tears, like a woman. And I would be *beneath* you in every way."

And in an instant he was ready again, thrusting in before she had caught her breath, driving her through the frontiers of passion. . . .

THE SCARLET PRINCESS

Romantic Reading from SIGNET

THE SCARLET PRINCESS

CHRISTOPHER NICOLE

A SIGNET BOOK

NEW AMERICAN LIBRARY

SIGNET TRADEMARK REG. U.S. PAT. OFF. AND FOREIGN COUNTRIES
REGISTERED TRADEMARK—MARCA REGISTRADA
HECHO EN CHICAGO, U.S.A.

SIGNET, SIGNET CLASSIC, MENTOR, PLUME MERIDIAN and NAL BOOKS are published by New American Library, 1633 Broadway, New York, New York 10019

First Printing, December 1984

1 2 3 4 5 6 7 8 9

PRINTED IN THE UNITED STATES OF AMERICA

CONTENTS

I

The Homecoming

1

The Train

"Adela," called Constance Wynne. "Do come and look. We can see China."

Adela Wynne obediently put down her book and left her deck chair to stand beside her foster mother at the rail. It wasn't just a matter of pleasing Constance, although this was important in view of everything that had happened; she was genuinely excited at the thought of seeing her home again after four years of such miserable exile.

And suddenly the sea before them was littered with islands. The SS *Mary Evans* had steamed past the rugged ten-thousand-foot-high mountains of Formosa two days previously, a sight to bring her passengers, sea-weary after having crossed the entire immensity of the Pacific Ocean, swarming on deck oohing and aahing. But Formosa, in this spring of 1911, was no longer Chinese; it had been appropriated sixteen years before by the Japanese as a result of their shattering victory in the war of 1895—the year after Adela had been born. She had not wanted to look at it.

After that the South China Sea had visibly shallowed, losing some of the bottomless intensity of the thousand-fathom depths over which the ship had sailed for six weeks, slowly changing from deep blue to green—but for more than another hundred miles there had been no land. Now it was there like a scattering of jewels flung carelessly across the calm horizon. But these too were no longer Chinese jewels. Hong Kong was firmly situated in the imperial crown of the new British king, George V.

Yet Hong Kong meant that China was indeed only a few miles farther on. For the first time Adela decided she could cease feeling angry at the seamen's strike in San Francisco that had forced them to embark upon a British ship and make this enormous detour to regain their Peking home. But then, in her heart, she had never truly regretted it. China, all China, even those parts *temporarily* alienated—she had no doubts that they would all be reunited eventually—was her home, and she did not know the South at all. This journey would help to remedy that.

So she smiled and said, "It really is quite beautiful, Mother."

And received a quick, almost suspicious glance in return. Because even after the intimacy of a six-week voyage together, Constance remained unsure of their true relationship, just as she had to be aware, Adela knew, of the grave mistake she had made in sending her adopted daughter away from her Chinese school to America at all, and certainly in sending her at so tender an age as twelve. Four years ago Constance, as she had told her, had been able to envisage nothing more important to a child, however mixed her heritage, than to grow up a proper American young lady. Now she was obviously becoming more and more aware that the little girl had changed into a most remarkably beautiful young woman, a superb example of Eurasian femininity at its best—and equally obviously she did not know what to do about it, or indeed, how long ago this had happened.

Adela knew her beauty; she could see it every time she looked into a mirror. Her face was a curious and delicious combination of the European and the Chinese, small, with pointed chin and tiny nose, high forehead and center-parted jet-black hair, but also with full red lips and only slightly almond eyes—while, wonder of wonders, her eyes were a splendid deep blue. They alone had been obviously inherited from her English mother, who had been plain Kate Mountjoy before she had been swept away by the glamour of the imperial Ch'ing. Adela's figure was still typically Oriental, for she was at once short, only an inch over five feet, and slender, and indeed seemed nonexistent when concealed beneath her European-style skirt and blouse, which she hated. But even her schoolgirl's outfit could not conceal the true crown of her beauty, the ever-present, almost indefinable arrogance that seeped through her every movement, every glance.

This awareness of her royal blood, her imperial heritage, was her proudest possession, even if she knew it had also been responsible for the disaster that had been school in Richmond. She supposed it might have been a disaster anyway, for Miss Evesham, who ran the Evesham Academy for Young Ladies, had obviously remembered Constance Drummond only too clearly. In the eyes of her contemporaries, Constance Drummond had married well, the famous missionary Henry Baird. Every other young woman in Richmond had been jealous of her, had wished her only misery in her tremendous good fortune. That her marriage should have failed had been reasonable and just; that she should have risen above that failure, and gone from strength to strength, was clearly inexcusable in Miss Evesham's opinion. Thus she had frowned at the definitely half-caste little girl and remarked, "And *this* is your daughter, Mrs. Wynne?"

Adela had bridled at the very tone, but Constance had patiently preferred to explain rather than take offense. "My *adopted* daughter, Miss Evesham. She is the child of my dearest friend, Kate Mountjoy, of whom you may have heard."

"The English lady who was murdered by the Boxers?" Miss Evesham had sniffed, as if to suggest that any white lady who got herself murdered by a Chinese mob had been no better than she should be.

"Yes," Constance had said, glancing anxiously at Adela. But the fact of her mother's ghastly death, any more than her father's suicide, had not then been a depressant; Adela could not remember what either of her parents looked like. Yet from that moment she had positively loathed Miss Evesham.

"Miss Mountjoy was the wife of a Manchu prince," Constance had gone on to explain, "who was Adela's father."

"And his name was?"

"Prince Ksian Fu."

"Ah." Miss Evesham had written busily. "Then the young lady's name is really Adela Fu. Or would you rather she was called Wynne-Fu?" She had actually smiled at her own joke.

Even Constance's determined good humor had shown signs of deteriorating at that; soon afterward she had left. But, with that unshakable determination that Adela knew had taken her to many triumphs, no matter how many heartaches she had also caused, she had not taken Adela with her.

And thus the disaster had commenced. The other young ladies at Miss Evesham's Academy, most of them daughters of the sons of ruined planters painfully regaining financial solvency fifty years after the war that had ended their dreams, had found it difficult to believe that a "colored" girl could actually be a princess, and more, claim to be a cousin of the ruling Manchu emperor, P'u-i, who reigned under the name of Hsuan T'ung; in introducing Adela to her classmates, Miss Evesham had felt called upon to explain that of course the emperor was only five years old, and was under the regency of his father, Prince Ch'un, as if this somehow alleviated the situation—Prince Ch'un was Adela's uncle.

But the girls had also found it impossible to resist the delights provided by someone named Fu—she was immediately nicknamed Foo-foo, which she loathed, as an insult to her imperial ancestors. Nor had they been able to resist the temptation of her hair, which, long and fine and black, brushed the backs of her knees, and cried out to be pulled or impregnated with any sticky substance that came to hand.

"Hair that length is absurd, of course," Miss Evesham had declared. "It must be cut immediately."

"Manchu princesses do not cut their hair, ever," Adela had explained as courteously as she could, but with the utmost firmness.

That had led to an acrimonious exchange of telegrams with Constance, but Adela had won her point, even if Miss Evesham had then set out to make her life as miserable as she could, and had encouraged her young ladies to do the same. Adela, conscious of her dignity, which required that, as a Ch'ing, she must always bear every cross without a murmur, had accepted her fate with perfect stoicism for very nearly four years. But the night her dormitory companions, rendered furious by an entertainment to which they, as the senior girls, had been permitted to attend, and at which the young men present had had eyes only for the lovely Mongol, had tied her to her bed by her hair, her anger had at last erupted, and when Miss Evesham, discovering a face missing at breakfast, had come to release her, informing her at the same time that the incident was clearly her own fault for possessing such hair in the first place, Adela had been unable to resist a temptation of her own, and had sunk her fine white teeth into Miss Evesham's hand with all the strength in her powerful little jaws.

A fresh exchange of telegrams had then produced this much-to-be-desired homeward voyage.

Yet she had been distressed to realize that Constance had seemed more disturbed, at least initially, by the fact that her foster daughter had been expelled from such a reputable ladies' school, than that she had acted as any red-blooded American girl might have done when faced with such provocation. The voyage had been very nearly half over before she had thawed in the slightest, and Adela was very anxious that the thawing process should continue. Rejected by her Manchu cousins, Constance was all she had. Besides, she genuinely loved the woman, and even more important, genuinely admired the way she had risen above the vicissitudes of her own life to her present eminence—at least in China. So she stood close to her foster mother and remarked, "I have always heard that South China is even more beautiful than the North. Do you think that can be true?"

"I believe it *is* far more beautiful," Constance agreed. "I can hardly wait to see it. But the people are different. Here they are nearly all Chinese. In Peking they are nearly all Mongols."

"And the Chinese hate us," Adela said, without thinking, and more with consideration than with regret or fear, as she stared down at the slowly greening water. "And will one day try to bring us down."

To her enormous pleasure, Constance put her arm around her shoulders and gave her a squeeze. "No one is going to bring you down, Dela," she said. "Not now, and not ever. Now, let's finish packing and get dressed. We'll be ashore in a couple of hours."

In a great many ways, Adela Wynne supposed, Hong Kong epitomized the history of China over the past half-century. Because now the ship was feeling its way past the Ninepin Islands to Tathong Point, and up the Tathong Channel to Cape Collinson, and then through the Leu U Mun into Kowloon Bay before the tugs came out to shepherd her alongside the docks in Victoria harbor. Hong Kong was a British colony, and therefore the Chinese and English names jostled together; farther north it would be possible to discover Chinese and French, or Chinese and German, or Chinese and Russian, similarly juxtaposed. The foreign devils had come sixty years ago, and despite all the obstacles placed in their way, the foreign devils had remained. That China officially preserved its independence, that the boy emperor remained on his throne, even three years after the death of the Dowager Empress Tz'u-Hsi, that vicious and terrifying old lady whose indomitable spirit had kept the Ch'ing great, and whose death had been regarded by most observers as the probable signal for a Chinese revolt against their Mongol overlords, was merely because the Chinese had remained overawed by the presence of so many foreign soldiers in their cities and foreign gunboats on the rivers, and because the Europeans had not yet been able to agree among themselves as to how this vast country, far larger than their entire continent, could be equitably carved up—as they had, for example, carved up Africa.

The Chinese, more so indeed than the Manchu, had always resented and resisted the outrage practiced upon them by the foreign devils. Only eleven years ago they had erupted into a paroxysm of hatred and violence

which they had supposed would finally destroy the
hated barbarians. Like all earlier such revolts, the
Boxers had been crushed, and for every white man or
woman murdered during those tumultuous days, a
hundred Chinese had found themselves dangling from
trees, having watched *their* wives violated and their
children turned out to starve. The Europeans might be
the most blatant of invaders, but they enjoyed the
happy belief that wherever they went and whatever they
did, they were carrying out God's will, and no
European, priest or soldier, doubted that a yellow
heathen who raised his hand to a white Christian was by
God's will worthy only of death. Adela could thank that
same God, and often did, that her own people, as she
regarded the Americans in equal proportion to the
Manchu, had taken no part in the despoliation of China
—yet the Americans had been as outraged as anyone at
the concept of armed Chinese resistance to white pene-
tration, and there had been an American contingent
with the multinational army which had machine-gunned
its way into Peking to loot the Forbidden City.

Constance, unlike Kate Mountjoy, had survived that
tragic period, and had in addition saved both her own
son and the infant daughter of her friend. She had also
survived the murder of her husband, to marry again, a
handsome young marine officer who had been among
that relieving army. Fortunately, Frank Wynne had
never truly had the heart of a soldier, and he was a
soldier no longer. Their decision to remain and live and
work in China had no doubt astonished many—all those
who could not understand feelings of guilt, a desire to
help a people who had been civilized when the Celts and
the Gauls had still been painting themselves blue. It was
a decision for which Adela was more grateful than she
could ever hope to express to them.

Yet she knew how difficult it must have been for her

foster mother to *make* such a decision. There could be no other white woman so widely known in China. It was not merely the fact that she had been a prisoner of the Boxers or that she had once been a friend of Tz'u-Hsi herself; it was because of her yellow hair—an imperial color and never to be worn by nonroyalty—which she still wore long and luxuriant, even in her fortieth year, allied to her determination and courage, which had led her time and again to challenge Chinese and Manchu absurdities, as she saw them. In fact, Adela guessed that her foster mother actually enjoyed her notoriety. Now, as they approached the shore, she could feel Constance bristling with anticipation, and with resolve always to *be* Constance Wynne, and Devil Woman, as she had once been called. So she dressed herself with great care in a pale green traveling costume with white collar and cuffs, its tunic neatly buttoned over her white lace blouse before descending to her knees, put on her fawn felt hat with its dark green-dyed ostrich plumes, and gathered her matching handbag and gloves. Beside her, Adela, in her white blouse and navy-blue skirt, her neat tie and her straw boater, felt positively dowdy, just as she felt utterly embarrassed as Constance instinctively took her place at the head of the line of passengers waiting to disembark. The SS *Mary Evans* actually carried only twenty passengers, with none of whom Adela had been allowed to become in the slightest degree friendly, even during six weeks of no alternative company. In Constance's opinion, casual acquaintances had always heard just enough about the Wynnes to make them unpleasantly inquisitive. Well, Adela supposed she was right. She gave a sigh of relief as she descended the gangplank to smile at the British immigration officer who waited beside the customs officials.

"Mrs. Constance Wynne," he remarked, and stamped their passports. "And Miss Adela Wynne.

Welcome to Hong Kong, Mrs. Wynne. Are you on a social visit, or is this business?"

"We are merely passing through," Constance told him. "We wish to go to Canton as quickly as possible, and take the train from there to Shanghai."

"The train?" He looked shocked. "My dear Mrs. Wynne, it would be quicker, and far more comfortable, to take a cabin on a coasting steamer. Believe me."

Constance gave him one of her colder smiles. "*We* wish to take the train."

He shrugged and returned her documents. "There is a daily ferry upriver, but it has already left. I'm afraid you will have to wait until tomorrow morning."

"That will be quite satisfactory, thank you," she said, "supposing we can find anywhere decent to stay," she remarked to Adela, and beckoned one of the waiting coolie porters, telling him in Chinese which were their boxes as they came off the ship. Her knowledge of Mandarin seemed to shock the officials even more. And Adela presumed she could just as well have spoken English. After more than half a century of British ownership, Hong Kong was hardly more Chinese, she supposed, than parts of San Francisco. It was in fact a singularly unattractive place, with narrow, noisome streets, crushed against the waterfront by the low hills which formed the center of the island, and teeming with life, both human and canine, spitting and smelling, gabbling and bargaining, urinating on the pavements. This last at least was Chinese.

"Perhaps I could be of assistance, Mrs. Wynne." The man was English, and quite young; despite his mustache, Adela doubted he was yet thirty. He was tall, perhaps a shade too thin, his narrow shoulders accentuated by the starched white suit which nearly all Englishmen seemed to wear in the tropics. His face was also gaunt, and the bristling little mustache suggested a bush growing out of a crevasse on a hillside. He was also very nervous, she observed from the sweat on his brow as he raised his topee. Of Constance? "My name is Osborne. James Osborne."

"My pleasure, Mr. Osborne," Constance said with obvious untruthfulness; she was looking at the notebook in Osborne's breast pocket and clearly realizing, with regret, that the news of their arrival had spread more quickly than she had anticipated. "Do you know of a reasonable hotel?"

He smiled, and gained considerably in attractiveness. "I know of *a* hotel, Mrs. Wynne. Shall I call a rickshaw?"

"Is it far?"

"A few hundred yards."

"Then we should prefer to walk, thank you."

He raised his eyebrows; walking was not a pastime indulged in by white ladies in the tropics, as a rule. Then he snapped his fingers, and addressed the waiting coolies in a remarkable language which Adela recognized as Pidgin English—perhaps every fourth word was identifiable *as* English, and a few others as derivations of the language. But the Chinese seemed to understand him well enough. "These fellows will see to your things."

"You haven't met my daughter, Adela," Constance said.

Adela allowed him one of her quick smiles, which she had observed in the past were very unsettling to strange men.

It certainly unsettled Mr. Osborne, whose nervousness appeared to grow. "The princess," he remarked.

Constance's face froze. "My *daughter,* Mr. Osborne," she reminded him. However much she and

Adela might share an awareness of the girl's heritage, she was determined the child should never be pilloried by inquisitive newspaper reporters.

"Of course, Mrs. Wynne. I do apologize." He walked beside them, Adela in the center. "It really is a tremendous pleasure having you in Hong Kong. But you're just passing through, I understand."

"We continue to Canton tomorrow."

"To take the train. May I ask why? Mr. Ollerearnshaw was quite right about its being more comfortable to travel by ship, you know."

"We do know, Mr. Osborne," Constance said. "We have just spent six weeks on one. But as we are in South China anyway, and for the first time in our lives, we wish to look at the country."

"Of course," he agreed again. "I . . . I saw you once before."

Constance's head turned sharply. She distrusted incarnations from her past.

"In Peking, in 1900. I was with the British relief contingent. I was a soldier then, not a reporter."

"Were you?" Now her tone was genuinely cold. Adela knew that Constance's memory of the British entry into the Forbidden City was of the empress's women being thrown to the ground and raped. As Constance had been with them, and dressed like them, she had only narrowly avoided a similar fate.

He flushed, as if able to read her thoughts. "But I chucked it after that. I'm a correspondent now. With the *Daily Mail.*"

A newspaper Adela had never heard of. Nor, she decided, had Constance. In Constance's eyes, that he was a correspondent at all, eager for a story or probably an interview, would be bad enough.

"This is the hotel." He held the gate for them, and they mounted broad, deep steps to a veranda off which jalousied doors led to a spacious, dark, polished interior. Immediately as they ascended above street level there was a whisper of breeze to dissipate the last of the odors, and inside the building there were slowly revolving ceiling fans—driven by electricity—and anxious Chinese footmen in white jackets with brass buttons, and a somewhat weather-beaten-looking English lady to survey them, and positively fawn when they were introduced.

"Mrs. Wynne," she cried. "Oh, dear, but this is an honor. You must sign the book, Mrs. Wynne. Oh, indeed. This *is* an honor. Harry, the front room. And for the young lady . . ."

"We'll share, thank you," Constance said. It was not merely a matter of wishing to keep Adela by her side. Frank Wynne's import-export business, like all businesses in a financially depressed world, was not making a lot of profit at the moment.

"Of course, Mrs. Wynne. Of course. Harry . . ." She gave a stream of instructions in Pidgin English, while James Osborne twisted his topee in his hands.

"Perhaps you would do me the honor of having a drink with me this evening, Mrs. Wynne? This hotel has a very popular bar."

He was looking at *her,* Adela realized to her embarrassment; because it was obviously to Constance's annoyance—Constance was not used to men looking at other women when in her presence. But then Constance obviously reflected that he *had* found them somewhere acceptable to sleep. "We will look forward to that, Mr. Osborne," she said. "Six o'clock."

Adela soaked in the tin tub as luxuriously as she could; there was not a lot of room, even for someone as diminutive as herself. And the water, having been enjoyed by Constance first, was no longer very warm.

But it was refreshing, and there were no dead nits floating in it, which was a relief. Just as it was a relief not to be assisted by any Chinese maid—that had been something Adela had been dreading. During the four years she had spent in Richmond, she had, despite having to share a dormitory with several other girls—or perhaps because of it—become a very private person. She did not like to be touched, not even by her foster brother, Charlie, who was very special to her.

Which was why, she realized, she felt strangely out of sorts, whereas she should have known nothing but happiness at being almost back in her beloved China: Mr. Osborne's gaze had had an almost physical quality, as if he *had* been touching her rather than looking at her. She had never been looked at like that before in her life. And she was not sure she liked it.

Adela indeed sometimes found it hard to accept that she was now actually an adult woman, despite the long slender legs, the rosebud breasts, or the gentle wisps of silky pubic hair that proved this to be a fact. She did not suppose anyone could really be considered a woman until she had the large breasts and height of Constance, who was, as usual, dressing herself with great care in front of the wall mirror. It really was quite ridiculous that anyone should wish to look at *her*, when there was Constance to be admired. A fact which had certainly not escaped her foster mother, either.

Adela sighed, and soaped herself thoughtfully and sensually. She knew so little about Constance and her history—and therefore about herself, really. Constance seldom talked about the past, gave the impression that she found it difficult to believe that some of the adventures attributed to her had actually happened. She *would* talk about Adela's real mother, Kate Mountjoy, telling her what a lively and vivacious and charming person she had been—which aroused a certain suspicion in Adela's mind, as she did not consider herself to be either lively or vivacious, or especially charming; these were not words one associated with a Manchu princess. But Constance would not talk about Prince Ksian Fu at all. Adela knew the facts, of course. Her father, sent abroad by his imperial aunt, Tz'u-Hsi, at an early age as an ambassador, because of his good looks and his intelligence, had succumbed so utterly to Western manners and mores that he had become a Christian. This had been bad enough in the eyes of the old Dragon Lady, as Tz'u-Hsi had been nicknamed— with good reason—but in addition, upon returning to China, he had promptly fallen in love with the daughter of an English missionary, and instead of merely taking her as a concubine, whatever the objections of herself or her parents, as Manchu custom as well as common sense should have dictated, had married her—in a Christian ceremony. Ksian Fu had been too brilliant a man and too important a personage to be banished to the ends of the earth. Instead the empress had banished him to Mongolia, to the city of Port Arthur as viceroy, ignoring the fact that as the continuing quarrel between the waning Dragon Empire to the west and the waxing Japanese Empire to the east had increased to the stage where war had been inevitable, Port Arthur, with its magnificent ice-free harbor, would be at the very center of the coming storm. Or understanding that too well. In either event, she had starved her recalcitrant nephew of the men and munitions needed to defend the fortress, and when the Japanese had come storming down the Liaotung Peninsula, sweeping aside such feeble Chinese resistance as they encountered, Ksian Fu had been unable to do anything more than resort to the time-honored recourse of his class and his people, and blow out his brains.

Constance held that in so doing he had been betraying

his defeated army, his post, his wife and daughter, as well as his religion. But Constance was also a Christian. So of course was Adela, but she had always been prepared to reconcile her Christianity to the Confucian concept of duty and honor. Constance, for all her own determined individuality, did not seem to understand that there was nothing else a Manchu prince could have done, following so complete a defeat.

This conflict between Chinese and Christian ethics was always confusing, and sometimes even frightening, because of the problems it created within her as she recognized the vast difference between her intentions and her instincts. She wanted to be as American as Constance wanted her to be, and yet, when faced with a crisis, she invariably reacted as a Manchu would do, and more, as a Manchu princess. And she felt the conflict within herself was only increasing as she grew older—and would come to a head very shortly, with the question of marriage.

In fact, Adela had already come to the conclusion that there was only one man in all the world she could possibly marry—her own foster brother, Charles Baird. This was not something she had ever mentioned to Constance, much less to Charlie himself. But there was simply nobody else. As a Manchu, she could not marry a Chinese—this was against Manchu law. As a princess, she could not marry a Manchu either, because she could not marry a commoner of her own people, and all the princes were her cousins. Constance had always indicated that she had no doubt her foster daughter would marry an American, but Constance had not been thinking of her own son. She regarded Charlie and Adela as brother and sister, and the idea would be abhorrent to her. Constance was obviously thinking of some man, hopefully wealthy, who would remove Adela from China forever.

But leaving China was unthinkable. Four years had been bad enough. If she had to marry an American—and she was not going to argue with that—it could only be an American who loved China as much as she did, and would wish to spend the rest of his life there. Only Charlie, so far as she knew, fulfilled that requirement. And he filled so many other requirements as well. He was three years older than she, and still at college, but he would be finished there in another year. Over the past four years they had spent the vacations together, living with Constance's widowed mother outside Richmond, riding and fishing, and just enjoying each other's company, as brother and sister. But Charlie was also growing into a very handsome man, as handsome as his famous father had reputedly been, but without any of the doubts that had apparently ruined Henry Baird's marriage.

So Charlie it had to be, even if that had to remain her secret for the time being. Had she *not* been Ksian Fu's daughter, but instead belonged to the family of some Manchu bannerman, there could be no doubt, with her looks, of which she was well aware, that a eunuch would by now have already called upon her father's house and taken her secretly into the Forbidden City to grace the emperor's bed, or at least his uncle's bed. That was how Tz'u-Hsi had begun, and Tz'u-Hsi had finished up ruling the entire empire. Adela did not doubt she was as intelligent and strong-willed and, if necessary, as ruthless as Tz'u-Hsi had ever been.

Or that someone like her was desperately needed to restore the fortunes of the tottering dynasty.

But those were dreams. As a princess born she was the most useless creature on earth. Her fortune was that her imperial relatives had followed the examples of the Dragon Lady and cast her out to be brought up by Constance Wynne.

To make whatever she could of the uncertainties of life.

"I am sure you will catch cold if you remain any longer in that bath," Constance remarked. "Besides, Mr. Osborne will be waiting for us."

Some twenty Englishmen and their wives were already gathered in the hotel lounge, sipping aperitifs, and that everyone knew who Constance and Adela were became obvious from the way all conversation stopped at their entry.

James Osborne immediately detached himself from the group with whom he had been sitting and hurried toward them. "Mrs. Wynne. Adela. I hope the rooms are all right?"

"The room is perfectly adequate, Mr. Osborne," Constance acknowledged.

"There are some people over here who are longing to meet you."

"Thank you, Mr. Osborne, but no," she decided. "We are both a little tired, and we have a long journey in front of us. We really do not intend to stay down very long."

"Ah." He looked intensely disappointed, and she took pity on him.

"But you may interview me, if you wish."

"Oh!" He blushed. "How did you know?"

"I really couldn't suppose you spend your time rescuing damsels in distress. Especially as we weren't actually *in* distress."

"Ah." The directness which had set the European community in Peking by the ears, and so grievously upset Constance's first husband, apparently, was upsetting Mr. Osborne as well. "A drink?"

"Thank you." Constance selected the vacant table

farthest from the bar. "I will have a whiskey and soda, please. Adela will have a lemonade."

"Of course." He bustled off, pausing to mutter apologetically to the people he had been sitting with.

"Mother," Adela said severely. "You are being quite beastly to that poor man."

"I think I am being remarkably generous," Constance said, "seeing that he admits to having taken part in the sack of Peking." Then she smiled and squeezed the girl's hand. "You're right, of course. The boy was only obeying orders. But I get so *tired* of people wishing to pry into our lives, Dela. Why us? As for showing us off to his friends like a couple of prize chimpanzees . . ."

"Because I am a princess," Adela said composedly. "And because we were prisoners of the Boxers."

"They treated us very well," Constance reminded her.

"But no one will ever believe that," Adela said, and turned her smile on Mr. Osborne and the accompanying Chinese waiter who placed their drinks before them. "I do . . . ah . . . hope I'm not intruding."

"Of course you are, Mr. Osborne," Constance said. "My daughter and I are traveling as private persons. As indeed we *are* private persons. We find it difficult to understand why we should be of interest to anyone."

"Ah . . ." Osborne touched his breast pocket, hesitated.

"By all means make notes if you wish," Constance invited.

Immediately the notebook was on his knee. "You see, Mrs. Wynne, you *are* of interest, to everybody. I mean, foster mother to a princess . . ." He gave one of his nervous glances at Adela. "And then, what a princess. I

mean, a Ch'ing . . . actually living outside of the Forbidden City . . .''

Constance was staring at him with arched brows. And
even Adela was totally surprised. She could remember,
when last she had traveled with Constance, four years
ago, reporters asking prying questions about what it had
been like to be a prisoner of the Boxers, implying everything from rape to unthinkable sexual mistreatment as
they did so. Never before had anyone shown any
interest in *her,* save as a child who had survived such
misfortune.

Osborne appeared to realize he had said something
wrong, without understanding what it might be. "I . . .
ah . . . I do assure you that my readers are interested in
anything to do with royalty, Mrs. Wynne,'' he said.
"Especially . . . well . . .'' Constance's face was not
relaxing. "May I ask where you have just come from?''

"The United States, Mr. Osborne,'' Constance said
grimly. "My home. I have been visiting my mother and
my son, Charles, who is at college there. He is nineteen.
I am speaking of Richmond, Virginia.''

"Of course. And . . .'' He looked at Adela.

"Oh, indeed, Mr. Osborne. Adela has just completed
school and is returning home for a holiday before we
decide on a suitable career.'' Constance avoided
meeting Adela's eye, as this remained a sore point
between them—Adela did not wish a career. She merely
intended to get married the moment Charlie had
completed college.

"Yes, of course. Mrs. Wynne . . . do you think I
could have a photograph?''

"I'm afraid I don't travel with one, Mr. Osborne.''

"Oh, I have all the equipment, Mrs. Wynne. I could
take it tomorrow morning, before you leave.''

"You intend to publish a photograph of me in your
newspaper?''

"Ah . . ." Osborne licked his lips. "Of . . . of you both, of course. It would go so well with the article."

What article? Adela wondered. Was he planning to write an article about her? And how could he, when he hadn't actually asked any questions? Of her, anyway.

But Constance had obviously decided that her photograph in an English newspaper might even be worth sharing with her foster daughter. "Why, if it is so important to you, Mr. Osborne," she said, "you may have your photograph. But it will have to be done early. I gather the ferry leaves at eight."

James Osborne actually took three photographs, two of Constance herself, and one of her and Adela. His paraphernalia, as much as the little explosions which accompanied every snapping of the shutter, fascinated the Chinese and drew a large crowd, which duly followed them to the dock where the ferry steamer was waiting, funnels puffing vigorously and depositing black soot over everything. Osborne assisted them on board with their boxes, and then brought on a small suitcase of his own. "I hope you don't mind," he apologized. "But I have been to Canton only once or twice." He flushed as Constance gazed at him. "Besides, two white ladies traveling alone through China . . ."

"Oh, come now, Mr. Osborne. Surely at least fifty Europeans travel by the train north from Canton every day. The China I . . . we knew, a dozen years ago, is gone forever. They understand only too well what assaults upon Europeans can cost."

"Well . . . actually, Mrs. Wynne, this could be something of a scoop for me." His flush deepened. "Actually to spend a day in the company of a Ch'ing princess . . . and you, of course, talking, and . . . well . . ."

"Mr. Osborne," Constance said, obviously regretting having agreed to the photographs, "you are spending no more time in our company at all. I assure you that Adela has *no* desire to have her privacy destroyed for the sake of some sensation-seeking English newspaper."

She removed herself and Adela to the far side of the little steamer's deck.

"I think he's soft on you," Adela said. She didn't really, but she wanted to hear what Constance thought of it all.

"Soft? Where *do* you pick up such peculiar expressions? Anyway, he is just a child. But I can tell you this, he has designs on *you.*"

"Do you think so?" Adela cried in delight. She had no desire ever to come within touching distance of James Osborne, but to have him keen on her, so keen that even Constance could see it . . .

"It is as plain as a pikestaff," Constance declared. "Newspaper article indeed. And I let him take a photograph of you. Well . . ." She squeezed the girl's hand. "We shall not even speak with him again. That's certain."

Adela sighed, because she had never actually met a man who might desire her before; the boys she had occasionally been allowed to dance with at very carefully chaperoned tea dances in Richmond had been exactly that—boys. And Charlie had not yet seemed to realize that they were obviously made for each other, although of course he would, as soon as he finished his studies; she intended to see to that. But until then . . . James Osborne was really quite an attractive man, even if his gaze did give her goose pimples. But she knew too well that once Constance made up her mind about anything, that was that. So Mr. Osborne would have to be forgotten. As he soon was in any event, as she became absorbed in the magnificence of the scenery as the ferry chugged its way up the estuary, through a perfect myriad of small islands, green and glowing in the morning sun, before it entered the Pearl River, while that afternoon, as the sun began to droop toward the west, they came upon Canton itself, huge and sprawling, the metropolis of the South, a city which revealed the true torment of modern China, as the twin spires of the French Roman Catholic cathedral, the most imposing structure to be seen, loomed above the teeming boat life of the waterfront, a city within a city, where the Chinese coolies, too poor to afford any dry land of their own, lived and spawned and died on their little sampans, the stench of their self-contained cesspool drifting across the evening air.

After the neatness and cleanliness and comparative affluence of American life, this first view of the teeming poverty which held so much of China in its grip was a disagreeable reminder that however much she loved this land, there was a very great deal wrong with it. The lot of the common Chinese was something about which no one had ever been able to do anything, certainly not those illustrious ancestors of hers who had ruled this land for two hundred and fifty years from the opulent splendor of the Forbidden City. It was all explained, she knew, by Destiny, that mysterious natural force which decreed that one man or woman would be born a peasant, and another a princess. But even more, which dictated the major events of each life as it came along, so that, unless Destiny had so decided it, it was useless for a pauper to attempt to better himself, just as, while she was prepared to dream and even make plans, she knew her future was entirely in the hands of some predecided series of events, which had to be accepted and made the most of as they happened. This was not, of course, a point of view held by Constance, as it did not exactly coincide with Christianity, and thus was an outlook Adela preferred to keep to herself. And yet, she thought, even Constance would have a difficult time explaining how she had survived so much, whereas others . . .

As they left the ferry, they both checked to give hasty glances at the wooden cage on the street by the dock, in which a stinking bag of bones and rotting clothes who was yet a man stood on tiptoe, his head protruding through the bars roofing the cage, and exposed his swollen, purple, moistureless tongue in agony. Whenever his feet gave way, he strangled. And soon enough his feet would no longer support him at all.

The sight made Adela's stomach turn, and yet it was common enough in China, where criminals not only were punished but also were seen to be punished and made to understand that they *were* being punished. And for a man to be condemned to such a slow and horrible death undoubtedly meant that his crime had been no less ghastly, probably armed robbery along with murder or at least rape. And yet . . . he was there, and she was here.

As was Constance . . . and Mr. Osborne.

In Canton the hotel was Chinese-owned and -managed, far more magnificent in appearance than the hostelry in Hong Kong, but far less clean; Adela spent the first fifteen minutes in her bedroom destroying cockroaches with the heel of her shoes, and before they could descend to dinner it was necessary for them to explore each other's hair to eliminate any nits which might have already sought a home—again aspects of Chinese life she had all but forgotten in Miss Evesham's house. While the dining room—there was no lounge— was filled with Mandarin-class Chinese, an entirely male gathering, proudly wearing their buttons of office, from the ruby of the first class to the worked silver of the ninth, conversing gravely as they sipped their jasmine tea, and giving long if surreptitious stares at the white woman and her daughter. Adela wondered if they would wish to kowtow to her, could they know who she was.

James Osborne sat by himself in a corner, drinking sake. "At least say hello to him, Mother, please," Adela begged.

Constance nodded in his direction, and concentrated upon her meal, seating Adela so that her back was to the Englishman. They had reached the stewed ginger when they were approached by the hotel proprietor, arms folded into the sleeves of his magnificent red silk blouse, bowing so low that his pigtail, which denoted a subject Chinese as opposed to a ruling Manchu, flopped over his shoulder. "I am Wang Mang," he said. "My humble establishment is honored, famous Mrs. Wynne. My son tells me you wish train tickets to Shanghai."

"That is correct, Mr. Wang," Constance said, smiling for the first time since Osborne had offended her.

"It is a long journey. Several days."

"So we will require a private compartment."

"Of course. It will be arranged. You will also need food. My cooks will prepare a hamper. A large hamper." He glanced at Adela with narrowed eyes. As he knew who Constance was, presumably he was working out who she had to be, or certainly that she had Manchu blood—here in the South the conquerors, even after two hundred and fifty years, remained simply conquerors, whereas in the North, even if intermarriage was forbidden and Manchus were not allowed to enter business or do any menial work, the two nations managed to live in reasonable harmony; she could feel his hatred enveloping her, and wanted to shiver. "For you and . . . the young lady," he said.

Adela refused to lower her gaze. "That would be very kind of you," she said.

"The train leaves at nine in the morning," the hotelier said, and bowed again. "It has been a great honor, famous Mrs. Wynne."

"What a nice man," Constance remarked, but frowned as she saw Osborne get up to talk with Wang. "Oh, really, that would be too much." She got up in turn, crossed the floor. "Mr. Osborne, you cannot seriously be meaning to travel to Shanghai?"

"I have never been there," he confessed. But he was flushing again.

"Do you know, I believe I could have you arrested for molestation or some such thing."

"But I am sure you will not."

She glared at him in baffled anger. "I am certainly not going to speak with you again. And if you attempt to take any more photographs . . ."

"I would not dream of it. However, if I can be of any assistance at any time . . ."

"Mr. Osborne," Constance said, "if you address me again, I am going to slap your face." She marched back to Adela. "We'll retire now. I think an early night is indicated."

"Is he really coming with us?"

"No," Constance said with determination. "But he is traveling on the same train. I hope *he* remembers to take some food." She realized the Chinese in the room were all listening to the altercation, and one or two were sure to understand English. "Oh, damnation." She held Adela's hand. "Come along."

They swept into the corridor, discovered Wang deep

in conversation with another Chinese man, whose face was half-lost in the shadows by the stairs. But they had been talking about them; before either of the men realized they could be overheard, Adela heard Wang say, "The daughter of Prince Ksian Fu. There can be no doubt of it."

Now he was bowing again, while the other man hastily sidled through the doorway. "Who was that?" Constance demanded. She had also overheard.

"Ah . . . my servant, Mrs. Wynne."

"What were you telling him about us?"

"Ah . . . that he must be sure to secure the very best private compartment on the train, Mrs. Wynne."

But he was obviously lying.

What *was* the fellow up to? Or was he up to anything? For the first time Constance wondered if she *was* taking a risk. The thought had simply not entered her mind before. Because everything she had told Osborne was true. The train from Canton to Shanghai was used regularly and consistently, according to her information, by Europeans, as it was engineered by Europeans and managed by them; railway building and operating, with the vast profits to be thereby obtained, had been among the main concessions wrung from the Manchus following the defeat of the Boxers. Just as it was also true that there could not be a Chinese or a Manchu in Eastern China who had not seen at first hand what the vengeance of the white people could accomplish. She had now lived in China for twenty years, and the last eleven had been spent in Peking, where there was at least as great a chance of meeting some demented fanatic as in Canton, and far more chance than on a European train, and she had spent those eleven years in total security, because her skin was white.

She had allowed that silly young man to upset her.

Well, that was absurd and would not happen again; she could only hope he had not equally upset Adela. And the next morning her fears seemed totally pointless, for all that it was pouring with rain, a heavy downpour which, as there was no wind to disperse the clouds, seemed likely to last forever.

"My humble establishment weeps at your departure, famous Mrs. Wynne," Wang Mang said, kissing her hand. "The heavens themselves weep at your departure. Will you not return again to see us?"

"Why, of course we shall, Mr. Wang," she promised. "But I can't say when. Is that our hamper?" She surveyed the enormous wicker basket with some concern; it looked frightfully expensive. "You will have to tell me what I owe you."

"Not a single string of cash, famous Mrs. Wynne," Wang said. "The hamper is given to you with the compliments of my staff and myself."

"Oh, really, Mr. Wang, I couldn't possibly . . ."

"Go, and prosper, famous Mrs. Wynne," Wang commanded. "And you also, Miss Princess. Your fortune is written in the stars, and can never fail."

"He *did* know who I was," Adela whispered as they splashed through the streets in their double rickshaw, watching the rain bouncing off the heads of the men drawing them, and getting increasingly damp themselves as the canvas hood flapped and allowed the rain to drip inside.

"I'm afraid everyone does that," Constance said sadly. "The sooner you are permanently in America, the better."

"But I am going to stay in China," Adela said, her face becoming set in firm lines.

"That is something we shall have to discuss with your father," Constance said equally firmly, if dishonestly—

Adela was well aware that her foster mother intended to make the final decision herself, confident that Frank Wynne would agree with her.

But then, *she* intended that the decision would be *hers*. And Charlie's, of course.

The train, or at least the first-class carriage, was remarkably neat and clean. The first-class conductor was a Chinese named Ting, who was inordinately proud of his position, no less than of the blue European-style jacket and trousers, and even more, the peaked cap, which composed his uniform. "You be comfortable in here," he announced, showing them how the settees converted into berths—the carriage was an American-made Pullman—and how to use the washbasin, and assuring them that they had but to ring if they needed fresh water for either drinking or tea. The toilet was just along the corridor, a place which immediately reduced Adela to helpless laughter, because the instructions were printed in both English and Chinese, and then, to aid the illiterate, were illustrated with line drawings.

"I'm sure we *will* be very comfortable," Constance agreed, and gave him an American silver dollar—worth its weight in gold to the average Chinese—as a tip. "Can you tell me if a Mr. Osborne is also traveling?"

"Oh, yes, Mrs. Wynne. He has the compartment next to you."

"Oh," Constance said, and drew the corridor blinds as she closed the door, before joining Adela at the window to watch the teeming thousands on the platform, many jostling for their places in the third-class carriages, where they would sit crammed six to a five-foot-long wooden board, without food or water save what they could carry in their arms, for the duration of the journey.

"Do you think," Adela asked, "that China will ever be like America?" She had been enormously impressed with American railways.

"One day, I should think, but not until . . ." Constance changed her mind about what she would say.

Uselessly. Adela knew her points of view too well. "Not until they expel the Manchus," she said. "And make themselves into a republic."

"Well," Constance said, defensively, "you have to admit that being a republic works for America. And that over the past hundred years or so your family has been a continuing disaster for China."

"That's not true," Adela shouted in sudden anger. "The Ch'ing conquered China and made it great. It is only since the Europeans came with their opium and their machine guns that we have had disaster."

"My dear girl," Constance protested, "I didn't mean to upset you. I'm sure you're right. But—"

"One day the Chinese *will* drive the Ch'ing out," Adela said in a lower tone. "I know they will." She gazed at Constance, and Constance saw there were tears in her eyes. She had not before seen quite such a display of emotion on the girl's part, about her family and heritage, and possible future. For the second time she wondered if visiting Canton might not have been a mistake, even as she realized her foster daughter had grown up more than just physically during her years in the United States.

But Adela was already smiling through her tears. "I don't mind being driven out," she said. "Not if it would be best for China. I don't mind all the Ch'ing being driven out. But, Mother, I don't want their heads to be cut off. I should hate that."

Constance sat beside her to hold her in her arms. "Nobody is going to cut *your* head off, my darling," she promised. "Not ever."

But cutting off heads of the vanquished was a Chinese pastime, and regardless of age or sex. So that is why, my dear sweet child, she thought, you *cannot* plan to live the rest of your life here. No matter how much you want to.

It was not in Constance's nature to remain angry with anyone for very long. When, just after they had eaten their luncheon, discovering that the hamper was packed with the most exquisite delicacies, and sufficient for a dozen of them for a week—supposing the food would keep that long—there was a knock on the door and Mr. Osborne looked in, she smiled at him without thinking.

"I have a bottle of champagne here," he said. "It's not very cold, I'm afraid."

"Why, Mr. Osborne," she said. "What are we about to toast?"

"Well . . . the journey." He gestured out the window. "China." The railway to Shanghai, unable to take a direct route because of the massive Wu-Ishan Mountains which lay between the two cities, began by following the valley of the Peh-Chiang River almost due north, for Shao-Kuan and Heng-Yang, some two hundred miles and a full day's journey away, before it would turn back to the east. Now they passed through level country, a mass of flooded rice paddies, into which the steady drizzle splashed endlessly, and in which the women, wearing the age-old Chinese flat hats to shelter themselves from the weather, and with their trouser legs rolled up to their thighs, waded as they sought the precious grains which were the wealth of South China. But already in the distance they could see the mountains of the Ta Shan to indicate that the scenery was soon going to change dramatically.

"Well," Constance said, "I'll drink to that."

Adela was really not in the mood for champagne. And besides: *"I'm* going to explore."

"Oh," Constance said. "Well, please do not leave the carriage."

She had expected, and half-hoped, that Mr. Osborne might offer to accompany her, but he did not, and so she merely stood in the corridor, just down from the compartment, and gazed out of the window. As she had left the door slightly open, she could hear almost everything they were saying. She knew eavesdropping was not exactly proper, but she had no doubt at all they were going to talk about her, and she did want to know if Mr. Osborne really liked her or not.

"Will she be all right?" he asked.

"I should think so," Constance said.

Adela listened to the cork popping. "You are a very confident woman, Mrs. Wynne."

"Perhaps I've just lived too long."

"You are an immortal." He sat beside her, touched his glass against hers. "I would like to apologize for my gaucheness these last couple of days. I . . . well, I suppose having you arrive in Hong Kong was about the biggest thing that has happened there recently."

"Oh, really, Mr. Osborne . . ."

"Fact. May I ask a question? Out of curiosity," he added hastily. "I haven't brought my notebook."

Adela could tell from Constance's tone that she was smiling; presumably it was the champagne, although Osborne could obviously charm a blind hermit. "Then ask whatever you wish," she said.

"The girl. Adela. She is a Manchu princess, yet she lives with you, as your daughter, here in China. I find that difficult to understand."

"It isn't really. Manchu princesses are two a penny. Once they were of *some* value, for marrying off to turbulent border princes, to buy peace for the empire.

Now, to their families, they are the most useless things on the face of the earth. They cannot marry Chinese, by law, they cannot marry inferiors of their own people, and they cannot marry or become concubines to their own cousins and brothers, so they just exist, hidden away in the Forbidden City. There is a whole legion of them, spinsters all, every age from a few months to ninety, extra mouths to be fed, extra extravagances to be catered for. Fortunately, in Adela's case, the dowager empress fell out with her nephew, Prince Ksian Fu, and she did not approve his marriage to a European, either. She refused to recognize the child at all. This suited me admirably, after Kate's death, and I became responsible for Adela. I hope to be able to allow her to live a normal life."

"And marry an inferior?"

"Whoever Adela marries, Mr. Osborne, is going to be her inferior. But I would hope to see her married to an American when she is a little older. Then perhaps we shall all leave China."

"Yet you are happy to live here now?"

"We love China, Mr. Osborne. Do you find that so difficult to understand? And Adela is not yet seventeen. There is time."

"Time," he remarked. "There is never sufficient time, Mrs. Wynne."

"Just what do you mean by that?"

"Have you any idea just how much the Manchu are hated by the Chinese?"

"Probably more than you, Mr. Osborne. And hated more than ever since they attempted to use the Boxers to get rid of us foreign devils, and then repudiated the movement when it was discovered it was not going to succeed."

"And that does not bother you?"

The smile was back in her voice. "The Chinese have

always hated their conquerors, Mr. Osborne. In most cases they have managed to assimilate them. The Manchu have always resisted assimilation, by such methods as forbidding intermarriage, making the Chinese wear the pigtail, and things like that. Which makes them even more hated. On the other hand, history tells us that there is an eruption of Chinese anger and misery roughly once in every second generation. The last took place in 1900. By the time the Chinese now living have forgotten what happened to them eleven years ago, and a new generation, prepared to risk it all happening again, has been born and grown to manhood, *we* shall all be dead. That is what I meant by having time.''

"Don't you believe it," he argued. "Things are changing. Since the Japanese beat the Russians in 1905, all the East is changing. The Chinese are wondering why they might not do as well as the Japanese, given modern weapons.''

Adela frowned at the window. She had always supposed that the unexpected ease with which the Japanese army and navy had overwhelmed the creaking might of Russia would have made the Chinese more afraid of the rising power to their east than encouraged them to emulate it; she *knew* this was the case with the dynasty.

"Those were exceptional circumstances," Constance said.

"Maybe," Osborne agreed. "But to the average Chinese coolie, only the fact remains. Russia tried to show the Japanese who was the boss, and the Japanese up and gave the Bear a very bloody nose." There was a clink as he refilled their glasses. "I didn't mean to upset you, Mrs. Wynne. No matter which of us is right, the Chinese are going to have to become a nation in arms, like the Japanese, before *they* are going to give anyone a bloody nose. And that is certainly going to take a long time."

Adela would never have supposed that Mr. Osborne would be capable of thinking so deeply about China and the Chinese. She would not have supposed he could be that interested. But certainly he had put forward points of view *she* had not previously considered. Disturbing points of view which kept her awake that night as the train continued to rumble on its way through the rain, and as Constance breathed slowly and regularly on the bunk bed across the compartment. She had not, of course, been able to discuss the reporter's ideas with Constance, as that would have meant admitting she had been listening. But she hoped to be able to bring up the subject soon enough. Because Mr. Osborne had almost seemed to be suggesting that he *knew* there was another revolt of some sort in the making, a revolt which would once again tax the dynasty, perhaps even bring it down.

That was an unthinkable thought. And surely a revolution was not possible as long as British gunboats patrolled the rivers, and each main city in the East contained a sizable contingent of European troops. Osborne was an alarmist, she thought, drowsily deciding that she did not like him after all. Just as he would clearly prefer to sit and talk politics with Constance than go for a walk with her.

She slept uneasily, awoke with a start as the train suddenly jolted to a halt. She sat up, listened to Constance move. "Mother? What *can* have happened?"

"There must be something on the line," Constance said. "It'll mean a delay for a couple of hours, probably. Go back to sleep."

But immediately there came a rapping on the door. Now Constance sat up in turn. "Who is it?"

"James Osborne, Mrs. Wynne. Are you all right?"

"Of course we are all right, Mr. Osborne."

"The train has stopped."

Constance sighed. "I know that, Mr. Osborne. These trains often do. Cattle wander across the line."

"I do think I should stay with you until we start moving again. This is wild country. I have a revolver, Mrs. Wynne."

"Oh, for God's sake," Constance snapped.

"He sounds really scared," Adela whispered. "Let him in, Mother." She rather looked forward to getting some of her own back for the way he had tried to scare them.

"Oh . . . wait a moment," Constance called. She got out of bed, put on her dressing gown and slippers, found the matches, and lit the oil lamp set on its bracket on the wall above her head. "Put something on," she told Adela.

Adela hastily pulled her dressing gown over her nightdress while Constance unlocked the door. "Really, Mr. Osborne," she said. "If you are going to rush in here to protect us every time the train stops, you may as well have Ting make up a bed for you. Where is Ting, anyway?"

Osborne had donned a topcoat over his pajamas; one side of the garment sagged beneath the weight of the revolver in his pocket. He looked excited, but not actually afraid. "I have no idea where he is," he said. "I went looking for him just now, to find out why we'd stopped, but I couldn't find him. I can tell you this, though: this train is surrounded by a large number of extremely unpleasant-looking fellows."

Adela frowned at him, her stomach doing a sudden somersault. There was a good deal of noise in the corridor now, as the other first-class passengers, nearly all Europeans, although there were no other English or

Americans, opened their doors and began shouting at each other in a variety of languages. Instinctively she turned to the window and released the blind, found herself staring at a Chinese man. He was dressed like any coolie she had ever seen, and wore a flat hat—but he carried a rifle and had a bandolier slung over his shoulder. There was also something else unusual about him, but for the moment she couldn't decide what it was. His expression as he stared back at her was sufficiently disturbing. Hastily she pulled the blind down again. "There's a man," she remarked, keeping her voice as even as she could. "Looking at us."

"For heaven's sake!" Constance reached for the blind, and was checked by Osborne's hand on her arm.

"Leave it, Mrs. Wynne."

She frowned at him, then turned back to Adela. "What sort of a man?"

"A Chinese man," Adela said, quite unable to keep the quaver out of her voice this time. "Standing there."

"He would have had to be on a horse, to look in the window," Constance decided; she had a tendency to fasten on detail in a crisis.

Osborne was locking the corridor door. "Maybe we should just turn down the lamp," he suggested. "And wait."

"Really, Mr. Osborne," Constance protested. "I am sure there is some perfectly rational reason for what is hap—" She gazed at the door, mouth open as the high-pitched conversation from outside changed into smothered screams and exclamations of alarm, and they listened to the thudding of boots on the floor. She stood up and put her arm around Adela's shoulders; the girl had also risen. Osborne drew his revolver as they all faced the door, which a moment later hurtled inward as someone put his shoulder to it, scattering glass over the floor. Constance choked a scream, and Osborne leveled the gun. "Stop right there," he shouted. "Or I'll shoot."

Adela stared past him at the men, six of them, like the man at the window dressed as coolies, but even better armed, with swords as well as rifles and bandoliers. In their midst Ting goggled at the white people in terror, afraid to speak but desperately trying to convey with his eyes that whatever he did, he was being forced to.

One of the men, clearly the leader, spoke in Chinese. "Shoot him," he said, pointing at Osborne.

"No," Adela shouted, freeing herself from Constance's embrace and throwing herself forward, knocking the Englishman's arm up before he could squeeze the trigger and precipitate his own death.

"Miss Wynne," he cried in consternation, as two of the men stepped into the compartment and seized him, tearing the weapon from his grasp.

"They would have killed you," she gasped.

"You are right," said the bandit leader, for she supposed they had to be bandits. "It would be a waste of a bullet to shoot him. Cut his throat."

"No," Adela begged again, throwing both arms around the young man.

Constance had by now recovered herself and was as usual attempting to rationalize the situation. "What do you want with us?" she demanded, showing very little fear. But then, Constance had encountered Chinese bandits before. "Our money? Take it. There is very little. Our jewels . . ."

The leader of the bandits drew back his lips from his teeth in the semblance of a grin. "We do not want your money, Mrs. Wynne," he said. "We have come for the princess."

2

The Warlord

Adela's jaw dropped as a wave of fear swept over her. But hadn't she known what they wanted from the moment she had seen the man outside her window? She hastily clamped her teeth together again. She could not possibly show fear to a bunch of Chinese bandits.

But they knew who she was. And now she realized what made these men different from any Chinese she had ever seen before in her life: they each had cut off the humiliating pigtail.

"You bastards." Osborne was still trying to free himself from the men grasping him.

Fortunately he spoke English, and the bandits did not appear to understand him. But he was still being a nuisance. "Get rid of him," the leader said again, and the reporter was dragged to the door, still vainly struggling.

"And bring the girl," the leader went on.

More of his men crowded into the compartment, and Constance's head jerked. Obviously she was remembering that she *was* Constance Wynne, of whom everyone in China had surely heard. "Wait," she snapped.

The leader looked at her in surprise.

"If you wish *us* to come with you," Constance said, "we will do so. But wherever the princess goes, so do I. I am her mother. And I must warn you that should you remove us from this train, you will all be hanged for kidnapping."

The leader looked more surprised than ever at the calm authority she had managed to get into her voice.

"And if you harm that young man you will also certainly be hanged," she went on. "You have taken his weapon. Put him in his compartment and lock the door."

The leader stared at her, and then nodded to his men. Osborne realized that he had been interceded for once again. "No!" he shouted. "Mrs. Wynne! Adela! I cannot leave you. I—" One of the Chinese hit him in the stomach, another in the face. He gave a gasp and was dragged into the corridor as he fell to his knees.

Adela found she was chewing a knuckle. Constance was obviously just as frightened, although she was trying not to show it. "I will remember that," she said. "Now, if you will give us a moment to get dressed . . ."

The leader nodded again, and two of his men stepped forward. Constance had half-turned away from them, and was unable to defend herself. One man held her hair, pulling her head back, while the other in turn hit her in the stomach. Constance gasped and retched and sagged, and the man released her hair and hit her across the face. Blood flew from her cut lip and she fell across the bunk, gasping and weeping.

"You come," said the leader, pointing to Adela.

She stared at Constance in total horror. She simply could not have imagined such a thing happening to Constance had she not seen it with her own eyes. Her instincts cried out for her to rush forward and hammer at the men with her fists. But she knew that would only involve her in a beating. Besides, she was a Manchu princess, and Manchu princesses suffered whatever fate had in store for them with stoic dignity.

Yet she could not go outside in her nightclothes. "My clothes . . . " she said.

"You come," the leader said again. "Or we carry you."

She inhaled. She could not doubt that to have them touch her would be the most dreadful thing she had ever experienced. But she couldn't just surrender. Surrendering would also mean surrendering to the sheer terror that was lapping at her mind. These things could not happen in China, in 1911. The Western powers had decreed that they should not happen. There had been a British gunboat alongside in Canton, only fifteen hours behind them.

But Constance was lying on her bunk, still gasping for breath, and with pain, as well, all her strength drained away in fear and humiliation.

"You *will* hang," Adela told the leader as viciously as she could.

He grinned at her. "You come. Now," he said a third time.

She hesitated, looked at Constance. But there was nothing she could say or do. Her business was surely to stay alive, if she could, until the ransom was paid or she was rescued.

She stepped into the corridor. Terrified white faces stared at her from the doorways of the other compartments, but she refused to look at them. Mr. Osborne continued to bang on his locked door. Poor Mr. Osborne, she thought; he had been quite ready to play the hero, even if it cost him his life. She reached the end of the corridor after what seemed a very long walk, stood on the observation platform, while the distinctly chill breeze drifting down from the mountains rustled her nightclothes and brought her flesh up in goose pimples, gazed at the men waiting there, a very large number of men, she realized, all very well armed, all mounted.

"You ride with me," the leader said.

"No," she protested without thinking. But to spend she did not know how long virtually in his arms . . . Yet to defy him . . . She tensed herself for a blow, but he merely grinned.

"You can ride?"

"Of course I can ride," she said.

"You," he said to one of his men. "Get down."

The horse was brought forward, and Adela realized she would have to sit astride, with nothing on under her nightdress. She sighed, grasped the saddle horn and swung her leg over, looked down at the grinning faces as she adjusted her dressing gown to hang on either side.

"You try to get away, and we beat you," the leader said. "You remember." He mounted the horse next to hers. "Now, ride."

At least the rain had stopped, and it was a crisp night. Or rather, Adela supposed, morning, because dawn could not be far off.

She shivered from time to time; the breeze remained chill. But she knew that at least part of the cold was caused by sheer fear. Of course it had only to be a ransom attempt. That man Wang Mang in Canton had recognized her and had clearly been in partnership with these thugs. They had not harmed her, and they would not harm her . . . but only if the ransom was paid. And who was going to do that? Her stepfather was not a wealthy man. No doubt these people thought they could make demands of Prince Ch'un himself. What would happen when the prince had their messengers decapitated, as he most certainly would?

Only Constance could save her. Constance and Mr. Osborne, by alerting the governor of the first town the train came to, and having troops sent behind her. She had to believe that, just as she had to be careful to stay alive and unharmed until that happened. That meant boldness, she was sure. Confidence. That was the only thing these people would understand. She *was* a Manchu princess. She must act the part, for the first time in her life, utterly and without reservation.

And she *must* not let them see how afraid she was.

She must not even show discomfort, and that was becoming a problem. She had not ridden a horse for any length of time since her last vacation in Virginia; the weeks at sea had allowed her muscles to soften, and in addition she was inadequately protected. Soon she chafed and was sure she was bleeding. But she was not going to ask her captors for a rest. Instead she tried to concentrate on where they were going as they followed a trail through the foothills of the Ta Shan, over rough country with few trees and an inordinate number of fast-running streams through which they splashed, maintaining a good pace in the darkness to show that her captors knew this country very well. Before they had gone very far they heard the clanking and hissing of the train starting up again, and going forward, to Shao-Kuan. There the outrage would be reported to the provincial governor, and then he would take such action as he deemed appropriate, always supposing that he was not also in league with the bandits.

But there Constance would leave the train, and get on the telegraph, and a European rescue mission would set out for Canton. She had to believe that.

Meanwhile they rode, up and down and over the hills, until her aching thighs were sure they could continue no longer, and the trail suddenly debouched into a valley, just as the first light swept over the hilltops, and Adela saw in front of her the huts and tents of a military encampment.

There was a vast number of people surrounding her, emerging from their sleeping quarters, women as well as men, even some children, and the inevitable numbers of barking dogs. If this was a robber encampment, it was larger than she had ever heard of; this was more like an army.

Could they be Boxers? Or something similar? Mr. Osborne had hinted at such a possibility. But if they were Boxers, then ransom did not come into it. They could have taken her off the train for only one purpose. Constance had always adopted the attitude that she was English first, by birth, American second, by adoption and upbringing, and Chinese a very poor third, by force of circumstances. But that was typical of Constance's arrogantly confused thinking. Adela was *Manchu* first, by birth, American second, she was prepared to grant, English third, by accident—and Chinese not at all.

And when she was in China, only the Manchu blood counted. Or would matter to these people.

Well, then, she was going to die. But even death had to be met as a Manchu princess, with a toss of the head and a smile of indifference. And a prayer that the terror which was gnawing at her belly would not overwhelm her and leave her groveling on the ground, begging for mercy.

The horses were brought to a halt in front of the largest of the wooden huts and the leader of her escort was gesturing her to get down. Her muscles were so sore she nearly fell, but she retained her feet by grasping the bridle.

The leader lifted an oxhide skin which served as a door to the hut. "You go inside," he said.

Her prison? She ducked into a low doorway, and found herself in a sort of antechamber lit by a single smoky lantern and occupied by several armed men. One of these promptly lifted an inner skin doorway and pointed. "Inside."

Adela ducked through this one as well, and blinked in the sudden light. Because in here there were several lanterns, and also some candles guttering in the drafts that came through the ill-fitting walls. Here too there were rugs on the wooden floor, and several divans, to give the impression of some comfort. And two people. Adela's nostrils dilated as she breathed; she did not doubt these were to be the arbiters of her fate.

One of the people was a young Chinese woman, not all that much older than herself, Adela thought. She wore what had obviously once been a most expensive costume, a form-fitting gown in crimson silk which gleamed in the light—but it was stained and crushed and clearly had not been washed in some time. The same suggestion of neglect and decay shrouded the woman herself. She had a perfectly formed face and head, not only because of the length and straightness of her midnight hair but also because she had splendidly delicate Oriental features, so composed they might have been carved from golden wood. She *should* have been beautiful, save that the body revealed by the clinging garment—Adela estimated she wore no underclothes—was pitifully thin, and the features were strangely loose; her lips kept parting to show her tongue, and she seemed unable to keep still, but trembled or jerked all the time as if in the grip of an ague.

Instinctively Adela knew the girl was an opium addict. Despite laws against the sale and use of the drug, it was a widespread vice, especially in South China, but she had even seen pitiful, emaciated, half-mad creatures on the streets of Peking, reduced to starving penury by their dependence on the poppy.

Thus the girl could not be as important to her future as the man, who was now rising from one of the divans to stand before her. He wore a khaki Western-style uniform, complete with brown cross and waist belts, from the latter of which hung a revolver holster. His peaked cap could be seen on the floor where he had thrown it to the left of the divan, and his brown boots were splashed with mud. This and the fact that he was fully dressed suggested that he had only recently entered the hut. He also was Chinese, his face large and bland, and decorated with a thin mustache, which could not hide the cruel twist of his lips. He was quite a big man, and running to stomach, although she did not suppose he was very old. But apart from his mouth, his eyes were too liquid for comfort, seeming to slide over her, while his lips parted in an even more unpleasant smile.

"The princess," he said. He took Adela's chin in his hand and raised her head to gaze into her face. "Ah, yes," he said. "I was told how lovely she is."

She hoped he was speaking to the girl, and not referring to her as a thing. She drew a long breath. Exhaustion and discomfort had to be forgotten. No matter what was about to be her fate, boldness and composure had to be her watchwords. "I do not know your name," she said.

The man released her and drew back his shoulders. "I am General Feng-so-lin," he told her with some pride.

"General?"

"Of course. You have seen my army." He realized that she might not have been sufficiently impressed. "Part of my army."

"Well, General Feng," Adela said, "I don't know what you are trying to accomplish, but if I am not back on that train by the time it reaches Shanghai, you will be a proscribed criminal.''

Feng gazed at her, almost in admiration. "Ha," he said. "She spits like a true Manchu viper."

"Give her to me," the Chinese girl whispered. "Give her to me, great Feng. For just half an hour."

"You are a vicious little monster, Pearl," Feng said. "I call her Pearl, Princess, because she is lustrous, but yet a *thing*. And what good would she be to me, or any man, once you had sunk your claws into her delightful hide, Pearl?"

"She will defy you," Pearl said. "That is plain. She will have to be *bent,* just a little, to your will."

Feng smiled at Adela. "Is she right, Princess? Are you going to defy me?"

"I am a Manchu princess," she said.

He gave her a mock bow, came closer, stood in front of her once again. "Such eyes," he said. "I have never seen such eyes in any woman."

"Eyes which will look on your *head,*" she hissed. "Stuck on a pole."

He smiled at her. "You are wrong, Princess. It is the Manchu's hour which has struck. They will soon be swept away like so much chaff before the wind, and *their* heads will decorate the gates of every city from here to Chungking, and beyond." Again he cupped her chin, turning her face up to look at him. "But you will ride at my side, in splendor, and look at these things."

She frowned, for a moment unable to understand what he was saying.

Feng unfastened her dressing gown, gazed at the thin linen of her nightdress, and reached out to take a clearly delineated nipple between his thumb and forefinger and pinch it, so that she caught her breath. "Will you not enjoy being my bride, Princess Adela?"

She stared at him in total disbelief. "Your *bride?*"

"We shall be married this very day."

"Married? You think I . . . would marry *you?*"

"It is what I have decided."

Adela tried to think; her brain seemed to have sunk into a whirlpool in which anger and pride were jostling hopelessly against common sense and her understanding that her business was to survive, not commit suicide. She tried Constance's invariable prop, legality. "You cannot marry me," she said. "It is against the law."

"Manchu law," Feng said contemptuously. "When I have destroyed the Ch'ing, *I* will make the laws. I will make the laws for all China, as I will unite all China, behind me, Feng-so-lin. I will unite even the Manchu bannermen behind me, because I will be married to a Manchu princess, and therefore my sons will be half Chinese and half Manchu. Because you will give me many sons, sweet princess. I will see to that." His hand slid down her side to her thigh, to squeeze, very hard. "Oh, I will see to that, this very night."

The anger won. Adela gathered all the saliva she could discover, and spat in his face.

Feng's head jerked back, and he released her. Then his hand slashed across her face, and she went stumbling to the floor. She bit her lip to stop herself from crying out, but her lip was already split from the force of the blow, and the pain was so intense that she did cry, silently, feeling the tears rolling down her cheeks, tensing her muscles for a yet more damaging blow as she saw the booted feet raised above her.

"What, then, will you stamp her to death?" Pearl asked.

The boots hit the floor. "Manchu," Feng said in disgust. "She is a Manchu. She will defy me. Well, I shall drag her to the ceremony, and afterward I shall—"

"Would you not rather she stood at your side, and even smiled at you, and afterward came to your bed willingly?" Adela saw Pearl's feet come closer. "Give her to me, great Feng, for only a few hours, and I will have her crawling at your feet, if that is what you wish."

"You will take her into that lair of yours and corrupt her," Feng grumbled.

"Not so. I will make her *eager* for your caress. Is she not the most beautiful creature you have ever seen, great Feng? And she is a princess. The blood of Nurhachi runs through her veins, and from her, will run through the veins of your sons. Is she not worth more than just rape?"

"Two men!" Feng called after the briefest of hesitations. Immediately two of the guards entered from the outer chamber. "You will take the princess to the smoke room," Feng commanded. "Do as the lady Pearl commands you." He pointed at the woman. "You may touch. But she must not be marked. Remember this."

Pearl nodded, and stooped beside Adela. "Stand up, Princess," she said. "Stand up and come with me."

Adela could not imagine what horrors were about to be inflicted upon her. She was suddenly in the center of a world which, if she had certainly known it to exist, at least in the minds of all the teeming millions of Chinese who hated the Manchu, had always existed securely beyond *her* consciousness, thanks to Constance, and Frank Wynne . . . and even Miss Evesham, she realized. But now, to go with this female monster . . . It came to her that she was not, after all, going to suffer with the stoicism of a Manchu princess, but that she was going to fight them with all the outraged anger of Constance Wynne's daughter. Because she wanted to hurt someone —hopefully Pearl, as she did not suppose she would ever reach Feng—more than she had ever wanted to do anything in her life before. No matter what happened to her after, she thought she could even die happy if she could hear Pearl scream in pain, just once, first.

She drew a long breath, reached her feet, and swung her hand with all the strength she commanded, striking the nearest soldier across the face. He gave a startled exclamation and staggered back. Adela turned to find Pearl, but the second man had already thrown both his arms around her chest, pinning her own to her side.

"Two more men," Feng bellowed. "Do not mark her," he shouted at the woman, whose lips were drawn back from her teeth so that she looked about to bite.

Adela attempted to kick her, but the second man had now recovered from his surprise and grabbed one of her legs, and now the other two men were in the room. They took a leg and an arm each and carried her, facedown, across the room and through the door. The daylight outside the hut hurt her eyes, but far more hurtful was the crowd which instantly gathered, pointing and laughing as only the Chinese could at the sight of another human being in torment. Adela no longer fought. She was too afraid of having her arms pulled out of their sockets, and equally of having her nightdress ride up even farther than it already had; besides, she wanted only to shut her eyes and not have to look at anyone. She had not managed to hurt a soul, much less Pearl. Her explosion of anger had resulted only in total humiliation. And worst of all, she had betrayed her heritage. She wanted the earth to open and swallow her up.

Instead she was carried a considerable distance, hair trailing in the dust, shoulders and thighs aching, nightgown fluttering in the breeze, and then through another doorway into a hut far more gloomy than Feng's, although of an almost equal size. Here Adela's eyes jerked open at the sickly-sweet smell which afflicted her nostrils, even as the amount of smoke in the room made her catch her breath. Now the men holding her legs released them to allow them to flop to the floor, and she knelt, her arms still held, to gaze around the room, almost empty of furniture, but filled with people, men as well as women, in various stages of undress, several quite naked, many obviously having been here for several days, from the excreta by which they were surrounded. Some of the people seemed asleep, others stared at the ceiling in abstract contemplation. Some were sufficiently active to make a sort of pawing love to each other, regardless of sex. One or two even turned their heads to look at the newcomers, but without great interest. And all smoked clay pipes or had allowed them to fall from their hands. Adela realized that she was in an opium den.

Adela instinctively shrank back from the ghastly scene, but she was dragged forward, across the room, and made to sit against the far wall, where there were rings set into the wood. To these her wrists were tied, her arms being pulled apart to leave her helpless. While the men were thus securing her, Pearl had been preparing a pipe, and this she now offered to her. "You smoke," she recommended. "Then you not fight with General Feng."

"Never," Adela snapped. "Never! Take it away."

At a signal from Pearl, one of the men held her ankles to prevent her from kicking, and the other grasped her jaw with one hand and forced her teeth apart by squeezing her cheeks. Pearl inserted the pipe into her mouth, and then the men let her teeth snap shut on the stem, holding it in place when she tried to eject it with her tongue. Desperately she held her breath, but Pearl merely smiled and began to caress her, pushing her nightgown up above her knees while she stroked the pale legs. Adela tried to kick, but her ankles were held by the other man. She gasped for breath in her outrage . . . and inhaled. She choked, and her mouth sagged open, but the man kneeling beside her head maintained the pipe pressed against her tongue, and now she had to breathe again. She once again choked, but at the same time felt a most peculiar sensation of relaxation seeping through her mind.

She realized her danger, tried to make herself think, to understand what was happening to her, to resist them, at least mentally. Pearl had by now pushed her nightdress and dressing gown up to her thighs, utterly exposing her. Her legs had never been bare in public in her life, much less her pubes. She knew she should be utterly horrified, and *was* utterly horrified. But she did not feel able to summon the energy to do anything about it, and besides, no one else in the room seemed to notice or to care, save for Pearl. Now she raised her head to smile. "You are beautiful," she said. "Truly beautiful. I will make you more beautiful, Princess. Why do you not just smoke the poppy? The poppy cures all things, relieves all ailments. The poppy is the greatest of flowers. . . ."

The room seemed to have lost substance, and to be tumbling through space. Adela no longer sat on a hard floor, but on a soft mattress, and her wrists no longer ached where she had been pulling against the ropes. While Pearl no longer seemed a devil incarnate, but rather a sweet and lovable child, a hermaphrodite lover who was now sitting beside her, Adela discovered, fondling her breasts while she also smoked a pipe. Before Feng, no one had ever touched her breasts save herself, and on one occasion at school . . . but then she had slapped the girl's face so hard it had never been tried again. Yet there seemed nothing indecent or unnatural about Pearl doing so, and she was inducing the most delightful of sensations.

Adela sighed, and her mouth sagged open; the clay

stem fell from her lips. Pearl herself replaced it; the men had gone. And Adela willingly clamped it between her teeth to inhale the precious scent, and again feel herself soaring through the air, in the very best of company, holding hands with Pearl. Even Feng had suddenly become a very pleasant memory.

She became aware that a man had crawled across the room and was staring at her crotch, mouth open and tongue circling his lips. That *did* annoy her; she belonged to Pearl, and later, to Feng. Not to any itinerant Chinese coolie. For a moment she did not move, because the last time she had attempted to move, she had been unable to do so. Then she drew up her legs. "Go away," she shouted, surprised at the sound of her voice. It seemed to come from a very long way away, so that it reached her only as a whisper, and yet at the same time seemed to be trapped within her own head, so that the words bounced back and forth from ear to ear, deafening her.

The man disappeared. Adela looked down. Pearl seemed half-asleep, leaning against her; she did not seem to have heard the shout. Adela realized that she was thinking lucidly, for the moment, gazing in consternation at her naked legs. Now was the time to spit out the pipe and stop breathing the noxious fumes, and return to normalcy and common sense and determined opposition to Feng's horrible plans, as well as total rejection of Pearl's obscene advances. Now . . . She opened her mouth, and the pipe fell from her lips into her lap. But Pearl had not been sleeping after all. She opened her eyes and sat up, picked up the pipe and looked into it, and then crawled away, to return a moment later with a fresh one. "You smoke," she commanded.

"No," Adela muttered feebly. But her brief spell of resolution was already fading. She *wanted* to smoke.

She wanted to stop wondering what was going to happen next. She wanted to soar into that wonderland where nothing mattered and everything was going to turn out to her advantage. She inhaled, and sighed like Pearl, and kissed the top of the woman's glossy black head, and saw boots, and raised her eyes to stare at the light which suddenly filled the room, and at the men who had come in behind the light, and were standing around her.

Adela realized that she was lying on her face across a bed, and that she had been vomiting. Her tongue burned and her mouth tasted bitter and her head continued to swing. But neither the taste nor her physical discomfort seemed important. Her brain was still clouded, still relaxed, still uncaring of what might really be happening around her.

She was hungry, and her throat was parched. She wanted to eat and drink, and have another pipe, so that she could dream again and wander through those heavenly paths, Pearl at her side. With an effort she rolled on her back and blinked in the gloom of the hut . . . at a man.

She tried to sit up, and fell back again. She tried to straighten her nightgown, with no more success. She stared at him, as he stared back at her. He was dressed like a Chinese peasant, in blue smock and trousers, muddy boots, and was unarmed. He was not a young man; indeed, she would have said he was older than Feng. But he had a handsome face, and in its flat mouth and rounded chin and above all in the deep black eyes, it was an enormously strong face, and by no means a brutal one, but the hardness of mouth and eyes and chin left no doubt that he was used to command. A coolie? It was all too incomprehensible for words.

"Drink this," he said, and sat beside her to hold a cup to her lips.

It was cold tea. It tasted as bitter as her saliva, and yet it cleared some of the fuzz from her mouth, and from her brain as well. "Who are you?" she whispered.

"I am Lin-tu," he said. "Has your mother never told you of me?"

She gasped, and spilled some tea. Lin-tu had commanded the Boxers outside Peking and in the assault on the mission at Chu-teh. As such he had been, at least indirectly, responsible for the murder of Kate Mountjoy. Yet he had saved the lives of Constance and her two infant responsibilities. Constance had always said it was because *she* had once saved *him* from the vengeance of the Manchu. But he had perished in the fighting against the Allied Relief Force, surely.

"We were told you had died," she said.

"It was a good time to be dead," he said. "Do you not remember me at all, Princess?"

She shook her head. She had been only five years old in 1900, and besides, it was not something she had ever *wanted* to remember. Memory was a kaleidoscope of screams, and smells, and noises—all dreadful.

"I saved your life," Lin-tu said thoughtfully. "And now it seems I have saved even more than that." He got up, went to the door. "Come," he said. "Let us deal with General Feng."

3

The Revolutionary

Adela's mystification grew, seemed an extension of her whirling mind. Lin-tu might have commanded the Boxers, but he appeared as nothing more than a coolie; Feng was a general, and this was *his* army, or so he had claimed.

Yet Lin-tu had already opened the door into the next room, and Feng stood there, his arms secured behind his back, and at the same time held by two of the soldiers. She realized that she had been carried from the opium den into an inner room of the general's house itself, without being aware of it.

And now . . . Feng was gazing at her, his face impassive, save for the hatred that radiated from his eyes.

"Did this man violate you, Princess?" Lin-tu asked.

She caught her breath. Lin-tu was definitely in command. And would avenge every wrong that had been done to her. The Manchu in her should desire only that, swift and merciless. But she had no wish to harm anyone, only to escape this place and try to forget that last night had ever happened.

"No," she said. "He did not harm me, really. He hit

me in the face . . ." She touched her lip, which was still swollen. "And he made me smoke opium. But he did not harm me."

"Yet he intended to marry you," Lin-tu reminded her. "Is that not true?"

Still she gazed at Feng. "That is what he intended, yes."

Lin-tu snorted. "You are fortunate, Feng," he said, "that the princess accuses you of no serious crime against her. Or I would have you castrated. But you are in any event condemned by your actions. Your madness is incomprehensible to me. Who could have given you such orders?"

"I give my own orders," Feng snapped. "We have waited long enough. Always it is wait, wait, wait, for this and wait for that. It is time to strike, *now*. With the princess as my wife, I would have rallied all China behind me."

"You condemn yourself out of your own mouth," Lin-tu said. "Have you anything more to say?"

"You cannot sentence me," Feng declared. "These are my people."

"You think so? We shall discover the truth of that," Lin-tu said. "You are a traitor to our cause. You are condemned by your own actions as much as by the evidence of Miss Wynne. You swore to obey Dr. Sun, and you have broken that oath. More, you have betrayed our very principles. We would make China into a republic, and you dare to dream of empire, of Manchu princesses, of perpetuating the evils which have for so long kept China in the dust. You are condemned. Take him outside."

The soldiers pulled him toward the door. Feng made no move to resist them, remained gazing at Adela. Who gazed back. She was still not sure what was going to happen.

Lin-tu looked at her. "Will you witness the sentence being carried out?"

"The sentence?"

"He is to be executed. Immediately."

"Executed? But . . . he didn't harm me, Mr. Lin. Not really."

"I am not executing him for harming you, Princess," Lin-tu said. "I am executing him for his treachery to our cause. Stay here if you wish." He opened the door and went outside.

Adela stared after him for a moment. But she could not possibly just stand here and let this happen. She looked down at herself. She was just starting to think clearly again, as the fumes clogging her brain began to dissipate. And thus she was just starting to realize what she must look like, in her filthy sweat- and earth-stained nightgown and dressing gown. But they were all the garments she possessed. She staggered to the outer door —the soldiers were gone from the antechamber—and looked out, inhaling the fresh evening breeze which swept down from the hills. *Evening* breeze? Had she really been in the encampment a whole day? In the opium den a whole day?

Almost the entire army seemed to have assembled before the house, facing Lin-tu and General Feng, who was still standing between his two guards. Instinctively Adela ducked back into the doorway. They were the people before whom she had been humiliated that very morning. Out there were no doubt the men who had held her while Pearl had assaulted her.

"Speak to them, if you wish," Lin-tu told Feng.

The general glanced at him, then drew a long breath. "This man seeks my death," he said. "For some imaginary crime. For seeking our destiny, in our own way, and when the moment calls for it. When I learned that a Manchu princess was on that train, unescorted, I made an instant decision. It came to me that here *was* the moment. We have been told for too long that we cannot yet fight the Manchu, because we are not as strong as they. But if your commander is married to a Manchu princess, if he has the right to call himself a prince of the Ch'ing, would the Ch'ing fight against him with all of their purpose? And when our victory is won, will they not then rally behind a man they can call their own? I seek greatness for China. And I will bring down the Manchu. I will lead you to the very gates of Peking, and beyond. But *I* must lead. I must decide how best we can gain the victory, because I *know* how best we can gain the victory. Now, release me, and bind this man, and send him back to Dr. Sun, to tell him that we will go our own way, to victory, and triumph.''

He paused, gazing at the faces in front of him. No one moved. They waited for Lin-tu. The general's face hardened. And yet, Adela thought, were they *not* his men?

Lin-tu smiled at them coldly. "He *will* lead you to victories," he said. "I *have* led you to victories already. You know me. I am Lin-tu. I am Dr. Sun's personal aide. I chose this man to be your field commander. I made a mistake, but it is a mistake I will now rectify. The moment word reached me of what this madman intended, I took horse to ride here with all possible speed, to prevent him endangering us all. He thinks he would divide the Manchu by marrying one of their princesses? The Manchu would laugh at him. This is not a true princess. She has been cast out by her own people because of her barbarian blood. No one in Peking cares whether she lives or dies . . . save the British and the Americans. Your general would stand before you guilty of the abduction of a white woman. The foreign devils would fight with the Ch'ing, against us. He tells you he will lead you to the gates of Peking, and beyond. But

those gates will be shut in your faces, and many will die
as you seek to batter them down. When Dr. Sun gives
the word, those gates will stand open, to welcome you.
Feng would give you triumph? The only triumph he
seeks is his own. We have sworn an oath, Feng too, that
we will obey the doctor in all things. Feng would break
that oath, and seek his own counsel. Is he worthy of
life? Can he ever be trusted again?''

The soldiers and their women watched, their faces
expressionless. No one dissented. But Lin-tu still had to
find the necessary executioners, Adela thought. That
would be the moment of truth.

Surely. Her heart seemed to constrict as Lin-tu
stepped up to one of the two men guarding Feng and
plucked the revolver from the soldier's belt. ''You may
speak again, if you wish,'' he told the general.

''You act without authority,'' Feng said. He did not
seem to be afraid.

''I act in the name of Dr. Sun,'' Lin-tu said, and
pressed the revolver muzzle against Feng's temple.
Adela gave a start of horror and ran forward, regardless
now of the watching people. But she was too late. The
revolver had already exploded.

The general's head dissolved. Blood and brains scattered across the men who were holding his arms, and yet
he stood there for what seemed an eternity before they
released him and he collapsed like a sack of coal, to lie
in a bloody heap at Lin-tu's feet.

''No,'' Adela whispered, standing above the dead
man. ''Oh, my God, no.'' If, living most of her life in
China, she had seen sufficient criminals on the point of
death, like the man in Canton, she had never before
witnessed the act itself, that she could remember. And
never someone she had actually known, who had

actually touched her. Yet, strangely, she neither felt sick nor wished to faint, as she had supposed might be the case. She felt merely light-headed, almost disbelieving, that Feng would never smile his sly smile again, never plan and plot and desire. . . .

"Bring the woman," Lin-tu commanded.

Other soldiers dragged Pearl forward; Adela had not previously noticed her. Now she saw there were bruises on the golden arms and face, and no doubt on other parts of her body as well. Pearl panted, and bared her teeth.

"No," Adela said. "Please, Mr. Lin. Not her as well."

"You do not know her," Lin-tu said. "She is far more evil than Feng. Feng was only misguided, and by *her*. She is a creature from the seventh pit of hell. An *unnatural* creature."

"I know her," Adela said. *"Please."* Why? she wondered. She knew he was right about Pearl, whereas she was not at all sure he had been right about the general. But Pearl, whatever her vices, was young and beautiful . . . and they had shared a brief dream, however horrible that dream now seemed in retrospect.

"Let the unmarried men have her," Lin-tu said. He raised his voice. "Be sure you use her well."

"Kill me," Pearl shouted. "Do not give me to those swine."

Lin-tu smiled briefly. "They may teach you something," he said.

A bath was prepared by some of the women in the bedroom of the hut. And clothes were laid out for Adela to wear, shapeless Chinese garments of loose trousers and a blouse, ill-fitting boots. The color of the clothes, a bright red, was as off-putting as the thought that they were almost certainly riddled with lice. But anything would be an improvement on her tattered and filthy nightdress.

Adela soaped herself long and carefully. She wished to wash Feng away from her mind as much as the dirt from her body and hair. Away and away and away. But also Pearl.

The women had left her alone because she had sent them away. But now one of them returned through the skin doorway, gazed at her with disinterested eyes. "His Excellency awaits you," she said.

Lin-tu? But he was not a man to be afraid of, surely, however she remained appalled by the way he had shot Feng. He had saved her life. And he would now wish to return her to Constance. Surely. "I will dress, and come," she said.

The woman gave a brief bow and withdrew. Adela dried herself, pulled on the clothes, dragged her fingers through her hair, tried to smooth it down on her scalp. Clearly she looked like a scarecrow, when she so wished to look like a princess . . . or at least like Adela Wynne.

She drew a long breath, then pushed the skin aside and stepped into the larger room. Lin-tu sat on one of the divans, gazing at her. He was drinking tea, and on the table there was a cup for her. She was ravenously hungry, rather than thirsty, but there was no food to be seen, and she was certainly not going to ask for any.

Lin-tu gave one of his brief smiles. "Now you look more like a princess," he remarked.

"In these?" She looked down at the Chinese clothes.

"They become you. I regret what has happened. You understand this?"

His eyes gloomed at her. Carefully she sat on the other divan, opposite him; she could feel the heat in her cheeks, but hoped she was betraying no other sign of emotion. It was the first time in her life she had ever been alone with a man who was not related to her. "I am grateful to you, Mr. Lin." she said. "For saving me from General Feng." He did not immediately reply, but continued to stare at her, and butterflies suddenly started to flutter around and around her stomach. She picked up the tea and sipped it. "Do you think I will have become an opium addict?" she asked.

She had intended to keep the conversation light. But he took her seriously. "No," he said. "You did not smoke enough of it. But it would be unwise of you ever to smoke it again."

"I shan't," she said. But here was a subject she could usefully attack. "I had never seen the effect it could have on people," she said. "It was quite horrible. Why do you permit it?"

He shrugged. "Opium smoking is a way of life in China. Especially here in the South."

"But cannot it be stopped? Surely these people cannot be of any use to you?"

"Indeed they can. As Feng sought to control the woman Pearl, so it is possible to control the strongest man, once you have made him an opium addict. As for stopping it, that would be an immense task. Everyone smokes opium, from time to time."

"Have you ever done so?"

"Of course. As have you."

There seemed no immediate answer to that. The woman came in with a fresh pot of tea.

"I saved your life when Chu-teh fell," Lin-tu observed.

Adela discovered she was breathless, but still without quite knowing why. "I know," she said. "My mother told me."

"I would have saved your mother's life as well, had I been able to reach her in time," Lin-tu went on. "I would have you know this."

"Thank you," she said.

"But I did not. So I saved your life, and the life of the boy, Charles Baird, and the life of Constance . . . Wynne." He spoke the last word, Constance's new name, with disgust. "I protected you all from the Boxers, and kept you safe. And when I went off to fight, she ran away from my encampment, with you. Why did she do that? Why did she betray me?"

Adela found her mouth was open. It was not something she had considered before. Even less had she considered that this man might so resent it. Because it had never been worth considering, as he was dead. But now it was necessary to think, to try to remember everything Constance had ever told her. But Constance had never actually told her anything. "She left because you were fighting *her* people," she explained.

"She left with Wynne," Lin-tu said bitterly. "I know of this. He was her lover."

"Her . . ." Adela bit her lip. Constance and Frank had certainly been friends before their marriage. But lovers? She took refuge in a sip of tea. "He is her husband," she explained.

"And Prince Ksian Fu?" Lin-tu asked. "Was he also her *husband?*"

"No, no," Adela said. "He was my mother's husband. He was my father."

"I know he was your father," Lin-tu said, and Adela stared at him. He was making the same deduction so many other people had made. Including herself?

"I loved Constance also," Lin-tu said. "I loved and admired and respected her, for her courage as much as her beauty." His face twisted. "I was never her lover. I loved her too much for that." He gazed at her. "Do you understand what I am saying?"

"Yes," Adela gasped.

"And now I hate her." He got up suddenly and

violently. "I hate all white people. Almost as much as I hate all Manchu." He pointed. "You are both a white woman and a Manchu."

Adela opened her mouth and closed it again.

"You understand that I did not wish this to happen," Lin-tu said. "Indeed, when I learned from Wang Mang what Feng intended, I came with all possible speed to prevent its happening. It is an overt act, and we are not yet ready for overt acts. But it has happened. We cannot turn back the clock. You are our enemy. And now you know our secrets. You understand this?"

Adela could only gaze at him. Her heart seemed almost to have stopped beating. She had supposed herself saved.

Lin-tu stood above her and touched her hair. Oh, my God, she thought. Oh, my *God*. "And you are so beautiful," he said. "To destroy you would be a terrible thing. But if you must be destroyed, should you not be enjoyed first?"

She raised her head. She had supposed herself saved from *that,* as well. Yet she wanted to live. After everything she had experienced during the past twenty-four hours, only life seemed important. So, forget Manchu stoicism, Manchu acceptance. Live, by whatever means. "Then enjoy me," she gasped. "And keep me here as your woman. But do not kill me."

She was instantly ashamed. Now she was not only betraying her Manchu heritage, she was betraying Constance as well. And everything she had always been taught to hold dear.

And she had even failed in that. Lin-tu released her hair. "I have devoted my life to the overthrow of the Manchu," he said. "In that cause I have risked death time and again, and I have done and seen many terrible things. I cannot shrink from doing other terrible things, if their accomplishment will bring the fall of the Ch'ing one day closer. But the decision is not mine. It rests with Dr. Sun, and he is here now." The sound of horses' hooves drifted through the window. "You will come to Dr. Sun."

He left the house without waiting for her. Heart pounding, mind curiously in abeyance, knowing that here *was* the true arbiter of her fate, Adela went outside, again acutely conscious of the people watching her, of the tangled mess that was her hair, the certainty there was no one present who did not know that she had been in the opium den, with all the horrors that lurked there.

The general's body had been removed, and the blood scuffed into the muddy earth. Of Pearl there was no sign; no doubt she was still with the young men. Would she still be fighting them, or would she have been beaten into submission by now? There was a wasted life, a microcosm of utter human misery, for all the splendor of her physical exterior.

The entire camp was drawn up in attention, several hundred soldiers, while their women and children waited in a group behind. Surveying them was a surprisingly young man, no older than Lin-tu himself, she estimated, neither tall nor large in any way, but most remarkably handsome, with neatly brushed black hair, worn in the Western style, and, like all his followers, conspicuously lacking the obligatory pigtail, broad, strong, and yet perfectly chiseled features, dominated by the powerful jaw and the neatly clipped mustache which extended just beyond the corners of his lips. Like his lieutenant, he was unarmed, but far more surprisingly, he was dressed in a Western-style suit, with a neat tie, worn beneath an astrakhan coat, and he carried a slouch hat and a silver-topped cane. The hat, he had just finished waving to his people, to their obvious gratification. Now Lin-tu, standing at his elbow, was saying something in his ear, and he turned to face Adela.

"Miss Wynne," he said in perfect English with a slight American accent. He held out both his hands, and Adela went forward to take them. "I cannot tell you how grieved and shocked I am by what has happened," he said. "Marshal Lin-tu has told me how he has found it necessary to have General Feng executed. I am afraid that much as I abhor arbitrary justice, I am forced to agree with his decision. The man appears to have become a mad dog." He sighed. "How little we know of a man's true nature until we give him command. But in Feng's case I suspect it was the poppy."

Adela found herself staring at Lin-tu in amazement. A marshal? Even if only of a revolutionary army? And he had not even considered it necessary to tell her his rank.

Sun Yat-sen was smiling at her confusion. "I understand that Marshal Lin is an old friend of your family's." He walked beside her toward the general's house, while she wondered if she dared trust the feeling of relaxation which was surging at her stomach. It was impossible to believe that this man, so gentle and well-spoken and obviously civilized, could ever indulge in wanton brutality. Yet he had just approved of Feng's judicial murder—but had she not also done that, at least tacitly? "But you did not perhaps know his exact position in our movement." He stood back to allow her to enter the house before him. "When we have triumphed, Marshal Lin will stand at my right hand. You may be sure of that."

"I am sure he will prove worthy of your confidence, Dr. Sun," Adela murmured, but her attention was taken by the trestle table that had been erected in the center of the room, on which women were laying out food and three bowls. There were rolls made from crispy pancake, and the inevitable pork, served in a variety of ways, which formed a part of every Chinese meal, at least in the South, and the even more inevitable bowls of rice, together with a pot of jasmine tea. Adela's nostrils dilated as the scent reached them— she could not remember ever having been so hungry in her life before.

"Dinner," Dr. Sun said, holding a chair for her. "I have ridden all day. I really am quite hungry. I am truly sorry that Marshal Lin did not get here in time to stop this crime even being attempted. But we only learned of its inception after the train had already left Canton. That is why I sent him on ahead." He smiled. "He is able to travel so much faster than I." His reassuring personality flowed over them as he poured tea. "Now I am sure you will wish to regain your foster mother as soon as possible. I will arrange an escort for you, to within sight of the walls of Shao-Kuan." He glanced at her. "I'm afraid we have no Western clothes to offer you, unless you wish to be returned to Canton."

Adela's mouth was full of pancake. She could only gasp in discomfort and look at Lin-tu.

"Miss Wynne will be able to lead the imperial forces to this valley," Lin-tu said.

Dr. Sun raised his eyebrows.

Adela could at last speak. "I will not do that, Dr. Sun. I give you my word. But . . . I will have to tell my mother what has happened. She may well insist upon telling the *tsung li yamen.*" Which was the Manchu Foreign Office.

"Why should she do this?" Sun asked.

The directness of the question took her by surprise. She could think of no immediate reply.

"Can you doubt that my people will manage things better than the Manchu?" Sun asked. "But I forget. They are your cousins."

"I . . ." Adela bit her lip. It was impossible merely to take a stance with this man. She had to defend that stance. "You plan a revolution. A revolution means bloodshed and destruction of property. China is but slowly recovering from the Boxer Rebellion. It has had enough bloodshed for this generation. And in addition, as you say, the Ch'ing are my cousins. I cannot leave my own family in ignorance of what is gathering about them."

"She is a danger to us all," Lin-tu growled.

Adela gazed at him as coldly as she had looked at General Feng. He was reminding her of her attempt to surrender. Of her humiliation.

"All Manchu are a danger to us at the present time," Dr. Sun said gravely. "But when *the* time comes, they will no longer be a danger. You think I should disband my forces, Miss Wynne, and creep back into exile, and wait for better times to be upon us? Well, perhaps in many ways we do have the expectation of better times. But those times will not come merely by waiting for them. They must be created, and that creation depends upon the elimination of the Ch'ing as emperors. I mean them no harm, if they are willing to accept that. If, however, they resist the coming change . . ."

"As they must," Lin-tu said, staring at Adela.

"Then the blood must be on their own heads," Dr. Sun observed. "But in any event, Marshal Lin, you know that it is not my purpose, and it will never be my purpose, to make war upon women and children. And especially upon a young lady as beautiful as Miss Wynne." He smiled at her. "You must do your duty, as you see it, Miss Wynne. I doubt that anyone in that cesspool that is Peking will listen to you, but we shall in any event of course move our encampment elsewhere. Yet I would ask you to consider well what you mean to do. I await the right moment. I intend to bring down the Ch'ing Dynasty, drive them from China, or at least make sure they can never again interfere in the affairs of the Middle Kingdom. Then I intend that it shall be a kingdom no more, but a great socialist republic in which all men will have equal justice, and equal opportunity. I seek these things, and I will achieve them. But I hope to achieve them with the very minimum of that bloodshed of which you spoke. Think well, I would ask you, before you bring about a bloodbath by forcing us to premature action." He finished his meal and nodded to Lin-tu. "Now, if you would be good enough to have horses and an escort prepared, Marshal Lin, I am sure our guest will wish to leave first thing in the morning."

"Oh, my dear child," Constance said. "Oh, my dear, dear child. To think . . . But Dela, are you sure . . . well . . ."

Because if being a virgin at one's marriage was not quite so vital to an American young lady as to a Manchu princess, to lose one's virginity was still the worst disgrace that could overtake any young woman, and to lose it in such a way . . .

But she could not tell Constance *anything* of what had happened between Feng and herself, or Pearl and herself, or even Lin-tu and herself. Because even if she had not been raped, she had still been reduced to something tarnished, something less than her ideal of herself, something *shared*. Recovery from that experience was a task for herself alone. Especially if she would still marry Constance's son.

"I am quite sure, Mother," she said. "Look, even the bruise on my lip is nearly gone. But, Mother . . . they *weren't* bandits."

Constance gazed at her from beneath arched eyebrows. It was the first time they had been alone together since her sudden appearance at the gates of Shao-Kuan. For the past three hours there had been officials, and reporters, and photographers . . . but surprisingly, and disappointingly, no Mr. Osborne. "He rode back to Canton for help," Constance had explained.

To them all, Adela had told how the bandits, when she had explained that she had no money, that her parents had no money, and that she was not really a Ch'ing princess, had put her on a horse and told her to leave. Eyebrows had been raised, at least on the part of the governor of Shao-Kuan—he knew his bandits. On the other hand, she was standing before him, obviously unharmed, and she *had* been taken from the train. Who was he to argue? And her reappearance at least saved him the necessity of mounting a rescue operation, as for the previous twenty-four hours had been hysterically demanded by the yellow-haired devil woman.

The reporters had been enchanted, at once by her obvious courage and her equally obvious survival.

Constance had been overwhelmed, until now, as Adela told her exactly what had happened, save that she suggested Lin had appeared much sooner—she omitted all reference to the opium den.

"My God," Constance said when she had finished, sitting beside her on the settee. "Lin-tu. I thought he was dead. I was *told* he was dead."

Adela waited.

"And you say . . . he hates me?" Constance gave a quick flush as she glanced at her foster daughter.

"Yes," Adela said. "Did you know him *very* well?"

Another quick glance. "I saved his life once." Constance got up, walked to the window, peered out. Adela watched her fingers twist together. "A very long time ago. But of course we never . . ." She turned.

"I know," Adela said. "He told me that."

"He was Chinese," Constance said, and flushed again. She was suddenly realizing that she was talking to Adela woman to woman, rather than mother to teenage daughter. "The important thing," she said briskly, "is what we do about the army, and Dr. Sun, and . . . well, everything. We will tell your father first, and see what he says."

"Will we tell Father about Marshal Lin-tu, as well?" Adela asked.

Frank Wynne himself came out in the sampan to meet the steamer from Shanghai as it dropped anchor beyond the bar that prevented deep-draft vessels from navigating the Pei-ho River. He joined them in their cabin before they had to face a new crowd of reporters and officials. "My darling," he said, holding Constance close. "My darling, darling girl. What on earth possessed you to go to Hong Kong, and then take the train?"

She clung to him. One of the most reassuring things about her foster parents, Adela had always found, was their obvious adoration of each other. With good reason, she supposed. Constance was her ideal of a woman, and Frank was very nearly her ideal of a man, allowing for his age. He was in his mid-forties, but was tall and powerfully built, handsome in an aquiline fashion, and debonair in spirit. He kept himself in the peak of fitness, as befitted an ex-marine who had remained in the reserve. She realized, with an almost guilty start, that he was every bit as beautiful in his Occidental way as Lin-tu was in his Oriental. Of course, she was seeing him for the first time in four years, and a great deal had happened in that time.

Constance was seeing him for the first time in four months, which seemed long enough. "There was a strike in San Francisco," she explained. "We couldn't get a passage direct to Tientsin. And we had never seen Hong Kong, and Canton, and the South. We wanted to explore."

"Knowing that the South is full of bandits?" He held her at arm's length, frowning through his happiness, seeking refuge from being overemotional in a mock censure.

Adela waited patiently. Nothing had happened to Constance at all, save a punch in the stomach. But she was used to this total isolation, even from those nearest and dearest to her. She was a nothing, she thought with a sudden surprising surge of bitterness. A microcosm of human irrelevance, who because of her parentage must cause trouble wherever she went. As everyone knew.

"There were no bandits, Frank," Constance was saying. "Adela has so much to tell you."

As last he took her in his arms. "You'd better wait until we can talk in peace," he said. And smiled. "But you didn't find it necessary to bite anyone, I gather."

She thought his attempt at humor was appalling. But how odd, she thought, that it had *not* occurred to her to bite General Feng. Or had she instinctively known that would be too dangerous?

"No, Father," she said. "There did not seem any opportunity for that."

He looked past her at Constance and raised his eyebrows. Even more than Constance, Adela realized, he clearly did not know what to make of this utterly lovely creature for whom he had so strangely become responsible—Kate Mountjoy had been Constance's friend, not his. Indeed, he had hardly known the English girl. "You must tell me all about it," he said. "When we're on the train." He held both their hands and escorted them outside to face the reporters.

The train from Taku chugged up the line toward the junction at Feng-tai before it would reach the terminus of the line at Hachiapo, just outside Peking. This was the starkest contrast to the journey north from Canton;

only the river running close by the tracks remained constant. Instead of rice, here in the North the fields were under grain, dry rather than wet—although the North China Plain was subject to horrendous inundations when the Pei-ho burst its banks—and instead of mountains, here was an endless flatness, the highest undulation only a couple of hundred feet. These were different people, too, in a way more hardy, because they were exposed to bitter winters which seldom troubled the South, but in another way less hardy because their daily lives were less arduous than those of their compatriots. It was no coincidence that almost all invasions of China had come out of the North, sweeping across the Great Wall, only a little more than a hundred miles away, and in places closer than that, and finding a submissive people on the plain. Equally it was no coincidence that the mountainous South had always been the most difficult to conquer, and that the Ch'ing, for all the military skill and energy of the eight banners, or tribes, led by the immortal Nurhachi, had never truly imposed their will upon the southern provinces. It was from the South that the Taiping had arisen in the middle of the previous century, to bathe all China in blood before they had finally been subdued, and it was also from the South that, on a far smaller scale, the Society of Righteous Harmony Fists—the Boxers—had come to sweep briefly across the land in an orgy of murder and looting. And once again, the South was stirring. But here in the North such passions and hatreds seemed far removed.

Adela had made the journey often enough, but the last time had been four years ago. And even had she made it yesterday, she thought, she would still have enjoyed every moment of it, looking at the farms and pagodas, smiling at the peasants who invariably gathered to watch this wonder of the white man's civilization puffing past. Because it was taking her to the high purple walls of Peking itself, the Tartar City, one of the most crowded metropolises in the world, where teeming humanity lived and loved and sweated and even died in a unique intimacy. A city which shimmered in the noonday sun, a city which was, above all else, alive, in such stark contrast to the city within, the Forbidden City, the home of the Ch'ing Dynasty.

A city into which Adela had never been admitted.

Peking was a place to love, and therefore in which to feel at home, or to hate, in which case to feel afraid all the time. Adela had always loved it. She had lived here ever since she could properly remember; memory before the age of five was at once confusing and nightmarish. And for all the violence she had seen here, for all the conflicting and totally unstable emotions she knew lay just beneath the surface, even the hatreds which she now knew were directed at her as much as at her family, Peking meant security to her. She knew it better than any other city in the world, even after four years in Richmond. She had never felt other than a stranger in Richmond, because she was so clearly of mixed blood. Here in Peking she belonged. Besides, everyone knew her as the daughter of the famous devil woman, and that was the greatest feeling of security one could possibly have.

Thus in Peking all that had happened seemed more remote and unbelievable than ever. It was something that she knew had to be thought about very deeply and carefully. But it was also something she did not *wish* to think about at all. It was too confusing, and too alarming. Not the physical danger or mistreatment, so much as the questions it had raised. Lin-tu was a blood-thirsty radical. But he was an honest man. And his master was clearly one of the most honest and dedicated men she would ever meet. Yet they were both her enemies. Because of the Ch'ing. She knew from first-hand observation just how corrupt and inept the dynasty was, but at the same time, as she had told Constance, she did not wish it destroyed, and equally she did not want the China she knew and loved to change much, and certainly not to explode into a crisp and brash new century filled with reform for the sake of reform, which would breed its own brand of corruption and injustice—as she knew would happen when Dr. Sun and his enthusiastic young men got control.

Even if they would also clean up the opium dens and all the other horrors of Chinese life?

These were not feelings and emotions she could convey to Frank, or even Constance. She confined herself to the plain truth, omitting only Lin-tu, and suggesting that it had been Dr. Sun himself who had taken her from the opium den and executed General Feng. Constance made no comment, and Frank also listened in silence. At last he said, "This Sun Yat-sen seems a remarkable fellow. Almost unbelievable."

Adela gazed at him. "You mean *you* don't believe me."

He smiled and ruffled her hair, an annoying habit which he had indulged since she was a little girl, and which was doubly annoying now she was trying to look her best. "I believe you, Dela. I mean it may be difficult to convince others. Especially that he can have been in China for some time, raising an army. There is a price on his head, you know. And as a matter of fact, the dynasty does take him seriously. They have made such representations that Japan, as well as Britain and France, the countries where he has been spending most of his time, have refused to let him in anymore. So has Hong Kong. And you say he is actually here in China? That will set them by the ears, *if* they believe it."

"They have to believe it," she insisted. "I saw it."

"But whom should we tell?" Constance asked as they drove in the trap from the station and through the Yunting-Mien, the south gate of the city, nodding rather than presenting passports to the soldiers on guard there.

Adela was well aware what was on Constance's mind: she wanted to keep Adela as far away from the dynasty as possible, now and always. Which was not a point of view she really disagreed with. However proud she was of her Ch'ing blood, and however much she regretted that she would never see the wonders of the Forbidden City, as described to her by Constance, who had been there often enough in the old days to take tea with the dowager empress, she also had no desire to be reclaimed by her family and be forced to endure the mind-deadening seclusion of a real princess, surrounded only by other women and eunuchs, allowed to know nothing of what was happening in the outside world, hardly even allowed any books to read. And it *could* happen, she knew, should Prince Ch'un ever meet her and realize at once how beautiful and intelligent she was. Of course Constance had a legal right to her . . . in America. But here in China it was the dynasty who made the laws.

Not, of course, that it ever *would* happen. Prince Ch'un would cheerfully surrender all of his unmarried cousins and aunts and nieces merely to be rid of the expense of maintaining them, to whoever would accept them. The real truth of the matter was that Constance was intent upon playing down every aspect of her foster daughter's Manchu and, even more, royal background, and was afraid, Adela was sure, that if she once saw the wonders of the Forbidden City, she might *wish* to live there.

It was just another aspect of the confusion which had always filled her life and which had so suddenly been brought into sharp relief by Feng. But at least now she was home; the house was coming into sight. It was the old Bunting house, which Frank had bought from William Bunting when he had decided to pack up and leave China forever in the aftermath of the Boxers. It was set back from the road, only a block from the legation complex, and just within the wall of the Tartar City itself. It was surrounded by a most delightful garden, a Chinese garden, full of whispering water and little bridges, broad floating lilies and quick-darting, brilliantly hued goldfish. And it was home. Once the gate closed behind their trap, it became even more than ever impossible to believe that a week ago she had been chained to the wall of an opium den.

But not yet to be fully enjoyed, apparently. For as she stepped down she observed there was a richly caparisoned horse standing by the front stairs. And Pu-Tang, the butler, hurrying down to greet them, and obviously overjoyed to see them both safe and sound after such a perilous adventure, was yet filled with self-importance. "It is the great viceroy himself, Mrs. Wynne," he whispered to Constance. "Marshal Yuan Shih-k'ai, come to discover if you are well."

Constance hesitated, glanced over her shoulder at Frank, who was following her, holding Adela's hand. "Yuan," she said, obviously delighted. "The answer to all our problems."

Frank frowned. "He is retired."

"He's still the most powerful man in all China. And he's our friend. He'll know what to do. Come on, Dela. You must tell the marshal what happened."

Adela allowed herself to be drawn up the stairs. As it was four years since she had been in Peking, it was also four years since she had seen Yuan Shih-k'ai; she could hardly remember what he looked like. But she did remember that he was a very old friend of Constance and Frank's, and had been for years. And if he was a Chinese rather than a Manchu, according to Constance he was the most remarkable man she had ever met, a member of the conquered race who by sheer force of character and ability had made himself indispensable to the Manchu, who had risen to high command in the army, and been entrusted with the highest diplomatic missions as well. Since the collapse of the Boxer Rebellion, to be sure, there had been rumors. It was said that although he had apparently wholeheartedly opposed the rebels at every turn, he had secretly encouraged them with money and words, just as it was said that when the dowager empress had finally seized all power for herself in 1898, she had done so with his tacit agreement, although he had sworn loyalty to her nephew the emperor, and, in commanding the only armed force in the vicinity of the capital, could have ended the coup d'etat with a single word.

The real reason behind his enforced retirement from the position of viceroy of Chihli Province, and thus Peking itself? The present regent, Prince Ch'un, was the brother of that hapless young man whose life had been bedeviled by the Dragon Lady.

All facts which suggested he was possessed of a true Chinese duplicity, quite apart from *being* Chinese, Adela thought; she was not in the mood for admiring any of the race. On the other hand, he was Constance's friend and had apparently once saved her life. He had even been one of the few people to encourage Frank and her to remain in China, following the revolt, for which she had to be grateful. And that he was undoubtedly as powerful as ever, even in retirement, because of the esteem in which he was held by everyone, was also certainly true.

Therefore, she reminded herself, it made sense to trust him as her mother and father did, especially as it was their wish.

Certainly the marshal made an imposing figure, standing tall—unusually so for a Chinese—and straight in his blue uniform, plumed hat waiting on the table beside him, revolver and sword belts resting on the settee. His face was broad and bland; his mustache was turning gray, and drooped to either side of his face; his pigtail was short enough to be considered a fad rather than an indication that he belonged to a conquered people. Actually he looked rather like a reassuring uncle as he embraced Constance, and then turned to her. "Adela," he said. "Adela! What a woman you have become. A wonderful woman."

He held open his arms, and after a moment's hesitation Adela allowed herself to be embraced. She told herself that it was because she was off all Chinese at the moment, but his eyes seemed to have the same sensually liquid quality as Feng's, which was most disturbing.

He gazed at her. "And such an adventure. . . . Tell me that what I read was not true."

"Not all of it, Marshal Yuan," she said.

"Thank the heavens for that."

"Actually, it is far more serious than it appears," Frank said. "I'm very glad you are here, Yuan. Adela has quite a story to tell."

He was still staring at Adela, and now to her distress she saw his eyes suddenly become opaque, almost as if a shutter had fallen behind the iris, although they continued to smile. "A story?" he asked. "For me?"

"It really is important, Yuan," Constance said. "Shall we sit down? Pu-Tang, some tea." Otherwise of course the servant would listen.

"You will sit beside me, Princess," Yuan said, patting the settee. He was still holding her hand, and still gazing at her. Despite the heat, she felt as if she had goose pimples all over. "Now, tell me everything," he commanded.

Like Frank, he listened in silence, never taking his eyes from her face. When she had finished, he continued to stare at her for some seconds before asking, "You are sure no harm was done to you? Quite, quite sure?"

She was utterly surprised, and embarrassed, because obviously he was thinking of rape, counted it more important than the revolutionary threat. "Quite sure, Marshal Yuan," she said.

"Well, then, all is well that ends well. What an experience. It makes me ashamed of my own country. But it is behind you now. We must make sure you never are in such danger again, eh?"

Almost as if he was going to look after her himself, she thought.

But by now even Constance was surprised at his lack of interest in the true importance of her tale. "What will you do about it?" she asked.

"You mean about this mysterious Dr. Sun? He is but an agitator, believe me. Tell me, Princess, did he have a fellow called Lin-tu with him?"

Constance caught her breath, and obviously needed a great effort to prevent herself from looking at Frank, who was filling a pipe beside her.

"Lin-tu?" Adela asked, keeping her face straight. "There was no one by that name, Marshal Yuan."

Constance had recovered herself. "Lin-tu? You mean the Boxer leader?"

"Why, isn't that the name of the fellow who held you prisoner for a while?" Frank remarked. "He was killed in the fighting before Peking, we understood."

"He *disappeared* in the fighting before Peking," Yuan corrected. "Recently I have received information to suggest that he may still be alive."

"But . . . this fellow Sun Yat-sen was never connected with the Boxers," Frank argued. "Was he?"

"Not directly. But neither was Lin-tu, actually," Yuan told him. "Lin-tu is one of Dr. Sun's young men. His paladins, if you like. His mission has always been to stir up trouble for the dynasty wherever it can be done. So naturally he joined the Boxers, and as he is an able fellow, immediately rose to command. Now, there is a dangerous man. Far more dangerous than Dr. Sun." He gazed at Adela. "If he were with Dr. Sun again, there might be some cause for concern."

"He wasn't," Adela said. But she knew he could tell she was lying. But then, she felt so many things about him. That she had told him nothing he did not already know. And even that terrifying thought was overlaid with the slowly spreading feeling that he was totally unconcerned, save perhaps to be disappointed that Lin-tu had not been there, that he might even welcome a revolution . . . because he was Chinese and hated the Manchu.

And that for all his caress and his gaze, his admiration and his reassurance, he hated her, too. The most powerful man in the country.

4

The Proposal

"Then you will do nothing about it?" Constance asked.

Yuan shrugged. "What action can I take? I cannot send my men wandering all over the Ta Shan. There are valleys there in which an army of over a hundred thousand might lie concealed. In any event, my dear Constance, I am not in office. And if I were, the Ta Shan is not my province."

"I must confess that my inclination is to pack up and go," Frank said, to Adela's total amazement, and to Constance's too, from the way she jerked her head. "It's actually something I've been considering for a couple of years. Ever since the empress died."

"Leave China?" Yuan was also displaying astonishment. "But why?"

"Because I can see nothing but trouble in front of us. This fellow Ch'un doesn't really know what he's doing. So the government is broke. That figures. So he's raised taxes, on a people who can hardly subsist anyway. And now this talk about nationalizing the railroads . . ."

"I agree that will upset the Europeans," Yuan said. "It is already doing so. So it will hardly come to pass."

91

"Maybe. But there's going to be trouble. Now, from what Dela has been telling us there already *is* trouble brewing in the South."

Yuan looked at Constance. *"You* feel like this?"

"Well . . ." She flushed. "Maybe I haven't thought about it as much as Frank. I've only just come back, you know. But he has a point. If Dela's life is in danger, as well . . ."

To Adela's consternation, Yuan put his arm around her shoulder to give her a squeeze. "Adela is safe here, and will always be safe here. Believe me, Constance, as of this moment I make her safety my own personal responsibility." He pretended to frown at her. "Provided you keep me informed of any intended journeys, I beg of you. As for the future, however uncertain it may appear at times, I will tell you this, Constance, Frank: of all the people in China, and there are a great number of them, you have the least to fear from *anything* that may happen. I give you my word on this. Stay, and prosper, and let your destiny take its proper course. I repeat, *you* have nothing to fear." To Adela's relief, he released her in order to lean forward and pat Constance on the knee. "You have both had a desperate adventure. But you tell me you are unharmed. And the princess says that she too is unharmed." Once again Adela had to suffer a squeeze. "And the true villain, Feng, has been executed." For just a moment his voice was filled with venom. "So, as I say, all is well that ends well, eh? But, Constance, the next time you wish to go exploring in the interior of China, kindly inform me first, and I will provide you with an adequate escort." He smiled at the girl. "I may even accompany you myself."

"How very odd," Frank remarked when the marshal

had left. "I almost had the feeling that he knows exactly what is going to happen."

"Yes," Constance said. "I felt that too."

"Because he means to lead a revolt himself," Adela said quietly. "And even become emperor himself."

They stared at her. "Yuan? That is absurd," Constance said. "He is not a Manchu, and he is of humble birth. Anyway —"

"Was not Nurhachi himself of humble birth, before he led the eight banners across the Great Wall and proclaimed himself emperor?" Adela demanded. "Was not every king who ever reigned, of humble birth, at some time in history? And were not there Chinese emperors before the coming of the Manchu?"

"Why, yes, I suppose that is all true," Constance conceded. "But . . . Yuan . . ."

"He is powerful, he is talented, he is ambitious, and he hates the Ch'ing," Adela insisted. "He is the most dangerous man in China."

"My dear Dela, how can you say things like that about the marshal? Hate the Ch'ing? Yuan was the empress's most devoted servant."

"Only because he needed her to give him power. Now she is gone, and the regent *fears* his power. Soon we shall discover his true feelings."

"Well," Constance said, obviously taken aback by her foster daughter's ability to show such an intensity of feeling about a subject which should hardly concern a seventeen-year-old. "*You* are the odd one. You were quite happy to sit there with this ogre's arm around you."

Adela shook her head. "No, Mother. *He* sat here with his arm around me."

"Well, probably like so many lonely middle-aged widowers, he has a weakness for young girls," Frank said, seeking to defuse the incipient quarrel. He ruffled the long, straight, glossy black hair. "And sure, Yuan is an ambitious man. But I think he is also supremely aware of what is practical and what is not. And where his own best interests lie. He knows this government will need to call on him again, when this crisis breaks, whether it is a financial one or a political one, or both together. And he is quite happy to await that call, as he will be to answer it. Then he'll probably be chief minister. That's his ambition. So you can be certain he has a vested interest in seeing that the emperor, or at least the regency, is a success."

"He cares *nothing* for the regency or the emperor," Adela said, and got up. "He is an enemy of the Ch'ing. *All* the Ch'ing." She left the room.

"What will you do?" Frank asked.

Constance stared into the darkness, listened to the barking dogs, the distant discordant music which was part of the Peking night. They lay together in their double bed, and naturally, as they had been separated for several months, he had wanted to make love. And so she had lain in his arms and pretended passion—and had found herself thinking of Lin-tu.

"Do?" she asked.

"I can tell you've a lot on your mind," he said.

"Oh . . ." She was grateful for the gloom. "Do you know, I feel as if the clock has been turned back fifteen years. Like when I was trying to warn people about the Boxers. Everyone treated me like a child. There, there, Mrs. Baird. You've had a nasty experience, but it was just an experience. Nothing will come of it. That's exactly Yuan's attitude to Adela."

"Well, I'm afraid I agree that he's probably right. At the moment. I think she's a little hysterical. And who wouldn't be, after an experience like that? What *I* don't like is the thought of this character Lin-tu being alive and active all over again. As I remember, he had quite a weakness for you."

"He never touched me," Constance snapped.

"Sure. But I've a notion he was working himself up to it. And then you ran out on him. I sure would hate to think of you ever bumping into him again. But the whole business, supposing even half of what Adela says is true . . . Connie, forget what I told Dela, how I went along with Yuan. I think we want to do some very careful and logical thinking, right this minute. We lived through the Boxers. We don't want to have to repeat the experience. And then there *is* Dela. God knows what she is really feeling, coming back from the security of Richmond, and being whipped off a train by a bunch of thugs. . . ."

"She hated Richmond," Constance said.

"Okay, okay. And she doesn't *seem* all that upset by what happened. But try thinking of the danger she'd be in if there was another revolution, and this one aimed directly at the dynasty. Like the Taiping, fifty years ago."

"Just what are you trying to say?" she asked, as if she didn't know.

"I think we should call it a day here in China."

"And go where?"

"Well . . . back to the States."

"The States? What would you do?"

"I could start another business. The other end of the stick, if you like, run a Chinese import-export agency from San Francisco rather than here. Heck, I know enough about China to make a go of that. And if we could get a reasonable price for the business here . . . I should, you know, what with the goodwill I've built up over the years. . . ."

"Peking is our home, Frank."

"We can make another home, Connie."

"Not until we have to. Okay, so Dela would be better off in the States. That's what I've been trying to organize for four years. But us . . . in Peking we're somebodies, Frank. In the States we'd be nothing at all. What are you so worried about? Yuan is right about this Dr. Sun, I'm sure. He's probably just another harmless agitator. I mean to say, think of the way he treated Dela. Does that really sound like a revolutionary leader? Or the vicar come to afternoon tea? So maybe he has managed to raise an army. But he's gone and executed his own general. If a single battalion of imperial troops were to move against him, or even into the Shan, that rabble would disperse so fast and so far you'd not even see their dust."

"As you say, he seems to have executed his own general," Frank observed. "That doesn't sound entirely like a softie to me."

"Oh . . . that was an act of justice. If only Yuan had agreed to do something. Do you know, the only thing about the entire business which seemed to interest him was whether or not Adela had been raped. He didn't seem upset at my being punched in the stomach."

"Well, these Chinese have odd senses of honor," Frank said. "Maybe if Adela, an imperial princess by birth, *had* been raped, he'd have felt called upon to do something about it."

"Oh, don't be ghastly. The poor child suffered enough as it is. And what about me being beaten up?"

"He probably figures you could stand it." His hand found hers and squeezed it. "*You* weren't raped, were you?"

Adela lay beneath the blanket on her bed and listened to the sounds of the Peking night. There was no wind, so every barking dog, every shrill cackle of laughter, every jangle of discordant music seemed to carry for miles, although they might all have been in the next street, so far as she knew. They were not sounds that disturbed her; tonight they delighted her. She had been away from them for too long, and suddenly she did not know how she had ever slept without such a cacophony to lull her into her dreams.

Just as she had been away from this house for too long. It was the only home she could remember, save for those vague, nightmarish shapes and sounds which must have been Chu-teh. She had spent an hour before retiring, just moving about her room, touching things she had almost forgotten, picking up her crayons—she had never been one for dolls—and her riding crop, amazed and delighted to find that for four years Constance had kept the room exactly as she had left it.

Dear Constance. Dear, confused, *unhappy* Constance. Because she *was* unhappy. Adela had never even considered that possibility before, but she would not have believed the way her foster mother had reacted to the news that Lin-tu was alive if she had not seen it with her own eyes. It was incredible to conceive that Mother could ever feel anything more than contempt for a Chinese. But then, Mother had always been proud to call Yuan Shih-k'ai a friend. What had she wished to call Lin-tu?

Thus tonight was not a time for sleeping. Or even for lying awake and feeling the contentment of having come home after so long and so many happenings. Rather was it a time for thinking. She still did not *want* to think right now. Because to think of what had happened, of Yuan and of what might still happen, was frightening. But she no longer had the time to wait.

Because whatever he had said to reassure her, Frank was definitely considering packing up and leaving China. And if ever she wanted to stay in China, it was now. Because supposing Sun Yat-sen *was* planning a revolution, and supposing Yuan, who she was prepared to concede was the only man who could truly prevent it, *was* as much of an enemy as she was sure he was, then . . . she didn't know what. She only knew that it could not be her destiny to run away from such a situation, away from her cousins—no matter how they had ignored her all of her life.

But how could she make certain of staying, if Frank managed to persuade Constance to leave? She knew that Constance loved China, and Peking, and this house, as much as she did. But she didn't know how Constance might further react to the news of Lin-tu when she had had time to think about it. She might well decide to run away from so important and apparently disturbing a piece of her past.

There was only one solution to the problem that she could think of. But it was also a solution which promised a sharing of her experiences, and a reassurance as to her future, which her emotions were crying out for. An alleviation of the sudden loneliness which had overtaken her. And even a tentative *shaping* of her future, before it was shaped for her, by Chinese revolutionaries.

Adela got out of bed and relit the lamp. Then she carried it to her desk in the far corner of the room, sat down, and started to write a letter.

By the time she had been back a week, Adela discovered, she might never have been away. The incident on the train might never have been, her four years at the Evesham Academy for Young Ladies only a distant nightmare. Even the mixture of suspicion and envy with which she was welcomed by the European community in Peking seemed normal, because, as usual, all their friends and acquaintances blamed Constance for everything that had happened. Constance had always been regarded as a troublemaker, a headline snatcher, and a thoroughly discordant element. Trust Constance Wynne to have her train stopped by bandits—still the official account—and actually lose her daughter, at least for a night, and then return to Peking, the heroine of the hour, the main story in the international press for at least a week. She and Frank were temporarily dropped from the dinner-party circuit.

They did not seem to care; they had many Chinese friends. Unfortunately, these included Marshal Yuan, who continued to be a regular visitor, and always insisted on sitting next to Adela to tell her stories of his campaigns against the Japanese and various Chinese rebels. Equally invariably he always contrived to put his arm around her shoulders and give her little hugs. Adela knew that Constance was afraid she would one day erupt and push him away in disgust, but however much she disliked both him and his attentions, she kept herself under careful control, and gave him a bright smile to convince him she really lived only from visit to visit.

Because she could tell that both Constance and Frank found his obvious desire to display to the world that the Wynne family was under his personal protection intensely reassuring. She did want them to be happy, and remain in China, and not to feel that she was too much of a burden. She could understand how much heart-searching must have been involved before Constance had made the decision to adopt Kate Mountjoy's daughter. And she knew it had not been easy for her foster mother. It would have been difficult even without the concomitant of her royal blood, because she had always been a lonely child. This had been inevitable, because she had such an ingrained mistrust of Chinese, because all Manchu children not actually in the Forbidden City were her inferiors, and because most of the white mothers in Peking regarded her as "colored." These things had never bothered her; she preferred her own company, as she preferred to spend her time drawing or reading or just thinking, as opposed to playing childish games—but she could tell that it upset Constance.

As to the future, which also seemed so to upset Constance, she had never been overconcerned about that, either. She had never doubted that one was not born a Manchu princess merely to live and die in obscurity—however Constance might insist that that was the invariable fate of those women trapped within the Forbidden City. It had not been the fate of the dowager empress, and Adela was sure that it was not going to be her fate, either. If she could remain in China. And if she had to engage in a little personal subterfuge to ensure that, and to ensure her position, then she was quite happy to do so.

But Constance was also clearly upset at that moment by more than just the train incident. Adela suspected that her foster mother would have liked to have been the one actually kidnapped, and received proof one day, about a fortnight after that safe return to Peking, when Constance suddenly asked her, when they were alone together, what exactly Lin-tu had said to her. Without thinking, Adela asked a question of her own in reply: "Do you love Marshal Lin-tu, Mother?"

"How absurd," Constance snapped, and flushed. "It . . . well . . . it is possible to feel an . . . well, an affinity for someone without loving him. It is of course very, very wrong to allow the person in question to know this, or to let him take advantage of such an affinity, certainly if you are married to someone else."

"But if Father were never to know," Adela pointed out, "it could never make him unhappy. So how *could* it be wrong? Although . . ." She had checked herself in time. Although not in time to stop Constance giving her a very hard look. Constance was well aware that to Adela, loving a Chinese was an impossible thought.

"Because some things are just wrong," she had snapped, thoroughly on the defensive.

Adela decided to smother her embarrassment in argument. "Because the Bible says so. But I do not believe that everything the Bible says is necessarily right. Or true."

"You don't," Constance remarked with heavy sarcasm. "Well, miss, all I can say is that the sooner we get you back out of this heathen country, the better."

She had been taken aback. "China is my home," she said without thinking. "And these are my people. It is possible that I may have an important part to play in their history."

Constance's smile had remained full of sarcasm. "I am sure that is possible, my dear. But equally I am sure you must concede that if you are to play such a part, you require the very best possible education, and that is something you can obtain only in America, so obviously the sooner you return there, the better."

She was clearly very angry—which had to mean that she was, or had been, in love with Lin-tu. Certainly Adela knew it was essential to make friends again as rapidly as possible. "You are probably right, Mother," she said. "But I hope *you* will agree that I cannot be blamed for being a little off traveling at the moment." She kissed her foster mother on the cheek. "I do not mean to quarrel with you, truly. If you still wish me to return to America, say at the end of next year, when I am eighteen, I will be happy to do so."

Constance was, as always happened when Adela turned on her very adult personality, left speechless. But utterly relieved. Of course Adela hated having to practice such a subterfuge upon the woman she loved so dearly, but it was necessary, and for the moment they were suddenly closer, and happier, than they had ever been together. Because suddenly they were women together, and if Constance never again raised the subject of Lin-tu, yet had it once been shared between them. Thus she wanted to share other things, much to Adela's pleasure, and if a very natural desire to discuss Adela's own emotional problems was embarrassing—Adela had no intention of discussing her true feelings or her true desires with anyone—there was still a great deal that could be shared. Even physical things. Constance wanted to redecorate the house, which had never been properly undertaken in all the eleven years the Wynnes had owned it. Adela was delighted to help, as they altered Harriet Bunting's stark white walls to soft pastel shades of yellow and blue, a different motif for each room. Not entirely for reasons of economy, Constance elected to do the stripping and painting herself—she clearly needed an outlet for her energy but she was equally delighted when Adela volunteered to help, even if the servants were scandalized and Frank amused by their unusual domesticity.

But more than anything else, both Constance and Frank were so transparently pleased and relieved at her bubbling fun and laughter, so un-Manchu and reassuringly American, and so convincingly suggesting that she had entirely overcome the shock of her misadventure, and even more, the resentment she had obviously felt against Miss Evesham and all her erstwhile schoolmates, and even, they suspected, against them for inflicting such misfortune upon her.

Nor was it all entirely playacting, because her destiny, she knew, was rushing toward her. The pair of them were working in the spare bedroom, wearing old clothes and paint-spattered aprons, their hair bound up in bandannas, on an August afternoon, when Pu-Tang came into the room gasping with excitement and pointing over his shoulder, unable to speak. Constance stood up in concern, and saw Charles Baird waiting in the hallway.

With manhood, Charles Baird had become more than ever like his famous father, at least physically—Henry Baird had been three inches over six feet tall, and built to match. But Charles was also handsome in a way Henry Baird had never been, mainly because the missionary had concealed his face beneath a heavy black beard, whereas Charles had so far resisted the temptation to grow even a mustache, and thus the big square chin and the wide mouth were exposed as much as the straight nose and the soft brown eyes. He seemed to have inherited all his father's good points, the basic gentleness of character, but also the determination, as well as the complete confidence—and up to now, at least, had revealed none of the twisted uncertainty which had possessed Henry Baird's soul and left him unable to reconcile his natural desires as a man with his self-appointed position as a mouthpiece for the Deity, and which had so often turned him into a monster of misogynistic hatred. Constance had always determined that so long as *she* had anything to do with it, Charlie would be educated to a completely natural and joyous approach to sex. But of course, she had to remind herself, he was still very young, and it was still impossible to say for sure how he would turn out.

Just turned twenty, she thought as she went toward him; just finishing college and ready to move to business school. Then what on earth was he doing here?

"Charlie?" she asked, and was passed by Adela, who threw her arms around her foster brother's neck.

"Oh, Charlie," she cried. "How marvelous to see you."

Charles kissed her on the forehead and then looked at his mother. He was wearing his best suit, but had grown out of it, and it was also somewhat the worse for wear. And instead of a suitcase, he had placed a canvas carry-all on the floor. Yet he looked fit enough. Fitter than ever before, she thought.

"Charlie?" she asked again.

He took her in his arms, held her close. "Mother! It is so good to be here."

"Yes, but what are you *doing* here?"

He put one arm around her waist, the other around Adela's, and walked with them both into the drawing room. "I've decided not to go back to college after this vacation."

"Not to . . . ?" Constance attempted to stop herself, and continued to be propelled along by the muscular arm around her body.

"Oh, my grades are good enough, I should think. But it really would be a waste of time. And how could I possibly sit behind a school desk after what happened to you on that train? When I read your letters . . . my God! My place is here, in China, with you and Dela. And Father."

"But . . ." As usual in times of crisis, Constance concentrated on detail. "How did you *get* here?"

"I shipped as deckhand on a merchantman."

"Deckhand?"

"It was a tremendous trip, and they even paid me for it."

"But . . . Oh, Pu-Tang, I'm sure we could all do with a drink," she called. "Make mine a brandy and soda." She sat down, staring at him as he sat on the settee, Adela beside him, her arm still around his waist. "What on earth are you going to do now?"

"Work with Father. It's what I've always wanted to do."

"But . . ." She seemed incapable of thinking straight. She gazed at Adela.

Who smiled at her. "Isn't it splendid to have the whole family together again in China?"

"Well, of course, Charlie, it will be a great pleasure having you in the business," Frank agreed. "As a matter of fact, I was just considering looking for another European clerk."

"I thought you were planning on *selling* the business," Constance said.

"Well, I was, but you were so firmly against it, I completely abandoned the idea."

Constance opened her mouth and then closed it again. Because she had been completely against it. She supposed she still was.

"And Charlie *is* going to inherit the company, Connie," Frank went on. "Sure, it was my idea that he learn something of the theory of business management. But there really is no substitute for practical experience. If he's prepared to start at the bottom, and work his way through all the aspects of the business, well, there can be no finer training than that."

"That's what I want to do," Charlie said.

Constance gazed at them both in impotent fury, realizing that she was being utterly outmaneuvered. She had no doubt at all of what was going through Frank's mind. Maintaining Charlie at business school would have been very expensive—and because Frank felt as guilty about Henry Baird as she did about Kate Mountjoy, he was never going to suggest that his stepson do as so many other young men and *work* his way to a degree. All that could now be avoided. And if it was what the boy wanted to do . . . But apart from Charlie, her only real hope of getting Adela back to the States—and keeping her there—had been for Charlie to be there as well, for the girl to turn to whenever the going got rough. "And what about Dela?" she asked.

"Well . . ." Frank hesitated, and glanced at Charlie, and Constance suddenly realized that the pair of them had already discussed *that* matter as well.

"Yes?" she asked, her voice ominously quiet.

"I wonder if you're not pushing this American angle a bit too hard, Mother," Charles Baird said. "Sure, one has to go to college if one is going to get anywhere in this modern world, in business or politics or anything like that." He grinned at her. "Unless one has something to inherit, like me. But Dela isn't ever going to go into business or politics. And if you're trying to turn her into a model young Virginia lady, forget it. She just isn't going to do that."

"She agreed to go," Constance insisted, sticking to the essential facts. "After everything, she finally agreed to go. She *had* agreed to go. Now . . ." She pointed at Frank. "You've always thought she should go."

"Well . . . maybe I was wrong. It does rather appear that Yuan may have been right about Sun Yat-sen being a storm in a teacup. Not one word of revolution has been heard since you came back. You know that. In fact, if that fellow Feng hadn't hooked Adela off that train, no word would have been heard then."

"Meaning she invented the whole thing."

"Of course not, Connie. Meaning that Feng stepped out of line and blew the whole thing, so Sun has decided to call it a day for another few years. As for Dela, well, I'll admit I felt she was growing up without sufficient counterbalances to the Chinese, or rather, I should say, the Mongol influences in her life. But with Charlie living here . . ."

Again the money, she knew. Frank was becoming a positive miser. Even if she could understand his reasoning. He was planning on investing every penny he could save against the rainstorm he still saw on the horizon, despite his reassuring words. "Do you really suppose Charlie is going waste his time on a seventeen-year-old girl? Who also happens to be his sister?"

Charlie smiled. "I can't think of anything I'd rather do, Mother. I think you're worrying needlessly about Dela. I think things are going to work out very well. Let's call it fate."

"Fate," Adela said. She walked her horse through the great pine park immediately south of Peking, Charles at her side. In the summer this was a place of singing birds and soughing branches, and also of a vast herd of sheep, the exact ownership of which had never been quite clear, although those of the Pekingese who laid claim to the animals certainly seemed to know exactly which belonged to whom. "Only the Chinese believe in Fate." She had to say things like this to Charlie, who like his mother was a total Christian in his attitude to the Unknown, even if *she* knew that Fate decreed all things. It was only necessary to recognize the hand of Destiny when it was revealed. "But it is a good argument."

"You believe in *making* things happen," Charles remarked.

"That is why I wrote to you, yes," she agreed. "Do you not think I was right to do so?"

"Oh, every time. Father and Mother are most definitely in a very agitated state. And that talk of selling out . . ."

"Your inheritance," Adela reminded him, as she had reminded him in her letter.

"Of course. Well, I think I've quashed that one. But, Dela . . . how did you know it would work for you?"

"Because Mother doesn't really want me to go to America. For one thing, as I mentioned in my letter, she can't afford it. Father can't, I mean," Adela said, expertly mixing sufficient truth with her fabrication to make it convincing. "And for another, she really would prefer to have me here with her. She's only been insisting on my going because she feels it's somehow wrong for me not to have an American education and background. All that was necessary was for you to come along and say it isn't necessary. As you did."

"You have a brain like an adding machine," he said admiringly. "I can understand your wanting to stay here for as long as possible. But, Dela, do you really mean to spend the *entire* rest of your life in China? Mother has a point, you know. I mean . . ." He flushed. "Supposing your aim is the normal one, you know, grow up, have a little fun, get married, well . . . boyfriends are going to be thin on the ground here in Peking."

The moment of decision, she thought. Charlie knew only what he had read in the newspapers, and the few additional details she had given in her letter. She had told him nothing of Pearl, or the way Lin-tu had looked at her—or the way she had offered to surrender everything for her life. How that haunted her.

Only Charlie could exorcise all of that, give her back her pride, and her womanhood. But more than ever she did not want to be touched, and caressed, which he would certainly want to do should she tell him the truth. Of course she did not doubt that she had done the right thing in writing to him, for his sake, at least. It was *his* inheritance Frank and Constance had so carelessly considered throwing away. And he was so obviously happy to be back.

But as regards herself . . . She knew he loved her, even if, being a boy, he had not yet gotten around to translating such things as pleasure in her company, shared thoughts, and a mutual love for China into emotions. He would, with the slightest encouragement from her, she was sure, and it was an encouragement she had always intended to give. But it would involve touching, and surrendering at least part of her body, with the rest to follow.

She did not think she was ready for that yet, at least partly because it would mean a quarrel with Constance. There could be no doubt about that. And she and Constance had only just resolved one crisis. The dust from that should be allowed to settle awhile before it got all stirred up again. And besides, now there was time, all the time in the world.

She touched her horse with her heel and galloped away from him. She rode sidesaddle, of course, her legs concealed beneath a voluminous skirt, and with a broad-brimmed hat tied securely beneath her chin, from out of which her hair floated in the breeze, and yet she seemed as much a part of her pony as if she had been astride. "I do not wish to have any boyfriends." Her voice filtered over her shoulder.

Charles had to kick his own mount to catch her up. "But you *do* mean to get married, one day?"

At last she turned her head to look at him; her face as composed as ever. "Why, yes, Charlie," she said. "That must be the idea of every young woman."

Constance sat in her little office and did the household accounts, listening to the drip of the September rain outside. The rain seemed to encompass the entire North China Plain in a vast gray mist. It had been raining now for more than a week, as it often did in the fall—and every time the weather settled into such an uneasy pattern, there came the risk of the Pei-ho and the Han-ho, the two rivers which drained the basin, bursting their banks and flooding, with consequent damage to property and risk to life. When that happened, even the streets of Peking were likely to be inundated, and getting about was next to impossible. There were very few places on the plain high enough to be safe from the waters.

But even the rain could not dampen her spirits. Because the two months since Charlie's return had been such a happy time. She had been terribly depressed when he had first appeared and had talked her out of sending Adela away. She had also been very angry at the way she had been conspired against by her menfolk. Even Frank. Her trouble was that she could understand all the arguments against her, and she could not help but admit that Charlie was probably right, at least judging by Adela's very obvious contentment with the new arrangement. Almost as if the girl had known it would turn out like this.

But Charlie had made a tremendous change in all of their lives, with the force of his personality, his unfailing good humor, and above all, his tremendous confidence—it was like a sudden fresh breeze blowing through a room which had been kept locked for too long. She found herself thinking of his father, and wondering why Henry could not have possessed just that spark of humanity which so elevated the character of his son. Because Charles was half her, and Henry had lacked that leavening? That was pride. Yet she had to suppose it was true.

Certainly there could be no gainsaying the difference he had made to their lives. Frank's often considerable pessimism had quite disappeared. Not that business had improved. Far from it. But Charlie had thrown himself heart and soul into the firm, and never doubted that a dramatic upturn in trade was just around the corner—and had Frank believing it as well.

While Adela . . . Only a week ago they had celebrated the girl's seventeenth birthday, and never had there been such a happy party. Adela was now quite superbly lovely, every facet of her small crisp features being offset by the uncanny sparkle of her blue eyes and her wide mouth, the whole framed in the straight jet hair which reached almost to her knees. For her birthday Constance had for the first time allowed her to put it up, and it had added several inches to her diminutive five-foot-one figure. But the beauty of her physical appearance was unimportant when compared with the serene happiness of her character. Constance realized now just how much the girl must have hated the prospect of spending several more years in America as a student. Once that threat had been removed from her life, she had seemed to find a whole new dimension in living, and there could be no doubt that she and Charlie were the best of friends, spending almost every spare moment together as they talked, and rode together, and planned for the future.

Because this was the most reassuring thing of all; Charlie had not merely put forward negative proposals —that was quite foreign to his nature. Constance would certainly have remained concerned about what shape Adela's future *would* take, if she grew to marriageable age here in Peking. But Charlie had all that worked out. Next year, when Adela would be eighteen, he suggested that Constance and he launch her into American society. "Forget Richmond," he said. "Richmond is a backwater. San Francisco is the place."

And amazingly, Adela had seemed quite pleased with that plan. Although, as she had *seemed* contented enough with Constance's original idea, Constance did not wholly accept her agreement now. Dela was really content just to go through life putting off decisions about the future. But then, was she not also? she asked herself. And Charlie's plan was certainly the best yet. Adela *would* have been miserably unhappy at college, far away from her beloved China, and her only true intimate, her foster mother—although there had been, Constance was realizing, much less intimacy between them over the past month, now that she had her foster brother to talk to—and it *would* also have been a waste of money. For less expense than it would have cost to keep her at school for a single year they could throw a splendid party in San Francisco and have every young man in the city falling at her feet, she did not doubt— and then the girl would be almost an adult, and could be left to make her own decisions. And *that* would be a great relief.

She smiled at her foster daughter, who was standing in the doorway holding a very ornately crested envelope in her hand. "That looks important."

"It's from Marshal Yuan," Adela said. "Addressed to you. In English."

"From Yuan?" They had heard nothing from the great marshal for nearly two months—since Charlie's return, in fact. But this was not unusual. All those Chinese wealthy enough to own country estates invariably escaped to them once the rains started turning Peking into a vast drain. She slit the envelope, discovered that the whole letter was written in English, and in Yuan's own hand. She raised her head. "The marshal says he knows how dreadful Peking can be at this time of year. He invites us all to spend a week with him at his home. It is south of the river, you know."

"A week? With Marshal Yuan?" Adela looked distinctly skeptical at the prospect. "However shall we get there?"

Constance glanced at the letter again. "He is going to send an escort for us," she explained. "I think it all sounds rather splendid."

And entirely in keeping with her mood of contentment.

* * *

Frank did not think he could get away, as he was in the midst of attempting to secure a large order for agricultural machinery for the new viceroy of Chihli, and was due to meet with him on the very Saturday for which they were invited. But he was quite happy to let Charles have the time off, and delighted that Constance and Adela should be enabled to take a break from the misery that was Peking in the rain. Charles was also delighted at the prospect of seeing some more of China, and Adela, as had become usual over the past few weeks, was happy to do anything Charles wanted her to. Had she not been his sister, Constance thought, she would have been a perfect wife for the boy, and often there was almost a suggestion of the intimacy of betrothal between them. But that was of course impossible and unthinkable. Even if there was no actual blood link between them, they had grown up as brother and sister . . . and Adela could have been her own daughter. It was the merest chance that she was not.

She was actually the most delighted of them all, and not only at the prospect of getting away from Peking for a few days. It was also the thought of going to visit with Yuan, of allowing that huge, confident personality to sweep over her and reassure her that she had done the right thing in abandoning the idea of immediately sending Adela away—he would most certainly do that—as well as telling her that all was well with China despite what people said.

Just getting there was a splendid adventure, the more enjoyable because it was undertaken at his behest and under his aegis. They took the train to Taku, as usual, but there boarded an ornately decorated sampan, in which they were utterly protected from the weather by a huge, high, embroidered canopy—the whole thing made her think of pictures she had seen of state barges used by

kings and queens of England and France in the sixteenth
and seventeenth centuries. In this splendid vessel they
were poled across the fast-flowing and turbulent Han-
ho, and thence entered the Grand Canal, the huge
waterway constructed some two thousand years before,
when China had been about the only truly civilized
nation in the world, to link the great Yellow River with
the rivers around Peking, and thus provide a quick
means of communication between north and south.
Here all was peaceful, save for the dripping of the rain
and the occasional rumble of thunder, as they slowly
made their way, now drawn by horses on the bank,
through clusters of water lilies growing so thickly that
one could almost feel them holding back the boat, and
on the second evening they came into a landing where
there were palanquins waiting for them, to convey them
the quarter-mile to the house, or rather, Constance
supposed, the palace of the marshal.

Here were hundreds of servants waiting to greet them
and escort them inside beneath brilliant parasols. And
here indeed was a palace, a place of pagoda-roofed
turrets, of great hallways, luxurious reception
chambers, all built around a large ornamental lake
studded with statuary and filled with fish, into which a
manmade waterfall rushed and seethed to set up a
constant rustle in the background. Here were bedrooms
each the size almost of their entire house in Peking, with
great divan beds which looked big enough and soft
enough to smother in, and more servants to help them
change their clothes and bathe and prepare for the
evening. Because here too was Yuan himself, waiting to
entertain them in the splendor to which he was
obviously accustomed.

They were given Chinese robes to wear to dinner, and
there was a message from their host requesting the ladies
to leave their hair loose, to which Constance could find

no objection. The marshal himself was also wearing Chinese dress, and in the weeks since Constance had last seen him he seemed to have explanded his personality, if that were possible, beaming and confident, himself taking them on a tour of the various apartments in the house, showing Charles his collection of weapons and armor, most of which, he smilingly confessed, he had actually worn in battle, and then Adela and Constance his collection of Chinese artwork, the most exquisitely brushed representations of birds and flowers. "Is it not a shame," he asked, still smiling, "for a single person to enjoy all this?"

Constance did not suppose he was that single. If his wife had been dead for some years, and his children had all grown up and had homes of their own, his servants included a large number of pretty young girls, and also, she observed, several equally pretty young men. She was not the least shocked, even if she had not expected his amusements to be quite so openly flaunted. But she had lived in China for more than twenty years. A Chinese took his pleasures on whatever scale he could afford, and Marshal Yuan could clearly afford almost everything his heart desired; like all his race, he did not suffer any of the unnatural sexual guilt imposed by the early Christian Church to haunt succeeding generations. If she had any doubts on the subject, it was a slight apprehension that he might discover too much attractiveness in the handsome young giant who was her son, but Yuan, regardless of the paths down which his lusts might occasionally lead him, was in public totally heterosexual, and as ever when in the Wynnes' company, appeared to have eyes for no one but Adela. And yet . . .

He seated Constance opposite him at the end of the huge European-style dining table, and while he divided his attention in the main between discussing business with Charles and telling Adela how beautiful she was, his gaze kept sliding up the table to find her own, and to exchange a quiet and private smile.

Suddenly she realized that there was more to the invitation than had met the eye. This was the first time she had ever been invited to the marshal's house, for all that they had known each other for so very long. It had indeed always been a source of mystification to her, as well as a certain pique, that of all the Chinese or the Manchu with whom she had come into contact, Yuan, although he had always been obviously attracted to her personality and enjoyed her company, had never once suggested that he might be attracted to her as a woman. For which, she had always reminded herself, she needed to be very thankful. But still a mystery. Which was about to be solved?

She was aware of the tremendous excitement. However wrong she knew it to be, however contented her eleven years with Frank, the thought of having men fall in love with her was irresistible. And when the man was Marshal Yuan Shih-k'ai . . . Of course, it was possible for her to be utterly mistaken. He had invited the entire family, including Frank. On the other hand, would not Yuan, who knew everything that went on in Peking, in naming a specific date also have known it was the one week when Frank would not be able to leave Peking?

And whatever he had planned, it was going to happen now. The meal was over and the last of the plum wine was drunk. Yuan was beaming at the children. "I am sure you will understand that the old people, your mother and I, have much to discuss," he said. "And I am sure there is much exploring you wish to do. My house is yours. Go wherever you wish, and have whatever you wish. You have but to clap your hands, and you will be attended."

They understood that he wanted to be alone with

Constance, however embarrassed they were by his suggestion of unbounded hospitality. But they left the room, and Constance, heart pounding, and wishing that she had drunk just a little less wine, was escorted into a small sitting room toward the back of the house, where the whisper of the waterfall was very loud.

"They are superb children," Yuan said. "Children such as I might have hoped to father." He sat her on the settee, waved away the hovering manservant, and himself poured brandy from a crystal decanter. He had become very Western in his habits. "Of course the boy Charles is your very own, so it is to be expected that he would take after you. But the princess . . . she may have inherited her beauty from her parents, but her character she must have obtained from growing up with you, Constance."

"Oh, nonsense," she murmured nervously, taking the goblet from his hand and drinking before she remembered that she had decided not to have another until this ordeal was over.

"I think that is very true." He sat beside her. "And her beauty is quite breathtaking. Tell me, am I correct in supposing that she has just entered her eighteenth year?"

"Why, yes," Constance acknowledged in surprise. "However did you know?"

"I have kept track of the years. Thus she is, by any standards, of a marriageable age."

"Well," Constance said doubtfully, "I suppose she is. We are more inclined to take eighteen itself as a marriageable age. But some girls do get married at seventeen. Adela, thank God, shows not the slightest inclination in that direction. She doesn't even have a boyfriend."

"One would not expect her to," Yuan said severely. "She is a Manchu princess. But I am still relieved to hear it. Just as I was nearly mad with concern when I heard of those 'bandits' who molested her last spring. Had she been violated, I think I would personally have torn the genitals from every man in that so-called army." He smiled at her. "You must forgive me. But I would have you understand the depths of my feelings. I have of course wished to discuss the future of the princess with you often in the past, and have several times nearly done so. But I have hitherto decided against it, as I had no wish to commit you, and the princess, to a course of action which might at any moment have been altered by Fate, for who can tell what one year after another will bring? But now I am sufficiently sure of the immediate future to feel at rest in my mind."

Constance could only stare at him. From being avuncular he was now sounding almost like a father, in the way he was assuming that he would have a say in whom and when Adela married. That was something she would never permit. If he supposed that, having been her friend and adviser for so long, he was to start exercising prerogatives he did not have, well, then . . . But she would have to dissemble. Offending a man like Yuan could only be a mistake.

Besides, she was curious to know what he had in mind. And who.

"And that is why you asked us here to visit?" she asked, feeling at once greatly relieved and somewhat disappointed. "To discuss Adela's future? My dear Yuan, believe me that I am most grateful for your interest, but I can promise you the subject is under constant discussion between Frank and myself. And I can also tell you that it promises to be a difficult one. You see . . . " She hesitated, because she didn't really know how to tell the marshal that she didn't want her foster daughter to marry an Asiatic, even if he had managed to locate a suitable prince.

Yuan smiled. "I can foresee no difficulty, Constance. We have both long known that she would become my wife the moment the time was right. Now it remains only for you to give us your blessing."

II

The Flight

5

The Revolution

Constance swallowed the remainder of her brandy and choked. Yuan lent her his own handkerchief while he delicately patted her back. "Did you *not* understand this?" he asked.

Constance gasped for breath. "I . . . I . . . It's not *possible.*"

He frowned artificially. "Why is it not possible?"

Because you're old enough to be her grandfather, she wanted to shout. Because you're a lecherous old man. Because you have a record of doing what is best only for Yuan Shih-k'ai. Because you are up to some devious and terrible scheme.

Because I would rather be dead than allow it. And because Adela would rather be dead too.

But he was Yuan Shih'k'ai, probably the most powerful man in China, not excluding the regent, and she was in his house and surrounded by his people. Even more, so was Adela. If ever she needed her Chinese experience of dissembling, it was now.

"Because it is against the law for a Chinese to marry a Manchu, Yuan," she said quietly.

"I do not think the point will arise, in this case," he replied.

"She is also a princess."

"And I am a commoner? But that point is also irrelevant. The Manchu do not consider her to be one of them, or they would not have allowed her to be brought up in your home. Therefore neither of those objections is valid. And that the country as a whole *does* regard her as a princess, well, I think that is all to the good. Constance . . ." He seized her hands. "I have great plans. Plans which I can see approaching maturity with everyday. The country, as we both foresaw, is racing to rack and ruin. Soon they will have need of me, more than ever before. Sooner than we perhaps realize. And this time they must give me what I want, absolute power to set things right. Then there will be no looking back, Constance."

He means to destroy the Ch'ing, and be emperor himself, Adela had said. But that was impossible. Just because he *was* Yuan, he would know what was possible and what was not. Then what did he *really* seek?

"Before the call comes," he went on, "I wish to have Adela at my side." He smiled. "Times have changed, you see, Constance. One no longer conquers an empire, or at least an empire like that of China, by leading eight banners across the Great Wall, or a rabble up from the South. One conquers by emerging from within, the man everyone *must* follow, because there is no one else. And when that man is also related to the ruling house, however distantly, well . . ."

My God, she thought; he seeks the regency for himself, or to become regent for the regent, a sort of Chinese shogun, after the Japanese model. But the Japanese had themselves abandoned the idea of a shogunate as unworkable in this modern age—forty years ago.

"I see you are dazzled by the prospects I envisage," Yuan said, and refilled her glass. "It is of course a confidential matter, but I know that you of all people can be trusted. And I promise you that it will happen, and that, as I have also promised you, Frank and you have nothing to fear, nothing to anticipate but prosperity. While for Charles . . . why, the whole world may well lie at his feet."

"Yes," she said. "Yes." If only she could have a moment to think, and plan, to decide . . . But what was there to decide? There was only one thing she could do, supposing she could ever escape from this palace. With Adela.

"So all that remains is to set the date." He patted her on the knee. "Do not worry, I shall submit to a Christian ceremony."

"Yes," she said. "You do understand, Yuan, that Adela has no inkling of your feelings?"

"Nor should she. Marriage is a matter for parents, not children. It is sufficient that she is aware of how fond I am of her, and that she has revealed her fondness for me."

"Yes," Constance said doubtfully. "But still, she has been brought up as an American . . . Oh, I anticipate no problems," she continued hastily, as the marshal began to frown, genuinely this time. "It is just that it would be dishonest of me, a betrayal of my relationship with the child, merely to confront her with a *fait accompli.*"

"Indeed? And how *are* these matters handled in America?"

"Well . . ." Obviously it would be a mistake to tell him that in most cases it was the young couple who sought their parents' approval, rather than the other way around. "I will have to put your proposal before her, you see, and ask for her agreement."

"*Ask* for her agreement?"

"It is only a formality," Constance assured him. "She will of course be dazzled at the prospect, the idea of living here . . ." She looked around her. "But she may just be overawed by the many responsibilities being your wife will entail."

"She is a Manchu princess. Responsibility is in her blood."

"As you say," Constance hastily agreed. "Once she gets over her initial surprise, she will be delighted. Nonetheless, I must beg of you, Yuan, to let me handle this in my own way. I would ask you to say nothing, or reveal nothing, during this week. Allow her to experience the utter happiness of living here as your guest. And then, the moment we return to Peking, I will talk with her and . . . arrange things."

Yuan's eyes were watchful. "I do not wish any delays," he said. "I have told you, the call to office may well come more quickly than any of us supposes."

"I should have thought all the . . . the arrangements could be made within a month," Constance said.

Yuan nodded. "That will be very satisfactory." He held Constance's hand. "And I give you my word that I shall say, and do, nothing to upset the princess during her visit here." He smiled at her, and refilled her goblet. "I have always admired you, more than any other woman I have ever known, Constance. I have often thought that you would make a man a superb wife, or even more, a superb concubine. Do not frown at me. I can say these things to you now, because we are going to be related. I have long looked forward to that. Indeed, the certainty that this happy day would come has helped me to repel all the thoughts of lechery which I have so often had concerning you. That is a compliment, you know. A very great compliment. But soon I will be paying you an even greater compliment." He kissed her fingers. "I will be calling you Mother."

* * *

In later years, Constance was never sure how she survived the week, for all that Yuan was as good as his word, and revealed nothing more than his normal considerable interest in and affection for the princess. But every night after dinner, when the children had been dismissed, he would talk to Constance of his plans, of the children he wanted, even what their sex was going to be and what he would call them. He made plans for Frank, too, envisaging him as a sort of minister for overseas trade in the government he had no doubt he would be called upon to form, while Constance herself, as the doyenne of European and American women in China, would apparently do little more than host a series of receptions and dinners and tea parties, and lend her personality and her authority to charitable functions.

It was an unceasing nightmare, even if she hardly slept when he finally let her retire. It was a nightmare because it was the sort of life to which she had always looked forward—nor could she doubt that Yuan *would* prove to be the man to bring China into the twentieth century with the least upheaval.

But of course it could never be. It would mean condemning Adela to a life of . . . servitude. To Yuan women were things, objects to be played with, and used, and thrown aside whenever their usefulness was ended. He did not hide his attitudes. Constance was nearly sick the morning he took her to watch the punishment of one of his young women, together with one of the young men. "They have misbehaved," Yuan explained as the pale yellow flesh reddened and then burst beneath the impacts of the bamboo cane, while the girl shrieked and the boy bit his lip until blood also ran down his chin. It was horrible to watch, not only because of the pain being inflicted, or because Constance herself had once suffered like that, but also because she could not doubt that Yuan would inflict such a punishment even on his wife, should *she* ever "misbehave." And who could doubt that a young woman as high-spirited and free-thinking as Adela would misbehave from time to time, at least in the eyes of the marshal?

Of course it was tempting to leave the decision entirely to the girl. Just as it was tempting that she might wish to accept, whatever the risks. Because if she were to do that, the future was suddenly enormously bright. But she wouldn't accept. She hated Yuan, of that Constance was sure. And therefore the future was suddenly more clouded than ever before. Because Constance entirely believed what he had had to say. He *would* soon be called upon to form a government, and thus his already immense personal power would be enhanced by that of the state. And this was the man she was setting herself and her family up to oppose. Worse, since she dared not openly oppose him in case he decided to take what he wished by force, this was the man she was preparing to betray.

She could hardly allow herself a full breath until they were once more safely on the train to Peking. And apparently Adela felt the same way. "Thank heaven that's over," she announced, taking off her straw hat and throwing it across the compartment.

"I thought it was all rather amusing," Charles said. "If a trifle boring. But he does live on some scale, eh? And Dela, he certainly dotes on you. Suppose he were to ask you to move in?"

Constance's head jerked upward. Could Yuan possibly have said something to Charles?

No, she decided; he was definitely teasing. But Adela did not look amused. "I would kill myself first," she declared. "He is an evil man."

"For admiring you? Does one necessarily follow the other?" Charles asked with gentle humor.

Constance took no part in the conversation, but she knew that there was no help for it. She could hardly wait to see Frank when they returned, taking him into her little study the moment he came in from the office.

"Well," he said. "You're all looking very fit, if a trifle overfed. I gather from Charlie that the marshal lives like a prince."

"He does everything like a prince," Constance said. "Frank . . . how soon can we leave?"

"Leave? For where? You've only just come back."

"I mean leave China. For the States."

"You mean you and Dela? My dear Connie, I do wish you'd make up your mind. When last I heard, you were staying here for another year. So I did some expanding. Well, I couldn't have afforded to take Charlie into the firm, certainly not to pay him what I am paying him, if I'd known I had to finance an American jaunt this year. Whatever changed your mind?"

Constance told him. He listened in silence, stroking his chin. "My God," he commented when she had finished. *"What* a bundle of problems we did take on, to be sure, when we adopted that little girl."

"We can't let it happen, Frank," she said. "Adela hates Yuan, and even if she didn't, she would feel she was demeaning herself. He's a Chinese."

"You've talked to her about it?"

"Of course not. But I know how she will feel."

"I'm not arguing that. Well, of course she'll have to leave. And of course you'll have to accompany her. Yes, indeed. I'll see what can be done. We have a month to play with, you say? I should be able to sort that out."

"Frank," she said, "we *all* have to leave."

He frowned at her.

"Frank, this is Yuan Shih-k'ai we're talking about. As far as he knows, I'm very happy about the whole idea. There was no other way I could think of to handle the situation, there in his house, with Adela absolutely in his power. When I leave with Adela, he's going to take it as a slap in the face. More than a slap in the face. As a complete betrayal. I can't count the number of times he told me how much he admires and respects, and above all, *trusts* me. Do you really suppose you and Charlie could stay here after I run out with Adela?''

"Now, really, Connie, this is the twentieth century, and Charlie and I are American citizens—''

"Oh, don't talk nonsense, Frank. Do you really think China has entered the twentieth century yet? If it had, I'd have been able to sit down and talk him out of it. This is *China*. Manchu China. Tz'u-Hsi's China. And more than any of those, it is soon going to be Yuan Shih-k'ai's China. If you stayed here with Yuan as an enemy, at the very best you'd lose all your Chinese customers. At the worst you'd wind up in a ditch one night with your throat cut, and no one would know who did it.''

"Connie, Yuan is our friend. He has always been our friend.''

"Only so long as it has suited him. He's apparently been planning on marrying Adela for years. Maybe ever since she was born. I don't know. I do know he claims to have had her guarded all the time she was in the States. Can you believe it? The effrontery of the man? He got quite touchy over my decision to return via Hong Kong and Canton this spring without telling anyone. Especially him, if you please. Endangering the princess, he said.''

"Well . . .'' Frank ventured.

"Okay, okay, so he's right about that one. I'm just trying to show you to what lengths he'll go. This is what he wants to have happen, and this is what he is going to *make* happen. And anyone who gets in his way is going to be trampled flat. Adela saw from the beginning that he was an evil man. And I'm beginning to think she could be right. Certainly to those who oppose him. As for when he *is* made prime minister . . ."

Frank scratched his head. "I have no idea what to say, Connie. You're the one who refused point-blank to leave China when I suggested it. Now you want to pack up and go, just like that." He snapped his fingers. "Have you *any* idea what you're proposing? I don't have a hope in hell of selling the business in a month. And the moment I put it on the market, Yuan will be the first to know about it."

"I understand that. You'll just have to forget about selling the business, Frank."

"You mean just walk away from it? Connie, that's impossible."

"Why is it impossible?"

"I just don't have that kind of money. I don't have more than five thousand dollars available in cash."

"Five thousand will get us to the States."

"And what do we live on then? I have maybe another ten invested over there. How long do you think that is going to keep us?"

"Oh, I don't know, Frank. Something will turn up." She gazed at him, and he gazed back. She knew what he was thinking. "The alternative is to condemn that girl, our daughter, Frank, to a life of utter misery and possible danger as well. Yuan may go up very fast, but in China people like him have a way of coming down even faster. And the catastrophe invariably involves their families."

"There is such a thing as the greatest good of the greatest number, Connie."

"Frank!"

"Okay, okay. So I'm being an ogre. But you're asking me to ruin everything I've spent eleven years in building up, and to ruin all of Charlie's prospects too.

You're planning to abandon your home and have us all set off into the world with hardly a cent to our name. Connie—"

"I am asking you to help me save our daughter from . . . oh, call it a fate worse than death, if you like. Frank . . ."

He grinned, and took her into his arms. "Okay, Connie, okay. You know I'll do what you want me to. I just wanted you to be sure you understood what's involved."

She kissed him. "It'll work out, you'll see. If we can just get away from the clutches of that real ogre."

"Your old friend?"

"I always knew he was an ogre," she said, and got up. "I just never realized how *much* of an ogre."

"Where are you running off to now."

"To tell Adela. I'm sure she'd like to know what's going on. If she hasn't already guessed."

"And suppose she's prepared to do it? You'll have to at least give her the choice."

Constance gazed at him, and then shrugged. "Then we're all sitting pretty, I would say. But it has to be *her* decision, Frank."

Adela regarded herself in the mirror as she brushed her hair. This was a nightly ritual, and a lengthy one. Often it was a tiresome task, drawing the brush through the long, silken black threads.

Tonight was different. Tonight, having locked her door, she had undressed as usual, but instead of putting on her nightgown, had sat before her mirror naked. To look at herself. And think. And wonder.

This was not a pleasure she had allowed herself very often over the past six months. Looking at her body made her think of General Feng's encampment, of Pearl and the opium den, brought back all the revulsion and the shame and the hideous feeling of defilement. And now she was in grave danger of being defiled all over again—and far more terribly than anything that had happened to her in the Shan Mountains.

She had reacted instinctively to what Constance had had to tell her, instinctively, that is, in the direction of what she had supposed would most impress her foster mother. She had wept hysterically, even while her brain had been tumbling with confused thought. But her initial reaction *had* been outrage. A miserable Chinese, asking for *her* hand in marriage. For the second time in six months.

This coincidence had not seemed to occur to Constance. Constance had clearly been too upset by the whole situation. While Charlie had exploded into a genuine anger that had matched her own. Which was intensely reassuring.

But her confusion was increased by her realization that Constance and Frank had been *so* taken aback by her distress that they must have been allowing themselves to think, and perhaps even dream, privately. Because she could, of course, stay. Constance had left the final decision up to her, and she could tell that both Constance, and far more, Frank, knew that that would be the solution to all *their* problems. For her they were apparently prepared to throw away everything they had been working for ever since she could remember, but obviously they would rather not have to. And there was Charlie as well. Wynne and Company was his only inheritance. There was even the fact, although fortunately they were unaware of it, that it had been *she* who had persuaded him to drop everything and come home in the first place. If she were to behave in the slightest way like one of the heroines in the romances Constance kept giving her to read, she would willingly sacrifice herself for their happiness.

It was even possible to see, in Yuan's proposal, the hand of Destiny.

She was well aware that Destiny had hitherto taken great care to smooth her way through life, in giving her English blood and Constance as a foster mother. These assets had taken her out of the cloistering atmosphere of the Forbidden City and allowed her a better idea of what life could be about than she could ever have obtained as a full-blooded Manchu princess. It was impossible to suppose that Destiny had done that without intending her to put that increased knowledge and understanding to *some* purpose.

Her problem was that she had never been able to decide what the purpose could possibly be. Almost from the earliest thoughts she could remember, she had been aware of two immense facts: that China, the China owned by her family, was on the edge of a total, chaotic collapse, and that, so far as she could estimate from listening to Constance and Frank talking—and Mother knew the Ch'ing family better than most—she had more brains and more gumption than all the rest of them put together, not excepting the dowager empress. No one else understood that, of course. It was a personal certainty, like knowing one could ride a horse better than anyone else, or bake a cake. Constance indeed was so unaware of it that she had never been able to conceive of a better future for her foster daughter than to submerge her in the vast mass of American womanhood and American motherhood, quite forgetting that *she* had always refused ever to be so submerged.

Adela had preferred to dream of greater things when she had been a girl. Only with the observations of adulthood had she realized that they could be *only* dreams. And yet she still felt, she *knew*, that Destiny would not have given her what it had, her brains and her beauty and her *awareness*, merely to spend her life rocking on a back porch. Thus it had been possible to consider her kidnapping as a manifestation of that Destiny, in that it had shown her the danger the Ch'ing were in. Certainly she had never doubted that she should remain, by whatever means, to help them if she could. Without any idea how. But now she was being offered a very definite role in the future. She *was* a member of the imperial dynasty, and her dreams had always been tinged with sufficient reality to understand that she could never save the empire, or even more, take it for herself, *by* herself. Even Tz'u-Hsi had had to rule through men, as had the great empresses of history, such as Wu Hou, infamous for her ruthless cruelty. And now she was being offered a man, and a man she could not doubt was capable of ruling an empire.

But he was Chinese, and thus, for all his fine words, dedicated to the destruction of the Ch'ing, just as she knew he was a man who would never be dominated, even by her, but would seek to use her to bear him sons who would belong to both nations, and then leave her locked inside the Forbidden City, without a vestige of power, just as he was a man old enough to be her grandfather and riddled with vice and perhaps also disease. Just as he was a man she had hated ever since she could remember. And just as he was the sort of man who would never even leave her as regent for his son, if he could father one. That had been Tz'u-Hsi's road to power. Yuan was more likely to leave a command that her execution should immediately follow his own death.

Fate could never have decreed that. Therefore this was no hand of Destiny, but an evil temptation to which she had allowed herself to be exposed. And yet a *fate* to which she was still exposed. Constance and Frank had worked out their escape in elaborate detail, and Frank had this afternoon left for Tientsin, on business, in the eyes of the world—or, more important, in Yuan's eyes —but in reality to find them passages for America. Once that was done, he would write Constance a letter saying that he had encountered old friends who were unable to visit Peking but who would be overjoyed to see her as well as Charlie and Adela, so why did they not all catch the train and come down to the coast for a day or two? They would time their departure from the city for the day before the ship was due to sail, when they could go on board almost immediately.

The American in Adela, and the memory of the four years she had spent in the totally civilized security of Richmond, told her these precautions were absurd. They *were* all American citizens. Surely all they had to do was go along to the American legation, not a block away, and ask for protection, at least down to the coast. But this was China, not Richmond. And while the minister hemmed and hawed and tried to decide whether to believe them or not, the news would spread all over the city, and thence to Marshal Yuan's mansion, and they would be very lucky to *reach* the coast, even if it meant an international incident.

She put down her brush and threw herself across her bed in a paroxysm of anxiety. Because, thinking like that, it was difficult not to conclude that Yuan, so omnipotent, so powerful, would not know exactly what they were planning, would not already have laid his own plans to prevent their leaving, to have her carried to his palace . . .

The gentle tap on the door had her starting up as if someone had touched her on the shoulder, kneeling on the bed, staring at the wooden panels. "Who is it?"

"Charlie," he whispered. "Are you awake, Dela?"

She scrambled off the bed, went to the door,

remembered she had nothing on, and went back for her dressing gown.

"Dela," he whispered again.

She unlocked the door, and was in his arms. It took her so completely by surprise that she did not even protest. Besides, it was a chaste embrace, an overflowing of relief, and love. Brotherly love.

"Dela," he said, pushing the door shut behind him, "I've been lying there awake, thinking, worrying. Oh, Dela . . . I do love you so."

Now he seemed to have surprised himself. His head went back as they stared at each other, while he slowly seemed to realize she was wearing but a single garment, which was opening against him; he was wearing only pajamas himself, and she discovered that the embrace was not so chaste, after all.

He flushed. "Dela . . ."

But suddenly she was glad to be in his arms, glad to feel him against her. This was what she had feared, so stupidly. Because here was gentleness, and love, and perfect manhood, and love, and total mutual understanding, and love.

Here was her Destiny, surely, as she had always known. And it was a Destiny which precluded all others, and all other temptations, too, if she yielded to it. Yuan would never even consider marriage to a girl who was not a virgin.

There was a totally bad, un-Christian, *improper* thought to be having at a moment like this. But it had passed through her mind, even as she knew she *wanted,* as she had wanted, she supposed, ever since Feng and then Pearl had touched her. She even understood now that it had been the wanting which had left her so fearful of the deed. But now she was no longer afraid.

"As I love you, my dearest Charlie," she whispered, moving backward until her knees touched the bed.

* * *

The lamp still glowed in the far corner of the room, but in the bed it was difficult to see. And in any event, she immediately realized, he did not wish her to see. Even less did he wish her to touch. He wanted to kiss her, which was delightful, because she had never been kissed on the open mouth before, and he wanted to enter, as quickly as possible. The haste disturbed her, and disappointed her, because surely this was something too immense for haste. Surely he should wish to touch her breasts, and her bottom, and various other places which she enjoyed touching herself. And surely he should wish to be touched. And surely, too, their eyes, their awareness of each other's beauty, was as important to the moment as touching. She had never seen a man before. If Chinese coolies were in the habit of urinating in the street without regard to who might be about, it was not something she had ever wanted to look at, even if she had not been taught by Constance, ever since she could remember, immediately to look the other way. But surely no Chinese coolie had ever looked like this, so huge and yet soft, so insistent and yet gentle . . . until he was actually inside her, and then the sudden sharp pain took her by surprise.

Yet there was more than just pain, and she knew the pain would end, and then there would be nothing but pleasure left, if he would just keep moving. But he had already stopped, and was lying on her chest like a dead-weight crushing the breath from her lungs.

She didn't want him to move, in case he would come into her again. But she just had to breathe. . . . He rolled off her, and she gasped, and again, filling her lungs to the utmost.

"Dela," he said. "Oh, Dela . . . I didn't mean to, really. I just . . ."

"I wanted you to," she said, and rose on her elbow to

look at him, and smile at him, and lean forward to kiss him on the mouth. Because if she was now his, then equally he was now hers. All of him. She looked, openly, even if she did not wish to embarrass him by touching—and anyway, the rod which had entered her had lost all its passion, and therefore its power as well.

"But, Dela . . ." He was suddenly anxious, and worried. And afraid? Oh, not Charlie, surely.

"Now we can get married," she said.

"Get married? But . . . Mother?"

"We shall have to tell her, that's all. We shall do it tomorrow."

"Tomorrow?" Now he was definitely alarmed. The clinical decision of her thinking was strange to him, even if he had always known she did think like that, in straight lines to her goal. "But, Dela, what about Yuan—"

"That's all finished now. Don't you see? I'm yours. Not even Yuan can take me now. He won't want to, when Constance tells him."

"But . . . won't he be angry?"

"So let him be angry. The fact is, I *cannot* be his wife anymore. The only person in the whole world whose wife I can be is yours, Charlie." She lay down with her head on his shoulder.

"Yes," he said doubtfully.

Destiny, she thought. It has to be Destiny. She could not possibly have made a mistake.

"Ah," Constance said. "I was going to ask you to come in anyway this morning. Both of you."

She was in her office, as usual, surrounded by books and accounts. Because, being Constance, although of course she had not been able to risk telling Pu-Tang or Cook what they were meaning to do, she was yet determined to leave them paid not only up to date, but with an extra fortnight to tide them over until they could find new jobs.

"Come in," she said. "And shut the door."

Adela and Charlie entered the room and closed the door. They stood before her desk, rather, Adela thought, as she had had to stand, on more than one occasion, before Miss Evesham's desk. She would have liked to hold hands, but Charlie apparently did not wish this. Charlie had indeed suggested putting off this moment, at least until they were safely on a ship to the States. He had explained he was sure their mother had too much on her mind at the moment to respond favorably. Adela had had to point out that what they were going to do would *relieve* Constance's mind, as removing her principal cause for apprehension.

"Now," Constance said, "I don't know how long it will take your father to find us that passage. Hopefully not more than a few days, but it all depends on whether or not there is an American ship actually in the Gulf of Chihli at this moment. So it could take a week, or even a fortnight. Obviously during that time it is terribly important that we live our lives exactly as normal. This is not only for the benefit of the servants. I have no doubt at all that Yuan is keeping us under surveillance; he claims to have been doing so for years and years. I'm sorry that we have to be dishonest about the whole thing, but there it is." She tapped the papers on her desk. "As a matter of fact, I have written to the marshal this morning, telling him that we have discussed his proposal and that you are willing to accept."

"Mother!" Adela cried.

"It is necessary, don't you see? We must use every weapon we have. I have also told Yuan that unfortunately Frank has been called away on a business trip to Tientsin—he will know that by now anyway—but that the moment he returns we will all get together to celebrate your betrothal and make plans for the wedding. Meanwhile, life as normal. You will go the office as usual, every day, Charlie, and you will take your normal rides in the park, Dela. And should Yuan come to call—"

"I will spit in his eye," Adela declared.

"Oh, Dela," Constance said. "It's only for a few days. And it is necessary."

"No it is not," Adela said.

Constance gazed at her in surprise.

"Charlie and I have come to a decision," Adela said, looking straight at her foster mother and refusing to allow any distracting apprehensions to interfere with what she was saying. "We would like to get married."

"You . . ." Constance actually scratched her head, something Adela had never seen before, no matter what the provocation—or how persevering the nits.

"It seems to us both," Adela went on, "that this is the solution to all of our problems. Quite apart from the fact that we love each other." She gave Charlie a quick look and a smile, but he seemed to have lost the power either to speak or to smile, at least temporarily. "We also think that you are making a mistake in attempting to deal with Yuan at all. One cannot deal with the Chinese. They are the most dishonest people on earth, and so they assume everyone else is being equally dishonest with them. I suggest that you tear up that letter, and write another, to tell the marshal that when you put his proposal to me, I explained that I could not accept, even if I wanted to, because I am no longer capable of being his bride. I am not a virgin. Then he will no doubt have us escorted to Tientsin and placed on a ship himself. Or tell us we can live here for the rest of our lives, which is what we all want to do anyway."

Constance's jaw had dropped. "Not a . . ." She looked at Charles.

"I'm sorry, Mother. But it just . . . well, happened."
He was flushed with embarrassment.

"You . . . " Adela had never before seen the expression which crossed Constance's face, a combination of
exhaustion, fear, disgust . . . and pure anger. "You did
that? To your *sister*?"

"I made him do it, Mother," Adela said. "I mean, I
wanted it as much as he did. And I am not his sister. We
are not related in any way."

"You wanted it? But why? In the name of God, why?
Just to escape Yuan, you—"

"Of course not," Adela said, continuing to gaze
straight into her foster mother's eyes. "I wanted it
because I love him. Because I wish to marry him,
Charlie, and no one else."

"And I love her," Charlie said, regaining some of his
composure.

"You . . ." Constance drove her hands into her hair,
quite destroying the pompadour, to bring golden streaks
trailing past her ears. "My God! Oh, my *God*! And you
think that now you can just tell Yuan that you cannot
marry him because you are betrothed to someone else?
To your own *brother*?"

"Charlie is *not* my brother," Adela said sharply.
"And Yuan will never take as a bride a woman who is
not a virgin, Mother. You know that."

"Of course I know that," Constance shouted. "He
also won't have any more reason to respect you, or help
you, or treat you as anything better than a *thing*. Tell
him you were not a virgin when he proposed, indeed.
Do you think he is a complete fool? My dear child, he
was making devious plans when you were still in your
cradle. And what do you suppose he will do to
Charlie?"

Adela bit her lip. These were points she hadn't really
considered.

"Do you suppose he is going to pat him on the back and say, 'Well done, I couldn't have managed it better myself'?" Constance asked, her voice low and hard.

"I . . ." It was Adela's turn to look at Charles in confusion.

"Now, wait just one moment," Charles said. "Yuan seems quite a reasonable fellow. If we put the matter to him fair and square—"

"Oh, God," Constance moaned. "Oh, God! Can you really be so innocent? Do you think you are dealing with some Virginia planter? Even if he smiled at you, you stupid boy, he would already be laying plans to have you waylaid and castrated. Yes, castrated," she shouted as he gasped. "Turned into a eunuch, a nothing. That is the very *best* he would do to you. I . . . I don't know what to say. Yes, I do know what to say, but I won't say it. You have both behaved abominably, and stupidly, and criminally. Now all you can do is *pray* that we get away from China in one piece. You, go to the office, Charlie. You, miss, go to your room and stay there. And pray!"

It was tempting to suppose Constance was being hysterical, through anger. Certainly she was very angry, Adela knew. On the other hand, Constance knew Yuan, and she even knew China, or at least the Chinese, better than herself, Adela was willing to concede. She could be right. She could certainly be right that it was a risk not worth taking.

So then, what difference had it made? They were still planning to escape. And at the end of it, she and Charlie would still have each other. She put this point to Charlie himself that evening when she went to kiss him as he came home. To her dismay, he pushed her away. "Please, Dela," he muttered. And when she tried to explain that nothing had really been altered, he just stared at her. "You don't understand," he kept saying, "You just don't understand."

Because of course, from his point of view, everything had been altered. Had they tried to escape yesterday morning, and been captured, Yuan would have shaken an admonishing finger at him—and taken her to bed. Were they captured now, Yuan would cut off that precious possession he had not let her touch. That either way *she* would have been sacrificed did not seem to matter.

Men, she thought. Was any one of them better than any other? She found herself thinking of James Osborne, who had so gallantly tried to defend her on the train. But was *he* any better? She had felt obliged to write to him, care of his newspaper in Hong Kong, soon after her return to Peking, to thank him and hope he had not been too badly beaten up by Feng's thugs. And had never had a reply. If he had been soft on her, she had been a passing flirtation. Or he had no wish to know her after Feng had taken her.

No doubt, she thought sadly, they were all the same. But being angry with Charlie was pointless. Because no matter how frightened he might be of having to face Yuan, he was still her man. Having allowed him to love her, she could never be anyone else's: that was Manchu law, as it was certainly American custom. And of course, if he was too upset to love her again as long as they remained in China, he would recover his spirits and his courage fast enough once they were on the ship to San Francisco.

So she continued to smile at him, just as she continued to smile at Constance. Neither of them ever smiled back. Constance's only remark was, "Oh, I wish we could hear from Frank." But the days became a week, and the weeks became a fortnight, and she could almost visibly see both of them mentally disintegrating beneath the strain. This *was* frightening, as she did not know how to cope with it, and even more, she was realizing how much of a rock Constance, in her certainty and her aggressive confidence, had always been. But this Constance was no less afraid than her son, stood in the doorway of Adela's room almost wringing her hands. "Have you seen Pu-Tang?" she asked.

"No," Adela said. "Isn't he in the kitchen?"

"He isn't," Constance said. "And neither is Cook. They've just disappeared." Her head jerked as there came a series of explosions from somewhere in the city. "God, listen to them."

"Firecrackers," Adela said. The Chinese set off firecrackers every day, for whatever reason might occur to them.

"I'm not sure they are firecrackers, all of them," Constance said. "I . . ." She turned in alarm as the front door opened and Charlie ran in, hatless, face crimson with exertion.

"Mother," he shouted. "There's something very odd going on. No one is doing any work, and there are huge crowds in the streets. I can swear there has been gunfire."

"Firecrackers," Adela said again, hoping to calm them both.

"From the Forbidden City? Anyway, I've closed up the office, and I think we should put up the shutters here too, just in case there *is* some kind of trouble."

"Trouble," Constance muttered. "Oh, my God! And the servants gone. If *only* Frank were here."

Adela thought that if she said that once more she would slap her face. "If there is going to be trouble," she said, speaking as quietly as she could, "I think we should go along to the legation."

"The legation?" Constance stared at her. Of course Constance had been one of those trapped inside the legation for several ghastly weeks during the Boxer Rebellion. But she had survived, as had all the white women who had reached that haven.

"You mean you think it may be *real* trouble?" Charlie asked.

"You're right," Constance decided, pulling herself together. "The legation is only a few yards away. We'll be safe there until whatever it is blows over. But we must lock up the house first, or it will be looted. Charlie, the front. Dela, the back. I will see to . . ." She paused, and turned, as they all listened to the immense *growl* of a mob, suddenly very close, and almost immediately accompanied by the shattering sound of their gate being forced.

And now they could identify some of the shouts, as well. "Death to the Manchu!" people were calling. "Death to the Ch'ing."

Constance stared at Adela, while Adela's entire stomach seemed to fill with lead. Was not *this* the nightmare which had been hanging at the edges of her consciousness ever since she could remember? The mob outside Chu-teh mission must have sounded very much the same.

As Constance could also remember. Her face had turned quite white, and she was breathing so hard Adela thought she might be going to have a heart attack.

The entire house trembled. "Run," Charlie bawled. "Oh, run."

Run where? Adela wondered, as the front door suddenly collapsed beneath the weight of bodies thrown against it, and she stared at the men.

6

The Conspiracy

It all happened with such a terrifying immediacy. Adela instinctively stepped forward, in front of Constance, both to be beside Charlie and if possible to protect the older woman. "You are breaking the law," she said, trying to speak calmly, gazing at their bloodshot eyes and yellow teeth, straggling hair from which the pigtails had been either chopped or released with untidy haste.

"Death to the Manchu," they shouted. "Dr. Sun, Dr. Sun. Lin-tu, Lin-tu. Death to the Ch'ing."

Dr. Sun? Lin-tu? Had the long-awaited revolution suddenly arrived? But if it was Dr. Sun's revolution, or Lin-tu's . . . "Wait," she shouted. "Listen to me. Dr. Sun is my—"

She was seized by, it seemed, a thousand grasping hands, lifting her from the ground, holding her arms and legs, scratching at her breasts and back, digging into her hair. They surrounded her with evil-smelling odors as she gasped for breath, suddenly more angry than afraid, and entirely winded so that for the moment she did not resist them as they carried her across the room and threw her on the floor by the settee before commencing to tear at her clothing.

She heard Charlie yelling, and began to fight viciously and angrily, kicking and scratching less to protect herself than to get at him. The men nearest her fell away from the violence of her sudden resistance, but they came back again, tearing at her blouse, snapping the straps of her chemise, throwing her this way and that as they grabbed at her, bruising and cutting her with their fists and fingernails, and then suddenly falling away from her to leave her sprawling on the floor panting and almost spitting, furious at being manhandled, because everywhere they had touched had become so private to Charlie and herself.

She gazed at the two men, clearly mandarins from their dress and bearing, who had come into the room and had checked the mob. "These are white people," said the first man. "Are you mad? Dr. Sun gave instructions that no European or American houses were to be touched."

"She is a Manchu," someone shouted, pointing at Adela.

"She is a Ch'ing," shouted someone else, far more damning.

"Dela!" Constance ran to her. She too had been thrown to the floor and her clothes torn; her yellow hair was flopping over her face. "Dela! Are you all right?"

"Where's Charlie?" Adela asked, and tried to go to him, as she saw him sitting up and rubbing his head, which was bleeding. But immediately her arms were grasped again.

"Manchu!" they chanted, spitting in her face. "Dr. Sun has said they shall be destroyed."

"You *are* mad," the mandarin snapped. "Dr. Sun has said that the dynasty must *fall*. I will take charge of these people."

"The white people," said one of the men. "We will keep the Ch'ing."

"Charlie!" Adela said as the boy reached his feet. He came to her, and she threw her arms around his neck.

"We will see to *her,*" a man snarled, and seized Adela's hair to pull her away. She exclaimed in pain and outrage, and the man tore the remainder of her blouse from her shoulders, leaving her panting with anger and humiliation, because her chemise had also collapsed and she was naked from the waist up. The Chinese cackled and pointed at her small, heaving breasts, and then surged forward again. The mandarins were thrust aside as they closed on the girl. Charlie tried to regain her and was also knocked down. Constance screamed as she saw the knives, while Adela's brain seemed to go dead; although her mind could accept the thought of death with inbred stoicism, the thought of mutilation turned her blood to water, and less because of the thought of the agony than of the destruction of her beauty, her sexuality . . . and therefore her Destiny.

But it was going to happen, she realized, as hands seized her breasts to pull them away from her chest in preparation for the cut, while the noise rose about her. The mandarins were helpless to control this mob. Charlie was being trampled on, and Constance could only scream, her memory no doubt going back eleven years to how Kate Mountjoy had died, in circumstances very like this.

But *she* was not going to die. She sucked air into her lungs, stared at the knives as they came closer. "Wait!" she screamed. "Wait!" she screamed, her voice cracking with effort. "Lin-tu!" she shrieked. "Lin-tu!" And wondered: Why Lin-tu? Because she knew he would be more effective than his master?

She had at least checked them; the knives were lowered. But they still held her like a sacrificial victim.

She gasped for breath. "You say you serve Dr. Sun?" she demanded. "Then you must also serve Marshal Lin-tu."

"Marshal Lin-tu commands the assault on the Forbidden City," someone acknowledged. "He will spit on your head."

"Marshal Lin-tu is my friend," Adela declared.

They stared at her.

"Take me to Marshal Lin-tu," she told them. "Take us all before the marshal, or beware his anger."

"Marshal Lin-tu has no friends among the Ch'ing," someone growled. But they were Chinese; they could not resist an argument.

"I am his friend," Adela insisted. "I am his woman!" She stared them down, even as pink spots gathered in her cheeks. "His *woman*! He will wish *me*, and my mother and brother, brought before him."

Still the men hesitated, but clearly she had won them at least a temporary respite with her devastating confession. The men holding her breasts released her, and the hands slipped from her arms; the knives were being put away. She gathered what she could of her tattered clothing about her as she sank to her knees against the settee; she could not stop the tears of mingled exhaustion and relief, anger and humiliation, from rolling down her cheeks.

The men argued, while others roamed the living room, seizing precious ornaments, shattering expensive vases. Constance also wept. She had thought all this was behind her. And if she had been prepared to abandon her house and flee, the thought of its being looted by such hands was overwhelming.

For the moment the exact import of Adela's words did not seem to have penetrated her brain, to Adela's relief, and at least the mob leader had sent someone off to see if he could locate Marshal Lin. The two mandarins had also gone off. Yet there were at least twenty men still in the room with them, grinning at them, laughing and making obscene remarks.

"My God," Charlie muttered, recovering some of his confidence now that they were no longer actually being manhandled. He took off his jacket and wrapped it around Adela's naked shoulders. "Are you all right?"

"Yes," she said. "Yes." Her tears were already drying as she stared at Constance, watching her foster mother's thought processes starting to work again. But Constance's reactions were the least of their problems at the moment. She tore a piece of material from her already tattered chemise to dab at the wound on Charlie's head—it was more a bruise where he had struck a table leg in falling.

"*I* am all right," he muttered, and glared at the Chinese. "Goddamned swine. Now, Mother, how do we get out of here?"

Constance looked at him, and then at the men watching them, her shoulders slumped.

"Mother," Charlies said urgently. "We must do *something*. That was a brilliant idea of Dela's, but even if this fellow what's-his-name does come, when he discovers that he doesn't know her, or us . . ."

Constance sat down with a sigh, allowing her back to slide down the wall; the settee was available, still, but it was as if she no longer felt the house or its furniture belonged to her.

"Lin-tu will come," Adela said. "And he will help us." She continued to stare at Constance. Because Constance had to take it from here, whatever her feelings. Lin-tu loved *her*. He hated the Ch'ing as much as any of his people.

"You mean you *do* know him? Well, glory be." Charlies sat down himself, next to her.

"Yes," Adela said. "We both know him. Mother . . ."

"It will be all right," Constance said. "I will make it all right."

Adela sighed with relief. Constance was herself again. She had asked no questions, uttered no recriminations, at the situation her foster daughter had placed her in. She *would* make it all right.

And she could relax, at last. She had never felt so exhausted. She knew she was suffering from shock, and it was not only the shock of her assault. Even if she had known for six months that there was another revolt simmering just beneath the surface of Chinese life, she had allowed herself to believe the confidence of others, and had taken refuge in the patterns of history. Certainly over this last week Sun Yat-sen's machinations had no longer seemed a relevant factor when compared with the menace of Yuan. But now . . . This was a revolt against the dynasty. Where were their plans now? And if it *was* a revolt against the dynasty, where were Yuan's plans now? Were they safe, or was *she* in deeper danger than ever?

"I wish I knew that the devil you two were talking about," Charlie grumbled. He had been watching the Chinese. More and more men were crowding into the house, and now that the word had spread, there were women and children here too, staring at them, pointing to where the white women's skirts had been torn to expose their legs, jeering and shouting. The spokesman had disappeared, and there seemed no one in authority. If Lin-tu did not soon come, or at least send instructions, it seemed likely they would be torn to pieces after all.

"Simply that you must remember you have your mother to care for," Adela told him, sounding rather like an elderly aunt, although she was pleased with the calm of her voice. "They do not mean to harm you, and will not, if you do not fight them. There is no point in attempting to play the hero, and losing Mother's life as well as your own."

He stared at her, and she stared back. Did she really mean that? Her system was still too shocked to know *what* she meant. Despite the quarrel with Constance, life had been going so according to plan; despite having to leave China, it had been possible to see even Yuan's menace as part of the forces driving her in the right direction. But it was also possible that Fate had only been playing with her, that she *had* no future at all; it was not possible to live without dreams and hopes, but that she was about to come to a full stop sometime very soon, a cord wrapped around her neck . . . or worse, torn to pieces by these people who were staring at her and chewing their lips in anticipation of again laying hands on her body. Compared with this mob, General Feng's soldiers had been the most perfect gentlemen. She could still feel those filthy hands on her breasts; her entire body felt dirty. Mother had died this way. Might not Fate have a repeat performance in mind?

But if that were to be so, then she *must* face it without fear. She was a Manchu princess. If she died, it would be because of that simple fact. Thus nothing that happened must bring the slightest murmur of complaint from her lips. Already she regretted having wept when she had realized they intended to cut off her breasts. That had been the Englishwoman in her rather than the Manchu, even if the tears had been caused by shame rather than fear. Yet her cry had saved her, if only for a few moments, because the end of her ordeal was at hand, one way or the other. The men were parting to let Lin-tu into the room, their strident cries sinking into mutters.

* * *

Unlike the last time she had met him, Lin-tu wore a uniform, khaki with a peaked cap, and with a revolver hanging from a leather waist belt. He had not bothered with any insignia, however, might have been a sergeant or a lieutenant rather than a marshal. But his authority was as usual evident in the way his people obeyed him and waited for his every command.

At the sight of him, Constance stood up, trying to straighten her gown, a hot flush spreading across her cheeks. Adela followed her example, holding Charles's jacket closed across her breasts, but too curious to see what would now happen between these two old protagonists to feel embarrassment. Charles glanced from one to the other, and then, understanding who the man had to be, also got to his feet.

Lin-tu ignored them all to gaze at the spokesman for the mob, who had reappeared. "What is the meaning of this?" he demanded. "Orders were given that no European or American houses or people were to be interfered with."

"We sought the Ch'ing woman," the man muttered.

"She is an American citizen," Lin told him. "You will be whipped for this." At last he looked at Constance. "So you had to send to me for help. *You* had to beg for *my* help. But this is not the first time you have begged me for help, devil woman."

Constance drew a long breath, but she refused to lower her gaze. Yet she did not seem able to speak. Charles was looking more mystified than ever.

"I sent for you, Marshal Lin," Adela said quietly. "It was me the mob wished to kill."

He turned his gaze on her, slowly taking in all of her, and she felt herself flushing in turn. "I also wished to congratulate you," she said. "On keeping your plans so secret."

"Secret," he marked. "The fools brought it on themselves. Now they are destroyed. The Forbidden City is ours. It could have been done years ago. I have always said this."

"You have destroyed the Manchu?" Constance was aghast.

Lin-tu continued to stare at Adela, and she almost felt her blood chill all over again. "They are our prisoners," he said. "Now they await the pleasure of Dr. Sun."

Constance's breath exploded in a gush. "Then you will talk with me," she said. "Please, Lin."

Lin-tu gazed at her for several seconds. "You have nothing to say to me, Mrs. *Wynne*," he said at last. "And I have nothing to say to you, save to curse you. I will talk with *you*." He pointed at Adela, and she caught her breath. "In there," Lin-tu commanded, pointing at Constance's bedroom. "Watch these white people," he said to the waiting men. "Do not harm them unless I say so." Again he pointed. "In there, Princess."

Adela attempted a smile at Constance. She intended to reassure, but Constance merely stared at her in consternation. Adela stepped through the bedroom door, and Lin closed it behind them.

"You attract calamity," he said. "As a steel pole attracts the lightning flash. By your very existence, you surround yourself with disaster."

She faced him as boldly as she could. "As you spend your existence *creating* disaster?" she asked.

He came closer. "Orders were given that all European houses, and American houses, and especially *this* house, were to be unharmed. Yet this has happened. Some of those men out there will have to be punished. Yet it has happened. Why should I not let events take their course, and *then* punish those men? Tell me that, Princess."

She would not lower her gaze. "Because you would be committing a terrible crime," she said. "And you would know it. But if that is what you mean to do, then *do* it. Open that door and tell those sewer rats to come in here and take me. While you *watch.*" She released Charlie's jacket, more in vehemence than with any intention of seduction, and hastily grasped it again as it swung open.

Lin's nostrils dilated. "So the Ch'ing have courage," he remarked. "This has never been disputed. Perhaps too much courage to die so miserably." He stretched out his hand to stroke her chin, and she kept still, refusing to shrink away from him. "Yet will you have to die, I think. You are too dangerous to live. You are too beautiful, and too bold, and too intelligent to live except as what you are. And that can no longer be."

She stared at him, trying to keep her breathing under control.

"Yet *will* it be a crime," he said, half to himself. "To destroy so much. It should at least be shared, that it should be remembered."

He wanted her to beg, as she had done in the Shan. He wanted her to offer herself, all over again. That he could take her? Or that he could again spurn her?

He was not going to have either pleasure. "You have the right," she said, "to give me to that mob. You have no right to take me for yourself, without being dishonored."

"Because you are a princess? The Ch'ing and their laws are no more. I could even announce you as my woman, and take you, forever."

"You could not, with honor," she said. "I am betrothed to another."

He frowned at her. "You?"

"I am betrothed to Charles Baird," she declared. "And our love is already consummated."

His gaze dropped down her body to her crotch, in the purest dismay. And suddenly she realized that she was not going to die after all. Or even be raped. Once again her courage had come to her rescue. Her Ch'ing courage, and presence. It was only necessary now to complete his discomfort.

"We are to be married," she said. "Constance's son and I. We were planning to leave this place within the next week and sail to America and be married."

He stared at her face. "And live in America?"

"Of course."

Again he allowed his eyes to wander up and down her body. Then he half-smiled, and sighed. "To destroy you *would* be a crime," he said. "Perhaps you have only the substance of a dream, to most men. To all men, except Charles Baird. Go to America, Princess Adela. And live, and be happy. But do not return to China. Never do that. China can only mean disaster for you." He went to the door. "I will dismiss these gutter rats and put my own men to guard this house," he said. "And I will inform you when it is safe for you to leave for Tientsin." The door closed behind him.

Adela soaked in a hot tub in her bedroom, felt the blessed water lapping over the cuts and bruises she had sustained, hurting her but bringing relief at the same time, making her feel clean again. If only it could lap at her mind.

Yet had she triumphed, and for them all. That simple fact was what she had to remember, always.

From the kitchen she could hear Constance and Charlie talking as Constance bathed and dressed her son's head wound. Poor Charlie. He was totally bemused. If he, like them, found it difficult to understand what had happened, he also found it impossible to understand how his sister, who was also his fiancée, after a brief conversation with a rebel had restored their freedom as well as their dignity.

Constance was not confused. Constance had no
doubt at all how it had been done, if not this morning,
then six months ago. That was something which would
have to be explained. But not now. Constance was not
in the mood, was still trying to accept the fact that a
man she had always supposed in love with her had
apparently transferred his affections to her daughter.
Constance had perhaps never truly understood the
conflict between honor and anger, self-respect and
Manchu-hatred, that made up Lin-tu's character.
Constance was angry.

It was of course something that would be resolved,
once they had the time. Once their emotions had settled
down. Once *her* emotions had come to grips with the
situation. Because over everything that had happened,
the invasion of the house, their manhandling by the
mob, her own very close brush with a ghastly death,
there hung a cloud of unimaginable blackness and
horror. A cloud that was blacker and more horrible for
her than for either Constance or Charlie. Because the
unthinkable, the impossible, had happened. The
dynasty had apparently fallen in a single morning. To a
peasant rabble led by the least imperious figure she had
ever known. Where was her Destiny now?

But, as she had been coming to realize, she had never
had a Destiny in China. She had had a dream, a chaotic
vision that even she had never seen clearly. And now it
was revealed for what it was, no more than a dream.
Whatever direction China was now to take, whatever
was going to arise on the ashes of this catastrophe, she
had no part in it. If she had a Destiny, it was with
Charlie. As his wife. As his *American* wife.

That meant that his reassurance, the reestablishment
of their love, was far more important than explaining
what had happened between her and Lin-tu. She got out
of the bath.

Charlie was clearly feeling much as she had felt. "It seems incredible," he was saying. "What happened . . . and then it just ended . . ."

"Nothing ever just ends," Constance said.

"When I think what they did to Adela . . ." He gazed at her as she came through the door wrapped in her dressing gown, water still dripping from her hair.

"What they *nearly* did," she said.

Constance raised her head; her eyes were cold. "Did not Lin-tu say he would send for us when it was safe to travel?"

"That's right. Mother—"

"Which could be at any moment," Constance pointed out. "And we must be ready." She looked around her shattered house. "Certainly there is nothing to remain here for. So I suggest you get yourself dressed, Adela." She had already changed her clothes.

Adela sighed. But she would have to sit this out, until the time was right for explanations. "Yes, Mother," she said, and turned back to the door, to check as there came the sound of horses' hooves in the yard, and barked commands.

The front door opened and one of the men Lin-tu had left on guard looked in. "The marshal comes," he said.

"So soon?" Constance said. "Oh, Adela, do hurry."

"Marshal Yuan Shih-k'ai," the soldier explained.

"Yuan?" Constance stared at him, and then turned toward Adela again, as if supposing she might have an answer to this too. And Adela stared back at her foster mother. Because she *did* have an answer, suddenly exploding in her brain like a bright light.

But it was too unthinkable to be believed.

She had never seen Yuan in all his military finery before, was amazed at the splendid figure he made. He wore khaki, but tunic and breeches instead of jacket and trousers, perfectly pressed, as well as highly polished brown boots. His leather belts and his revolver holster and scabbard also gleamed with polish. His peaked cap was a mass of gold leaf, as was his sword hilt, and there was gold leaf in his epaulets; red tabs on his collars, together with the ruby badge of a mandarin of the highest rank, completed his ensemble as a commanding general.

He seemed totally out of place in what was suddenly a rather small and poky drawing room, even had it not also been a pile of rubble. "Constance!" he said, but he had eyes only for Adela, who had remained waiting in the inner doorway, still in her dressing gown, her towel now wrapped around her hair. "Princess Adela! When I heard . . . I have commanded one man in every ten out of that mob to be beheaded immediately."

Adela stared at him in horror. But then, she would have done so anyway. Yuan Shih-k'ai! She had always known him to be an enemy, but he had always at least paid lip service to the dynasty.

"One in *ten*?" Constance cried. "But, Yuan . . ."

"They did not actually do us any harm, sir," Charlie explained. "Beyond a few bruises. And some insults."

"They laid their filthy hands on the princess, and as you say, they insulted her," the marshal pointed out severely. "They did these things to my future wife." He glanced at Adela. "You know of this?"

Adela's head moved up and down in what might have been a nod. Oh, for the power to *think,* to combat this new catastrophe. She looked at Constance, but the truth of what had happened was apparently just dawning on her foster mother. She was speechless.

"You will all leave the city and come to my encampment," Yuan declared. "My forces are concentrated just without the walls. I'm afraid the country is in such a state of turmoil you will have to stay in the camp for a few days, as only there can I guarantee your safety. But I will soon have the situation under control, I promise you. And then, my dear Princess, you are never going to be in danger again. I promise you that too. So if you would like to get dressed, and gather your things together . . ."

"Under control?" Constance asked, obviously making a great effort to come to terms with the situation. "You mean you have put down the revolt? Please tell us what has *happened*."

"Ah, the whole thing was grossly mismanaged, as are most things planned by Sun Yat-sen," Yuan said, disparagingly. "There were no plans for an uprising against the Ch'ing until next year, when I would have been ready. But of course that absurd episode in April, when the princess was taken from the train, had to be reported by the viceroy at Shao-Kuan, and the government was alerted that *something* was brewing in the Ta Shan, and obviously also in Canton. Canton has always been a nest of revolutionaries. So they sent their agents all over the South, and one of these spies stumbled upon the headquarters of the Kuomintang—that is Sun's organization, you know—which was not in Canton at all, but in Hankow. The government immediately arrested everyone they could lay hands on, and discovered a great many papers containing information that would have incriminated me, as well; can you imagine, leaving material like that lying around to be captured by imperial spies? Well, Sun panicked, as is usual with him. Messengers were sent to me, warning me of what had happened, and to this imbecilic army commander of his, Lin-tu, who happened to be in Peking. Before I could even decide what to do, Lin-tu had taken it upon himself, not to command the Peking organization to go to ground and himself leave the city, but to launch the revolution here and now. Of course, it has all turned out very well. But when I think . . ."

Constance sat down on the settee; she rather collapsed, as if her legs would no longer support her. "You?" she asked. "And Dr. Sun? Plotting together?"

Yuan sat beside her. "We have been in correspondence for years, my dear Constance. It always pays to be in touch with people. Especially those who have *ideals*." His tone was contemptuous. "Sun Yat-sen dreams of becoming a popularly elected president of a democratic China." The contempt grew. "Democracy. Truly, the Greeks have a lot to answer for."

"But . . ." Understanding was obviously slowly filling Constance's brain, and tearing it apart. "The train . . . the man Feng . . ."

"Yes," Yuan said grimly. "Would you believe that man was a protégé of mine? I took him from a private soldier, and I made him an officer. I made him a general. I recommended him to Sun to command the army he was trying to form in the Ta Shan. He had talent, and I knew that anyone with the remotest idea of military discipline and tactics would be preferable to this madman Lin. But more than that, Feng had been a friend. An intimate," he added darkly. "I had made the mistake of telling him what I had planned. And so he thought he could forestall me."

"Oh, my God," Constance said. "Oh, my God."

"Do not reproach yourself, my dear Constance," Yuan said. "You could not have known the risk you were running. And besides, by taking that train journey you at least made the traitor reveal himself. He must have acted on the spur of the moment, when he learned that the princess would be on that train. Well, he is dead. Do you know, I regret that? I would like to have him still alive. For him I would have revived the death of a thousand cuts, and *kept* him alive, for three years, while every day a sliver of flesh was removed until he would be counting his own ribs." He patted her hand. "Forgive me. We Chinese do not easily forget those who betray us. We are not taught, like you Christians, to turn the other cheek. Nor do we believe that a man's sins are punished in hell, sufficiently. We prefer to hear him scream while he is yet on this earth. But that is the end of Feng. You will not hear his name again."

Constance could only stare at him, and then turn her gaze on Adela. Her thoughts were easy to interpret. Even this new horrifying suggestion of what could be Charlie's fate were Yuan ever to find out what he had done would be less important than her slow understanding of the terrifying web he had been weaving—for how many years? While serving the Ch'ing with apparent absolute fidelity, accepting their decrees, even that of his own dismissal from his viceroyalty, without the slightest demur. The army massing in the Shan, which he had turned aside as a joke, had been virtually his own. No doubt *he* had ordered its dispersal, all without a change of expression, the day after he had smiled at her and told her to forget about it.

Even Adela found herself breathless at the magnitude of the conspiracy in whose coils they had lain for so long, because even she had only half-suspected the truth. And now the coils were slowly tightening about them. Lin-tu had promised to send them under escort to Tientsin. But Lin-tu served Yuan. And he knew nothing as yet of Yuan's marriage plans.

And she had betrayed herself to him!

Her brain tumbled, and raced, and suddenly settled. There was a way . . . because Yuan had no idea of her true feelings for him, of her long-felt suspicions. And in arrogantly boasting of his double dealing, he had given her an opportunity.

He was expanding even now. "At least it is all over and done with," he was saying to Constance. "The

Ch'ing are in the dust. They collapsed like a house of sand. They were always a house of sand."

Adela screamed, "Traitor!" and ran at him, swinging her small fists, her dressing gown flying open and the towel slipping to the floor to allow still-wet black hair to scatter across her shoulders.

Instantly the guards charged into the room, but Yuan had already risen and seized her wrists to stop her scratching his face, holding her at arm's length as she tried to kick him.

"Princess!" he shouted in amazement. "Control yourself, Princess. You," he shouted at Charles. "Take your sister."

Charles seemed to awaken from a deep sleep, hurried forward to hold Adela's arms and pull her away.

"Traitor!" she shouted again. She dared not look at Constance; she could only pray that her foster mother would understand what she was doing, what she was hoping to achieve.

And act on it.

Constance could not immediately make up her mind if Adela was acting or not. Her senses had received so many sledgehammer blows today, and even before today, that she only felt like going to bed for a month, putting her head under her pillow and refusing to acknowledge the existence of any other human being.

But to attempt that would be to die. And if it was her criminal act which had gotten them in this position in the first place—Constance had no doubts the girl had led Charlie on—Adela was still certainly prepared to fight to the last second of her life. Thus she could not now be let down, however much she deserved a good thrashing . . . but Constance knew she was thinking of Lin-tu at least as much as Charlie in her anger.

And if she *was* acting, she deserved to be on the stage. Her cheeks were pink; her entire body, tantalizingly glimpsed through the swaying dressing gown, seemed to be heaving with emotion, and there was even a tear rolling down her cheek.

Certainly she had won them a considerable advantage. Yuan was looking quite bemused, no doubt, Constance thought, both by the girl's reaction and by the beauty which was being revealed to him, and which he assumed would soon be his. "I do not understand," he confessed. "This behavior . . ."

"Take Dela into the bedroom, Charlie," Constance commanded. "Talk to her." If it was an act, she couldn't risk its not being sustained. "My dear Yuan," she said, "this house of sand of which you speak was inhabited by Adela's cousins. She is very conscious of her imperial heritage."

The marshal sat down as he watched Adela being dragged, still fighting and shouting, "Traitor!" through the door; apparently he did not object to her being manhandled by her own foster brother. "That child?" he demanded. "Has any member of that family ever recognized her? Ever treated her with anything but contempt?"

"Why, no," Constance acknowledged. "But that does not mean she is not proud of being Ch'ing. Were she not, would you wish her as a bride? And today she is of course quite distraught anyway, and not only from the attack on her. Can you imagine a young girl being exposed to such an experience?"

"I have punished those responsible."

"But she is deeply upset by what has happened to her family," Constance insisted. "By the thought that they may have been imprisoned, or even murdered."

"No one has been murdered inside the Forbidden

City,'' Yuan insisted, now definitely on the defensive. "At least to my knowledge. And if there has been, then more heads will roll. I can promise you that.''

"Nevertheless,'' Constance pressed on, "Dela is in a very delicate frame of mind. And now to learn that for years you have been conspiring against her family, and are prepared to boast of it . . . That was a grave mistake, Yuan.''

"You asked me.''

"That was careless of me, too. But of course I had no idea what you were going to reply. Or that you could possibly reply as you did. Now . . . I am afraid that after all of my work, right this minute Adela hates you.''

"She will recover,'' Yuan said.

"I can't be sure of that. She is a very emotional girl. And a dreamer. I wonder if it would not be best to abandon—''

"I am going to marry the Princess Adela, Constance,'' Yuan told her. "It is something I have planned almost since her birth, it is something I have told my people I would do, and it is something I *want* to do. She is the most desirable creature I have ever seen.''

Creature, Constance thought bitterly. But she was realizing that she might have overplayed her hand by hurrying too fast; there could be no mistaking the deadly seriousness in Yuan's tone.

"And if she is an unwilling bride,'' he went on, "then I will accept that, and trust to our lives together to reconcile her to her situation.''

"Yes,'' Constance said, and decided to try another approach. "Of course, her present feelings will not last. They are complicated by so many others. For one thing, she is terrified by what happened this afternoon. And with good reason. She doubts—*I* doubt—that in the present state of Peking even *you* can guarantee her safety.''

"Me? I am Marshal Yuan Shih-k'ai."

"You appear to have no jurisdiction over people like this monster Lin-tu and his rabble," Constance pointed out. "And I can tell you that *he* would willingly murder all the Ch'ing. I did not tell you this before, but Adela has told me how in the camp of General Feng he wished to execute her, along with the general."

"How can you know that is true?" Yuan remarked. "Did she not deny that Lin-tu was in Feng's camp at all? But I shall keep an eye on Lin, never fear."

"Yuan," Constance said. "Listen to me. I cannot help but feel it would be far safer if Adela were to be removed entirely from Peking, at least until this situation settles down. It would be better for her, too. Away from the city she will be more easily able to come to terms with what has happened, realize that you did only what you had to do, remember how much she has always admired you and respected you. Even loved you. Give us an escort and send us down to Tientsin."

"Tientsin?" His eyes narrowed.

"To the European quarter. There we . . . *she* would be safe, even from Lin-tu. Frank is down there on business. My God, he'll be beside himself with worry when he hears what has happened here. But there we would be safe until you feel it would be all right for us to return."

Yuan continued to regard her for several seconds, while her heart pounded and she prayed her fear did not show in her face.

"You are afraid of Lin-tu," he remarked at last. "There is no need to be. He is a rabble-rouser, not a true leader of men. You will be safer here than anywhere else in China. I will send word to Frank that all is well, and I will send an escort to bring him back up to you, as soon as it is safe to do so. As for Lin-tu's master . . . he is due in Peking today. He thinks he is arriving to assume complete control of the Chinese state. I think we should return to my encampment and await the coming of the illustrious Dr. Sun. As soon as the princess is dressed, of course. I would like her to be there when I disabuse the doctor of his ridiculous ambitions."

Had Constance succeeded in making any sort of a point? Adela could not be sure—they were allowed no time alone together, and could only exchange a hasty look and a half-smile. At least they once again understood each other.

Horses were provided, and they rode beside the marshal himself, surrounded by his soldiers, down the Grand Avenue and through the Yun-ting-Mien. The streets were still crowded, rifles were still being fired into the air, firecrackers were still being exploded, but none close to the cavalcade. Instead, as Yuan and his entourage approached, the crowds melted sullenly down the side streets, leaving only dead bodies to make the horses whinny and step aside; some of these unfortunates had been shot, but several had been decapitated and their heads removed, no doubt to be mounted on the gates.

"It has of course been necessary to execute looters and rabble-rousers on the spot," Yuan explained. "To restore order." He turned to Adela. "Those men who would have harmed you are among them. I am sorry you have to look upon their miserable carcasses."

Adela tilted her chin defiantly; she had allowed herself entirely to regain her composure, had now to make sure that she not only preserved her anger toward him but also acted the Ch'ing princess at all times. "They are those who revolted against the dynasty," she said, and left him to make what he could of that.

But clearly he was in no mood to be put down by anybody. If it was not in the Chinese nature ever to reveal one's true emotions, Adela could yet tell that Yuan Shih-k'ai was a very happy and confident man. Yet she could not understand the reason behind his ebullience, his confidence. This was Dr. Sun's revolution, no matter how much contempt he had for the man; he had himself admitted that he had been caught quite unprepared—it had indeed been a marvel of effort and organization for him to mobilize his little army in time even to come in on the tail of the rising. And the people of Peking, if clearly temporarily overawed by the smartly dressed—they wore blue jackets and white trousers, blue peaked caps and gaiters, to appear almost European—and very well-armed soldiery, as well as by the reappearance in their midst of the man they had for so many years known as their viceroy, with powers of life and death over them, were nonetheless the same people who a few hours earlier had shouted their support for Dr. Sun. However confused they might be by the absence of their leader, or even his deputy, Lin-tu, she did not doubt that were either of them to appear and command the destruction of Yuan and all his people, that destruction would follow immediately. Which was obviously understood by Yuan himself, and was the reason he was removing them, and himself, to the safety of his troop concentration.

It was just getting dark when they reached Yuan's army, which was encamped in the imperial pine park just south of the city, but even in the gloom Adela could see that it bristled with machine-gun emplacements and even a battery of artillery, and looked very well defended, while the gleam of the torches and lanterns made it seem considerably larger than it probably was. And here too, to her surprise, waiting outside the largest of the tents, was Dr. Sun, apparently just arrived by train from the South, and with him Lin-tu and several other officers, mostly very young and very fervent in their admiration for the great man. But to have brought him here? She realized immediately the reason behind Yuan's confidence. These men, including the doctor himself, much less Lin, did not truly understand with whom they were dealing. They still believed in trust, where the good of China and the downfall of the hated Manchu might be involved.

She almost felt sorry for them.

This evening Sun wore a uniform, of the loose-jacket-and-trouser variety; he carried no weapons, but there was gold leaf on his peaked cap. And he looked happy enough, and confident, too. "Marshal Yuan," he cried, holding out his arms to embrace his ally. "A great day. The greatest in Chinese history. And by fulfilling your promise to me of nonintervention, you have helped to make it so. Believe me, your name will ever be honored in the history of our people."

"I thank you, Doctor." Yuan gave a brief bow as he dismounted, and then turned to assist Adela from the saddle; she accepted his hand as if it were a red-hot poker. "You have already met the Princess Adela, I believe? My betrothed? Now I would have you meet her foster mother, and Mr. Charles Baird."

Sun ignored Constance and Charlie, to stare at Adela. "Your . . . betrothed?" he inquired.

"The Ch'ing girl?" Lin-tu snapped, stepping forward. Adela stared at him, knowing that her life, all of their lives, was suddenly in his hands.

"Why, yes," Yuan said, smiling blandly.

Lin glanced at her, and her heart almost stopped beating. She could only beg, with her eyes, for at least a respite from immediate denunciation. Lin looked at Yuan again. "It is not possible for a Chinese to marry a Ch'ing," he declared.

"The dynasty has been deposed, and is to be reduced

to the status of private citizens," Yuan said. "This is what we agreed. All laws concerning intermarriage between Manchu and Chinese are to be abolished. This is also what we agreed. Therefore the Princess Adela is fully able to become my wife."

"But you keep referring to her as a princess," Lin-tu insisted. "She is no longer a princess."

"In law, perhaps, Marshal," Yuan said, still with the utmost composure. "But when one has been born a princess, one remains so throughout one's life, regardless of laws which may be passed by humble men like ourselves."

Lin glared at him for a few moments longer, and then looked at Adela again. And again she begged him with her eyes.

"This is unnecessary and unseemly bickering," Dr. Sun said. "Such as I had hoped would never affect our councils. Miss Wynne, I congratulate you. But then, I should congratulate the marshal also, on securing so beautiful a bride. Mrs. Wynne, to you also my congratulations. Now, if you will excuse us, there is much to be done."

"The essentials are already in hand," Yuan assured him. "My men are now engaged in restoring order in the Tartar City and in taking control of the Forbidden City. By tomorrow morning all will be ready for our official entry."

"Restoring order?" Lin demanded. "Taking command of the Forbidden City? Those are my soldiers in there, already in command."

"The people you stirred into action are in there, I agree," Yuan pointed out. "Committing mayhem. I cannot feel, in view of everything that has happened"—he glanced at Constance—"any confidence that they are capable of preserving the lives of the imperial family, even if they wish to do so. As for the Tartar City, it is your people who are being disciplined. We cannot afford to leave Peking in the hands of a mob."

"A mob?" Lin-tu shouted. "They are the ones who carried out the revolution. While your soldiers stood by and did nothing."

"As we agreed," Yuan reminded him. "My soldiers will now assume their proper function, as guardians of the state."

"Guardians of the state?" Lin cried.

"Gentlemen, please," Dr. Sun said, glancing right and left in some embarrassment, not only because of the presence of Adela and Constance and Charles but also because he was aware that the altercation was being overheard by several of Yuan's officers. "I will have no more quarreling. Nor can I permit you to exceed your authority, Marshal Yuan. As Marshal Lin has said, while we agreed that you would resume your position as viceroy of Chihli province, with responsibility for law and order, those are our own followers within the city. I fully agree that order must be restored, and life and property preserved, and of course I do not wish any member of the dynasty's blood to stain the reputation of the revolution, which is why it is criminal for us to stand here arguing when there is so much to be done. Tomorrow morning is too late for me to be seen to be grasping the reins of power. Now, Marshal Yuan, I have here a paper which I would ask you to sign, as it has already been signed by all my provincial commanders, agreeing that I should be appointed provisional president of China pending elections, and that until such elections are held, all the executive power will lie in my hands and the hands of those appointed by me."

He held out the sheet of foolscap paper, covered with Chinese characters. Yuan raised his hand, and one of his aides hurried forward to hold a torch, flaring in the night air, for the marshal to read by.

"It would be far more convenient were we to move inside," Sun suggested gently. "The sooner that document is completed, the better. I will then enter the city myself, this very night, and make the necessary arrangements for restoring order. I will also interview the regent and arrange for the retirement of him and his family, and the formal abdication of the emperor, as well as for the safety of all the Ch'ing." He smiled at Adela. "Poor people, they must be beside themselves with worry."

Yuan had completed his scanning of the paper. Now he raised his head. "This document is worthless," he declared.

Sun frowned at him.

"It is signed by people of whom I have never heard," Yuan declared. "People of whom no one in China has ever heard."

"And I suppose you imagine that everyone in China has heard of you?" Lin-tu demanded.

"I *know* everyone in China has heard of me," Yuan told him.

"Which is why your signature is so important to our plans," Dr. Sun explained placatingly.

"Yes," Yuan agreed. "I must also inform you, Dr. Sun, that I do not feel this entire operation has been properly carried out. It has been ill-organized, ill-coordinated, and utterly haphazard."

"Ill-organized? Ill-coordinated? Haphazard?" Lin shouted. "It has been the most perfect revolution ever mounted. The *perfect* revolution. When in all history has a dynasty fallen in a single day? You mean *you* were unprepared, and lagged behind."

"I mean what I have said," Yuan repeated, speaking

with the utmost mildness. "All of which has raised in my mind a question as to the fitness of Dr. Sun for the immense role in which he has cast himself. You succeeded here today only because the forces opposed to you were in even more disarray than yourselves. They will not always be so. The forces which will in the future oppose China, a resurgent China, will need more than opportunism to overcome."

Sun gazed at him. "Be careful what you contemplate, Yuan Shih-k'ai," he said. "My people pervade all China. They pervade all Peking. They are all around your camp. They are millions, whereas you number your followers in thousands. And I have your sacred oath to be true to the principles of the revolution."

"My sacred oath is to *my* destiny," Yuan said. "And nothing else. And you may have a million men ready to do your bidding, Dr. Sun, but in the absence of *your* bidding they will obey whoever gives them their orders. In this camp, you and your generals are but as drops of water into a lake—and the lake is *mine.*"

Slowly and with great deliberateness he tore Sun's document into strips and dropped them on the ground. Lin started forward with an exclamation of anger, and was followed by several of his companions—but they all checked at the deafening *click* of a hundred rifle bolts.

"I have therefore decided," Yuan said, still speaking quietly and calmly, "to take control of this revolution myself. Regrettably, I must begin by placing you and your associates under arrest."

7

The Betrayal

Adela could not be sure whether tearing the document had been a signal or whether there had been a pre-arranged moment in time, but now, as she and Sun and Lin and the revolutionaries looked from left to right, they suddenly became aware that they had been surrounded by a very large number of armed soldiers, some carrying flaring torches which made the scene even more dramatic, but most with rifles pointing at Sun and his people. Even if she had known what was going to happen, the calm certainty with which Yuan had gone about his treacherous coup d'etat took her breath away.

This man she had to escape, somehow, before he destroyed her in turn.

"Do you suppose this can endure?" Sun asked in a low, passionate voice. But he was sweating.

"It will endure," Yuan said. "I too have prepared a document, you see, which awaits *your* signature, Dr. Sun. It sets out that, having deeply considered the matter and having observed your inability properly to control your people, you, Dr. Sun, have reached the inevitable conclusion that you lack the skill or the experience, and even the courage, to undertake so

momentous a task as the restoration of China. Therefore, ever with the good of your people and your
country at heart, you wish to resign the *provisonal*
presidency you have been offered by various *provincial*
leaders, and require instead that all Chinese patriots,
and all men who would subscribe to the overthrow of
the hated Manchu, take an oath of allegiance to the one
man who possesses the necessary skill and experience,
and who in addition commands the only viable armed
force in the empire, the Marshal Yuan Shih-k'ai."

There were several seconds' silence while Sun and his
followers gazed at the marshal. Adela discovered that
Constance was holding her hand; she could almost feel
the older woman's bubbling outrage.

"This is treachery," Lin-tu said in a low voice. "The
deepest, darkest treachery in all history."

"It is an act of necessity, Marshal Lin," Yuan said.
"And an act of self-sacrifice which will greatly redound
to the credit of Dr. Sun."

"And do you suppose the foreign powers will ever
recognize you? Do you even suppose they will stand by
and let this happen?"

"Did you suppose they would recognize *you*?" Yuan
asked.

"Of course. We represent the will of the people. That
is democracy."

"Democracy," Yuan said contemptuously. "Let me
tell you, Marshal Lin, the foreign powers will not only
be eager to recognize me, they will be the first to *congratulate* me. When China became convulsed with
revolution, when the streets became filled with the
hordes commanded by the bloodthirsty Lin-tu, a man
still closely identified with the Boxer outrages of eleven
years ago, when indeed a repeat of the Boxer
catastrophe seemed imminent, I stepped in with my
soldiers and restored order, saved the lives of the

Europeans''—he smiled at Constance and Adela—"and also of the Ch'ing, even if I was forced to recognize that they could no longer rule, and thus, regretfully, determined that I must devote my declining years to saving my country.'' His smile widened. ''That is how the foreign powers will think of *me*. And that is how history will *write* of me.''

There was another silence, as Sun and his men realized just how conclusively they had been outmaneuvered, how Yuan, like a skillful chess player, had looked just one move further ahead than they.

''And if Dr. Sun refuses to agree to such a betrayal?'' Lin asked, still in a low voice.

Yuan shrugged. ''You all die. Here and now.''

There was another brief silence. Adela discovered she was holding her breath, as was Constance, she thought. While Charlie as usual seemed to have been turned to stone; perhaps only today had he truly begun to understand the immense forces with which he had unwittingly become involved.

''If I sign your paper,'' Sun said at last, his voice trembling with emotion, ''I would like to put upon it the projected date for the elections we have promised the people.''

Yuan turned his smile on his victim. ''When that will be is impossible for any man to say for certain. Elections must be prepared, and the people must been seen to be ready for them.''

''You seek a military dictatorship.'' Lin seemed to spit the words out.

Yuan merely gazed at him with increasing contempt. How little they still understand, Adela thought bitterly. How little they *know*.

Sun sighed and looked from left to right at the waiting soldiers. Adela felt sorry for him, even if he was her enemy by definition. He had striven so hard for so long, known so many disappointments and disasters. But this last week, as he hurried north to be in at the death, summoned by Lin-tu to set the seal on their joint triumph, he must have felt sure that his years of waiting and frustration were finally over. Now he was again defeated. More by his own gentleness and trusting qualities than even Yuan's machinations; had their roles been reversed, Yuan would certainly have had him assassinated the moment the revolution proved a success.

Now: "My life?" he asked.

"Is safe, the moment you sign," Yuan said. "You are a revolutionary hero, even if you are unable to control the forces you have set in motion. An escort is awaiting you to take you down to the coast, where a ship also waits you."

"You are sending me back into exile?"

"I am sending you back to Europe," Yuan said. "Where you are so well known already. I am sending you to represent the cause of China. I am sure you will do well. But I must warn you, Dr. Sun, that if I am to restore this country to greatness, I will need to rule with apparent harshness, and punish those who oppose or resist me, or fail me, with the utmost rigor. Nor can I allow myself, whatever my personal inclinations, to show mercy even to my closest associates. I am giving you a great task, which will bring much honor upon you. But it must be carried out. Any ambassador sent abroad by me, who speaks against my government or myself, who engages in any subversive activities against my government or myself, or who returns to China without my express permission, will be instantly condemned to death. And should he be unavailable to take his punishment, it shall be visited on all those of his family who are in China, or in the absence even of those, on his closest associates."

Sun's gaze flickered to Lin. "Then my officers are not *immediately* to be executed," he said quietly.

Yuan smiled. "They too are revolutionary heroes. Execute them? I will give them positions on my staff, that they may learn what soldiering is really about."

"They are to be hostages for my behavior."

"You think in the darkest terms," Yuan said jovially. "They will assist me in what I have to do, and they may even advise me in certain directions. But more important, they will *remind* me of you. Now, come, you will sign the paper, and then we will tour the city together, and then . . . why, then we will celebrate."

The plates were gold, as was the cutlery; the goblets were crystal rimmed with gold. The napkins and table-cloths were purest damask. It was a setting, and indeed a meal, such as Adela had never attended in her life before, and made even the appointments in Yuan's palace south of the river seem like a hovel. Nor did she think Constance had ever experienced anything like this, either; however often she had visited the Forbidden City in the past, she had never done more than take tea with the empress.

But this was the day of days, the most remarkable day in Chinese history, when three thousand years of imperial rule had come to a full stop. The emperor himself was not present, of course, but this was merely because he was a child and unable to enjoy adult pleasures.

The ex-emperor.

Prince Ch'un, the ex-regent, was here, with all his male cousins and nephews. This was sufficiently unique. But there were females present also, commanded to attend by the all-powerful warlord. At one bound Yuan Shih-k'ai had reached out and dragged China into the twentieth century, as represented by Parisian manners and customs. In the presence of the regent, staring glumly at his plate; of his male relatives, gazing angrily around the room at the whole men who guarded the doors and stared at the women, where only eunuchs had ever been permitted before; of the female cousins, too abashed and horrified at what had happened to them even to taste their food—which no doubt they supposed was poisoned in any event; of his senior officers, determinedly keeping up a flow of conversation; of Dr. Sun, hardly less glum than the regent; of Dr. Sun's officers, such as Lin-tu, endeavoring to match the anger of the Manchu gazes but yet unable to overcome their awe at being in such surroundings, and such company, at all; and of Constance and Charlie and herself—seated at Yuan's right hand and wearing an imperial yellow silk gown, slit from the ankle to the knee to allow her to move, as it fitted her so tightly it might have been a second skin, with her hair swept up and her fingers covered with jeweled rings, carelessly taken from the imperial treasury, and no doubt once worn by Tz'u-Hsi herself; but most of all in the fact that this banquet should be taking place within the palace itself, in rooms where only the Ch'ing and their servants had ever been permitted to tread, Yuan was demonstrating the extent and scope of his triumph, as well as the immense power he had with a sudden single contraction gathered into his own two hands.

Her knowledge of history told her that something like this *must* have happened before, but not for two hundred and fifty years, since the day the great Manchu general Dorgun, acting for Nurhachi's son and successor, Huang T'ai Chi, had driven the last of the Ming from the city and proclaimed his master Ch'ung Te emperor of China. For the Ming there had been left only the silken cord of suicide or a shameful death. But for Prince Ch'un and his family Yuan had promised an honorable retirement. This much had civilization advanced in two centuries, although she had no doubt the marshal was more interested in impressing European and American observers with his moderation and justice than in what happened to the deposed dynasty. But to those who had enjoyed Dorgun's legacy for eight generations, what was now happening had to be unbelievable. And even more unbelievable was it that Yuan should be parading her, his future bride, before them all. She did not doubt she was the most beautiful woman in the entire room. But equally she did not doubt that she was the most hated, by the Manchu, for her apparent act of usurpation, and by the Chinese, because she was a link with the hated past.

And by Lin-tu, who knew her secret, but had so far not betrayed her. Why? She could not believe it was through any sense of honor. And yet she had recognized in him a certain honor.

But he hated her and all the Ch'ing. If he had not betrayed her, it was surely for some purpose of his own —either that or he waited for Yuan's wedding, and the subsequent explosion, with cynical amusement.

She felt almost physically sick. And not merely because of Lin-tu and the threat hanging over her. Not even because of the events of yesterday, the mob and the manhandling. It was caused by the sheer pace which had suddenly overtaken her life, the mad kaleidoscope through which she was being unceasingly whirled.

Yuan had insisted she ride at his side when they had entered the Forbidden City this morning. Even had she been taken on a secret conducted tour, she would have been overwhelmed. She had been told so much about the Forbidden City by Constance, and here at last it was, the broad, clean, and empty avenue—in such strong contrast to the busy, teeming, filthy streets of the Tartar City—which had stretched in front of her all the way from the Gate of the Zenith past the various temples to the Imperial Palace. To either side, white-walled buildings with exquisitely carved balustrades and pagoda roofs were shaded beneath huge and spreading banyan and silk cotton trees; on the verandas, white-gowned women had looked down at her and fluttered their fans, and whispered to one another, while in front of her a coterie of eunuchs had hurried by, still going about their duties while their secret world had collapsed. The only *men* normally allowed inside this place of silent shadows were the high officials of state . . . and the emperor and his brothers and cousins.

And then to see the famous Dragon Staircase, the broad flight of steps which gave access to the throne room, and on which the imperial dragon had been painted, so skillfully as to suggest that the creature lived and moved as she walked over it—this *was* her heritage.

But to enter the city at the side of the warlord, to be presented to Prince Ch'un and watch that bland mask of resigned defeat twist with anger at the thought of this outcast cousin being raised above him, to stand and look at the infant emperor when her every instinct cried out to her to fall to her knees in the kowtow, to watch and listen as Yuan informed the Sons of Heaven of their reduction to ordinary citizens—these things had been almost more than her reeling mind could stand. And now to sit at his side as he hurled his personality across everyone who had ever been anyone in China, and several who had only dreamed . . . she felt that she was herself in a dream.

And all of this was being offered to *her,* by a man she loathed and detested and feared, a man who had destroyed her family, humiliated it and reduced it to the dust from whence it had first arisen three centuries before.

But also a man, the only man, who could possibly restore China to greatness. She could no longer doubt that.

One half of her mind was actually crying out for her to accept, to take his love, to stand at his side as he rebuilt the country, while all the time twisting that love, and twisting his ambition too, until his life dwindled in anguished despair. The other knew that she could not succeed, not with a man like Yuan, and therefore that she would be committing a betrayal, not only of her family and her people, but of everything she had always supposed to be of value in the world.

And Charlie? Because of course she no longer had the choice. She knew that Charlie, seated several places to her right, was staring at her and willing her to stare back. Because Charlie was afraid she might do or say something to betray them both, and because they had been allowed no time together, to reassure each other and hold each other close. But Charlie had no inkling of the turmoil which was her mind, the temptations with which she was faced, almost the horror with which she looked back on her surrender to him, which had forever *robbed* her of the choice.

But *she* had made that decision. Thus she had no course left to her but to sustain her loathing. And pray that Yuan would be so repelled by her anger he would himself decide to throw her out. It was her—it was *their* —only hope of survival.

The marshal leaned toward her, while still smiling down the table in benign command of everything he saw. "You are the only Ch'ing who deserves to rule," he said. "You are the only truly imperial Manchu remaining. For you I will make all China scintillate as this room does tonight."

She turned her head to look at him. "I hate you," she said. "I hate you and I will always hate you, should you kill me for it."

The smile never left Yuan Shih-k'ai's face. "To marry a woman of such spirit," he remarked. "What more could a man possibly ask?"

"Thank you," Adela said. "You may leave me now."

The eunuch looked totally disconcerted. But he had already been put out, when she had declined to be bathed. Because he had obviously intended to superintend the business himself.

The thought was utterly repulsive. It was symbolic of all the decadence that had pervaded this sensuous enclave and finally brought down the dynasty. She did not even wish him near her, although she understood that it was his duty to sleep outside her door.

Now he gave a nervous bow and backed from the room.

"And you," Adela said to the waiting maids. "I will undress myself. You may leave also."

They gazed at her. They knew that she was the betrothed of the warlord, and therefore the most powerful woman in the land at this moment. But they also knew that she was virtually a barbarian, and clearly an ignorant barbarian, at that.

"Lady cannot undress herself," one said.

"Lady should not retire without bath," said another, emboldened by her friend.

"Lady's hair must be brushed," said the third.

"And lady must be prepared for sleep," said the first, with terrifying mysteriousness.

Adela looked from face to face. "I will undress myself," she said firmly. "I will brush my own hair. I had a bath this evening, before dressing to come here.

And I will prepare *myself* for sleep." She pointed. "Now, go."

A last hesitation, and then they filed from the room; she had the power to have them all whipped if they angered her. No doubt her nauseating habits would be whispered throughout the palace, but they would just have to put up with it.

For how long, before they could smile behind their fans as her head was mounted on a stick?

But she was inside the Forbidden City. Inside the palace. And she was going to sleep here. For at least one night. Was that not something she had always dreamed of doing?

And now she hated it, and trembled at every sound.

She sat on the bed and listened to the explosions of firecrackers from the Tartar City. Yuan had declared a holiday to celebrate the fall of the Ch'ing and the installation of the new military dictatorship. He had decreed that there was to be no more violence, that all the inhabitants of China were to be as one beneath his rule. And to this end he had sent his messengers by train and boat and horse, in haste to every corner of the vast empire, informing everyone of the new situation. But Adela did not suppose any Manchu would sleep easily in his bed tonight—supposing he was allowed to sleep at all, and supposing he was ever to see another dawn.

A situation undoubtedly anticipated by Yuan, to be used to his advantage. If a Manchu were murdered, then a provincial mayor or even viceroy could be held responsible, and removed from office or executed in turn, with the utmost legality and the plaudits of the civilized world. Unless of course the mayor or viceroy happened to be a staunch supporter of the marshal's, in which case the crime would clearly have been that of a subordinate—in those circumstances Adela could not see him lacking universal support.

Just as he would also have foreseen that there would certainly *be* resistance to his coup d'etat, however scattered and uncertain. No doubt he also knew already which of the viceroys were at once willing and able to oppose him in arms, and which would continue to fight in Dr. Sun's cause, and in their direction arresting officers or assassins were by now already on their way. None would survive, because none possessed Yuan Shih-k'ai's powers of decisive action and complete political amorality—and no one in all China possessed an army to compare with his.

She realized that she was exalting him into a demigod. Which was no way to continue the fight against him, with any hope of success. But did she have any hope of success, anyway? No matter what she said, apparently, he was going to marry her.

And then execute her. And Charlie. And no doubt Constance as well. She wondered what *they* were thinking about, surrounded by their handmaidens and eunuchs. Charlie, surrounded by handmaidens! Or would he be too frightened to appreciate it?

The most depressing thing of all was their inability to be together, and talk, and perhaps even plan.

To escape? She got up, restlessly moved to the window. But the window merely looked down into a courtyard, and in the courtyard there was a soldier patrolling. The window, the courtyard, and the soldier symbolized her helplessness. She was in a box within a case within a trunk, and even if she got out of the box, she had no idea where Constance and Charlie were, and even less idea how to lead them out of this dismal labyrinth.

She threw herself across the bed in a paroxysm of despair, wishing she could weep, but she had never been able to do that at will. Wishing she could follow the example of her father, and commit suicide? But to do that, to tie a cord around her neck and then suspend it from a beam, this so beautiful neck which connected this so beautiful face to this so beautiful body . . . to end all those vital thoughts and ambitions and *desires* which tumbled through her brain. It would be done soon enough by an executioner.

She heard a sound, and raised her head, heart thumping as she supposed an assassin had already entered her chamber . . . and gazed at Lin-tu.

Lin-tu put his finger on his lips as she would have cried out in sheer amazement. She controlled herself with an effort. "How did you *get* here?" she whispered.

"The Forbidden City is no longer barred to men," he said. "And eunuchs, like men, are both capable of holding political opinions and ambitions for wealth. This fellow on your door is a supporter of Dr. Sun. But I am still risking my neck. You know this?"

"To come to me?"

He gazed at her. "I had supposed you might wish to speak with me." He crossed the room and sat beside her on the bed. "Do you not?"

"I . . . I wish to thank you, certainly, for preserving my secret."

"Is your maidenhead truly taken?"

She hesitated, and then nodded.

"And do you suppose the marshal will not become aware of this, after taking you to his bed? After having married you, before the eyes of the world? Have you any idea of his rage when he learns that he has been duped?"

She could only gaze at him. He was putting into words things she dared not even think about.

"And yet you persist," Lin-tu went on. "When surely a confession of the true situation . . ."

"It cannot be," she said.

"Ah." He half-smiled.. "As I supposed. You are not betrothed to Charles Baird. You accepted his embrace. Yes, I have heard this of Western women. They are shameless. Your foster mother is shameless. I know these things. And you accepted your brother's embrace *after* Yuan had proposed marriage. Do you know, even I cannot imagine his anger when he learns of this. They will hear your screams in Canton."

She tilted her chin. If he had come to gloat, she had to meet him as a princess. "I am not afraid to die," she lied.

He shrugged. "What is death, indeed, Princess? It is what precedes the moment when the spirit flees that is difficult to consider. There was once an empress named Wu Hou. Have you heard of her?"

Adela's head flopped up and down.

"Her husband, the then emperor, took a concubine, whom she imagined he loved more than her. She could do nothing while the emperor lived, but when he died and left her as regent for their young son, she revenged herself. She had the girl seized, and her ears, her nose, her lips, her breasts, her feet, and her hands cut off, and then had her thrown, still alive and bleeding, onto a trash heap, to die slowly and in the utmost agony, watched by the common multitude, and mocked by them."

Now she did feel sick. She wrapped both hands around her throat and stared at him in horror.

"That will be a marvelous sight," Lin-tu observed. "When it is your beauty being displayed and destroyed. No one present would ever forget it."

She gasped, and he smiled. "But it is a fate you would rather avoid, I imagine. And it would be a great waste of beauty, and accomplishment, and charm."

Her head jerked, and she frowned at him. "*You* can help me?" she whispered.

"Do you imagine I wish to remain here? Yuan will send Dr. Sun away and pretend to our millions of followers that this is part of the agreement they have reached, which he is so honorably implementing. Thus he will reduce him to a nothing. He knows all our secrets; it will be a simple matter for his agents to infiltrate our most private societies, and then destroy them and arrest our leaders. Once that is done, he has no more need to keep Sun alive, because he will be valueless even as a martyr. Before then he will have lost any need to keep *me* alive, certainly. I must leave here while I still have a head on my shoulders."

Her heart was pounding so that she could hardly think. Could he possibly be offering . . . ?

"I would take you with me," he said.

Once again she gasped; she had been holding her breath.

"As my woman," he said.

Her heart slowed. But had she not known it was coming, without being prepared to believe it?

"I belong to another," she said.

"You belong to no one, Princess Adela, save the common executioner. It is a choice between me and him."

"You would take me, defiled?"

He smiled. "I would take you even had Feng given you to his entire army."

She gazed at him. Suddenly the fear and the sickness were gone. She could feel her brain settling into its normal pattern of quick and accurate thinking. He was in love with her. No, not with *her*. He could not be. He was in love with the idea of possessing a Ch'ing princess. And no doubt with the thought of possessing her beauty as well. But he would know those were transient pleasures. Therefore he wanted more than that. He wanted to defy and taunt Yuan Shih-k'ai. To take something that the marshal considered precious. Because if she went with him, Yuan would not know she had not been a virgin when she left. Then his anger would be the rage of frustration, and as he had announced his intention to the world, it would also be the anger of humiliation.

And Lin could even offer her back, slightly tarnished, in return for some future concessions, so that the marshal could *then* mutilate her and cast her on a dung heap.

To go with Lin would be merely to postpone her death to an even less acceptable moment. But yet . . . he could take her out of the Forbidden City. She did not doubt this. He had been a revolutionary who had been in and out of Peking all of his life, without being caught, according to Constance. If he could do that, then surely he could also take Constance and Charlie; certainly she could not abandon them. But then she would have promised herself to him. She would have *promised*—to a man who she knew hated her and would destroy her without a second thought, if he felt it would be to his advantage. Could a promise to such a man be binding?

She was aghast at her own duplicity. But it was certainly how a Manchu princess would think. If it could be done.

"I see the idea attracts you," Lin-tu said.

She bit her lip. She had not sufficient practice at controlling her expressions. And she must not appear overeager. "I would know what you intend," she said.

"To worship at your shrine, Adela."

She tossed her head. "I meant, I would know how you imagine we can escape from this place. From Peking. If I am going to be captured and executed, I would rather at least celebrate my marriage first."

"But you will come with me?"

"Perhaps," she said. "If it is possible."

Lin hesitated, and then shrugged. "We cannot just walk through the gates, Princess. But there is a way which is not guarded, simply because it has never been thought necessary. We will leave by the Ornamental Water."

Which was the name of the artificial lakes which lay on the northwest side of the Imperial Palace.

"The water? But how?"

"It is fed from the canal which surrounds the Forbidden City," Lin explained. "It is simply a matter of wading, and sometimes swimming—"

"I cannot swim."

"Then I will tow you," he said. "Unless you are afraid, Princess."

"I will not be afraid," she said.

"Then there is no difficulty. The lake will lead us to the canal, and the canal will lead us beyond even the outer walls. There I will have someone waiting with horses. We shall leave tomorrow night. It must be done as quickly as possible, while Yuan is still in a state of euphoria, and before he can impose his will on the entire country. I need only twenty-four hours to prepare."

"And where will we go then?" she asked.

"To the coast. I have many friends in Tientsin, among them sea captains who will take us, secretly, back to the South. To Canton, where my people are. There we will plan Yuan's downfall."

Tientsin, she thought. She could hardly believe her ears.

"Well, then," he said. "All that remains . . ."

"I will come with you," Adela said, speaking very quietly, "if you will take my mother and brother as well."

"Your . . . That is impossible."

"Why is it impossible? Can you not gain access to their apartments also?"

"Of course. But it will be dangerous. The more of us there are, the more chance there is of being taken. Anyway, why should I?"

"Is not Constance your old friend?"

"She was once my friend," he said. "No longer." He smiled. "And Charles Baird is my rival, is he not?"

"I cannot leave them to die, Lin," she said. "If they stay, I stay."

"And what am I to do with them, after we escape?"

"You say we are going to Tientsin," she said. "Leave them there. They can gain the European quarter. My father is there as well. They can leave China."

He gazed at her, eyes narrowed. Oh, my God, she thought. He suspects.

"And I will come with you," she said. "To the South. To fight against Yuan."

He continued to regard her for several seconds. Then he said, "Reveal to me the prize for which I am risking so much."

Her head came up.

"Undress," he said. "Prepare yourself for bed, Adela. Is that not what you were about to do? I would watch."

"You will not touch me," she said. "Until after my mother and brother have been placed in safety."

He shrugged. "I would not wish to, until lovemaking can be the *only* thing on our minds. All else is but tinsel. But I would still see, that I may anticipate." Again he smiled. "And dream tonight."

"Is it not beautiful?" Yuan Shih-k'ai walked across the exquisitely arched bridge and thence onto one of the islands of the archipelago which studded the

Ornamental Water. Adela walked to one side of him, Constance to the other—etiquette demanded that he not be alone with his bride until after their marriage.

Yuan's entourage of secretaries and guards followed a discreet distance behind—unlike all the other rulers who had promenaded here, he had no wish constantly to be surrounded by useless women or even more useless eunuchs. Now he placed his hands on his hips as he surveyed the waters and the statuary and the darting fish beneath him. "Even that is beautiful, of its type." He pointed at the famous stone replica of a Mississippi paddle steamer, life size, towering out of the still waters, a grotesque representation of the childlike interest the dowager empress had found in the wonders of the Western world, even while she had hated all they stood for. "Our navy! Do you know, when an enormous sum was voted for the creation of a new Chinese navy, following our defeat by the Japanese in 1895, the money was appropriated by the empress to build *that*. Truly, that woman had so many crimes to answer for, had we taken her alive when the Forbidden City fell—had she still *been* alive—it would have been necessary to hang her a hundred times to atone for them all." He smiled at Constance. "I forget, she was a friend of yours."

"At times," Constance said. "Yet you will retain this monstrosity?"

She spoke quietly and calmly. Adela had no idea of her feelings or her knowledge. They had exchanged but a single glance when they had met half an hour ago, with Yuan already present. There was no means of knowing whether or not Lin had been able to contact her. But he must have, she thought. Thus the calm.

She wondered what Constance or Yuan would say if they knew that not twelve hours ago she had stood naked before a Chinese brigand. The thought made her knees quite weak. But then, the thought of having done it at all left her feeling weak. As the light in her bedroom had been poor the night Charlie came to her, and as she had not actually removed her dressing gown, last night was the first time she had stood naked before any man. And what a man.

But a man who would help them all to escape, because in his arrogant contempt for her and all her family, white and yellow, it never entered his mind that they could oppose him or attempt to betray him.

The thought filled her with a wild, anxious courage—even as she also felt sick at what she had to do.

"Oh, indeed I shall keep it," Yuan was agreeing. "Because it is a beautiful reminder of the bad times which have gone forever."

"Forever, Yuan?" Oh, certainly Lin had spoken with her. This Constance was as confident as Adela could ever remember her.

"You doubt that, Constance? You are a typical American, afraid of words. You are frightened by these words people are applying to me, 'military dictator.' What is there to be afraid of in that? A military dictator at least by definition controls the army, and therefore the country, and is therefore able to do whatever he wishes. It is only when he wishes to do evil things that he is himself bad. Not by merely being."

"I was reading something the other day by some English professor of history, to the effect that while all power corrupts, absolute power corrupts absolutely."

Yuan smiled at her. "How democratic you are. The man of whom you are speaking is hardly just a history professor, my dear Constance. He is an English lord. Lord Acton. And he should know about the corruptions of power, because his grandfather was once virtually dictator of Naples."

As usual, the extent and depth of this man's knowledge left Adela's brain reeling. He knew so much it was difficult to suppose he did not know *everything*. And thus was able to prevent anything happening that he opposed.

He continued to smile. "No doubt he was thinking of his own family. I would concede that a man who suddenly finds himself in power, by an accident of history, or before he has properly considered his ambitions, and more important, what he will do with them, is apt to lose his head, metaphorically speaking, before he loses his head physically. The one leads to the other, you might say, because of the excesses he practices in the enjoyment of success." He chuckled at his little joke. "But I . . . I have prepared for this ever since I can remember. Certainly since Tz'u-Hsi gave me my first appointment, since I was first able to see for myself what pale shadows of the past were the Ch'ing of my own time, I have known my destiny. You will forgive my saying these things, Princess Adela. But they are true, and must be recognized. Only in rare instances, such as in your own father, and through him, in yourself, has the energy and ability of Nurhachi reemerged in his descendants."

He waited for her to reply, and when she did not, strolled across the grass, the two women beside him. "But you, Princess, you will be the founder of a new line of princes, men with energy and ability, and power, and knowledge, who will take this country of ours back into the forefront of Asian and, indeed, of world affairs. You understand what I intend?" The question was directed at Constance.

"To sacrifice to heaven? I think you are taking an enormous risk. The Western powers—"

"You can forget the Western powers, Constance. They are of no account anymore. They are too concerned with themselves, in Europe. Almost every day they move closer to war with each other. Only recently,

France and Germany all but came to blows over the presence of a German warship in a French colonial port. Only a few weeks ago a high-ranking British minister, Lloyd George, made a speech in which he virtually told Germany that if she builds any more warships Britain will smash her fleet before it becomes powerful enough to challenge her own. Oh, they no longer have the time or the inclination to interest themselves in our affairs. If they think of us at all, it is to pray earnestly that China remains at peace with itself and all the world. Thus it will be as I told Sun Yat-sen, that they will praise me for checking a revolution which could have convulsed the country, and required their intervention, for perhaps ten years, like the Taiping. But they will praise me even more for declaring myself emperor. Like us, only perhaps even more so, they are the slaves of tradition. It is impossible for any European statesman to imagine a prosperous and peaceful country not ruled by a king. Only the United States is the exception. But your country had never *had* a king, and indeed deliberately rejected the idea at its inception. Europeans dislike the words 'military dictator' as much as you do; they start to think of Napoleon Bonaparte. They will be greatly relieved when China again has a king, an emperor, and they will be even more relieved when they realize that this emperor intends to *rule,* and will not be at the mercy of his eunuchs or his aunts.''

Was he right? Adela thought that he might very well be. And *he* was so certain, it was difficult to doubt that he had thought the matter through to the last detail—or indeed that he might not have already held secret conversations with European emissaries.

"But I did not bring you out here today to talk politics," he said jovially. "I am sure such matters bore the princess. I have brought you here to discuss the matter of our wedding. Because I must, alas, warn you that there may have to be certain delays." He caught the glance which was exchanged between the two women, and laughed gently. "There is no cause to fear, my dear Constance, my dear Adela. Do you suppose I could possibly change my mind? No, no. Life without you, sweet Princess, at my side, cannot be contemplated. But to marry you now would be a nothing. You must marry me when I am already emperor, and therefore you will immediately become an empress. Our nuptials will be a state occasion to which even royal princes will come, from England and Germany, Russia and Japan, and it will also be an occasion of the utmost symbolism, as we shall together, and before the eyes of the world, unite the men of Han and the Manchu, and signify to all men the emergence of a new and stronger Chinese nation and empire. Believe me, were it left to my passion alone, I would wed you this afternoon. Whenever I look at you, my manhood rises within me until it is fit to burst. But I, we, must also do what is best for China. It will not be for very long, I promise you. What I must first do is go through the forms of . . . democracy, I suppose you would call it. There can be no doubt that Sun-Yat-sen, or at least his ideas, command a considerable following in the country. Besides, it will impress the Europeans. And so I intend to go along with what he intended, and summon what you might call a parliament, at least an assembly, which will meet here in Peking and endorse me as leader of the state. That done, I will put my views on the best form of government for China before them, and they will then invite me to conduct the sacrifice to heaven, and become their new emperor. Unfortunately, such is the vastness of our country, and so backward our means of communication, the summoning of this assembly may well take several months."

He paused, and Adela, her heart suddenly tumbling, could not resist a dig. "What will happen if the assembly refuses to agree that you should become emperor?''

Yuan's eyes took on the sleepy expression she had come to know and fear so well. "I am sure, my dear Princess, that when they are here in Peking, able to see and hear me every day, able to understand the grasp which I have on the affairs of my country, they will be only too happy to agree to anything I wish. I am far more concerned about the delay in fulfilling your dreams of happiness. Will you not reassure me, my dear Adela, that a brief delay will not wither all your hopes?''

Adela gazed at him, refusing all temptation to look at her foster mother. But Constance would have to be thinking the same thing she was: here was a reprieve of several months. Several months in which anything could happen. And most of all, several months in which she need not make a decision. But the decision had already been made, and if she did not go tonight, Lin-tu would not wait for her. More, he might reveal her secret there and then.

"Or does the princess still hate and fear me, who desires only to worship at her shrine?" Yuan asked.

Adela looked into his eyes. "The princess will be pleased to wait upon your excellency's pleasure," she said.

The bath was sunk into the center of the stone floor for some four feet; it was also about eight feet square, and so there was a great deal of room for splashing about and even for shallow swimming. The water was heavily scented, and heated to just the right temperature. But so was the room itself, and there was no trace of steam. The room seemed full of people, but it wasn't really, because they were only present in mind, as required. Thus the four maids stared vacantly into space like statues. They sat together on a marble bench against one wall, and remained fully dressed; two carried a voluminous towel, and the others had the princess's nightclothes, folded on their laps, ready for her use.

The two eunuchs were also fully dressed, but with their sleeves rolled up to their elbows. No doubt they had bathed imperial princesses before, and were not disconcerted by her sudden darts from one side of the pool to the other, splashing water, or by her sudden movements as they soaped her, sometimes sinking to the bottom and sometimes standing straight, which sent their hands perhaps not entirely where they had intended.

But Adela could not have kept still even had she devoted every muscle to that purpose. That she would have done this, be doing this, cavorting naked before four young women and two . . . things? Whatever would Miss Evesham say?

It had been an enormous act of will. But an act of will in keeping with her mood, her almost hysterical indecision, her desire to snatch at the life which was being offered her but which she dared not take, and which was to last only a few hours more.

To snatch at sexual dominance, too. She gazed at the impassive faces, wondered if they *did* possess no animal feelings at all. It was quite impossible to suppose that a human being could touch her breast or slide his hand down her belly or between her buttocks and feel *nothing*. The very idea was insulting. Besides, she had heard sufficient tales of how the ladies of the court—or of the harems in Muslim countries—used their eunuchs to provide sexual pleasure, at least by massage. Surely the man had to feel *something* when he felt a woman responding under his touch?

Her brain seemed seized by a gigantic confusion. Partly it was sexual. She had spent so much of the past year thinking about sexual matters. Before Feng and Pearl, sex had been an *awareness,* as it was also clearly a very useful weapon, perhaps a woman's *most* useful weapon; Constance had certainly from time to time used her sexuality as a weapon, very successfully.

But Constance had lived so long, experienced so much, *enjoyed* so much. *She* had only turned the first few pages of the book of her life, certainly of her sexual life. As she had only turned the first page of luxury. And of the power of having a strong man desiring her. All of which she must now abandon.

The eunuch's soft hands slid over her shoulders. "Lady should come out now," he said, his voice, as ever, contradictorily harsh. "Lady should not allow her skin to become wrinkled. And lady should retire early."

"I will come out when I wish to," Adela replied, and pushed herself away from the side of the bath, so that she skidded across the surface of the water, arms outstretched, and legs too, body only faintly distorted by the rippling liquid, black pubic hair suggesting marsh grass peeping from the sweetest of pools, chill-hardened nipples just cutting the surface, like tiny sharks' fins. She wanted them to see her, and want her, and know that they could never have her.

Because no one could ever have her now. Save Charlie. Dear, sweet Charlie. The boy she had always wanted to marry. And still wanted to marry, deep in herself, no matter how afraid he might be of what he had done. Surely. Charlie. . . . Could she ever imagine Charlie ordering a score of men to be decapitated for laying their hands on her? Would Charlie ever have stood there and calmly told five men that they must obey him or die— and have the five men know that he meant it? Would Charlie ever have the tremendous effrontery, the self-confidence, to seize an empire?

Would *their* wedding be attended by princes, and go down in history? Would Charlie *ever* be able to give her such luxury as she was presently enjoying? Or such a feeling of unrestrained pleasure?

Upon which she must now turn her back. There could be no question about that. She had grown up amid the careless brutalities of Chinese life and Chinese justice, but even without Lin-tu's sadistic suggestions, she could not *imagine* what punishment Yuan might decree for her when he found out that she had betrayed his bed.

Yet the temptation remained. Yuan loved her. He said he did, and he appeared to do so. Life without her at his side could not be contemplated, he had said. He looked at her as no other man had ever looked at her before, certainly in a way Charlie had never revealed. And if he loved her, would the fact that she had been entered by another man be *that* important? It wasn't as if Charlie were some common Chinese—or even a Manchu. He was an American, someone apart. She had not become pregnant. She really could not understand what all the fuss was about, some little membrane which was surely merely a nuisance.

Might it not be possible even to fake it?

So deep was she in thought that she left the bath without being summoned again, was wrapped in her warm towels, which were pressed against her body by her maids, chattering now as they were fulfilling *their* role, while the eunuchs left the bathhouse, no doubt to dream of her, she supposed. Now her hair, hitherto piled on the top of her head and encased in a vast waterproof bag, was released, to tumble past her shoulders. It had yet to be brushed, so bed was another half-hour away.

She sat in front of her dressing mirror while the girls slowly and carefully drew the hog bristles through the midnight silk strands; were they to give the slightest tug, she might order them to be whipped. Power! Such power! She stared at herself in the mirror. Would any man, but especially Yuan Shih-k'ai, wish to destroy so much beauty, or even to lose it? *Could* any man? And especially Yuan, who needed her not only to cement the two peoples over whom he would rule—marriage to any Ch'ing princess would accomplish that—but also to give him the strong, healthy, and above all intelligent sons he had to have to perpetuate his dynasty. Yuan had spent too many years observing the imbecilic ninnies produced by generation after generation of Ch'ing women to suppose *any* full-blooded Manchu princess, her powers and those of her husband diminished by years of inbreeding, could accomplish *that*.

But it was a risk she dared not take, because a mistake would be unthinkable, and because she loved Charlie, and was betrothed to him, and was committed to turning her back upon Peking and all it stood for.

And yet . . . She chewed her lip, and one of the maids clucked her tongue warningly—the slightest blemish would be held against *them*.

But the sound reminded Adela that she had her own part to play in their escape. "Enough brushing," she said. "Leave me. I would retire."

They bowed and withdrew, turning down the lamps, closing the door behind them. She could hear them talking with the eunuch who would spend the night outside. She suddenly realized that he was the eunuch in Lin-tu's pay. The same eunuch who had assisted at her bath? Who must know what they were planning? Was her life in the hands of such a creature?

She lay on her stomach across her bed, watching the door and sliver of light which seeped beneath it. Her stomach was suddenly rolling with nervous apprehension. If the eunuch were to betray them, she could find herself facing an executioner by dawn.

She listened to a sound at the door. A question, and then a cough. Nothing more. Instantly she was on her feet, staring at the door, watching it open, gazing at Lin-tu.

"You are not dressed," he said angrily. "You were supposed to be dressed."

"I did not understand how late it was," she said. "I will dress now."

She gazed at him, but he never moved. And did it matter, after last night? She dropped her nightdress on the floor, pulled on her riding habit, sat down to lace her boots, reached for her straw hat in the gloom.

"Hurry," Lin said. "Your mother awaits us. And Charlie."

She stepped to the door, checked, staring down at the body, her stomach seething in horror. "He was in your pay, you said."

"He was," Lin-tu said. "But could I leave him behind, to tell Yuan what happened?"

She raised her head to stare at him. Now was the die irrevocably cast. And this man, with a bloodstained dagger still in his belt, was the one she was planning to betray.

8

The Escape

"Dela!" Constance whispered, holding her close. "Oh, Dela!"

Charlie, also waiting in the gloom, said nothing. She wondered if he would ever speak again. They were both clearly in a state of high tension, and even, she suspected, some shock—and wondered how many murders *they* had had to witness to reach here. Constance had the added trauma of being asked to place her life in the hands of Lin-tu . . . but were not all their lives in those hands?

Those very capable if bloodstained hands. Lin-tu was absolutely calm, absolutely in command. "Now," he said, "I am told the princess does not swim. You will have to tow her, Mr. Baird, as I must lead. Quiet, now."

Charlie stared at her, and she gave him a quick smile. She wondered when it would occur to him, and to Constance, to ask *why* Lin-tu was doing this for them.

But such uneasy reflections were soon submerged by the trauma of the escape itself. She had not considered it very deeply before, had told herself she would surmount each problem as it arose, as she had done with problems all of her life. Now, in the utter darkness, it took all of her resolution to enter the water. It was an element she was not the least familiar with. Her childhood had been spent in Peking, where bathing in the canals, at least among Europeans, was regarded with abhorrence; her girlhood in Virginia, where there were clean rivers enough, had done nothing to change her attitude—Miss Evesham would have expelled any of her young ladies reported bathing in the river. Now there was no saying what lay beneath those turgid depths. It was also very cold on the November night; water crept up her legs as she was slowly lowered, soaked through her habit, and lapped at her chin; even at the edge it was five feet deep.

"Quickly," Lin said. "You *must* tow the princess, Mr. Baird."

Charlie grunted, and held her shoulders.

"Turn on your back," Constance instructed. "And do not be afraid, Dela." As if her own voice were not shaking.

Actually, once Adela realized that her face was not going to be immersed and that Charlie was not going to release her, was in fact obviously a very strong swimmer, she found it possible to relax. Even the cold was more bracing than debilitating, and it was necessary for them to move at a good speed—which helped to keep them warm—although they dared not risk any splashes.

Constance stayed beside her, smiling at her. Constance was actually being very brave, and revealing enormous powers of concentration, in view of the questions and doubts that must be tearing at her mind. Equally she had to be very worried about Frank. They did not even know where he was, if he had managed to leave Tientsin, and had fallen in with a revolutionary mob. As far as they knew, Yuan had not yet sent for him—the countryside was still in a state of confusion, and the Chinese peasants, as they usually did in times of strife, had apparently torn up considerable lengths of the railroad track. Yuan intended to send a mounted patrol down to fetch Frank as soon as he regarded the journey a safe one, but even if the soldiers left at dawn, they could hardly make the coast before dusk. It was up to Lin to get *them* there first.

But surely it would be a mistake even to consider the future until they were safely away from the Forbidden City.

It was necessary for them all to swim the last fifty yards, where the lake finally deepened just before the juncture with the canal, and the canal itself was deeper than the lake. Now Charlie found the going more difficult, and Constance had to help him with the tow, while Adela felt herself bobbing about, her feet sinking —her boots were quite filled with water—and from time to time her head being ducked as well. She could not help but gasp and splutter, while she fought back the desire to throw them off and drown or survive on her own, and the desire too from time to time to scream her fear to the world.

"Good girl," Constance kept saying. "Oh, good girl. Isn't she the bravest girl you ever met, Charlie?"

Charlie grunted. He was obviously still very afraid himself. And aware that she knew it.

But always they made progress, following Lin's unerring lead. Slowly they swam under the wall of the Forbidden City itself, then through the Tartar City, gasping and panting but surrounded by the midnight sounds and smells of Peking, standing motionless up to their necks in water—Adela's arms wrapped around Charlie—whenever any late wanderer approached the bank, more than once being showered with urine as someone relieved himself above them, until they had penetrated the outer wall as well, all without receiving a single challenge or hearing a single disturbance. Yuan had not imposed martial law, but in Peking, at least, his victory was obviously complete and recognized to be so.

It seemed they had been swimming all of their lives when, with the walls at a safe distance, Lin finally turned to the bank and climbed out. He seemed tireless, but he did not offer to help them, indeed walked away into the darkness. Charlie had to help Constance out, and then she took Adela's arms while he pushed at her thighs to get her onto the bank. She lay on her face, gasping and shivering in the night air, aware that the others were as exhausted beside her. But now there were feet, and hooves. She raised her head, saw that Lin had returned with a man, who led five horses. "We must hurry," Lin said.

Adela rose to her knees. "We must move," she said.

Charlie just lay there gasping.

Adela shook his shoulders. "Come *on,*" she insisted. "You cannot afford to be tired now. We must *move.*"

Constance was already on her feet and being assisted into the saddle by Lin; they would have to ride astride. Charlie sat up, looked at her, then shrugged off her hand and pushed himself to his feet. Adela chewed her lip. Almost she could suppose that he was angry with her. But why? When they were free of the city. Even if enormous dangers still lay ahead of them?

She turned away and mounted, following Lin into the night. But Lin was too much a master of avoiding capture to risk riding all the way to Tientsin. He knew that Yuan would send behind them the moment their escape was discovered, which could hardly be much after dawn. And he knew too that there was the telegraph, or if that had also been pulled down, the heliograph, which could be used to flash messages to soldiers in front of them, once the sun was high enough.

Therefore, after they had ridden around to the south side of the city and reached firm ground where their tracks would not be easily deciphered, they again dismounted. Lin's follower now led the five horses south at a gallop, as they would have done had they actually made their escape that way, while they stole across the fields toward the river, shivering in their soaked clothing. On the banks of the Hei-ho a sampan waited for them, and by dawn they were on their way down the turbulent current, apparently laden with produce for the Tientsin market, whatever the political upheavals that might be shaking the country. Lin, dressed as a Chinese coolie, and two other men handled the great sweep oars, while the three white people hid in the bottom beneath the piled bags of corn and fruit.

To begin with, it was a blessed relief to be able just to sit and stretch exhausted limbs and try to believe that they were actually on their way to freedom. But very shortly the cold became unbearable, and Adela sneezed.

"You poor child," Constance said. "Here . . . I've found some sacking. Wrap it around you."

Adela hesitated, and then knelt to take off her habit.

"Dela?" Constance asked in concern, glancing forward.

"Does it matter, Mother?" she asked. "I am sure Lin-tu has seen a naked woman before." She bit her lip as Constance's head jerked. But she would not change her mind, and indeed, once she was wrapped in the sacking, she felt much better, and distinctly warmer, even if she immediately began to scratch. Constance, after watching her for a scandalized moment, followed her example. There was a great deal of sacking, and she offered some of it to Charlie, but he merely turned away from her.

Adela felt almost angry herself, almost wished he *would* catch cold. And she could not for the life of her understand what was the matter . . . until she remembered that of course they had not actually been allowed a moment alone together since the revolution had begun, three days in which he had had to watch her always at the marshal's side, uncertain what might be happening between them in private—apparently unaware that the marshal would never lay a finger on his affianced bride until after the wedding ceremony—and three days also in which, as he would have been attended by eunuchs, he would be wondering just what the half-men might have done for her.

The great oaf was jealous of whatever she might have experienced.

She touched his arm, and he turned his head. "It's all over now, Charlie," she said. "It's all behind us."

He turned away again, and she sighed and leaned back against the side of the sampan. Let him be a stupid man. He would get over it, and she was too exhausted to pursue the matter further. She could feel waves of blessed relief spreading over her as she too closed her eyes. For the moment they were safe, and however cold and uncomfortable, she felt they *would* get down the river. And then . . . her eyes opened again. She had actually not thought about it, about what she would have to do, at all. She had allowed herself to assume that once they gained Tientsin, all would be well.

She watched Constance, her eyes now accustomed to the darkness. She could see that her foster mother's hands were clenched, and *she* was certainly not sleeping, however tired she might be. Constance was beginning to think, and wonder—and *she* had no idea what Lin-tu might have said to her.

She would of course have to be told, as would Charlie, if they were all to escape. But when? Because Adela was realizing she had no idea how much she could rely on them. It was incredible, after all these years she

had lived with them. But it was true. They had revealed
sides of themselves these past few days which had made
her aware of how little she knew them at all. There was
no doubting Constance's courage, but it had been
revealed over these days as a passive courage. Constance
could absorb enormous misfortune, even enormous
mistreatment, and come up smiling at the end of it; she
had surely proved that in her youth with the Boxers. But
active courage, such as might be needed were they to
have to fight their way to freedom . . . While Charlie . . .
She just did not know about Charlie. But she could not
help but reflect that of the three of them, if it came to a
showdown with Lin-tu, only *she* would be certain of
what would have to be done. And it was possible that
only she might have the decisive courage to do it. The
girl who could have been empress of China, she thought
bitterly. Or just a girl who had inherited a determination
her family lacked? Both her families?

Daybreak brought a more acute awareness of their
situation. As the sun rose and the air heated, it became
tremendously hot in the bilges of the sampan, which was
in any event a place of ghastly odors and seeping black
liquid. Lin brought them rice to eat and a cup of tepid
water each, but there was no means of preparing tea,
unless they were going to put in to the bank, and he was
not going to risk that. So they lay and sweltered, seldom
speaking, each wrapped in his or her own thoughts.
Although even thought was confused by uncertainty
and apprehension, as they were unable to look out and
see where they were, and what was happening. A great
deal obviously *was* happening. However easily Yuan
might have managed to subdue the people of Peking,
out in the countryside there were still large numbers
turbulently unsure of what had happened, of who, if
anyone, was now their master. Only the fall of the
dynasty seemed universally accepted, with a resulting

spasm of anarchy. Often they could hear the sound of horses' hooves galloping along the banks of the river, and sometimes even of rifle fire, while now and then shouted voices rose above the swish of the water. Once or twice they were challenged, and once at least rifles were fired at *them,* but Lin always extricated them from possible danger by promptly taking the opposite side of the stream from the hubbub, and with the fast-running current they were soon beyond the reach of any local pursuers. So fast did they travel, indeed, that he was able to tell them, as dusk began to fall, that he could see the lights of Tientsin in the distance.

By now their clothes had dried and they were able to dress themselves, even if the garments still stank of canal effluvia. And now Adela knew she could wait no longer; Constance's agitation was visibly growing. "Mother," she whispered, "you must speak with Lin and persuade him to take us directly to the European quarter."

Constance's head turned abruptly. "Will he not do that anyway?"

"He may not," Adela said, looking into her eyes.

Constance returned the gaze for several seconds, and then suddenly flushed. "You . . . What payment is he expecting for saving us?"

Adela drew a long breath. "Me," she said.

"You?" Constance's voice nearly rose, and she looked at Charlie. Who as usual said nothing.

"He offered, and I accepted," Adela said. "I could think of no other way to save our lives."

"But . . . my dear child . . ."

"I will not go with him," Adela said. "I will not have to, if he will take us to the European quarter."

"You mean . . ." Constance stared at her with her mouth open, then looked forward, where Lin continued to work his oar. Adela wondered if she was shocked at her foster daughter's ruthlessness, or if she was re-membering how *she* had deserted this man eleven years ago.

"But *you* must talk with him," Adela said. "If I do so, he will be suspicious."

Constance hesitated, almost visibly summoning her courage and resolution. Then she nodded and went forward. Adela gazed at Charlie, and as usual he looked away. More explanations, she thought. Why could he not just *trust* her?

"I have been thinking," Constance was saying. "It would be best if you were to take us directly to the European quarter. Safest."

Lin shook his head as he continued to walk to and fro with the enormous bow sweep; he seemed quite tireless, as did his companions. "We will spend the night in the Chinese city. It will be quite safe, because no one will know we are there. Yuan's people will in fact *suppose* we will have gone to the European quarter."

Constance bit her lip. But she had been foolish to suppose it would be at all easy. "But I must make sure my husband has not yet left Peking," she said. "Should Yuan lay hands on him, after our escape . . . You must see that cannot be, Lin."

Lin hesitated, and then nodded. "I will discover what is happening with Wynne," he said. "If he is in Tientsin I will bring him with me, to meet you and your son, and take you away."

"And the princess?"

His eyes gloomed at her. "She comes with me. You know of this?"

"Yes. Lin . . ."

"She comes with *me*," he said again. "She is mine. You were mine once, Constance, and I did not take you. I was a fool. I was young, and I dreamed. Now I am older, and I know better than to dream. I will take the princess, and I will use her as my woman, and I will be avenged, not only upon you but also upon the entire Manchu nation. That is our bargain, and that is what she agreed. Now, be quiet and lie down until we are in among the other boats.''

Her shoulders sagged as she ducked back amid the fruit. "He will not do it," she whispered. "He says he will go and find Frank for us. But he means to take us to his friends in the Chinese city."

"Well, that's it, then," Charlie said.

Adela gave him a quick glance. She could not tell whether he meant they were all finished, or only her. But her brain was too excited to worry about Charlie at this moment. Because there was still a chance. "You say *he* will go and fetch Father?" she asked.

"That is what he said. But we will be left under guard."

"He is totally confident," Adela said. "He considers us two women and a boy."

"Well . . ." Constance glanced at her son and flushed.

"So he will leave only these two men."

"Two *men,*" Charlie muttered. "And one of them has a revolver. Didn't you see that?"

"We must *try,*" Adela said. She gazed at him. "Or are you willing to let me go?"

He returned her gaze, then looked at his mother.

"Of course we must try," Constance said. "We shall. I will work out what we will do."

Adela opened her mouth, and then closed it again. She had always followed Constance's lead before.

They waited, their bodies tense, as the sampan nosed in amid the other river craft, while a hubbub of conversation rose about them. Lin came to kneel beside them while his companions made fast. "Here you will be safe," he said. "These are all Chinese, and they are all friends of mine. I will leave now, and discover what has happened with Wynne, and also make contact with the junk captain who will take the princess and me to the South. I may be gone for several hours, but do not worry, I will return before dawn. By dawn you and I will be at sea, Princess." He grinned at Constance. "And perhaps you also. It has all gone very well up to now. It will continue to do so. I am in charge."

Once again he gazed at Adela. By dawn, she thought, he expects me to be in his arms. And by dawn I shall *be* in his arms, unless I am prepared to die.

Which meant, she realized, that she must be prepared to kill.

She could not speak, but this did not seem to concern him, and he left the boat, having to cross several others to reach the shore. The two Chinese men grinned at them and gave them rice to eat before they withdrew to the bow to have their own meal and chat with the people on the adjacent boat.

Adela studied their situation. They were on the outside of a raft of about seven sampans, so far as she could make out in the gloom, which was all to the good —had they been in the middle, escape might have been impossible. But there were innumerable other rafts about them, swaying to and fro on the edge of the current. On the other hand, once they freed themselves and drifted away from their own raft, the current should seize them and whip them down the remaining quarter of a mile to the European dock; their real problem was how to avoid being swept past where they wanted to disembark—there was no way just the three of them were going to be able to row back up against such a current.

"When?" she asked, swallowing the last of her rice.

"I think we should wait until they settle down for the night," Constance said. Her voice trembled.

"It has to be *now,* Mother," Adela said. "If another boat should come and moor outside us, we shall not escape at all. Can you release the stern line?" she asked, as Constance still hesitated.

"I think so."

"Then do it as soon as I shout. Come with me, Charlie."

He hesitated, then followed her to the bow; she dared not look at him, could only hope he would be able to find *some* resolution.

The two Chinese gazed at them in mild surprise. "Have you no tea, no sake?" Adela asked, crouching beside them.

"Sake? No sake. But tea . . ." He turned to the woman on the next sampan, with whom he had been talking before the interruption, and Adela saw that there were several other girls on the little boat, but only one man. There was a stroke of luck—they were clearly prostitutes who had been negotiating prices with Lin's men. "You have tea for the white lady?"

"Tea?" the girl repeated. "Oh, yes, you will have tea, great lady."

Clearly they did not know who she was, which was another stroke of fortune. "Then would you fetch some, please," she said, as imperiously as she could.

The girl hesitated, and then turned to go aft, standing up as she did so.

"Now," Adela shouted, and pushed the man nearest to her. He gave a startled grunt, fell backward, and then regained his sitting position on the gunwale of the sampan. But as he had fallen backward his blouse had ridden up to reveal the revolver thrust into his waistband—and now both his hands were clutching the gunwale while he stared at her in amazement. Adela grasped the pistol and pulled it free, at the same time jabbing the barrel hard into his chest. He gave a shriek of pain and alarm and tumbled over the side. In falling, he grabbed at the gunwale of the neighboring boat, causing it to rock violently; the standing girl was taken off balance and also fell over the side, to a chorus of screams from her companions.

Charlie had pushed the other man over the side with less difficulty, and Constance had already released the stern, so that the sampan was commencing to swing out into the current. Adela pulled at the bow rope, but the knot jammed on the cleat, while one of the Chinese men grasped the gunwale and tried to clamber back on board, causing *them* to rock dangerously.

"Stop him!" Constance cried, running forward. Adela released the rope and hit the grasping fingers with the butt of her revolver. The man gave another bellow of pain and released the boat, to fall away in the darkness. But by now the entire fleet of sampans was in an uproar, and the prostitutes had all scrambled forward to reach for Lin's boat, still held by the jammed bow warp, although the stern had by now swung wide into the stream; the sight of Adela's brandished revolver sent them tumbling aft again, losing their balance and causing chaos among the men from the other sampans who were trying to come to their aid. Adela discovered that Charlie was kneeling beside her, releasing the jammed rope with a jerk. They drifted into the darkness, and immediately collided with another sampan, causing a fresh chorus of shrieks and shouts.

"The sweeps," Adela cried, using her feet to push their latest adversaries away. "Charlie, Mother, the sweeps."

Fortunately the men on the sampan were more concerned with regaining control of their own vessel than with grappling with the white people, and the two boats drifted apart. Constance grasped the nearest sweep, thrust it over the side—it was tied to its oarlock, and could not slip free. She dug the broad blade into the water and felt a tremendous pull as the bows came straight, then nearly went over the side herself before she managed to whip the heavy wooden spar up and repeat the sequence, desperately trying to remember the quick, forceful movements which Lin had performed so expertly. On the other side, Charlie was also heaving up and down, and by now, in the grip of the current, they were fairly sailing along. But in front of them were two more sampans, cast adrift from another raft and filled with shouting and gesticulating Chinese. Constance, back in the bow to commence her next sweep, was momentarily paralyzed as she saw them heading straight for the screaming men.

"Move," she shouted. "Get out of the way, or we'll . . ."

She heard the short, sharp bark of the revolver from beside her. Adela had not wasted the breath to threaten, but had fired into the mass blocking their way. One of the men in front of them gave a gasp and fell overboard, while the others hastily grabbed their own sweeps to get out of the way.

"My dear girl,' Constance shrieked. "Oh, my dear girl."

"The sweep, Mother!" Adela bawled. "The sweep."

The sampan was swinging sideways. Constance dug her oar down to bring them straight, looked forward, at the empty river, and at Adela, kneeling in the bow like some avenging goddess, her hair floating in the breeze, the revolver still in her hand. She had calmly shot a man, reaching back into the un-Christian inhumanity of her Mongol ancestors, to whom life had always been so cheap. And she did not seem to have turned a hair. Of course, when she realized what she had done . . . But what a tower of strength she was proving at the moment. It was a strength which deserved only to be matched, to ensure their own safety.

So Constance rowed with desperate energy, together with Charlie, while Adela encouraged them both. They covered the five hundred yards downstream to the wharf fronting the European quarter in a few minutes, turning their sweeps to drive the sampan full tilt into the wooden piling, smashing the bows and sending Adela rolling aft, at last releasing the revolver, while Charlie leapt ashore, carrying the painter, and hastily made it fast. And was immediately challenged by a British marine sentry.

"I am Mrs. Constance Wynne," Constance told him, helping the gasping Adela onto the deck. "From Peking."

"From Peking?" The man peered at her. "Well, glory be. Everyone's been in a tizzy here for the last couple of days, wondering what's been happening up there. The garrison's been put on full alert. Was it you causing that hubbub upriver?"

"Yes," Constance said. "Will you please take us to your consul or to my husband?"

"Mrs. Wynne, you say? The American lady whose daughter was kidnapped by bandits?" He stared at Adela, as if understanding for the first time that she had to be the daughter in question. "Hey, your Dad's been going spare asking about you."

"Where *is* my husband?" Constance demanded, resisting an urge to hit the fellow.

"At the hotel when at last I heard, madam. Hey, sarge . . ." He summoned the sergeant of the guard, and a few moments later they were hurrying toward the hotel under escort, running up the front steps and into the lobby, where there was quite a crowd of white men and women surrounding and shouting questions at, Constance saw with a pounding heart, four Chinese soldiers.

Yuan's men! Either they had made very good time or the telegraph wires had not been destroyed after all. Clearly everything would depend on how much *they* knew of what had been happening in Peking.

She paused in the doorway, suddenly terribly aware of how exhausted she felt and what an utter mess she must look, but still flanked by Charlie and Adela, and with three armed marines at her back, for which she was truly grateful. But what to do? She had an awful temptation just to turn and run. She couldn't make out Frank in the throng, and she wasn't at all sure how safe they were, even in the company of the marines, if the British were under orders not to oppose the regime without proper cause, and if the soldiers claimed, as they well might, that Mrs. Wynne and her children were wanted in connection with the murders of three eunuchs in Peking.

Then she saw Frank emerging from the rear of the room, hurrying, his face a mass of conflicting emotions. "Frank!" she shouted.

Her voice cut across the hubbub as every head turned toward her.

"Connie!" Frank shouted back.

"Mrs. Wynne!" People surged at her.

"These fellows say . . ."

"What's been happening in Peking, Mrs. Wynne?"

"The roads . . . ?"

"The telegraph . . ."

"The legations . . . ?"

"The dynastry . . . ?"

"You must come with us, Mrs. Wynne." This from the officer commanding the Chinese soldiers. "And the princess, also."

"Connie!" Frank at last managed to fight his way through the throng and reach her, to hold her in his arms while he grasped Charlie's hand and smiled at Adela. "Oh, Connie! We've been so worried. Nothing but rumors. And now these guys . . . I tried to get to you yesterday, as soon as we heard of the revolt, but the train was out. I managed to get through to the legation by telegraph, and they said that the house had been attacked, that no one knew for sure where you were, but that there was a rumor you'd been taken into the Forbidden City on the orders of Marshal Yuan, so far as anyone knew." He glanced left and right, aware that everyone was listening. "So I stopped worrying," he went on loudly, "knowing that Yuan is our friend. But now these fellows . . ."

"Mrs. Wynne must come with us," the Chinese captain said again. "She is wanted for crimes against the state. You may accompany her, Mr. Wynne. But the young ones must come also."

The white people stared at them, and Constance could hear Adela's breath whistle in her nostrils. To have fought so hard, and risked so much . . .

"Frank," Constance said. "Listen. Yuan is trying to hold us against our will. He knows, Frank. He knows everything. We must leave. You can't let them take us back."

"Mrs. Wynne must come," the captain repeated.

Frank looked past him at one of the white men. "You can't really allow my wife and children to be marched off by these thugs, Richards," he said.

The Englishman, clearly the British consul, stroked his mustache and decided to take refuge in legalities. "I'm afraid I shall have to inspect your warrant," he said.

"Warrant? No warrant," the captain said.

"My dear fellow, you cannot arrest someone without a warrant," Richards said.

"I do not need a warrant," the captain declared. "I serve Marshal Yuan."

"Nevertheless, you must have a warrant. Unless, perhaps," Richards said with obviously helpful intent, "you have a specific charge to level against Mrs. Wynne?"

The captain blinked. "There will be a charge," he said.

"But you do not know what it is?"

"I am to take Mrs. Wynne and her son and the princess back to Peking," the captain insisted.

Richards shook his head. "I'm afraid I cannot permit that, in the absence of a specific charge. Even if you possessed a warrant, Mrs. Wynne and her family fall under the law of extraterritoriality and are subject only to the jurisdiction of the American consul. He will have to countersign your warrant. When you get one, of course."

The captain stared at him.

"But the American consul is not in Tientsin right now," Richards said sympathetically.

"The marshal will be angry," the captain declared. "The marshal rules all China, and his will is law."

"Not to Europeans it isn't," Richards pointed out. "Or to Americans. I'm sorry, old man, but there it is. You will have to telegraph Peking and obtain an order for Mrs. Wynne's arrest from the American minister. Until then she is free to do as she pleases."

The captain gazed at the waiting men and women, and then at the bewildered British marines. But he was outnumbered and outgunned at the moment. He turned his gaze on Constance. "The marshal will be angry," he repeated. "You will suffer for this, Mrs. Wynne." He beckoned his men and left the lobby.

There was a moment's silence; then the hubbub

started again as more and more questions were asked. Richards waved his arms for silence. "I am sure you fellows can see that Mrs. Wynne and her children are quite exhausted. I think a few brandies and soda wouldn't go amiss. On the British consulate." He summoned the waiters and gave the necessary instructions, which effectively diverted everyone's attention. "And then," he went on in a loud voice, "I think a hot bath and a good meal and a soft bed are indicated. I believe the hotel is full. Mrs. Richards will be pleased to put you up." He smiled at the assembly and ushered Constance to the door. "She can tell you all about it tomorrow."

"But . . ." Constance protested.

Richards continued to smile at the anxious people as they slowly dispersed toward the hotel lounge and the drinks were brought. "I entirely agree, Mrs. Wynne," he said in a low voice. "I don't think you should hang around here a moment longer than you have to. But it would be a mistake to let *anyone* know that you intend to run for it. Didn't you tell me, Wynne, that you've cabins booked on the *Amelia Johnson,* out in the gulf?"

"That's right," Frank said. "And she's already delayed her sailing for several hours to see if I could get any news from Peking."

"Well, I would say you've received all the news you need," Richards told him. "Gather up your wife's belongings and get out of here before the chap does get a warrant, or before he decides to use force. I don't know that my government would back a military action in your support, especially if your wife did . . . shall we say, tread on a few toes in getting out of Peking. These marines will escort you to the dock, and I'll come along as well. I'll arrange for you to use my government launch to get out to the ship. But let's get on with it."

"We don't have any things to gather up," Constance told him. "We left Peking in what we're wearing."

"Then there's nothing to wait for," Frank said, and hurried them into the street, carrying his own small valise. "Oh, Connie, Charlie, Dela . . . if you knew how worried I've been . . ."

"We're here now, Frank," Constance said. "We're here." Explanations could come later, when they might all be able to work out exactly what had happened.

If he would wait that long. "But . . . I wish I could understand," he said. "I've just been speaking with the chap Lin-tu—at least that's who he said he was. You remember Lin-tu? My God, I suppose I should have gone back and told him that we didn't need him anymore. But the fact is . . ."

Constance checked; she dared not look at Adela. "Lin-tu? You've been speaking with Lin-tu?"

"He came to the back door of the hotel. Dressed like a coolie. I couldn't make head or tail of it. I must actually have been talking to him when you all reached there. He told me you were waiting in the Chinese city and that he would take me to collect you. But then he said something quite amazing. He said that only you and Charlie would be coming, that Adela had agreed to remain in China as his woman if he helped you get out of Peking and down to the coast." He gazed at Adela, but she did not speak, so he went on. "Do you know, I nearly punched him in the nose? But then I figured the thing was to get to you first, and sort him out after. So I went back into the hotel to get some help, and there you were. Do you have any idea what he was talking about?"

Adela drew a long breath, but Charlie got there first. "It was Adela's plan, to get him to help us," he explained. "It was the only way."

"My God!" Frank said. "But . . ."

"He apparently has the same idea as Yuan or Feng," Constance explained, also hurrying to the rescue. "That possession of Adela will somehow enable him to rally both the Manchu and the Chinese behind him."

"Good God!" Frank remarked again, and gazed at his foster daughter. "And you pretended to go along with him? You really are a remarkable young woman, Dela. But I wouldn't like you to run into this guy ever again. He really believed it."

"If he had not believed it, Father," Adela told him, "he wouldn't have helped us, would he?"

The explanations had not even begun, she knew. But Charlie had rallied, and so had Constance. If *they* were prepared to understand, then despite all, despite the man she had shot—she dared not think about that—she almost felt she could breathe again. And even that would be understandable, and perhaps acceptable, once they were off Chinese soil.

They had reached the dock and Richards was giving orders for the British consulate steam launch to make ready to take them out to the American steamer. "It takes a little while to raise the steam," he explained. "But you'll be on your way soon enough."

"I can't tell you how grateful we are, Mr. Richards," Constance said. "You really are saving our lives. Are you sure there won't be any repercussions for you?"

Richards kissed her hand. "None I can't handle, Mrs. Wynne. They had no right to take you without a warrant. What you decided to do between those Chinese leaving and returning *with* a warrant is none of my business. Besides . . ." He winked. "As far as I'm concerned, they weren't going to get you, no matter what you'd done. As one of your navy captains said once on this very river, blood is thicker than water. But if you *have* fallen out with Yuan Shih-k'ai, and he has taken over the government, then I think the sooner you say good-bye to China forever, the better.''

"I'm sure you're right," Constance agreed.

Forever, Adela thought. Her country, her people, her Destiny. All gone. Forever was a very long time.

She turned away and prepared to descend the ladder to the launch behind her foster mother. Constance moved slowly and carefully, and it was necessary to wait for a moment. Adela gazed at the crowd of Chinese coolies who had gathered to see what all the excitement was about. Surrounded as she was by armed British marines, even the sight of all those yellow faces did not frighten her anymore . . . until she saw, standing in their midst, staring at her with enormous angry eyes, Lin-tu.

9

The Suitor

How familiar the noise of the ship's engines rumbling up through the deck. Six months ago that had been a happy sound, carrying her home to all the sights and sounds and smells with which she was familiar, with which her life had always been associated. Now the sound was reassuring, taking her away from her enemies, from the people who would destroy her.

But it was an unhappy sound, because it was also taking her away from China.

Adela lay on her narrow bunk, only inches from the deckhead—Constance had opted for the lower berth, predictably, as Frank had been able to afford only two cabins and thus had decided to segregate the sexes, as yet unaware that there was no necessity for that—and stared into the darkness. Exhausted as she was, she could not sleep. If she had summoned all her reserves of mental and physical strength to carry her through the ordeal of the past twenty-four hours, and if indeed she had had to draw on even more reserves of strength during the preceding three days, she had been quite unable to subdue the tumultuous thoughts which filled her mind by simply boarding this ship and getting into this bed. Because what had happened was the most immense occurrence in all history, for her. And in her entire life, as well. She had made a bitter enemy whose memory would haunt her for the rest of her days. And she had killed a man. At least, she supposed he was dead. Certainly her escape had involved the deaths of at least two eunuchs. She had made these things happen, to burst free.

But looming over even these personal calamities was the overwhelming fact that the dynasty had fallen. China was in the hands of a warlord. No doubt observers had said the same thing of Nurhachi two hundred and fifty years before, and out of the confusion and bloodshed and civil war had emerged the Ch'ing. It was possible for a dispassionate observer now to suppose that out of the present maelstrom might arise a new dynasty, again to rule for two and a half centuries.

But it would not be *her* dynasty, her family. If there was one unchanging law in Chinese history, it was that once a dynasty fell, it never rose again. Not even the immortal Koxinga, last of the Ming admirals, who had held out against the Manchu for a generation, had been able to restore his masters to their thrones. She, lying in this bunk and listening to the throbbing of the engines, was a perfect example of what had happened, exiled from China, fleeing for her very life, with nothing more than the clothes she had come on board in to call her own.

The end of an era.

But far more, for her. Because she might have been the hinge of the future, had she not snapped away to leave the doorway helplessly open and empty. It was impossible, looking back on her life, and even more, on the lives of her parents, the way she had been conceived at all by two people of such differing backgrounds and races, not to suppose that she might after all be the child of Destiny. How that thought kept coming back to haunt her. Yet it was inescapable. She might have been created especially to bridge the gap between the Manchu and whoever would follow, in the persons of her children. That future, that Destiny, she had rejected. Her instincts rejected it still. Marriage to Yuan could never have been more than a personal disaster for her. But of how many famous queens, and more important, famous mothers of kings, could that not be said? Where Destiny, the Destiny of an entire nation, beckoned, what right had any individual to set personal feelings before it?

She had done so, and in a most irrevocable fashion. Willfully and consciously she had slapped Destiny in the face. Would Fate ever forgive her? Could her life now be anything more than a disaster, even with Charlie? Even with Charlie, she thought bitterly. Behaving like a jealous schoolboy. She had expected him at least to hold her hand when they had finally boarded the ship, after the way he had come to her aid in answering Frank's questions. But he had not even looked at her.

He would get over it, of course. But even if she were disposed to forgive him, and at the moment she was not, Fate was already surrounding her with misfortunes to haunt her every waking moment. This evening she had shot a man. She had known all along that they would never escape unless *she* made it happen, because she had known that both Charlie and Constance would wish to avoid the ultimate, as long as possible. Actually, Constance had behaved magnificently. But even she had faltered at the crucial moment. *She* had never doubted. If they had been going to escape, then *nothing* could be allowed to stand in their way.

So she had killed a man, entirely by instinct. He had been in her way. It was not a thought, presumably, to

disturb a would-be empress. She could not imagine
Tz'u-Hsi or Wu Hou giving it a thought; each of those
formidable ladies had caused the deaths of thousands of
men, women, and children. But she was not going to be
an empress, and now the whole future was unthinkable
as she was chased through the years by the almost
physical intensity of Lin-tu's hatred.

A tear trickled down her cheek as she finally fell
asleep.

How empty the sea. No, not empty, Constance
thought. The horizon was still ringed with mountains,
Korea, Japan. . . . Only China itself was already lost to
view. But soon even the distant mountains would disappear. And with them, half of her life. All of her life
that mattered. She had gone to China as a girl of nineteen, she was leaving as a woman of forty, with what to
show for it? A wealth of experience, certainly. A wealth
of memories. And among both experiences and
memories were some very bitter ones indeed.

But also a family, and a husband. She felt rather than
heard Frank come to the rail beside her. It was just
dawn, and chill; one of the ship's officers had lent her a
greatcoat in which to wrap herself. She had fallen into a
very heavy sleep almost the moment she had reached her
bunk last night, and woken up only a few hours later
shivering as Lin-tu's face had hung before her, glowing
in the darkness. Because she had also seen him standing
in the crowd by the dock. How remarkable that Adela
should have been able to sleep so soundly, after everything that had happened, everything she had *done*. She
was truly a remarkable child. And a frightening one.

She shivered, and Frank put his arm around her. "It's
all over now, Connie. There's nothing to be afraid of
anymore."

She sighed and rested her head on his shoulder. "And

I want you to know," he went on, "how magnificent you've been. How magnificent you all have been. Charlie told me how Adela shot your way out of those sampans. A seventeen-year-old girl. And he's been great too." He waited, but she didn't reply. Because to reply might lead her down culs-de-sac she would not know how to escape. Such as confessing that she was jealous of her own foster child? That she was even angry, and certainly intensely disappointed, that Lin-tu should have approached Adela instead of her?

"I guess you don't really want to talk about it," Frank observed.

"No," she said. "Not right now. It's all been a nightmare, Frank. I'm just about afraid to close my eyes, even for a second."

His arm flexed, to hold her tighter. "You're going to sleep again, Connie, and sounder than ever. Because it *was* just a nightmare, and you're awake now. Once we're in San Francisco you won't be able to believe it ever really happened. And there'll be lots to do, you know, finding a new house, finding a job for me, finding something for Charlie to do, seeing to Adela . . ."

Getting them married just as soon as possible, Constance thought. It was difficult to see how the girl could ever settle down in America, in civilization and without fear, after her experiences of the past few days. From nearly being shamefully mutilated by a mob to sitting beside the Bonaparte of China at dinner to having to shoot a man to make good their escape, all in seventy-two hours. And all at seventeen. But she loved Charlie, and Charlie loved her. It was absolutely vital to believe that now, and therefore to believe that together they would be able to solve any problems that might lie ahead.

She had sufficient of her own. She nestled in Frank's arms. "Tell me about America," she said. "Tell me all about it, Frank. I've just about forgotten what it's like to live there."

"It's like a dream," Charles Baird said. He stood leaning on the rail of the very brief promenade deck of the *Amelia Johnson*—she was a freighter, not a liner—and watched Adela brushing her hair; the wind kept snarling it and whipping it to and fro—she really would have done much better to tie it up and leave it until they reached America. But she had nothing else to do, and her hair was her most precious possession. So she spent hours combing it and brushing it, sitting in her deck chair, watching the white-crested blue swell surging by.

And today, at least, she had company. His company. She felt that he was almost a stranger. Of course she had always known he would get over whatever it was that had been upsetting him, and if it had taken several days longer than she would have supposed possible, well, she also knew that she must be a sight, with only the one riding habit to wear, and that starting to give at the seams and snag at the hems. But somehow there seemed to have been erected between them a barrier far more solid than she would ever have expected possible, considering the intimacy, mental as well as physical, that they had shared during the last month in Peking. And then, they had now been at sea for ten days, and in all that time he had not once sought her bunk. That would have been impossible anyway, with Constance about, but even when they were utterly alone, as now, he showed no interest in lovemaking, even with words.

But she had absolutely refused to become angry. She reminded herself time and again that undoubtedly he had had an even more unnerving experience than she herself during the revolution. Perhaps he even felt he had let her down, let them all down. It had been she who saved them from the mob, and it had been she who extricated them from Lin-tu's clutches. She felt that she could help him there, reassure him . . . but not right now. She did not want to talk about these things right now.

And at last her patience was being rewarded. He was here, alone with her, and at least talking. Now was a time to forget the past altogether and think only of the future. Of *their* future. She smiled at him. "In another couple of weeks or so we'll be in San Francisco," she said. "Then it *will* be a dream. Something to tell our children about."

He turned away from her to rest his elbows on the rail and look out to sea. Oh, dear, she thought, I have embarrassed him.

But that could not be possible, in their circumstances. "Well," she said, "I rather thought we should get married the moment we land. I know it would please Mother, after . . . well, everything that's happened."

"I cannot marry you as soon as we land," Charles said without looking at her.

Adela put down her brush to gaze at the back of his head.

"I . . ." At last Charlie turned, his face crimson. "We have to get settled in first. I have to get established first. I cannot possibly take a wife until I have a job, a regular income . . . until I have something put by."

Still she gazed at him. She was not sure what she wanted to think or do. She was only aware of having been kicked in the stomach by a mule. Because without Charlie, she might as well have stayed in China.

"And there's you, too," he went on, gaining in confidence as she had not replied. "You're very young, Dela.

Terribly young to get married. I . . . well, I think you want to be absolutely sure that you love me. That you wish to spend the rest of your life with *me.*"

"I am perfectly sure," she said. "Or I would not have let you . . ." She bit her lip.

"Oh, *that.*" He gave her a cheery smile. "Of course that was magnificent, tremendous. I shall never forget it, Dela. But in this day and age, being . . . well . . . being a virgin on your wedding night doesn't really matter all that much. At least in the States. If you found someone that you loved better than me, believe me, I wouldn't stand in your way."

Adela gazed at him for some moments, then got up and went below. She prayed the cabin would be empty, so that she could weep to herself.

"I would like you to tell me," Constance said, "what has happened between you and Dela."

"Eh?" Charles asked.

"I found her in our cabin, not ten minutes ago, sobbing her heart out. Do you know, I have never known Dela to cry before? Not aloud like that. And God knows she has had cause, from time to time."

"Well," Charles said, "she did have a pretty grim experience. Maybe it's just getting to her."

"We all had a pretty grim experience," Constance said with a patience she did not feel. She had at least supposed her children had something to look forward to. "Now I would like to know what you and she have quarreled about."

"We haven't quarreled," Charles protested.

His mother gazed at him, and he flushed. "I suppose she's a little upset."

"What about?"

"Well . . . I felt I had to point out to her that we

couldn't get married the very moment we land in San Francisco. She was assuming we would go straight from the ship to a church."

"I had also been assuming that," Constance said. "At least to have the banns read."

"Oh, *Mother*! You must see that is quite impossible."

"You'll have to tell me why," Constance said.

"Well . . . I'm not yet twenty-one. And Dela is only seventeen."

"That didn't seem a problem a couple of weeks ago."

"And I have to get a job," Charles went on as if she hadn't spoken. "You must be able to see that, Mother. I know how tight things are going to be until Father can find his feet, believe me. I can't impose a wife on you until I can afford to keep her."

"You will be imposing nothing we don't already have, you silly boy," Constance said. "Dela is a part of the family whether she's married to you or not. Oh, I understand that you're at last realizing what a big step you're contemplating. It's a pity you didn't consider it earlier. Has it occurred to you that she may be pregnant?"

"Oh, really, after one—"

"Ah," Constance said. "I'm rather glad of that."

"Well . . ." Charles flushed. "There wasn't . . . well . . . but the fact is, Mother, well . . ." He pulled his nose. "We don't really know each other all that well."

"Only all your lives."

"We've known *of* each other all our lives. But we've really been apart for the past six years, since I went to school. Okay, so we spent the odd holiday together in Virginia, but that isn't really the same thing. And . . . well . . ."

"You've discovered she's not quite the girl you thought she was."

Charles's head jerked.

"Oh, I know *that,*" Constance said. "She's not quite the girl I thought she was, either. I guess we've all been inclined to forget that she's half Manchu, or that she's half royalty as well. She doesn't look at things exactly the way we do, for all her upbringing as one of us. And she doesn't react to situations exactly the way we would, either."

"You can say that again," Charles agreed. "I mean, the way she fired into those men, without turning a hair . . ."

"If she hadn't done that, we would probably all be dead."

"Okay, okay, so she's a heroine. But what about Lin-tu?"

At last, Constance thought, we're getting down to bedrock. "She never meant to go with him, Charlie. That too was a pretty brave thing to do."

"Of course I know that, Mother. But . . . well . . . don't you suppose . . . well . . ."

He may have wanted something on account?" Constance asked. "Haven't you asked for that?"

"It's not the sort of thing one askes a girl," he said. "Certainly not Adela. But . . . what I mean is, if she felt it would have helped us escape, she'd have done it. You know that."

"I imagine you're probably right," Constance said. "And that being so, you no longer want her as your wife?"

"I didn't say that. I love her. Oh, I love her. But . . . well . . . I suppose you think I am being every possible sort of cad."

"I think you are setting up to behave like a cad, certainly," Constance said. "But I don't think you *are* one. I think you've just jumped with both feet into a situation you'd never expected to have to face. I think you *should* do some serious thinking about it. Like remembering that you've taken her to bed."

"Oh, Mother, in this day and age—"

"If you genuinely believe that, Charles Baird, then you are not only a cad. You're a scoundrel as well." She allowed her tone to soften, rested her hand on his arm. "Charlie, you must remember that everything that has happened, *everything*, mind, has happened just because she let you make love to her. Right now, without you, she has nothing. Nothing at all. Remember that, Charlie."

But how could she advise him *not* to run like the devil? she wondered. Because Adela was still the Princess Adela, the daughter of Prince Ksian Fu, and the official betrothed of Marshal Yuan Shih-k'ai, dictator of China. Could the world ever be big enough to enable her, or her husband, to forget that?

"A remarkable tale," remarked Mr. Glenning. He was a stout, florid man who seldom lacked a cigar stuck between his teeth; ash dotted the front of his brilliantly decorated vest, and there were scorch marks all over his polished oak desk. His hair was receding, but he endeavored to make up for this by sporting a walrus mustache.

Yet his smile was genial, and the atmosphere in his office very relaxed. He was the federal agent for Chinese and Japanese immigrants, of whom, despite the recent tough laws, there remained quite a number, and had been the man recommended by the San Francisco City Hall for Constance to go and see—no one else had had any idea what to do about her problem, or even if she had a problem.

"You know," Glenning went on, "I sit here, and I go down to the docks, and I see one hell of a lot of Chinks, begging your pardon, Mrs. Wynne, and I talk Pidgin English at them, and they jabber back at me, and I have no idea what they've come from, really. I always meant to visit China, but I never got around to it, and after what you've been telling me, I think maybe I'll give it a miss for a while longer."

"Yes," Constance said, keeping her smile with difficulty; she had just too much on her mind to listen to pleasantries. "About Marshal Yuan . . ."

"Well, now," Glenning said, flicking ash. "I've heard of the guy, of course. And I reckon Washington has too. And I'll forward what you've had to say to them. Mind you, I can't tell you what they'll do about it, if anything. Unlike the limeys and the krauts, our attitude is that China is an independent country and should be allowed to get on with it. If they want to be ruled by some power mad dictator—that's what you called him, right?—well, that's their business. Looking at their history, I don't think it'll be all that much of a change."

"I'm sure it is their business, Mr. Glenning," Constance agreed. "I am only concerned about *my* business. I want to know what you are going to do if Yuan sends for us."

"You mean if he makes formal application for extradition? Well, as I see it, he can't, Mrs. Wynne. There's no treaty between China and the United States calling for extradition in any event, but in addition, you and your family are United States citizens. Of course, if, as you say, the guys helping you out did in a couple of his people, well, I reckon he might be able to make a case as accessories against you, in the consular courts. But even then, if he's got it in for you, I guess we could insist on having the trial held here. Or at least string it along with enough legalities for him to get bored with the whole idea." He smiled at her encouragingly. "There ain't no way this here government is going to allow any American lady to wind up in no Chink prison, Mrs. Wynne. I can guarantee you that."

"Thank you," Constance said. "I had never supposed I would. Nor do I suppose for one moment that Marshal Yuan will waste his time and energy trying to have us brought to trial. I would like to know what the procedure is should he send some of his thugs after us. Where do we go for protection? I've been to the police department, and they weren't entirely helpful. They laughed at me."

"Well . . ." Glenning seemed to be having trouble in not doing so himself. "You mean he might actually send some guys to bump you off? Say, that would be going it a bit. Maybe you'd better tell me exactly what's between you and this Chink, why exactly you had to flee China with him behind you. And why he wants to get hold of you so bad."

"That is my business, Mr. Glenning. But I can tell you that Marshal Yuan is quite capable of going it a bit, as you put it."

"Yeah? Well . . . my advice to you, Mrs. Wynne, is to get hold of a couple of good revolvers and blow the head off any Chink who comes too close."

"You'll support us if we do this?"

"Shucks, Mrs. Wynne, you won't need my support, if you're acting in your own self-defense."

"You're a very reassuring man," Constance said, and stood up.

"Glad to be of help. All well with you?" Glenning asked. His gaze drifted over her obviously cheap dress, the single thin wedding band on her finger, the absence of gloves on a cold January morning which left the fingers themselves blue and puffy. "I mean, apart from this Chink business?"

She met his gaze. "Yes, Mr. Glenning," she said. "All is perfectly well with us, apart, as you say, from this Chink business."

She closed the door behind her and drew a long breath. All is well, she thought bitterly as she went down the stairs. She wondered if all was ever going to be well again. Somehow, compared with the problems of escaping Yuan, and then Lin, and then China itself, the problems of beginning afresh in California had not seemed so immense. She had in fact not considered them at all, except in passing. But now, as Frank had promised her, China, and Yuan, and Lin all seemed nothing more than dreams here where she was entirely surrounded by white faces and heard nothing but English spoken . . . and where nobody had any idea who she was, and cared even less.

Perhaps this was part *of* the problem. But the main problem was sheer existence! She didn't seek all that much. Her parents had not been wealthy, mainly because James Drummond had drunk most of the meager inheritance he had salvaged from the wreckage of Virginia in 1865, six years before she had been born. She remembered her childhood as a sort of genteel poverty; she had never actually gone hungry, but there had never seemed quite sufficient money, at least for Mother and Father, who had both been able to remember better days. Marriage to Henry Baird had changed all of that. Henry, as a missionary, had never been rich, but on Chu-teh, their own mission, with more than a hundred Chinese converts all anxious to play their parts, they had lived on a very good scale indeed, with all the food they wanted, and several seamstresses to make her clothes. Besides, on Chu-teh, where fashion was nonexistent, and the only white women she had ever seen—except on her rare visits to Peking—had been the two Mountjoys and the nuns from the neighboring missions, money had never appeared a problem, or even a necessity. Nor had it following her second marriage, to Frank. He had taken over a thriving business from William Bunting, and if again there had never been quite *enough,* so that trips to the United States, for instance, had always had to be carefully budgeted, she had never lacked clothes to wear or food to put on the table . . . or the servants to put it there.

Forty was a bit of an age to come face to face with actual poverty for the first time in her life.

The trouble was, she could see no end to it. If they had

not expected to be greeted by a brass band when they landed, they had never doubted that someone with Frank's background and ability would be *wanted,* in some capacity. Well, perhaps he was. After a month of answering advertisements and meeting people and talking with them, he had secured a position as clerk in a company which traded with China, had dealings with the local Chinese, and could use someone who both spoke and wrote Mandarin fluently. The pay might have been just sufficient for a single man to live on comfortably, but it did not really stretch to four.

Frank of course was convinced, or pretended to be convinced, that the setback was temporary. "Heck," he would say, "I know more about China than any other living American. Except you, of course." And he had written off to Washington, reminding both the State and War departments of his valuable military service and his experience, and his fluent Chinese, of how he had once penetrated the Boxer lines disguised as a coolie, with total success, and seemed to feel sure he would, eventually, obtain a satisfactory reply leading to a government post. Constance was equally sure he wouldn't, even if he would, she had no doubt, be far more efficient and sympathetic than Mr. Glenning for instance. But while his military service might indeed have been valuable, his record would be studded with references to his adulterous affair with Mrs. Henry Baird, an affair which had eventually led to his being transferred from the China Station to Manila. That he had managed to make things morally right by marrying the said Mrs. Baird would hardly make up for his reputation as a man who would go his own way regardless of propriety, and she also had no doubt that a full, if inaccurate, report of recent events in Peking, laying the blame for any unpleasantness experienced by any European squarely on the shoulders of the Wynne family for having mysteriously angered Marshal Yuan, had already been forwarded by the American minister. In fact, she would have been happier had Frank not contacted Washington at all; now that she had ascertained that looking after themselves was entirely their own problem, she felt the sooner they were forgotten by the State Department, the better—nor did she wish their address to be generally known.

But without that very faint promise of better times to come, what was there? She had dreamed of so many things, a house of their own overlooking the bay, of putting Adela through at least a couple of years of college or at least domestic science, and thereby hopefully weighting the American half of her against the Manchu, of persuading Charlie after all to go to business school, of making a little social circle for herself, of perhaps indulging in some charitable work. . . .

Instead of which she had no house, but a couple of miserable rented rooms. Her clothes, and Adela's, were the cheapest that could be bought anywhere in San Francisco. Christmas, so suddenly upon them after landing, had been the bleakest and coldest and most miserable she could ever remember. Now Frank was gone from dawn until dusk. Charlie spent his time looking for work—as going to school again was obviously out of the question—and also looking more miserable every day, entirely because of Adela. Constance did not doubt that he loved his foster sister—she could tell that from the way he looked at her. But she also knew that he found it difficult to accept that Adela was, quite seriously, a superior being to himself, with quicker reactions, more determination, probably more basic intelligence, and certainly a greater awareness of herself and her powers than anyone he had ever encountered—not excluding himself. This was a considerable admission for a mother to have to make about her own son as against a foster child, but it was true.

Therefore, would not marriage between them have to be a disaster? And he *was* her son. Yet Adela was her responsibility. If only, she thought, some handsome millionaire would come along and sweep the girl off her feet and remove her from their own limited orbit.

And allow a little bit of happiness to creep into their lives.

"We trade with Panama City, and Callao, and Santiago," Charlie explained. He stood in the midst of the tiny rented living room, and threw his arms wide as if embracing the world. "Right up and down the length of South America. It's a long trip, but not that long. We'll be away six weeks at a time."

"Six weeks?" Adela asked.

"Not really a long time, as seamen go," Frank said. "Steamships, are they?"

"No, as a matter of fact. Windjammers," Charles said. "Very romantic, really. I've always wanted to sail on a windjammer."

"That really does sound exciting," Frank agreed. "You know, if I were twenty years younger I'd come with you."

"But . . . you mean you'll have to climb masts and stand on spars and things?" Constance was horrified.

"It isn't a problem, really, Mother. I'm not afraid of heights, and the pay is good. Oh, really tops for a volunteer." He grinned. "Most of the skippers around here have to shanghai their crews. You know, kidnap them when drunk, to lick them into shape. But I'll be one of the chaps doing the shanghaiing."

Adela rose and left the room. Charles stared at his parents.

"I think you had better go and speak with her," Constance suggested.

He hesitated, then squared his shoulders and followed

her into the tiny box which served as her bedroom. "Dela . . . I told you I would have to make my own way. And I have. Now that I've got a berth . . ."

Her eyes were dry. She sat on the little cot which was her bed and gazed at him. "You'll be able to earn some money," she observed.

"That's exactly it, Dela. And after a voyage or two, why, we'll be able . . . well . . . we'll be able to think about getting married."

Still she stared at him. A voyage or *two*. *Think* about getting married. "If you still wish that to happen," she said.

"Want it?" he cried. "My darling Dela . . ."

He checked, because she was still gazing at him, willing him to remember, as he was remembering, that this was the first time he had been inside her bedroom in the three months they had lived in America.

"Dela," he said, and dropped to his knees beside her, "I do love you so. I adore you. It's just that . . . I'm so afraid. You know, of hurting you. Of . . . well, suppose you were to become pregnant before I had a good job. It would be dreadful."

"I know, Charlie," she said softly. "You are so afraid."

He gazed at her, then pushed himself to his feet and left the room.

"Of course not," Constance said. "Get a job? I have never heard of anything so absurd. You? You are a Manchu princess. Have you forgotten?"

"I am *trying* to forget that, certainly, Mother," Adela said.

"Well, I should not, if I were you," Constance declared, apparently forgetting herself that this was an entirely different point of view from that she had previously held and expressed. "One should never forget one's heritage. You are a Ch'ing. So your family no longer rules China. There are many royal houses about the world who no longer rule. They do not go out and work as shop girls. We have enough, especially with Charlie making his own way. And besides, I like to have you at home, to help me. And when Charlie comes back . . ."

But even Constance could not finish that sentence. Because Constance did not know what would happen when Charlie came back. Any more than Adela did.

Charlie, Adela thought. The man she loved. Because she did, actually. It occurred to her that it was perverse of her. Something to do with that background of which Constance had suddenly become so proud. As a Ch'ing princess she did not *want* to be dominated, to be mastered, to be swept to the side of the stage of life. That had been the reason for at least part of her feelings of revulsion for Yuan. If she dreamed, it was of Tz'u-Hsi and Wu Hou. They had been vicious monsters. Well, so, according to the history books, had been Mary of England, or indeed, even her sister the famous Elizabeth, when crossed. That was history. The important point was that they had ruled, small, fragile, inadequate women, by dominating the men with whom they were surrounded, by making them fall in love with them, so that each man would die for them, without hesitation. That was the sort of devotion *she* wanted. And if she could never now hope to dominate a court or an empire, then at least she wanted to have the whole love, the unrestrained love, of her husband.

Charlie would love like that, could he stop being afraid, she knew. But *would* he ever stop being afraid?

She sat on the seaward side of Golden Gate Park and looked out past the Seal Rocks at Point Lobos and then the Mile Rocks Lighthouse, which marked the southern entrance to the Golden Gate itself. She came here almost every day, because there was nothing else to do,

and their stuffy little rented apartment was next to unbearable . . . and because this was the nearest she could
get to China. Incredible to think that she had now been
away again for several months. Not a great deal of news
came from there. Yuan Shih-k'ai was apparently in
complete control. Nothing was said in the American
press about his marriage plans—she did not know if the
betrothal he had announced so grandly had ever been
publicized over here; certainly, according to Constance,
people like Mr. Glenning had never heard of her. Thus
she did not even know if Yuan hated, and dreamed of
her, and of possessing her, either to love or to torture
into oblivion. She did not even know if she *wanted* him
still to be thinking of her.

That was the past. If only she could discover a future.
Her nature cried out for her to embrace whatever she
attempted with all her heart and soul. That was how she
had embraced their escape, and apparently terrified
both Constance and Charlie by doing so. Charlie was
too upset to see that that was how she would embrace
their marriage, as well. Or he did see that all too clearly,
and it was that thought that was terrifying him.

But she was not being allowed to embrace America
either, as she wished. She had not wanted to do so at
Miss Evesham's Academy. Then she had been an exile
from China, but only temporarily. Now she knew she
must turn her back on the Dragon Empire forever, if
only because the Dragon Empire was no more. This was
to be her home from now on, and that being so, she
wanted to embrace it with all of her strength.

But how could she do that if Constance persisted in
keeping her as something apart, would not let her go out
to work or mix with any ordinary Americans?
Constance had always found her royal heritage an embarrassment—in China. But now that that royal
heritage was all she had, all any of them had salvaged

from the wreckage of their lives, Constance thought it was the most important thing in the world. And as Charlie painfully tried to struggle up the ladder of success, Constance wanted him to feel, and no doubt to tell the world, that he was at least married to a princess. And not a shop girl.

So it all, once again, came down to Charlie. He was due back in a week. From Panama City and Callao and Santiago de Cuba, just names on a map to her. He would be sun-bronzed and wind-bronzed, and hopefully his mind would similarly be bronzed, with the physical confidence of a fore-topmast hand. And he would have money in his pocket. Enough to get married? Probably not, in his eyes. As if one needed money to pad out a love mattress? She wanted. Oh, she wanted, both the sensation and physical love and the emotional satisfaction of possessing and belonging, all at once. It was more than the only half-remembered sensation of having had, once, briefly and unsatisfactorily. It was the feeling that there was nothing left in life. She had turned her back on greatness, and luxury, and wealth, and power. Only love and, through love, motherhood and contentment were left to her. And if it were not to be with Charlie, then it would have to be with someone else, and soon. Or she would go mad.

She sighed, and picked up her parasol, and heard a gentle cough, and raised her head . . . and gazed at James Osborne.

A totally prosperous-looking James Osborne, every inch the gentleman, from his brown felt bowler hat—which he was now raising—through his brown herringbone tweed coat to his dark brown striped worsted trousers and his brown leather boots; he even carried pale brown kid gloves and a cane, and his silk tie was white with brown spots.

"Mr. *Osborne*?" she asked in amazement.

"My dear Miss Wynne." Pink spots flared in his cheeks. "My dear, *dear* Miss Wynne. At last I have found you."

"At last? Found me?"

"I have been searching for you for months, my dear Miss Wynne." Before she could protest, he had taken her elbow, was walking her through the park. "Will you have a cup of coffee? I'm afraid they don't appear to serve tea in this place."

"Coffee?" But she did feel like a cup of coffee. She felt like a cup of coffee every day she came here, but had never had one, because she had never had any money. But how she wished the heels on her boots were not quite so down, or the material of her gown not quite so shoddy. No doubt he had already noticed these things. When last they had met, she had been the Princess Adela. Now . . . But he had been *looking* for her?

She felt obliged to wait until they had been shown to a table and given their orders to a very interested waitress, obviously unable to deduce the relationship between this handsome, very well-dressed young man and a shabby young girl. Then she asked, "Looking for *me*?" She wondered if she should be afraid of him, and decided that it was impossible to be afraid of anyone in a San Francisco coffee shop, and even less of Mr. Osborne.

"Well," he said, "when I heard how you had to flee China because of the monster Yuan, I was horrified. Do you know, when my new position was offered to me, I told them—"

"New position?" She hardly knew whether she was standing on her head or her heels.

"I am to edit the *China Gazette*," he said carelessly. "One could say that it will be the *Times* of China. I intend to make it so, certainly. But as I was saying, I told them, I will accept your offer, gentlemen, but not until I have found Miss Wynne."

"But . . . found me for what?"

He gazed at her with that peculiar intentness she remembered from Hong Kong, and she realized she was flushing. "I have something for you," he said, and from his pocket took a photograph. She stared at it in amazement; it was one of the three taken on the dock in Hong Kong, more than a year before. The one of Constance and herself, which had been enlarged several times. And it was a good photograph, although she could hardly recognize the totally confident young woman in the white blouse and blue skirt, the white panama hat with the ribbon, and the quiet smile, as herself.

"Why, Mr. Osborne," she said. "Did the others turn out as well?"

"Why, yes," he said. "They did."

"Have you got them?"

He shook his head. "Well, I have them somewhere, I suppose. I'm a newspaperman, you know. I never throw away a photograph."

Once again the long gaze. "Well," she said. "That was a delicious cup of coffee. And I'm sure Mother would be pleased to see you again, if you'd care to call." She stood up. "I'm afraid we haven't really found anywhere quite suitable to live, as yet. We had a nice place," she invented desperately, "but it was only available on a short lease, and when that was up we had to move into . . . well, rather a shabby place for the time being. It's only temporary, of course. Mother and Father are buying a property. But these things take time."

Still he gazed at her. Oh, Lord, she thought; he knows I am lying.

"Miss Wynne," he said. "Adela! I have just traveled six thousand miles to find *you.*"

"Ah . . ." She couldn't think of anything to say.

"And now that I have found you," Osborne went on, "you don't really suppose I am going to sit here and let you walk away from me? At least let me see you home."

"Oh . . . I . . ." Again she didn't know what to say. James Osborne. A man she had met only once in her life. But a man who had once tried to *save* her life, at risk of his own. And a man who had traveled six thousand miles to find her. Had he really done that?

A man who would make her feel like a woman, even a princess, all over again. Was already doing that, in fact.

"That would be very kind of you, Mr. Osborne," she said.

"The *China Gazette,*" Constance remarked, pouring tea. If she had clearly been taken aback by the young man's reappearance, and even more by having to receive him in such unfortunate surroundings, she had recovered with her usual rapid self-confidence. "How remarkable. Why, that is a *very* good position, Mr. Osborne. But . . ." She frowned. "Isn't it at least partly owned by the government?"

"Wholly owned now," Osborne said. "The marshal felt the government should have its own English-language mouthpiece, so to speak. But we also produce an edition in Mandarin, of course."

"And *you* are to edit it? But . . . forgive me, but I did not even know you had ever met the marshal."

"Well . . ." Osborne flushed. "I hadn't, when last *we* met. I met him for the first time when he offered me the position, as a matter of fact. He really is a most pleasant fellow."

"You said he was a monster," Adela reminded him.

He smiled at her. "And one should never criticize one's employer? But he is an old monster, even if a charming one. And as your mother has said, he offered me a very lucrative position, as well as a prestigious one, so . . ."

"And having offered you this position, he sent you over here to find Adela," Constance said grimly, glancing around the room as if in search of a weapon.

"Good heavens, no, Mrs. Wynne. But he was delighted when he heard what I intended. He willingly gave me leave of absence. Mind you, I have to be back by the end of August. I *do* have a newspaper to edit."

"I'm afraid I do not understand you at all, Mr. Osborne," Constance said. "Have you any real acquaintance with the reasons my family and I were forced to leave China? I should have thought Yuan himself might have enlightened you."

"Well, he did, eventually. When I went North, of course I had no idea. I did hear you had to get out in a hurry. But no one in Tientsin really knew why, so I traveled to Peking to find you. Really a very fortunate decision, as a matter of fact. Marshal Yuan and I took to each other immediately, and when he heard what I had to say, why, that's when he offered me this job."

"What you had to say?"

"Well . . ." Osborne colored again, and put down his teacup. He got up, took a turn up and down the tiny living room, stopped and faced them. "I'm afraid I have been very presumptuous, Mrs. Wynne. I do not know that you will ever be able to forgive me. But you see . . . the marshal was really quite upset at your precipitate departure."

"Quite upset," Constance murmured. "Oh, indeed, I'm sure he was."

"It was not merely that you had fled, and with such a scoundrel as this bandit Lin-tu—there is a price on his head, incidentally—or that a couple of eunuchs had been murdered. I mean to say, what are a couple of eunuchs to a man like the marshal? It was not even, believe it or not, so much that you had taken Adela with you. It was that he didn't know *why* you had acted as you had. Do you know, he nearly sent after you, here to America?''

"Nearly?"

"Well, when he reflected, he realized of course that he couldn't, that it wasn't really the thing a head of state can do, and keep his dignity. I mean to say, Yuan may be a monster, but he is trying to make China into a civilized country, and thus of all Chinese, *he* must be seen to act in a civilized and proper and, above all, dignified manner. But he was still very perplexed and, I am bound to say, angry.''

"Yes," Constance said. "Yes, I suppose he was. And he told you all this when you applied for this job?''

"Good heavens, no, Mrs. Wynne. I didn't apply for any job. I went to Peking seeking some information as to what had happened to you and the princess, of course. Well, before I quite knew what was happening, I found myself closeted with the marshal. He was very courteous, merely asked me if I knew you, and of course I said yes, and when he asked me what I thought of you, I naturally replied that I thought you were one of the finest people I had ever met. ''

"You are too kind, Mr. Osborne."

"I always endeavor to tell the truth, Mrs. Wynne. I also told the marshal that Miss Wynne, the princess, was the most perfect woman I had ever met.''

"I cannot imagine how you existed before our landing in Hong Kong," Constance remarked. "And once you had told the marshal all this, he promptly offered you a job.''

Osborne quite refused to be put off by her sarcasm.

"No, no. He told me just how you had betrayed him. I'm afraid he put the blame entirely upon you, assumed that the decision to flee Peking was yours rather than Adela's."

"It was," Constance said.

"Well, he offered me the job when I explained the situation to him."

"You explained the situation to him, Mr. Osborne?"

"Well, you see, Mrs. Wynne, when I learned the truth, I mean about his feelings, about how angry he was, and how betrayed as well, I was very upset. Because, well . . ." He gave Adela an apologetic glance. "I . . . well . . . I do not suppose it escaped your notice in Hong Kong and again in Canton how, ah, taken I was with the princess. With you, Adela," he said, turning to her. "My God, when you were taken from that train by those thugs, I was nearly mad with anxiety. And when I heard that you had been returned safe and sound, I was equally nearly mad with joy. I sent you a telegram, but never had a reply."

"I never got it," Adela said. "I wrote to you, though. And *you* never replied."

"I never received your letter," Osborne said. "My God! But what about all of my letters?"

"Yours? You wrote to me?"

"I wrote eight letters, Adela."

"Eight?" Adela cried. "You wrote to me eight times?"

"Every month up to your departure from China, and even once after that, care of the consul in Tientsin. I had hoped he would have a forwarding address. When you never answered, I was in despair. But I could not believe you disliked me that much."

"Disliked you? Oh, my." Adela stared at her mother.

"That was very kind of you, Mr. Osborne," Constance said. "It seems remarkable that none of them ever reached us. But you were telling us about Marshal Yuan."

"Well . . . it really is a delicate subject," Osborne said. "I don't know where to begin. My only thought was to prevent the marshal from doing anything dramatic, such as after all sending after you, or something like that. So I told him I could explain what had happened."

"You could explain?" Adela and Constance spoke together.

"Yes." Osborne looked from face to face. "I . . . ah . . . explained that you were actually betrothed to me." He hesitated, and as both the women merely stared at him, hurried on. "That this happened during your stay in Hong Kong. I suggested you had actually been there for some time before taking the train from Canton. I also explained, you see, that it had been a private understanding between you and me, Adela, and was unknown to you, Mrs. Wynne. So that of course when the marshal proposed marriage, you were happy to agree on your daughter's behalf, and it was not until after you returned to Peking that you discovered that Adela was already bespoken. I suggested that you then, ah, lost your head and decided to flee rather than risk angering him by telling him the truth." Another quick glance from face to face. "Of course, I don't know what *did* make you change your mind, Mrs. Wynne, although I suspect, and indeed hope, that it was Adela's decision that she could not possibly marry someone like the marshal. I mean, quite apart from everything else, he's old enough to be her grandfather. But I don't mean to pry, really. I'm just explaining that I had to make up the story virtually as I went along, and as he started asking questions, well, one thing led to another."

Adela hastily drank some more tea. Constance merely gazed at Osborne. "But the marshal believed you."

"He did. Believe me, Mrs. Osborne, he was merely looking for some explanation of the situation. He trusted you, Mrs. Wynne. To a quite remarkable extent, if I may say so. And then you just fled, without a word of explanation. I may say that he was still considerably upset to learn that you so *mis*trusted him you would not go to him with the facts, for fear he would not understand."

"He said that, did he?"

"Oh, indeed. But he quite understands now. I have a letter from him in which he expresses his happiness that Adela and I should have reached an understanding, and in which he entirely exonerates you, or any member of your family, from any blame for what happened, including the death of the eunuchs. He writes that he has no doubt at all you were coerced or perhaps even kidnapped by this scoundrel Lin-tu. He remembers that Lin-tu held you captive once before, during the Boxer Rebellion. Believe me, I wouldn't like to be in that rascal's shoes when Yuan's men finally catch up with him."

"You said something about a letter."

"It is in my pocket. Would you like to see it?"

"May I?"

Osborne held it out. Adela hurried around to read over her mother's shoulder. There could be no doubt that it was Yuan's handwriting, or that it was under his seal, as well as that of the government of China. Nor that it expressed exactly the sentiments Osborne had outlined.

"Well," Constance said. "It is of course extremely gratifying to learn that the marshal is no longer our enemy, although I doubt it can make any difference to us now. I may well write to him, although . . . Of course, we must be grateful to you for bringing this about, even if by such, shall I say, unorthodox means. I shall have to inform the marshal that your engagement to my daughter has of course been terminated, but . . .''

She had stopped reading. Adela had continued, still over Constance's shoulder. "It says he would welcome us back," she said. "Me back, anyway. As . . ." She raised her head. "Your *wife*?"

"Well . . ." Osborne gave another of his flushes. "Of course, that is what he assumes will happen. But, Miss Wynne . . . Adela . . . you may believe that I have followed you six thousand miles for no other purpose than to ask for your hand."

"How well off do you suppose he really is?" Frank Wynne mused. He sat beside his wife at a table in one of San Francisco's finest hotels, enjoying both the sea breeze that wafted through the open windows to disperse the late-afternoon June heat, and the ice-cold whiskey and soda he was sipping. Like Constance, he watched the dancers whirling around the floor to the strains of the orchestra, and one couple in particular. Then he sat up straight. "Good heavens! What on earth are they doing?"

"It is called the tango," Constance told him. "I believe it comes from South America. And it is very close to being obscene, throwing your partner from arm to arm like that."

"He does it very well."

Constance gave him an impatient glance. Frank seemed to have fallen entirely under the spell of the man. Of course she couldn't entirely blame him. She knew that, like her, and even more, like Adela, he was enjoying to the full this glimpse of the life they had expected to be able to live. She did not know if Mr. Osborne was actually courting Adela or not, in a physical sense, but he did not seem the least interested in being alone with her. Wherever they went, she and

Frank were invited along, and not merely as chaperons; Mr. Osborne apparently enjoyed only places where she and Frank could also enjoy themselves. During the past fortnight they had been to several plays, and out to dinner on half a dozen occasions, and to these tea dances, a pastime lately imported from England, which were becoming all the rage—always at Mr. Osborne's expense. She had, she had to admit, been having the time of her life. Clothes had been a problem to begin with, but Mr. Osborne had approached the matter with that remarkable candor which was his greatest asset, combined with his boyish smile, which he varied so easily with sudden intensely serious moments, which made one suppose that although he took life as he found it, prepared to enjoy every second of it, he was also capable of coping with any difficult situation, as well. Thus he had said, straight out, to Frank and herself, on the second occasion he had come to call, "Look, Mr. Wynne, believe me, I hate to impose, and if you think I am stepping out of line, you have but to say so, but . . . well, I do understand the situation. I think it is diabolical, and you may be sure I will tackle Yuan about it right away the moment I return to Peking, and see if your business can't be opened again. I have no doubt at all he'll agree. He really is most anxious to come across to the West as a dictator with a heart of gold. Would you like that?"

"Well . . ." Frank had glanced at Constance. "That would be very welcome indeed."

"Take it as done. So therefore anything I may say, well . . . there is absolutely no need for you to, shall we say, go short anymore. I know you are going to get your business back, and frankly, since my old uncle the duke died, I have thousands of pounds just lying around the place looking for a good investment. I would take it as an honor to be allowed to advance you a sum to tide you over until you can return to China. We'll discuss repayment and interest after you are set up again in Peking."

Constance had been dumbfounded. Frank, after a nervous glance at Adela this time, had accepted.

Constance had then wanted to be insulted, but how could she be? Mr. Osborne had been able to see at a glance how desperately they needed the money. Of course, the scoundrel was shamelessly trying to buy his way into their affections, but even that he was smilingly willing to confess. "How can I lose?" he had asked. "I am investing in my future parents-in-law."

Thank heaven that had happened after Charlie's shore leave. Yet Charlie's return had been difficult enough, because he had obviously not liked Osborne, even if he had equally obviously not for a moment regarded him as a possible rival. But at the same time he had clearly not yet resolved his own feelings for his foster sister. During the week he had remained at home, Adela had declined all invitations from the Englishman. But Charlie had not taken her anywhere.

And the day after he had returned to sea, she had once again accepted Osborne's invitation to a play. With her foster parents, of course.

What was actually going through the child's mind was difficult to estimate. She certainly enjoyed Osborne's company, and the constant entertainments to which he took them all, just as she certainly enjoyed the new clothes they had been able to buy. Yet on the day he had proposed she had looked him straight in the eye and said, "I am very flattered, of course, Mr. Osborne, but I am afraid I cannot accept your kind offer of marriage, because I am already betrothed."

Mr. Osborne had raised his eyebrows and glanced at her left hand, which had led both Adela and Constance to attempt explanations at the same time, with a good deal of embarrassed confusion. But Osborne had certainly gathered that the engagement remained unofficial, although Adela had suggested that it would almost certainly become official the day Charlie returned from his current voyage. Which had been the one he had then been about to complete.

The situation had not appeared to bother Mr. Osborne at all. Without ever becoming oversentimental or demanding, he claimed to have fallen in love with Adela at first sight, and to have grown more and more in love with her with every passing day, hence those so mysterious and unfortunate letters—had they been intercepted by Yuan's people? It was quite possible. Certainly the photograph he carried about with him was sufficiently dog-eared to lend *some* credence to his tale, even if Constance refused to believe either in love at first sight or in masculine faithfulness over a long period of time—and certainly when it was not being requited. Yet he *had* undoubtedly come six thousand miles simply to find the princess. And try as she might to dislike him, Constance had to accept that he was almost the embodiment of the type of man *she* would have selected as a husband for Adela—if she had never met him until a fortnight ago. Of course, he was English and not American, but then, Adela was half English. And he lived and worked in, and would take her back to, her beloved China. But that was the point. "It's all just too pat," she grumbled. "I am *sure* Yuan hates us. And then, Osborne himself. I mean, if we were asked to choose any man in the world as a husband for Adela, someone like Mr. Osborne would have to come near the top. And when you think that he's related to the nobility as well, *and* wants to take her back to China, it's all just too . . . well, perfect."

"There you go again," Frank said with a gentle smile. "Seeing sinister shadows every way you turn. Wouldn't you agree that Adela has had a pretty tough life?"

"Of course."

"So isn't it about time that some trumps turned up for her?"

"But . . . Yuan . . ."

"What *about* Yuan, exactly? Do you remember that I said at the time you were overreacting to his proposal?"

"Yes," she had to agree. "You did."

"I'm sure if you'd just told him the facts . . . He's always struck me as being a most reasonable and decent fellow," Frank went on. "And I have never seen or heard of him being otherwise. Nor, apparently, has Osborne. Have you, truly?"

"Well . . . that day at his camp . . ."

"He was pulling off a remarkable coup d'etat. I have no doubt at all he is as hard as nails when it comes to politics or warfare. Or he wouldn't be where he is now. But so was Grant, or Lee, or Lincoln for that matter."

"It was just a feeling I had . . ."

"Sure. But it *was* just a feeling. And now, what's your *feeling* about Osborne? That he was sent by Yuan to assassinate Adela? For God's sake, Connie. The man's an English gentleman. You can see that just by looking at him. And anyway, if he'd wanted to assassinate her, wouldn't he just have done it? Not squired her every day for a fortnight, and in the most public places, allowing everyone to see his face and know just who and what he is. I think you just have to pull yourself together, old girl. I know how many terrible experiences you have had in your life. And I even think I know how you were affected by the reappearance of that scoundrel Lin-tu."

Constance shot him an alarmed glance, but he obviously knew nothing of her private thoughts.

"And yet it was *he* you decided to trust, when it was obvious he was the one who intended to get his hands on Dela by hook or by crook. No, no, my dearest girl, the

Boxers were eleven years ago, and were the last of what might be called pre-twentieth-century China. Those days are gone. As for Osborne, well . . . you have to admit he'd make Dela a marvelous husband. And all the . . . well, oddities would be resolved. I'm not blaming Charlie for anything that happened. I feel as you do, that she probably led him on, and he's a young fellow with red blood in his veins. Now he's realized what a mistake it was, and a lot of other things besides, and doesn't know how he can decently get off the hook. But he's not in love with her—you can see that by looking at them together. That being so, wouldn't marriage between them be a case of piling one mistake on top of another? Wouldn't you be happier if they didn't?''

Constance chewed her lip.

"I may as well confess that I've discussed the matter *with* Osborne,'' Frank went on.

Another startled glance.

"Well, he felt called upon to raise it with me, as he is asking for my daughter's hand in marriage. And I put our point of view to him very straight—our fears, if you like. And I have to say that he removed them entirely. He quite understands how we must feel, but apart from his friendship with Yuan, whom he trusts absolutely, by the way, he pointed out that he is not only English, but a very influential Englishman now, both in China and, apparently, since the death of his uncle, in England as well. Yuan is still desperately trying to obtain the full support of Great Britain for his regime, and that's why, Osborne points out, that Yuan is so anxious to be friends with him. Can you really believe, in those circumstances, Yuan would *dare* lay a finger on any Englishwoman, even if she didn't happen to be Osborne's wife? And even if he were actually so inclined? Unlike Washington, you know, the British government has never been averse to sending the odd gunboat, or even a fleet squadron, to put their point of view into perspective. In fact, it's always been rather a hobby of theirs."

"Adela is not English." Constance as usual seized upon the main point of detail.

"Osborne will have her become a British citizen once they are married. She did have an English mother, after all."

"After they're married," she muttered.

Frank squeezed her hand as the music stopped and the dancers started to return to their tables. "I think it's something you should discuss with her, Connie. It would be a tragedy if she and Charlie married each other out of some misguided sense of loyalty to . . . well . . ." He flushed. "The first person each of them went to bed with. And you must admit that it would be marvelous if you and I were to be able to go back to Peking and get back on our feet. Wouldn't it?"

"Everything that you say is perfectly true, Mother," Adela acknowledged. "But for one point. I don't happen to be in love with him."

Constance put down her sewing. "And you do love Charlie, is that it?"

Adela hesitated, gently moving to and fro in her rocking chair. "Yes," she said at last. "Yes, I do."

"Then I don't quite understand," Constance said. "You love Charlie, but you're quite happy to be escorted everywhere by this man."

"Aren't you?"

"Why . . . of course I am, but that's different. I'm married. I'm older than he is. And I'm always accompanied by my husband."

"As I am always accompanied by you both."

"Oh, for heaven's sake," Constance snapped. "You know what I mean. He gives you presents," she said triumphantly, gazing at the new gold watch pinned to Adela's bodice.

"He likes giving me presents."

"And you like accepting them, obviously. Has he never tried to make love to you?"

"Of course not," Adela said. "He is the most perfect gentleman."

"But he has proposed marriage. More than once."

"Yes."

"And don't you think it's a trifle dishonest of you not to tell him about Charlie?"

"I have told him I consider myself betrothed, time and again, Mother," Adela said with great patience. "He just doesn't seem to believe it."

"Because *he* loves *you*. Now, do you suppose Charlie loves you like that?"

Adela stared at her foster mother with her mouth open.

"Oh, I'm not forgetting what you did," Constance said. "But believe me, I can understand only too well how it happened. You were distraught, and you are a truly lovely young woman, you really are, you know, and so . . . well . . . and when something like that happens at your age, you *need* to believe that you are in love. But it doesn't always work out that way, alas."

"Meaning that you don't think Charlie loves me."

"Well . . . not *that* way. He doesn't act very like it, does he?"

Adela gazed at her for several seconds more, then picked up her own sewing. "And will Mr. Osborne still love me when he finds out I am not a virgin?"

"Oh, I am sure he will, if he loves you now. Mr. Osborne is a man of the world, sophisticated. I don't think you have to worry about him. Anyway, you know, you don't *have* to tell him." She flushed as Adela's head came up again. "What I mean is, it hasn't made any difference to *you*, has it? And white men, Englishmen in particular, are not really the sort who inspect the sheets after the first night, or have midwives in to examine their brides, and that sort of thing. Nor would you be being dishonest, really. I mean, all that fuss used to be to ensure that the firstborn, who used always to be the sole inheritor, had to be the husband's and no one else's. But now that so much more is understood about conception . . . It isn't as if you have ever been promiscuous. What happened with Charlie happened once, and very nearly a year ago. It has never happened since. There can be no doubt that your children by Mr. Osborne will be *his* children." She paused somewhat uncertainly while Adela reflected that it was quite remarkable how Constance could adopt *any* point of view with an almost religious fervor, however unacceptable it might always have been in the past, once she convinced herself it was the right thing to do.

She could not even be angry. Constance had at least been consistent in her total opposition to and abhorrence of the idea of a marriage between her two children. If she had decided to go along with it, it had been because there had been nothing else she could do. But now there was a chance it need not happen. And she had also managed to convince herself that Charlie did not want it to happen. And of course only Charlie really mattered; he was her son.

Not for the first time in her life Adela had that feeling of belonging nowhere, of being a total outcast. It had not mattered when there had always been Charlie to fall back on. But Charlie was no longer there, only Mr. Osborne.

But could she pretend that marriage to Mr. Osborne would be nothing better than a long purgatory? He was certainly very wealthy, and very charming. He would take her back to China, and the life she loved, and on an even higher scale than she had ever known. Why, it was even possible once again to see the hand of Destiny . . . But she was never going to think of Destiny again.

Far more important was it to remind herself that he also certainly seemed to love her. "Adored" would be a better word. Which was what she had always wanted.

But she didn't love him. He aroused no passion in her at all, no desire to be held in his arms. But could that not be because she had never allowed herself to think that way, because of Charlie? If Charlie were definitely not going to marry her, and if Mr. Osborne did love her . . .

If only . . . She sighed.

"I do think you ought to give it some thought," Constance said. "Of course, Frank and I are thinking only of your happiness, and we'll go along with anything you choose to do, but . . . there isn't much time, if Mr. Osborne is going to be back in China by the end of August."

It was already the first week of July.

"I know," Adela said. "I will think about it, but, Mother, Charlie comes home next week. Cannot I just wait until then? I promise you, I'll make a decision then."

"I see that fellow Osborne is still hanging about." Charles Baird had certainly benefited from two voyages. He had filled out, and his muscles rippled as he moved. His skin was tanned and he walked with a jaunty step. Men stepped aside when he approached them on the sidewalk.

Adela had almost to run to keep up with his long strides. But at least they were walking together, even if his kiss had not been at all probing and his embrace hasty. "Yes," she said.

Because there was no use in beating about the bush.

Constance had engineered this walk in the park. She might not be able to engineer another tête-à-tête.

"Father says he's lent him money," Charlie said, standing with his hands on his hips staring out at the sea. "It's going to blow tonight."

"How do you know?" Adela asked, getting her breathing under control.

He pointed at the sky, to where the afternoon sun was beginning to droop toward the western horizon. "See the sun? See how it looks as if it were surrounded by a watery vapor? That means trouble. Wind as well as rain, sometime within the next twelve hours. At sea we'd shorten sail if we saw a sunset like that."

"It must be terribly exciting," she said, "having to watch the sky all the time, and make decisions all the time."

"It is," he said. "Rather odd, don't you think? Osborne hanging about all this while, and lending Father money?"

"Not really," Adela said, feeling her heart begin to pound.

"Oh? Why not?"

"Because he wants to marry me." She gazed at him. And he gazed at her. *"Osborne?"*

"Yes."

"But . . . he's old enough to be your father."

"Not really. I believe he's thirty-one. I'm going to be eighteen next month."

Charlie found a vacant bench and sat down.

"That's why we're here," Adela said, sitting beside him. She knew she would never be able to lead up to it slowly and subtly. That just was not her nature. "Mother feels we should discuss what we're going to do. You see, Mother feels I should accept."

"Mother feels that?"

"She thinks that you don't actually want to marry

me," Adela explained, pronouncing each word with great care. "I know she's wrong, of course, but I promised to talk with you and . . . well, find out."

"Mother told you to do that? Or you decided to do it?" he demanded, suddenly flushed—with anger, she realized.

"All right," she said, equally feeling a sudden anger. "I want to discuss it. Mother feels you and I should break it off. That we're not, well . . . truly in love with each other."

He said nothing.

"But I still love you, Charlie," she said. "You're the only person I've ever loved, or ever wanted to love. If you want me, I'll wait for you as long as you wish. Just say it, Charlie. Say it."

She would never have believed that she, Adela Wynne, princess of the Ch'ing, would utter such words to any man. And suddenly she knew that she need not, and should not, have done so. As with Lin-tu that day in the Shan Mountains, she had humiliated herself, for no reason at all.

Charlie cleared his throat. "Well," he said. "Of course I love you, Dela. More than any girl I have ever met. And of course I know that I shouldn't have . . . well, that it was very wrong of us to . . . well . . . I *am* your brother. Of course I know there's no blood between us, but the fact is that we grew up together, and that in every way, well . . . Have you told Osborne about us?"

Adela gazed at him. Nothing she could say would matter now. He was just looking for any way out. And he would find a way out, if not this time, then the next time. She had taken a year out of her life, and torn it up. And perhaps even more than that. She had confronted Destiny with her own decisions, and been made to look a fool.

"Yes, I have," she said.

"And what did he say?"

"That it didn't matter. He loves me, you see."

Charlie gazed at her. "And you love him. I can see it."

Adela opened her mouth, closed it again, and hurried through the park. After five minutes she slowed to a walk; she knew he could easily catch her up if he wished.

When she reached the road, she looked back. He was still sitting on the bench.

"I think I'm going to cry," Constance said. "Again."

Frank handed her his handkerchief, turned her away from the sea, began to walk her home. Every night for the week since Adela and Mr. Osborne had left for China, Constance had insisted on walking down to the park, to stand as she had stood on that first night and watched the ship departing, slowly sinking beneath the horizon, and every night she had wept, as she had wept that first night.

Frank's own feelings had been total relief since Adela had accepted Osborne's proposal. He had never questioned Constance's decision to adopt the child after Kate Mountjoy's murder. Quite apart from his love for his wife and his determination only to make her happy, he doubted he could have brought himself to abandon a five-year-old waif, unwanted by the Ch'ing, hated by the Chinese, even had he been on his own. But there could be no denying the fact that Adela had brought them nothing but misery over the past few years. All that fuss and expense of maintaining her at Miss Evesham's Academy, and cables that had raced to and fro because of her various quarrels with her headmistress, culminating in her expulsion . . . Constance had been deeply upset about that. And then, this kidnapping and marriage business, and then to seduce

Charlie . . . Trying to imagine what next she might get up
to or become involved in was a nearly impossible nightmare.

But now she was married. To a man who was wealthy
and who adored her. And was prepared to help them as
well. But the important thing was the fact of her
marriage; from that moment on she was someone else's
responsibility. Constance had pretended to be somewhat disturbed by Mr. Osborne's haste once Adela had
finally said yes. No doubt she had been looking forward
to a big white wedding, with all the attendant frills . . .
and all the attendant expense. Osborne had had more
sense. Presumably he would even have advanced the
money to pay for the wedding, had he thought it would
be a success. But of course he had quickly realized that
they knew no one of any consequence in San Francisco,
and that any attempt to have a church wedding would
be a most miserable fiasco. So he had pleaded the
necessity for haste, with Frank's blessing, and not
altogether falsely—he did have to be back in China
pretty soon—had found a ship that was sailing for
Tientsin only three days later, and had secured a special
license for that day. From the courthouse the happy
couple had gone straight to the ship. Leaving Constance
weeping.

Because somehow she felt guilty at having pushed
Adela into doing something she did not really want to
do. That was a total absurdity. All young girls needed a
good push in the right direction from time to time—
Constance herself, he recalled, had required several
pushes in her youth—and there could be no doubt that
Adela was going to be very happy. All her doubts had
very obviously been swept away in the mad rush of
those last three days, the frantic buying of clothes, the
excited counting of the hours . . . and now, he thought,
she is honeymooning on a Pacific crossing. Could any

girl ask for anything more romantic? And there would be no doubt that Osborne, being Osborne, would do it in style.

Leaving them, for the first time in eleven years, free. "I've been thinking," he said as they walked down the lane to their apartment building, "that perhaps now we can try looking for something a little better."

Constance, having dried her eyes, glanced at him. "Now?"

"Well . . ." He unlocked the door, closed it again behind him. "With my salary, and the money I still have from Osborne's loan, and with both Charlie and Dela off our hands, I think we can relax a little, have a better standard of living. It isn't as if we need to save anymore. Osborne promised he'd have a chat with Yuan as soon as he got back, and have all the charges against you formally lifted. We could be back in China by the end of the year."

"I'd like that," she said. "Oh, how I'd like that."

"Then look forward to it, because it's going to happen." He poured them each a whiskey. "And for God's sake, stop moping, my darling. You've got that little bundle of confusion settled at last. Better than I had ever expected, I can tell you. Now is the time for you to sit back and enjoy life just a little. Without anything on your mind at all." He turned his head as there came a rap on the door. "Now, who the devil can that be?"

He crossed the room, unlocked the door, stared in total amazement at the two very well-dressed Chinese men who stood on the landing. "Yes?"

"You do not know me, Mr. Wynne," said the shorter of the men. "But I am well acquainted with your family. My name is Dr. Sun Yat-sen."

"Dr. Sun?" Frank looked at Constance, who had also risen.

And now hurried forward. "Dr. Sun?"

"And this is my personal aide, Captain Chiang Cheng," Sun said, introducing the other man. He was very young, and very tall for a Chinese; indeed, at six-feet-plus he would have been tall for an American. He was also very thin, and had a peculiarly bleak face. It occurred to Frank that he was less an aide than a body-guard. And no doubt a formidable one.

"Do come in," Constance said. "I really am most pleased to meet you again, Dr. Sun. I have never had the opportunity to thank you for saving Adela's life from that monster Feng."

"A disastrous affair, which brought disaster for us all in its wake. But it was the least I could do for such a lovely and courageous young lady. She is not here this evening?"

"She's married." Frank had gone to the liquor cabinet. "Will you have a whiskey?"

"Well . . . a very small one, thank you, Mr. Wynne. To toast the princess. Married? I am absolutely delighted. To an American?"

"Well, an Englishman," Constance told him. "The next-best thing."

"Of course." Sun sat down, raised his glass. "To the health and happiness of the Princess Adela."

Chiang regarded his drink rather as if it might be poison, and then took a cautious sip.

"But actually," Sun went on, "I am pleased the princess is not here, much as I would have liked to see her again. I have heard, of course, of how you had to flee China because of that treacherous villain who now seeks to rule our country. It was to save the princess from his clutches, was it not?"

"Ah . . . yes," Frank said. Sun had been present, according to Constance, when Yuan had announced his betrothal, so nothing could be gained by prevaricating.

"I too have suffered most grievously at his hands," Sun went on. "As you may have heard. Yet have I not given up the fight. I cannot, for either my own sake or the sake of China itself. If you had any idea . . . But you, at least, Mrs. Wynne, know what Yuan is really like. You were present when he launched his traitorous career. Things have gone from bad to worse. Do you know, he called an assembly, as he had sworn to do, but when the delegates would not immediately endorse his plan to become emperor, he had their spokesman murdered?"

"Yuan did *that*?" Constance cried.

"He did not actually pull the trigger, Mrs. Wynne. But there is no doubt he paid for the bullet. Thus again we must take up the sword against a tyranny that will be worse than that of the Ch'ing, if only because Yuan is a far more able man than any of the recent Manchu emperors. My agents are already at work in the South, seeking to raise a new army to bring the despot down. In a few weeks I will be joining them. Now, Mr. Wynne, I also know, if you will permit me to speak of it, that you have found it hard since coming to America. That is the way of the world, where talent is so often neglected. But *I* can recognize talent. Especially talent such as yours, the talent of a soldier, and of a soldier who knows China and the Chinese."

Frank stared at him in consternation.

"Are you offering my husband a *job*?" Constance asked, equally dumbfounded.

"Well . . . I cannot pretend it may not occasionally have an element of danger," Sun said. "But Mr. Wynne's place would be on my staff. I am a man who attempts to learn from his mistakes, Mr. Wynne. And I have made sufficient of those in my time." He gave a quick smile. "Now I am getting too old to afford too many more. One of the handicaps I have always suffered from is an inability to find efficient aides. Captain Chiang here I would trust with my life, but he would be the first to admit that he lacks experience."

Chiang sat very straight. He had finished his whiskey, and might not have been present, save that his eyes constantly moved, searching the room, watching the doors and windows, on the lookout for any sign of hostility or treachery.

"This I am afraid applies to too many Chinese of talent. Even Lin-tu, who stood at my shoulder for so long, appears to have degenerated into a mere bandit. The Manchu kept my people in submission for too long. So now I am attempting to raise a staff of Europeans, or Americans, and Chinese, in equal numbers, to give me the benefit of their advice and their knowledge. Of their experience, Mr. Wynne."

"Good God!" Frank said.

"You would therefore not be expected to take part in any actual fighting, Mr. Wynne," Sun went on. "But you would yet be striking a blow for freedom, and a blow against the tyrant Yuan. I cannot of course offer you any great pay for your services, but I can promise to establish Mrs. Wynne in Hong Kong, where you will be able to visit her from time to time." He paused, looking from face to face, and realizing that they were not entirely receptive to his idea. "It is a great and glorious cause, Mr. Wynne," he said softly. "And one in which we will eventually triumph, to the great good of all China. Of all mankind. Yet I must be honest with you and tell you that I also cannot promise to restore the Ch'ing after we have defeated Yuan. Their day is done forever. This is why I am relieved that the princess is not here. Yet do I make you *this* most solemn promise, that their lives and their dignity will always be respected by my government."

Frank gazed at Constance; he had a sudden desire to

laugh. Because if this man had come to him two months ago, would he not have accepted his offer without a moment's hesitation? After nearly a year of being a clerk in San Francisco, the thought of going back to soldiering was simply magnificent. But now . . . "I am of course enormously flattered to think that you might wish me to fight at your side, Dr. Sun," he said. "That you should think I am capable of offering you any worthwhile help. But I'm afraid it is impossible."

"Ah," Sun said.

"It's not anything you may suppose," Frank said. "Believe me, I would help you if I could. But the fact is . . . well, things have changed, you see. In fact, Mrs. Wynne and I will be returning to Peking very shortly to resume our home and business there." He smiled. "You will have to be careful, next time you launch a revolution, that you *do* have your people avoid our house."

Sun frowned. "You have made your peace with Yuan Shih-k'ai?"

"As a matter of fact, yes."

Chiang made a startled exclamation and reached for an inside pocket, but Sun rested his hand on the young man's arm and gave a quick shake of the head.

"Oh, don't worry," Frank said. "I shall never repeat a word of this conversation to a soul, or tell anyone of your visit, but you do see . . . ."

"Yuan will have you back in China?" Sun was incredulous.

"Yes," Constance said. "We think so, anyway. It is because of the princess, really. She has married this Englishman, as I told you, who is a great friend of the marshal. In fact, she and her husband have returned to China to live, already. They will prepare the way for our own return. So you see, we could not possibly *fight* against him now."

"An Englishman who is a friend of the marshal?"

Sun's frown deepened. "May I ask the name of this man?"

"Why, yes. His name is Osborne," Frank told him. "James Osborne. He is to edit the *China Gazette*, the government newspaper."

"James *Osborne*?" Sun turned his head to look at Chiang, who nodded briefly. Sun turned back to the Wynnes. "My dear Mr. Wynne. My dear Mrs. Wynne. There has been the most ghastly tragedy."

Constance's head jerked. "What do you mean?"

"Mrs. Wynne, James Osborne is well known, at least in South China, as Yuan Shih-k'ai's leading agent. He is the marshal's absolute *creature*. In Yuan's name he has carried out some of the most terrible crimes that can be imagined. And you say the princess is *married* to him, and has returned to China?"

Constance could only stare at him in horror.

"My dear Mrs. Wynne," Sun said gently, "I have to tell you that if the Princess Adela has gone back to China with James Osborne, whether as his wife or not, then she has been kidnapped, and is undoubtedly on her way to execution, for opposing the tyrant."

III

The Emperor

10

The Trap

"Now, let me get this straight," said Mr. Glenning, flicking ash onto his vest. "You are claiming that your daughter, who just happens to be a Manchu princess, has been kidnapped by this Marshal Yuan Shih-k'ai, and taken back to China, to have her head chopped off? Although she is actually and legally married to this English guy James Osborne, who's going back with her?"

"That is all part of the kidnap plot," Constance said, a growing feeling of desperation creeping over her; she had met this attitude from everyone she had approached. "And she is my foster daughter, not my actual daughter."

"Yeah? Now, you tell me why this guy Yuan should want to cut off the head of some little girl."

"Because he wanted to marry her himself, once," Constance shouted. "She is a Ch'ing princess."

"So you been telling me. Now, how come you *didn't* tell me all this when you were here before?"

"Because I didn't think it was necessary. But that is the reason we had to leave China in a hurry, the reason I was afraid of Yuan sending after us. I couldn't let her marry him, you see."

"Why not?"

"Because . . . because he's *evil,* and would have treated her abominably. Because she hated him. Please, Mr. Glenning, you must help me. Adela is in deadly danger."

"For refusing to marry a guy? Come now, Mrs. Wynne, that's going it a bit."

"Not a *guy*. Yuan Shih-k'ai. Dictator of China. A man who commits murder with a snap of the fingers. And there's more than just a refusal of marriage involved. Dela . . . Well, she was engaged to be married to another boy, and well . . ."

"You mean this chick of yours has been putting it about? Say, you have *some* secrets locked away in your family closet, Mrs. Wynne."

Constance drew a long breath. "Mr. Glenning, I am not here to defend my foster daughter's morals. I'm here to save her life. Yuan Shih-k'ai believes that, having promised herself to him, she ran away because she had had an affair with another man, and to a Chinese that is an unforgivable personal betrayal."

Some hope at last; Glenning was actually nodding in agreement.

"So he had sent one of his people to get her back. Don't ask me how I know Osborne is one of his people; I just know. The whole thing has been done with quite diabolical cunning, to avoid any suggestion of a kidnapping. But that is what it was. And Yuan can want her back for only one thing. To execute her. And he will do it in the most horrible fashion you can imagine."

Glenning gazed at her. "You know what I think, Mrs. Wynne?" he said at last. "I think you came back to live in the States just in time. I reckon China was getting to you. It can happen, in these queer places."

"Mr. Glenning . . ." But there was no point in losing her temper at his insinuations. "Listen to me. I am not asking you to do very much. I have sent a cable to the British consul, Mr. Richards, who is a personal friend of mine, asking him to intercept Adela when she lands at Tientsin. I have also cabled the American consulate, and I have sent a cable to Adela herself, to be handed to her on arrival. All I am asking you is to send a backup cable to the American minister in Peking, explaining the situation and asking him at least to interview Adela, Mrs. Osborne, when she arrives, before she is taken into the Forbidden City. I would like her placed in protective custody until my husband and I can get there and ascertain the truth. Am I asking too much? She is my daughter. And let me tell you, once she enters the Forbidden City, she will never be heard of again."

Glenning's cigar had gone out. He relit it with great deliberateness, and then leaned foward again. "Now, you listen to me, Mrs. Wynne. God knows, I've tried to treat you as a sane and sensible human being, no matter how many times you've come into my office with a load of hysterical drivel. Now I have to tell you some of the facts of life. I know all about you and your shenanigans, because I've done some investigating, see? You and your husband fled China because some close friend of yours bumped off a couple of guys and you were afraid of being implicated. Sure, you almost admitted that yourself when you first came in here. But you never told me the guy who did the bumping off was a well-known Chinese outlaw. Okay. No sweat. I guess we all have some queer friends. But having fled, you found the going a little tough over here. I've kept my eye on you, you know, just in case there *was* any funny business. Then this English guy, rich, I've been told, comes along and woos your stepdaughter or whatever she is. As I understand it, they got married with your blessing. Now you've changed your mind. Maybe you've learned this Osborne ain't quite as wealthy as you thought. Maybe he even left you with a couple of rubber checks. I don't know and I don't want to know. But I do know, just as you know, that the guy works for a Chinese newspaper, a newspaper owned by the Chinese government—that is, this guy Yuan whatever. So you want me to cause a diplomatic breach with China to get your daughter back. Lady, you have to take me for a fool. You have to be taking the whole United States government for a bunch of fools. Let me tell you something, in case it's slipped your mind. In a couple of months' time there is going to be a presidential election in this country, and you know what Mr. Taft is going to tell the people? That for the past four years we haven't gotten embroiled in any foreign monkey business, and God knows there has been enough of it about. And he's going to promise the people that we ain't *going* to get embroiled during the next four years, either. And that is what the Democrats are going to have to say too, if they have any hope of muscling in. Not that they have, in this man's opinion. Because peace and prosperity, and being friends with all, is what this country happens to want. And you want to cause trouble over some chick who ain't worth a damn and who ain't even pure-blooded American? Mrs. Wynne, I don't know what you got up to in China, and what the real situation is between you and Yuan Shih-k'ai. And I don't want to know, see? This man's government ain't rushing to no confrontation with the Chinese on your say-so. You bring me proof positive that this young lady of yours has been kidnapped, like a ransom note, and maybe I'll think again. Until then, you sort out your own domestic problems. And leave me alone. I have work to do."

"There's no need to look quite so blue," James

Osborne said, putting his arm around Adela's waist and resting his head against hers, to watch with her the lights of San Francisco dwindling in the distance. "It isn't as if it's disappearing forever, you know. You can come back whenever you wish. Save that hopefully you won't have much reason, once your mother and father are resettled in Peking."

His reassurance drifted over her like a warm breeze, made her feel quite ashamed of having left the dining table to rush on deck the way she had. Of course it was ridiculous for her to feel homesick about leaving the United States when she was actually going to *her* home.

But her uncertainty was compounded of several things, not just departing California. Of things as irrelevant as this ship, which was smaller than any she had ever been on, and flew the Chinese flag, and had a Chinese crew, although the captain and the chief engineer were both British.

"They're friends of mine," Osborne had explained. "She trades regularly with both Hong Kong and Tientsin. And the Chinese are just as good seamen as the British or the Yanks, you know; they also happen to be a darn sight cheaper. I was delighted when I discovered she was sailing tonight. Besides, I thought you'd want to get back to Chinese customs and Chinese cooking as quickly as possible."

They appeared to be the only passengers, as well. But surely, again as Osborne had pointed out, that was an advantage, as they were on their honeymoon.

But there was also the fact of leaving Constance. Of course, she had left Constance five years ago, in a purely physical sense. But even in Miss Evesham's Academy she had never actually *left* Constance. Constance had always been there in the background, at the end of a telegraph machine, as Miss Evesham had found out, making the world rotate to her ideas. Now

Constance could never be in her background again. Even when she and Frank returned to Peking, *her* place would be that of Mrs. James Osborne. She gave a little shiver; she had not yet properly considered her new name.

But most of all, she was aware of guilt. Because she had not, after all, told Mr. Osborne about Charlie. And in just a little while they would be retiring to their cabin. Something to be excited about, surely. James loved her, and he was an experienced man—there could be no doubt about that. He would most certainly make her very happy, at least physically, of that she was both sure and anticipatory, even if he had been most remarkably forbearing up to now—in their entire relationship he had only once kissed her on the lips, and that had been five hours ago, when they had been pronounced man and wife. And his lips had remained closed.

But as Constance had said, there was no way he was ever going to know . . . But he *had* to know. He was her husband, and between them there could only be complete mutual understanding and trust. Surely.

She certainly didn't want a marriage on any other terms, and she had drunk just sufficient champagne with her dinner to make her feel that it could not help but turn out all right.

"Well," Osborne said as the lights commenced to fade, "I suppose that's that. Now, my darling, I know how tired you must be, and how upset you are too, at actually leaving your home and family, so . . ."

"James," she said. "There is something I have to tell you."

He smiled at her. "You have false teeth," he said. "So have I. Two."

"James," she said again. "Please listen. I . . . I should have told you before. But there was so much going on, and I didn't . . . well, I didn't want to spoil everything.''

His smile had changed to a frown. "What are you trying to say?" he asked. There was a distinct edge to his tone.

She was going about it entirely the wrong way. But then, she went about everything entirely the wrong way. And as usual, by the time she had realized that, it was too late to change her tactics.

"Tell me," he said, and now his voice was definitely sharp.

Adela drew a very long breath. "I . . . well, you knew that I had been betrothed to my foster brother, Charles.''

"Your father told me it had never been official."

"Well, it never was. What with leaving China and everything. But before we left China, we, well . . ." She bit her lip, because he was staring at her as if he had never seen her before in his life. Her shoulders rose and fell helplessly. "It just happened. After Yuan had proposed. We were all so scared and upset, I suppose, and . . . it just happened." She raised her head. "Nearly a year ago, James. And only once. We . . . we both regretted it right away. But that's why we thought of ourselves as engaged, until you came along."

Oh, Lord, she thought, I am making the most awful mess of this. She thought he might shout at her, or even slap her face. But she wasn't prepared for the way, after staring at her for several seconds, he turned and walked away.

Osborne went forward and climbed the ladder to the bridge, without looking over his shoulder. Adela hesitated for a moment, then ran behind him. She couldn't leave things the way they were. She had to . . .

A Chinese sailor descended the ladder and stood before her. "No walk on bridge, missee," he said. "No passenger walk on bridge."

"But . . . my husband just went up there."

"Mr. Osborne friend of skipper," the sailor explained.

"And I am Mr. Osborne's wife. Therefore I am a friend of the captain's too."

"Passenger no walk on bridge," the man said stubbornly, and gestured at the white-jacketed Chinese steward, who had just emerged from the saloon. "You take missee cabin," he commanded.

"If you will accompany me, Mrs. Osborne," the steward said in very good English.

"I wish to speak with my husband," Adela told him.

"Of course, Mrs. Osborne. And undoubtedly he will come to you in a few moments. But the captain is still navigating the ship through some shoals, and he cannot be interrupted at this moment. I will tell Mr. Osborne that you are waiting for him."

She hesitated, biting her lip in anger. But there was no point in making Osborne even more angry by forcing herself on him. As the steward said, he would come to her as soon as he had got over his . . . what? Anger? That was the strange thing, she thought as the cabin door closed behind her and she sat on the lower bunk. He had not seemed to be *angry*. Rather totally taken aback. Totally disconcerted. Totally . . . afraid?

That was impossible. In the darkness she had not been able to see his face properly, and thus she had gotten entirely the wrong idea. And she had certainly made a mess of things. Well, she would just have to make it up to him. They were married, after all. And the voyage had another four weeks or so to go. He could hardly remain angry, or whatever it was, for all of that time. In fact, she doubted he would remain angry for more than a few minutes, knowing that she was waiting for him. Thus it was up to her . . . She undressed, brushed her teeth, put on her new lace nightgown, and sat down to comb her hair. He would find that an irresistible sight when he came in, she was sure.

She combed for perhaps three-quarters of an hour, until her arm was exhausted. In all that time she tried not to think, listened to the throb of the engine beneath her, the swish of water past the hull. It was a perfect night to be beginning such a voyage. It *should* have been a perfect night.

Her new watch showed eleven, and he had not come. And she was getting quite sleepy; it had been an exhausting day. She pulled on her dressing gown and stepped into the corridor. The electric light bulbs glowed, and reflected garishly from the white paint of the bulkheads. She went along the corridor into the saloon, and found the steward sitting down and smoking. He hastily got to his feet as he saw her, stubbed out the cigarette. "Can I fetch you something, Mrs. Osborne?"

"I am looking for my husband," she said. There was no point in pretending. He would know Osborne was not with *her*.

"Mr. Osborne? Mr. Osborne retired about half an hour ago, Mrs. Osborne."

"Retired? Retired where?"

"To his cabin, madam."

"But . . ." She wanted to scratch her head, instead turned and looked back along the corridor. "Which is Mr. Osborne's cabin?"

"Number Three, madam."

She was in Number Four. He was behaving as ridiculously as Charlie might have done. No doubt he expected her to bang on the door and beg to be let in. She would see him damned first. "I see," she said. "Isn't it fortunate the ship is so empty."

"Madam?"

"I meant," Adela said, "isn't Mr. Osborne fortunate, to be able to sleep in any cabin he chooses."

"That *is* Mr. Osborne's cabin, madam," the steward explained. "It was booked for him several days ago."

"But . . ." She gazed at him, then looked back along the corridor.

"At the same time that he booked Number Four for you, madam," the steward explained.

"My darling girl! Did you sleep well?"

Adela turned away from the rail in surprise, heart leaping, all the resolutions she had spent the night in making seeping away like water from a holed bucket. Osborne had not appeared for breakfast, but now last night need never have been, judging by his expression, his smile, the light in his eyes.

Before she could stop herself, she was in his arms, and he was kissing her on the mouth. "No," she said. "Not very."

He held her away from him to look into her eyes, then squeezed her hand and walked her to the two deck chairs the steward had placed at the after end of the small promenade deck. "You must forgive me," he said. "It was something of a shock."

"It is you who must forgive me," she insisted.

He sat beside her, arranged a rug over her feet; even in August the sea breeze was cool. "You know, a girl like you, a Ch'ing princess . . . well, one would have supposed you prized your virginity more than anything else in the world. More than life itself."

"I do. I did. But I have always supposed I was going to marry Charlie. Don't you see, James, that is why we fled Peking? The story you told the marshal was absolutely true, except that instead of you, it was Charlie I was betrothed to. But it was even true that Mother knew nothing of it until after the marshal's proposal."

Once again he stared at her in consternation. Oh, dear, I've done it again, she thought. But at least this time he hadn't walked away from her. She laid her hand on his. "I know it was stupid, and wrong, and wicked of me, James. I can only beg your forgiveness."

"Then what eventually happened, between Baird and yourself?" His voice was thick.

Adela hesitated, sighed, and shrugged. "I guess we were just too young, after all. We . . . we realized we didn't love each other. But we didn't know what to do about it after . . . And then you came along."

"Very conveniently," he said. "For you both."

Adela bit her lip. "I suppose I just don't put things very well," she said. But now she knew that she was still going to need all the resolutions she had made last night, because this situation could not possibly endure for four weeks. It had either to end, or begin all over again. "James . . . I married you in good faith. What happened between Charlie and me happened once, that's all. I think we both knew right away it was a mistake. I want to be your wife, and if you will let me, James, I'll be your wife in every possible way. If . . ." She drew a long breath. "If what I've told you has made you feel I married you under false pretenses, then the marriage can be annulled." She gave a twisted smile. "It hasn't been consummated, after all."

He gazed at her for several more moments, then got up and went to the rail to look at the sea. While she waited. Her heart had slowed. Everything she touched seemed to fall to ashes in her hand.

At last he turned. He was smiling. Her heart gave a

tremendous leap. "Of course I do not wish the marriage annulled, my darling," he said. "You are the most adorable creature, and I love you." She mentally winced at his usage of the same phraseology as Feng and Yuan, but she reflected that perhaps all men spoke like that; certainly he did not seem to notice that he might have hurt her. "You will be thinking that I am the most awful stuffed shirt. I suppose I am. It's from being brought up in my uncle's house, you know, the castle. The British upper classes take this sort of thing very seriously. But I love you. I promise you, I will not refer to the matter again."

Her brain was in turmoil; his choice of words was most odd. But she managed a smile, and stood up and held out her hand. "Then . . ." She bit her lip as he didn't move. "Shall we start again? On our honeymoon?"

"Ah . . ." He flushed. "I don't really think . . . Dela . . ." He came to her, held her hands, kissed her again. "I do love you. I want you to understand and believe that. I do love you, and I intend to make you the happiest woman on earth. But you must give me time. When we get to China itself, to Peking, why . . ."

"To Peking?" she cried. "But . . . that's *weeks* away."

He looked into her eyes. "What are weeks, my darling, when we have our whole lives together?"

"Peking," she whispered. "Not until Peking." Then a deep frown took possession of her face as she realized that he had *never* meant to sleep with her on this voyage, whether he had found out about her and Charlie or not. "Is that why you booked separate cabins?" she asked.

"Come on, come on," James Osborne cried. "The sampan is waiting. We can be ashore in half an hour."

He was like a schoolboy. But he had been becoming more and more excited with every hour, as the land had approached. Could it be possible that he loved China even more than she did?

That was impossible. She could hardly contain *her* excitement. Because apart from its being China, it promised so much. Thus she had dressed with particular care in an outfit she and Constance had bought together just before her wedding, which she had never previously worn. It was in imperial yellow—and why not, as the dynasty was deposed and she *was* an imperial princess, however confused those two thoughts might be?—a full ankle-length skirt worn under a splendid three-quarter-length coat of the same color and material, but with black velvet hem and cuffs. Her blouse was white silk, and her felt hat was also yellow and black, with a black plume. Her gaiters were white and her shoes black patent leather. She thought she had never looked more elegant, and being an old married woman, she had also put her hair up into an enormous pompadour. But James, being a man, was interested only in getting ashore, and gave her no more than a glance as she finally joined him in the gangway.

"Our things . . . ?"

"Will follow on later. Oh, don't worry about them, Dela. Don't you want to set foot on Chinese soil all over again?"

"Oh, yes," she said. "Oh, yes." Because she did, and she had to believe that everything was going to be all right soon. When they were ashore. He had said so, and she had to believe him.

The remarkable thing was that it would have been the most superb voyage, had she not been married. The ship, however small, had been very well-appointed, the officers and crew obviously experts. They had had almost no bad weather. The food had been magnificent, and every night James had ordered a bottle of champagne. "After all," he would say, "we are honey-mooning." Then he would correct himself. "We are *approaching* our honeymoon."

For he had been the most splendid companion—as a friend rather than a husband. He was knowledgeable and urbane, anxious only to please her and be with her and talk with her about every possible subject, from the British and European aristocracies, most of whom he claimed to know personally, through European politics and the possibility of a general war, which he considered very likely but which he said could not possibly affect them in China, through shrewdly critical remarks on America, which he equally seemed to know well, to informed comment on China, and what he presumed Yuan was trying to accomplish. He was, she discovered somewhat to her surprise, a supporter of Yuan's concept of a new empire. And not merely because Yuan was by way of being his employer, or so he said. "A country as vast as China," he pointed out, "*can* be ruled only by an absolute despot."

A point of view with which she herself agreed, even if she would not have used the term "absolute despot," and even if she could not agree that Yuan was neces-sarily the right man to do the ruling. But she never voiced her own opinion, because she had no wish to argue with him about anything. Not that, she supposed, it would have made any difference to their relationship. Because here they were, about to land in Tientsin, and he still had not consummated his marriage.

She had refused every mental summons either to anger or despair. Because at last she understood what truly lay between them, and even if she from time to time reflected that life would have been so much simpler had he been as honest with her as she was with him from the beginning, yet the relief was so great she would have forgiven him anything. For James Osborne had a secret, which was every bit as disastrous in a European community as hers had been in a Chinese. It was not a secret he had meant to share with her at any time, she supposed—hence the separate cabins. But she had known within three days of leaving San Francisco, simply because of her own experiences, which had enabled her to recognize the smell and the symptoms: her husband was an opium smoker.

In her relief that the obstacle to their happiness lay in him rather than her, and was in addition so simply a physical matter, she had not even been disturbed, much less shocked, merely reminded herself that it was presumably an occupational hazard for anyone who lived too long in South China. She had told him she knew, told him she understood, told him there was no real necessity for him to keep to a separate cabin, after all—indeed there had been no necessity for one in the first place—told him too how Pearl had made her smoke the poppy as well. And told him she would help him to fight the habit, if he wished.

She had feared he might be angry. But he was not. Rather had he seemed relieved that she had found out. "My dear Dela," he had said. "My, dear, dear Dela. Then you understand everything."

She hadn't, actually, and he had not elaborated— and he continued to keep to his cabin. She presumed opium addiction in some way lowered the sexual urge, possibly even induced impotence. Although remembering what she had seen in Feng's opium den, and even more, her own feelings that had led her almost to accept Pearl's advances, she was sure this had to be psychological rather than real—despite Constance's disapproval, she had recently become a keen reader of the writings of the Viennese "quack" Sigmund Freud. But the fact was that however much James kissed her or even fondled her, which he seemed to enjoy doing more and more as the voyage progressed, she could tell that he was never really ready for sex. Once, indeed, quite early on, becoming herself aroused by his caress, she had indulged in a wifely privilege to touch the front of his trousers while he had been kissing her passionately, hoping for *some* response, and had found nothing, while her wrist had been held so tightly that she had supposed he would break it.

Yet still had he not been angry. "You are a *devil*, Dela," he had said. "But you must be patient. That is all I ask of you, my darling girl. Patience."

When he was as charming and persuasive as that, she almost felt she loved him. Indeed she knew she *would* love him when they finally *made* love together. Certainly she was prepared to be patient, because China was always coming closer. And here at last it was. The steam-powered sampan was crossing the turbulence of the bar, where the Pei-ho, reinforced here by the flow of the Han-ho, tumbled out into the Gulf of Chihli. And there, looming above the reed banks which lined both sides of the river, were the roofs of Tientsin. Not quite a year before, she had fled this place in terror. Now . . . For a moment she wondered if Lin-tu would be in the crowd to greet her, and gave a little shiver. But James immediately put his arm around her shoulder to give her a squeeze. "Soon, my darling," he said. "Soon."

To her surprise, she saw that they were not going to land at the dock in the European quarter, but were being taken to the other side of the river, to Taku, where the train was waiting, already impatiently puffing in its anxiety to begin its journey. And indeed a glance at her watch told her that the train would normally have left half an hour before now. "It's not waiting for us?" she asked.

"Of course it is."

"But . . . how?"

"The ship has a radio. I sent a message ahead to tell the train to wait. I've also arranged things with customs and immigration. So there is no need for us to stop in Tientsin at all, you see. I am in haste to reach Peking. Aren't you?"

"Oh, yes," she said. "But . . . they will do these things for *you*?"

"I am the editor of the *China Gazette,*" he pointed out, and gave a roguish smile. "And also a friend of Marshal Yuan's, which is far more important."

She gazed at him in wonder, and then at Taku itself in wonder, for there seemed to be an unusually large crowd of people waiting for them. At least a platoon of soldiers, wearing the smart blue-and-white uniforms she remembered Yuan's men displaying, but also several Europeans.

"Whatever can *they* want?" James muttered, half to himself, and then gave her a bright smile. "Newspaper reporters, I imagine. You will not object, my darling, if I send them off with fleas in their ears? We don't want to be plagued with reporters, do we?"

"No," she agreed. "We don't."

The boat puffed into the dock, and she was handed up the ladder, to face Mr. Richards, the British consul. "Miss Wynne," he said. "Thank God!"

Adela raised her eyebrows. "I think you mean 'Mrs. Osborne,' " she said, and showed him her ring. "I had no idea you were expecting me."

"Miss Wynne," he said. "Mrs. Osborne . . ." He glanced at the other white men, most of whom *were* reporters, she could tell from their notebooks, although she thought there were one or two other consular officials there as well, and then at the Chinese soldiers, standing stiffly to attention, as was their captain, but watching Richards with great interest. "I must speak with you alone."

James had by now reached the dock beside her. "Richards?" he asked with distinct coldness. "I really must ask you to stop badgering my wife."

"Badgering?" Richards demanded. "Why, you—"

"It's all right, really, my dear," Adela said. "Mr. Richards just wants to have a word."

"Well, he shall not," James declared. "Mrs. Osborne has nothing to say to you, sir." He took Adela's arm. "Come along, my darling."

"Why, you impudent scoundrel," Richards cried, and was joined by another man.

"Mrs. James Osborne? Calthorpe, from the United States Embassy. I would like a word too. I have a cablegram here for you."

"A cable? How splendid," Osborne said, before Adela could speak, and plucked the envelope from Calthorpe's fingers.

"Here, you," the American shouted.

"Now, you look here, Osborne," Richards said.

Osborne smiled at them. "Gentlemen," he said. "My wife and I have a long journey ahead of us, and we are anxious to get started. We have kept the train waiting for half an hour as it is, and it is not going to wait very much longer. So, if you will excuse us . . ."

"I insist upon speaking with Mrs. Osborne," Richards said. "In private."

"What do you suppose he wants to tell you, my darling," Osborne asked, "that he cannot tell me as well? That something has happened to your mother and father?"

"Oh, my God," Adela cried. "That isn't it, is it, Mr. Richards?"

"Of course not, my dear girl. But—"

"Then nothing else can be of the slightest importance," Osborne declared. "Do you really wish to wait here talking with these people, and certainly miss the train? Peking, my darling. Peking! I can hardly wait to get there." He put his arm around her shoulder and gave her a hug and a kiss on the ear. "Don't you understand what they want to tell you?" he whispered. "That I'm a dope fiend."

Of course! She should have realized that right away—Mother must somehow have found out, and being Mother, was overreacting like mad. "I do apologize, Mr. Richards," Adela said. "But we are in a frightful rush."

Osborne was already half-dragging her toward the train, and the conductor was holding the door for them.

"Mrs. Osborne," Richards shouted, running behind them. "This man is a scoundrel. Mrs. Osborne . . ."

She was inside the train, and the door was closed. She looked through the corridor window at Richards. "You are speaking of my husband, sir," she said coldly. "Just because he smokes opium. You should be ashamed of yourself, sir, trying to come between husband and wife. Mr. Osborne and I have no secrets from each other. Pray allow me to be the judge of whether or not he is a scoundrel."

Richards gazed at her with his mouth open as the train began to move out of the station.

"This is your compartment," the conductor said. "You be comfortable here."

"I'm sure we shall," Adela agreed, because it was quite the most luxurious compartment she had ever been in, for a day trip. It was several times the size of any ordinary compartment, to begin with, and instead of settees there were several leather-upholstered armchairs, while at the far end was a very fully stocked bar.

"This Marshal Yuan's own special compartment," the conductor informed her. He tapped the walls. "Nobody either side. Nobody in entire carriage, save you and Mr. Osborne. You talk, and shout as much as you wish. No interruptions." He placed a full ice bucket on the bar, in which there was an opened bottle of champagne. "You   drink,"   he   recommended. "Celebrate." He closed the door behind him.

Osborne poured them each a glass of champagne. "Might as well enjoy it while we can," he said enigmatically. "You handled that situation very well, Princess. You really are a most courageous and quick-witted young woman. And a loyal one. It's a crying shame . . . ah, well." He handed her a glass and sat down, one leg thrown over the other. "What shall we drink to, a short life and a merry one?"

She frowned at him. He was in a most odd mood. "What was in the telegram?" she asked.

"Do you know, I haven't read it?" He took it from his pocket, slit the envelope, glanced at the words, and gave a short laugh. "Now, how the devil did she discover that? Here." He held it out. "You may as well read it, seeing as how we've actually arrived. One telegram is worth a host of explanations."

Adela sat down, placed her glass in the holder beside her chair, and studied the words:

ADELA MOST URGENT YOU LEAVE OSBORNE IMMEDIATELY AND TAKE REFUGE AMERICAN OR ENGLISH LEGATION STOP WILL ARRANGE REPATRIATION TO AMERICA STOP OSBORNE YUAN AGENT STOP YOU HAVE BEEN KIDNAPPED REPEAT KIDNAPPED STOP PLEASE ACT IMMEDIATELY STOP CONSTANCE.

Slowly she raised her head. "Is this some sort of joke?" she asked.

Osborne drained his glass, got up, walked to the bar,

and poured himself another. "No joke, my darling, delightful princess. But I wonder how your formidable mama found out so soon."

"No joke? But . . ." She felt physically sick, and too bewildered to think straight. "Yuan . . ."

"Sent me to fetch you back. He sent me, to atone for my sins, you might say, in not properly protecting you against Feng. He actually wants you for a concubine, my darling Dela. He loves you. He adores you." He stopped next to the chair to stare into her eyes. "Or he thinks he does, at the moment. When he finds out what I have to tell him, I should think he is going to peel the flesh from your bones himself. Slowly."

11

The Prisoner

"You mean you have done nothing?" Charles Baird stood in the center of the small living room and gazed from Frank to Constance.

"Now, simmer down," Frank said. "We have done all we could. But . . . well . . ."

"We thought she'd be stopped at Tientsin," Constance said, her voice dull with misery. "We arranged for her to be. But this arrived yesterday." She held out the cablegram.

Charles read the words:

OSBORNES MET AS REQUESTED STOP MRS. OSBORNE REFUSED PRIVATE INTERVIEW STOP SEEMED PERFECTLY CONTENT WITH HUSBAND STOP QUITE UNHARMED AND VERY HAPPY STOP IS IT POSSIBLE YOU ARE MISTAKEN SITUATION QUESTION REGARDS RICHARDS.

He raised his head. "What does it mean?"

"I don't know," Constance cried. "Oh, I suppose I do. Osborne is still hoodwinking her. We must only pray that the minister in Peking will get to see her before she's taken into the Forbidden City and that something has alarmed her by then."

"Pray," Charlie said disgustedly. "Why aren't you *there*?"

"Now, steady on, Charles," Frank said. "We couldn't possibly be there yet. And while at sea we'd be completely out of touch. Even more important, what are we supposed to do when we get there? I can tell you that your mother wanted to catch the next boat across the Pacific after hearing what Sun Yat-sen had to say, but I talked her out of it."

"Why?" Charlie shouted. "In the name of God, *why*?"

"Because she'd be putting herself in danger as well. Don't you see, our being welcomed back into China was only on Osborne's say-so. Now we know that isn't worth a can of beans. We'd be seized and imprisoned, and probably executed as well, the moment we set foot on Chinese soil. Why, Yuan must be hoping we'll do that very thing. Then he'd have scooped the pot."

Charlie sat down, his head in his hands. "Oh, God," he said. "Oh, Jesus Christ. So we just sit here and do nothing. We wait for her head to be sent to us in a box."

"We'll go on *trying*," Constance said. "The American minister . . . and Mr. Richards won't give up when I cable him back and—"

"And what good is all that going to do Adela?" Charlie shouted.

"You just have to get a grip on yourself, old son," Frank said. "One would almost suppose you were still in love with the girl."

Charlie raised his head. "Don't you think I *am*?"

"Well . . . you haven't given much evidence of it recently."

"So I was mixed up," Charlie shouted, getting up again. "I was . . . I only wanted her to be happy. I knew *I* couldn't give her that right now. She . . . she's so much *older* than me, in her mind. But . . . God Almighty, the thought of her in Yuan's hands, being . . ." He gazed at his mother with enormous tear-filled eyes and then ran to the door.

"Hold it," Frank shouted. "Just what do you think you're doing? Don't you think Yuan will be happy to have your head as well? And other bits of you. Anyway, if he does mean to murder Adela, she'll be dead long before you can even reach China."

Charlie had already opened the door. Now he looked over his shoulder. "I am going to find Dr. Sun," he said. "I can still avenge her death."

Adela gazed at Osborne for several seconds, then propelled herself from the chair and ran for the door. To her surprise he made no attempt to stop her. Why, she discovered when she slid the panel aside and gazed at two Chinese soldiers—and there were several more in the corridor.

She looked past them. "Help me!" she shouted. But as the conductor had told her, there was no one else in this carriage. She turned to face Osborne, panting.

"Come in and sit down," he commanded. "Why anticipate it? Oh, bring her inside," he told the soldiers, now speaking Chinese. "And you better secure her to her chair, for her own safety. Don't hurt her, now. The marshal would be angry."

A hand touched her arm. Adela turned her head from side to side, gazing at the superbly appointed carriage, through the windows at the so familiar countryside rushing past . . . and wanted to scream and scream and scream. It could not be happening. It could not.

"You *can* scream if you like," Osborne invited,

watching her expression. "I shan't mind. I should rather enjoy it."

She sucked air into her lungs, and was propelled across the room by the soldiers, placed in an armchair. A silken cord was produced and passed three times around her body and arms, above her elbows but below her breasts, to pin her arms to her sides; the rope was then taken twice around the back of the chair and passed beneath it, to emerge in front, where it was made fast to her ankles and then drawn taut, so that while not uncomfortable, she simply could not move—they did it with such gentle courtesy that her hat did not even come off. While her brain teemed. She didn't fight them; she could remember too well the humiliation that had followed her attempt to fight Feng's men, but there had to be some way, some . . . The door had closed, and Osborne ws gazing at her, drinking champagne. "Do you know," he said, "I nearly anticipated it for both of us when you told me your unhappy condition as we left San Francisco. I lay awake that entire night. I thought: Why not go in there and beat the bitch to death and then throw her overboad and jump in behind her. It was a temptation." He sat in the chair next to hers. "And then I thought: While there's life there's hope. After all, I was told to deliver a princess, and I am doing just that. I cannot be held responsible for the odd tarnish. And after *all,* what can Yuan do to me that he hasn't already? And at least I will have the pleasure of watching *you* die."

She looked into his eyes. "But . . . you *hate* me," she whispered.

"Oh, I hate you, Princess. Of all the women in the world, I want to hear *you* scream."

Adela shook her head in desperate incomprehension. "Why? What have I ever done to you? James . . ." She had to fight back the tears.

"I will tell you," he said. "No, I will *show* you, my *darling.*" To her consternation he got up, opened his jacket, released his belt, and slid his trousers and drawers down to his knees. She stared in horror at the twisted flesh, only slowly raised her eyes to his face. To his smile. The smile of a demon. "Yuan's people did that to me," he said. "Do you know why? Because I did not prevent Feng's men from abducting you."

"Oh, my God," she said. "Oh, my God. But . . ."

"Your stupid foster mother," Osborne said, to her relief pulling up his pants, "decided to change her mind at the last minute in San Francisco, canceled your bookings because your ship was delayed, and transferred to a British vessel. The agent Yuan had traveling with you became confused and was left behind. *He* has been executed. So I received a wire to attach myself to your party in Hong Kong and accompany you to Shanghai. Yuan assumed you would pick up a coastal steamer, you see, as anyone else would have done. When your mother decided to travel by train, I had no time to organize proper protection. I could only come with you myself, and hope for the best."

"Then those photographs, the newspaper . . ."

"I had to have a reason for accompanying you, Princess. You may believe that I wished then I could have been anywhere else in the world rather than Hong Kong. But when Marshal Yuan commands, those who work for him obey. So it was me against those thugs, and thanks to your mother and yourself I was not even given the opportunity to die defending you. Because Yuan does not accept failure, Princess. Had I died, he would no doubt have spit upon my corpse, but at least I would have been beyond his reach. Do you know what he had his people do? Can you guess? Oh, I am not a eunuch. I feel, and I want, as much as any man. And I can hardly relieve myself with my own fingers. They strapped me down, Princess, and a pretty girl aroused me until I was on the point of ejaculation, and then they *broke* it, Princess. It is not bone, you know. Only flesh filled with blood vessels. When the heart pumps those vessels full because of desire, it becomes as hard as a bone, almost, but the slightest suggestion of ill treatment or pain and the blood flows away and leaves it soft and flaccid. But Yuan's man had been a professional wrestler. He held it so tenderly that it stayed hard, and then a single twist . . . Even now I can feel the pain. And do you know, Princess, he did it again the next day. And again every day for a week, until manhood was beyond me, no matter how *I* desired. I screamed, Princess. Oh, I screamed. In humiliation as much as pain."

Desperately Adela licked her lips; again she felt physically sick. But she had to think, because there was so much here that she did not understand. So much she had to decide, to try to use. "He did that," she said. "Yet you continue to serve him?"

"How may one not serve Marshal Yuan?" he asked, lips twisted, "when one has been chosen? I am at least still alive. Oh, I have the privilege of ending my own life, when I choose. I *must* do that, before *he* chooses to execute me. Slowly. So you see what a risk I am now taking."

"But . . . you came after me."

"I told you, he sent me. He cannot afford any international incidents at this moment. But he wanted you, above anything else. And he could send *me* to secure you, certain that you would still be a virgin, even after five weeks alone with me. Or as much of a virgin as you were when our marriage began. Supposing you were ever one at all. Now you are my wife, my *darling*. Certainly in the eyes of the world. Where I go, you go.

So we both go where Yuan wishes. He thought it all out. Do you know, I have a notion that he still means to marry you? He wants *you*, silly old man, because he imagines himself in love with you. Can you stomach that? But he still also feels that you may be able to help him gain what he really wants, the right to sacrifice to heaven. The fool! He has the reality, but he must also seek the pomp and glory. The Chinese will never allow it. They have had enough emperors. But he won't accept that. So he is even toying with the idea of having our marriage—*such* a surprise to him, my dear—publicly annulled on the grounds of nonconsummation, with all the gory details of my 'riding accident' being released to the international press, and then marrying you himself, as he always intended. Now, you will just disappear, and I will have to tell the world how you died of a fever, while your shrieks are still echoing through the Forbidden City.''

"And you would permit that?" she whispered. "Listen to me, Mr. Osborne . . . James. You are taking us both to our deaths. But does anyone on this train know that? To them I am your wife, and we are both the favorites of the marshal, so far as anyone is aware. James! We could leave the train and regain the coast before he even knows we have landed. Mr. Richards will protect us and put us on a ship for America. I would not betray you, James. I would be your wife. I would help you. Oh, God, I would help you.''

Did she mean any of it? She wanted only to win him, to persuade him, to do anything . . . and as had happened before, it did not matter whether she meant it or not. Because he was not going to be won or persuaded.

"Do you not suppose he would seek us out?" he asked. "Can you suppose there is a place on earth he would not find us and bring us back? Have you any idea what it is like to be tortured to death by Yuan Shih-k'ai? *I* have some idea. I have seen it happen. I have *felt* it happen. You will have an idea soon enough. You will also watch it happen, Princess. You will also *feel* it happen. To yourself."

"And what of you?" she shouted, nerves at last cracking under the strain. "Will you not lie there, screaming beside me?"

"He sent me to fetch you," Osborne said. "I have done as he commanded. I did not, I could not, know your obscene condition. I am innocent. Even Yuan must see that." A tremendous shiver ran through his body. "Even Yuan," he whispered. "Even Yuan."

His terror was horrible to watch. But then, everything about him was horrible. James Osborne, a man she had been prepared to *love*. She wondered if in the whole wide world there was any man *worthy* of her love. And was left with the sad reflection that perhaps there was only Yuan.

But even that reflection was a cause for hope. She had to hope, or she would die of sheer despair. She must think, and plan, and make some effort to combat the evil that seemed to hang around her like a shroud. Yuan was an evil man, a hateful man, and a vicious monster . . . but he loved her. Osborne had said so, and she had seen sufficient evidence of it with her own eyes. She had once thought: Would he really wish, *could* he really wish, to destroy so much beauty, on account of a single mistake? Surely Yuan, who had been a soldier and a diplomat all his life, used to weighing what small advantage could be gained here or might be lost there, could never be so much at the mercy of his passions. She *was* a Ch'ing princess. She *could* give him strong and healthy sons who would be half Manchu, half Chinese. He had to be persuaded of these things.

And then she would go to his bed, Yuan's bed, like a lamb to the slaughter. But what did it matter, if only she could survive? Survive until Constance organized her rescue. Because this time there would be no Dr. Sun, no Lin-tu to come to her aid. There was only herself, and Constance. But Constance at least knew the truth of her situation, that was obvious, and Constance would never give up. Constance had already provided for her rescue, and she had stupidly refused to accept it. But Constance would realize that she had been hoodwinked, and would try again. So she must survive!

This was a far cry from the haughty acceptance of Fate required of a Manchu princess. She had become Americanized. But survival depended on her at least *acting* the princess, now and always. Only that way could Yuan know what he could obtain, and what he could so easily lose forever, by a moment of senseless anger.

It was time to take control of herself, and her Destiny, once again. Besides, she was becoming acutely uncomfortable. "Will you release me, please," she said.

Osborne stared at her.

"I understand the situation, Mr. Osborne," she said. "Equally I understand that I cannot escape my Destiny. There is no need to bind me any longer. I am a princess of the Ch'ing. I am quite prepared to meet any fate which may overtake me. I will give you my word, *as* a Ch'ing princess, upon the souls of my father and mother, that I shall make no further attempt to escape. I wish only to proceed in comfort, while I may." She arranged her features into a smile. "Is that so much to ask, as it is for so little a while?"

He hesitated, then produced a pocket knife and cut her bonds. "If you try anything . . ."

"I have given you my word." She walked up and down the compartment a few times to restore her circulation. Then she went to the bar and poured herself a glass of champagne. Osborne, slumped in a chair, glowered at her. "He will peg you out on an ant heap," he said, "after coating your slit with honey."

She regarded him with cold contempt. "Your vulgarity was presumably learned in your English castle," she remarked. "Or is that part of your background also a tissue of lies?" But of course it was. How ever could they have been so taken in? Because they had *wanted* to be taken in. Frank and Constance, aware only of the problems with which they had been confronted in this unwanted foster child, would have accepted a leper if he had promised to provide her with a comfortable home.

But being angry with them, with anyone, was self-defeating. The coming battle, she knew, would be as much with her own temperament, her own nerves, her own courage, as with Yuan or any of his executioners. And that too was a battle that had to be won.

She drank her champagne, and sat down with her back to Osborne, gazing out the window. There was a hamper also waiting in the bar, and at lunchtime she helped herself to food, forcing herself to eat to maintain her strength for the coming ordeal, and discovering that she was quite hungry.

Osborne made no attempt to join her; neither did he speak. He was sunk into his own presumably terrified thoughts.

She welcomed his silence. Because she had a great deal of thinking of her own to do. Her principal problem, as she sat in the comfortable chair, eating crispy pancake roll and sipping champagne, gazing out the window, was to make herself believe she *was* living this nightmare at all, that this *was* actually a train journey to her own execution. Out there was everything she remembered from her childhood, the farms and the pagodas, the fields of wheat and the unending river—

and the people, with their children and their dogs, waving at the train as it passed. Familiar sights, familiar sounds, and all too soon Fengtai, and then Hachiapo itself, with the walls of Peking somber in the dying afternoon beyond. And a platform, and a fresh escort of soldiers. And an officer, clearly of field rank from his red tabs and his braided cap, standing in the doorway of the compartment and saluting. Almost, indeed, she thought he was with difficulty restraining himself from performing the kowtow. "Princess!" he announced. "General Chang Hsun, commander of the marshal's Imperial Guard, at your service. Welcome to Peking. You have long been awaited."

He had a peculiarly harsh face, the expression of a professional soldier. Indeed, it was a face she could even remember; she had seen it in Yuan's encampment the evening he had overthrown Sun Yat-sen, and he had been present at the banquet the following night in the Forbidden City. Clearly one of Yuan's most trusted aides. Yet of his admiration for her, as a princess rather than a woman, there could be no doubt. Obviously he knew nothing of the true situation. She glanced at Osborne and received a desperate waggle of the eyebrows. But then, of course, at this moment no one knew anything of the true situation. Not even Yuan. For a few minutes, at the least, she could live like the princess she was.

"I thank you, General Chang," she said. "It is good to be home."

She stepped past him and out of the carriage onto a red carpet. Here there were soldiers drawn up to either side, presenting arms. Beyond them, the other passengers, among them several Europeans, were craning their necks to obtain a glimpse of this obvious celebrity with whom they had been traveling. So why did she not break away and run to them and beg for their help? Because she knew that they could not help her? Or because it would not be acting as a Ch'ing princess should?

At the end of the carpet there was a totally enclosed palanquin, the draperies of which General Chang Hsun now held open for her. "It is but a short distance, Princess," he said.

She hesitated but a moment, looked over her shoulder to where Osborne waited, his face twisting. General Chang certainly knew something of what was in his master's mind, as she was not to be allowed to travel with her husband. For which she was utterly thankful. Apart from the misery of his company, Osborne was already entirely in the past. Her only concern was with the present. Only that would matter, once she entered the Forbidden City.

"Only a short distance," Chang said again. "To the marshal."

The palanquin stopped moving, and she knew they had arrived. She had resisted the temptation to peep through the draperies during the journey; she had been able to tell well enough, from the sounds and the smells, whereabouts in the city they were, and the last challenge had been succeeded by silence, save for the footfalls of the men carrying her, and her escort; then she had known she was in the Forbidden City.

She had had too much to think about to wish to look out. Her brain was still a jumble of emotion, one-third threatening at any moment to give way to screaming terror when she thought of the fate Osborne had suggested she might be made to suffer. That was impossible. But had not Osborne himself suffered almost as terrible a punishment?

Another third kept telling her that this could not be happening, that it was all a mistake, that she had but to explain the situation to Yuan to have her misery ended and find herself on the next available boat to San Francisco. But the final third reminded her that only by being everything Yuan had dreamed of for the past year and more, by being twice as beautiful and desirable as he remembered, could she avoid catastrophe.

It was on this she had finally determined to concentrate, to the exclusion of all else, this role she must play to the very end. She thanked her lucky star that she had elected to wear her most elegant gown and that she had resisted the temptation to fight the soldiers and thereby become disheveled. They had even left her her handbag. It was dark within the palanquin, but she could just make herself out in her vanity mirror, could ascertain that her hat was on straight and that her hair had not started to come down. Of course her skirt was crushed and a trifle dusty, but there was no way it could be otherwise after an all-day journey. She was also again hungry. She wondered when next she would be allowed to eat.

If ever.

But the moment was at hand, because the draperies were being drawn, by General Chang himself, and she was stepping out into the flaring light of myriad torches, held by eunuchs, while gathered at the top of the steps was a bevy of young women, all clapping daintily as she emerged.

"Where is Mr. Osborne?" she asked. It was terribly important that she have a few moments alone with the marshal before Osborne could tell his story.

"He follows, Princess," Chang said. "He will soon be here. Come. The marshal awaits you." He gave her his hand and she mounted the steps, while the women clapped again. Behind her she heard the sound of another palanquin arriving, but she dared not turn her head. Her time was now down to precious seconds.

The double doors before her were swinging open, and Chang was escorting her into a huge room with a polished wooden floor and some rugs, but no furniture to be seen save for a large high-backed and ornately carved wooden chair at the far end; she was in an imperial reception chamber. And sitting on the throne there was Yuan himself, in his full-dress blue uniform, several aides and eunuchs at his back. Once, she recalled, he had had no time for eunuchs. Not yet a year ago.

But now he was standing and gazing at her, while Chang bowed low and the women sidled into the room on either side. Adela discovered she was holding her breath, let it out slowly as Yuan approached. "Adela," he said. "Princess! You were stolen away from me. By that *woman*!" For a moment his face hardened. "No doubt she thought you were too good for me. How can any man have been so deceived by a smile and a promise? But now I have brought you back. Adela." He held open his arms, and after a brief hesitation she went forward to be embraced. Her brain was teeming, all her plans and resolutions jostling against each other in uncertainty. But there was no time for cowardice now; Osborne was right behind her.

Yuan kissed her forehead. "Osborne has explained the situation?" he asked in a low voice.

"Yes, my lord," she said. "My lord, I must speak with you in private—"

"My lord," Osborne said from behind her. "I must speak with you on a most urgent matter."

Yuan looked from one to the other. "A domestic tiff?" he asked. "There are no urgent matters this night." He tucked Adela's arm under his. "Tonight we shall dine. Oh, you shall come too, James. What, should a man not dine with his wife? We shall dine, and talk, and plan. And dream of love. Have I ever told you, my Princess, that you are the most beautiful woman in the world?"

She could think of nothing to say or do. Her tongue seemed stuck to the roof of her mouth.

But not, unfortunately, Osborne's. He ran forward. "My lord," he said in hardly more than a whisper. "It is *most* urgent. It . . ." he inhaled. "It concerns the princess."

Yuan frowned at him, then at Adela. "What would he tell me?"

She tried to think. "I . . . I would beg of you to hear me, my lord."

"Listen to what *I* have to say first, my lord," Osborne said. "Then to the princess, if you choose."

Yuan looked at her again, and then released her. "If this is some caprice on your part, James, you will suffer for it." He spoke softly, but Osborne's face paled.

"It is a matter with which my lord must be acquainted," he repeated.

Yuan walked away from Adela's side, into the middle of the room; Osborne accompanied him, their backs turned to her. She stood absolutely still, trying to get her breathing under control, dreadfully aware that all the people in the room, guards, eunuchs, officers, and women, were staring at her as she stood there, isolated. Awaiting her fate. Her knees touched, and she was equally aware of sweat trickling down her back. And then of the sudden anger which so often came to her rescue. She was a Ch'ing princess. And as Yuan had just said, she was the most beautiful woman in the world. No matter what was about to happen to her, she must be remembered as just those things. And besides, it was her only hope. She sucked air into her lungs, and held her head high, and gazed at Yuan as he slowly turned toward her.

"You," he said, pointing to General Chang Hsun. "Take this . . . this *thing* outside, and strip him, and *whip* him. Whip him until he bleeds. And when you are finished with his back, whip his front. *Lacerate* him, from neck to ankle. Whip him until he can scream no more."

Chang signaled four of the soldiers.

"Mercy, great Yuan!" Osborne fell to his knees. "I but carried out your orders, mighty lord. I have brought you the princess. As she was when she left China."

Yuan struck him across the face. "Hold your miserable tongue. Take him out. Whip him!" He smiled. "But do not kill him. As he says, he brought me the princess. Give him his worthless life, until I can find some use for it."

Osborne seemed incapable of movement. He remained kneeling, his mouth open and his tongue lolling in sheer terror, while the guards seized his arms and dragged him across the floor and through the door; Adela could hear his knees and toes bumping on the stairs outside. Now she could hardly breathe. Because now it was to be her turn.

"Leave us," Yuan said. "Everyone. Leave us. Not you," he snapped at the eunuchs as they started to file to the door. "I will have need of *you.*"

The women fled the room, whispering to each other, casting fearful glances at Adela. The remaining guards hesitated, and were dismissed with a wave of Yuan's hand. They too left, and the doors clanged behind them. The eunuchs—there were a dozen of them—had gathered in a terrified group behind the throne.

"Have you nothing to say?" Yuan demanded. "No denial to utter? Do you not wish the midwives summoned, that you may prove your *innocence*?"

She could not speak. She had nothing worthwhile

to say. If only she could have five minutes to think.

"Fetch me the bamboo," Yuan said.

Adela's knees nearly gave way as one of the eunuchs hurried from the room; she thought she would kneel as Osborne had done. But if she knelt, she would also beg, as Osborne had done. She was never going to do that. She made herself gaze at him. "If Osborne told you the truth, my lord," she said, "then you will understand that when you made your proposal to my mother, I was already betrothed to another man. Already belonged to another man."

"You are a liar as well as a prostitute," he said, slowly coming toward her. She bit her lip before she could stop herself, because she *was* lying in claiming she had given herself to Charlie *before* the proposal. "You are no better than that miserable creature I sent to fetch you back," Yuan said. "On your knees, *Princess*. On your knees and perform the kowtow before your master."

Adela raised her chin still further. "I am a Ch'ing princess," she said. "A Ch'ing princess kowtows to no one, save the Son of Heaven himself."

"And am I not the Son of Heaven?"

"You are a Chinese *bandit*!" she spat at him.

He stared at her. She realized that in all probability no one had ever so addressed him in his life before. Then he snapped his fingers, and two of the eunuchs hurried forward to seize her arms. "Make her kneel," he commanded. "Make her kiss the floor."

Adela did not resist them. Survival! She had remembered this, too late, in Feng's camp. And she had yet survived. They forced her to her knees and carried her body forward, bending it by exerting pressure on her arms. The brim of her hat touched the wood of the floor and the hat fell off. Then her forehead was on the wood; she could feel her pompadour starting to collapse, realized that she still held her handbag, and released it. She was going to need all her strength for herself alone.

"Now, confess," Yuan said, standing beside her head. "Confess, if you still possess a shred of honor."

Adela drew a deep breath . . . but now she was again angry. If he wanted defiance, then he would have defiance. "Very well, then," she said. "I took Charles Baird as a lover *after* you had asked for my hand. I took him so that I would not have to marry you. For how can a Ch'ing princess marry a Chinese bandit?"

For several seconds the room was silent, and pinned to the floor as she was, her arms almost breaking, she could not see the expression on his face. But she heard a door close, and knew that the eunuch had returned with the bamboo.

"Prepare her," Yuan said. He spoke quietly, but that he was in the grip of a powerful emotion could not be doubted.

Adela, still kneeling, tensed her muscles, but was totally unprepared for the sudden kick she received in the thigh, a paralyzing blow that took all the strength from her muscles; before she could stop herself, she was lying flat on her face on the floor, while two of the eunuchs were pulling her arms above her head and holding them there, one to each wrist; two more, she realized, were holding her ankles, pulling them not only away from her body but also away from each other, spread-eagling her so that she felt she was about to be torn into two halves. Then she felt other hands on her shoulders. Somehow that upset her more than anything that had yet happened; it had been such a lovely gown. She wanted to ask them to leave it, and she would take it off herself. But she dared not speak for fear her voice would break from discomfort and terror. So she lay still while the material was ripped, the tunic and the blouse, the skirt and the petticoat, the drawers. There was shame. But shame was meaningless now, when she was about to suffer more pain than she had ever known before. When she was about to be destroyed. Because she knew that even if she survived the coming flogging, once the bamboo had bitten into her so precious flesh, even once, she would never again be a Ch'ing princess. Or even a proud woman. She would be a thing, like Osborne.

"Show her the bamboo," Yuan said, still standing by her head; he was breathing heavily. Perhaps, she thought, he is appreciating what he is about to throw away.

She had supposed the cane would be held before her eyes; but that would have been too easy—she could have closed her eyes. Instead the cane was placed between her legs, to separate her most intimate secrets, and then slowly drawn upward, parting her buttocks in turn, scraping her with the point, until the point itself continued up her backbone to her neck. She could not stop herself giving a shiver, felt the tremor course through her muscles to her toes, knew that she was holding her breath and closing her eyes as tightly as she could, waiting, anticipating the blow that would mean the end of the Princess Adela forever and ever.

And realized that nothing had happened. And that her wrists had been released. For a moment she thought she must have lost consciousness and be in a dream world. Then she heard Yuan's voice. "Haste!" he was commanding.

She wanted to lie still forever, to become a part of the floor. But she could not resist opening her eyes and raising her head to watch the eunuchs scurrying through

the door, leaving her alone with the marshal. The
bamboo rod was on the floor beside her. She rose on
her elbow, turned to her side to gaze at his face, mottled
with blood, while he seemed unable to control his
breathing. Now he pointed at another door. "In there!"
he ordered. "Haste!"

When she hesitated, he kicked her in the buttocks.
What new and even more terrible punishment had he
devised for her? But she wanted to move, and run. She
wanted to feel alive, and enjoy her health and strength,
and beauty, even if for just a few moments longer. She
scrambled to her feet and ran for the door, her shoes
slipping on the polished floor, the remnants of her
clothes falling about her. She pushed the door open, ran
inside, stared at a most luxurious bedroom. She
checked, and received a push on the back which sent her
stumbling forward to fall across the huge divan bed. She
rolled, turning to face him, and saw him divesting
himself of his robes. He wanted her. Oh, how he wanted
her. Even if he thought her a whore, he wanted her.

Without thinking, she sat up to unlace her gaiters,
while she tried to think, to plan, and received another
push which stretched her on her back again. She looked
up at him, huge and demanding, as he knelt above her.
"Creature," he muttered, and pulled her sitting again,
as he sat, cross-legged, and scooped her forward into his
lap. Desperately she knelt in turn, parting her own legs
for his thrust. Survival. No matter what, survival.
"Thing," he said, stroking her hair. "Such beauty, such
wantonness."

He gripped her thighs, and brought her down on him,
and she braced herself for the shock of entry, and felt
only softness, and a terrifying surge of despair through
his fingers into her body. He tore at her, pulling her
buttocks apart, driving his fingers between, bringing
them around in front to squeeze and caress her breasts,

before throwing her away from him with such force that she rolled right across the bed and landed on the floor on the far side.

"Thing!" he screamed, and left the bed to run back into the outer chamber and pick up the rod.

Adela sat up, gasping, knowing that she might have only seconds to live. To think. To understand. Yuan was impotent. Permanently? But he could not be, or he would not have tried to enter her at all. If that was so, if it was caused by age or illness or even sheer desire, then . . .

He stood framed in the doorway, holding the cane in both hands. "I shall *take* you," he said. "If I have to thrust this into your very womb. I shall—"

Adela stood up. "I had supposed you wished to *love* me," she said. "At least first."

He stared at her, and she tensed her muscles, used her own hands, sending them sliding down her body to her pubes, fluffing out the hair, and then slowly drawing them up her sides to her breasts, holding the breasts themselves, up and away from her body, just touching the nipples so that they became hard and pointed. Still holding herself, she walked around the bed and toward him, wishing she could discard gaiters and shoes with a kick. But there was no time for that now, and the heels at least gave her an added three inches of height, so that she matched him. She stood beside him, released herself to hold him instead. "Make love to me, Yuan," she said, feeling him stir beneath her fingers. "I will help you. Make love to me, Yuan. And then do with me as you will."

She listened to the cane striking the floor. Survival. Because she *was* surviving. As she *would* survive, could she but make him come to her.

12

The Plot

Adela made love to him the only way she knew how, the way Charlie had made love to her. She gathered, from the grunts, that Yuan had never used the uppermost position before. But he entered her without difficulty, and climaxed with an enormous surge of power, almost moaning his pleasure. She had been so tense she had been dry, and afraid he would notice, but he did not, nor did he seem aware of the pain he was causing her; she had to bite her lip to stop from crying out. But now it was done. She could only wait, to see if she had gained a victory or not.

He pushed himself off her, lay on his back beside her. "You are a devil," he said. "Are you sure the devil woman is *not* really your mother?" He raised himself on his elbow, looked down on her face. Then he touched her breast, stroking his finger around the nipple before moving down her body to her groin, again to stroke, and sift, so gently. No man had ever touched her like that before. Almost she felt desire.

As he certainly did. "A miracle," he muttered, watching himself. "I could take you again. Youth. There it is. Youth!" He got up, walked to a silken bell cord, pulled it. He did not trouble to dress himself, and she remained, not daring to move, hardly breathing.

A eunuch appeared, bowing low, hands lost in the sleeves of his blouse; he did not look at the bed or the girl. "Prepare the Lotus Apartment," Yuan said. "And send me the woman Pearl."

Pearl? Adela sat up, without intending to. Pearl! Then she was not going to survive, after all. Pearl . . .

Yuan came toward her. "You are as I supposed you would be," he said. "The woman who could give me back my youth, my vigor, my energy. And you are debased and valueless. Is not that the true hand of Fate, to give and to take away in the same movement? She gave me strength and vigor as a young man, courage and brains as I grew older. I used these things to their best advantage. Thus in the course of time I achieved my every ambition. I became master of all China. And in that very moment I began to feel the vital forces seeping away from me. Then I sought you, and lost you. Now I have regained you, and you can be nothing to me, save a bedmate. Not even a concubine. But I need the bedmate, Princess. You may keep your miserable life, for a while."

"And I am grateful, mighty Yuan," Adela said. "But . . . I knew a woman named Pearl once. In Feng's encampment."

"This is the same woman."

"Then if you give me to her, great Yuan, I shall be dead within the hour."

Yuan smiled. "Because she hates you? Oh, she hates you more than you know, Princess. She has *cause* to hate you. But that is good. She will watch over you, and because she hates you so, she will not succumb to your charm. But she will not harm you." He reached for her again, grasping her arm to bring her against him, holding her close so that she could feel him, and he could feel her. "You will live, Princess. Do not suppose I have forgiven your crime against me. Do not suppose I shall ever do that. Do not suppose that when I decide to take your head you will not suffer the full extent of the wrath of Yuan Shih-k'ai. But you will live for a while. As long as you continue to give me pleasure and make me feel young. Now, go with Pearl."

The door was open, and Pearl stood there. Pearl? Adela knew immediately that it *was* the woman from Feng's encampment. The figure was the same, as was the hair, and the way of standing. But the face . . .

"I had her face stamped on," Yuan said. "I believe both her jaws were broken, and other things besides. But they have healed, even if perhaps not as she might have wished. You remember the Princess Adela, Pearl? The cause of your punishment?"

Pearl inhaled; it was impossible to discern any change of expression in the distorted mask of a face, but the eyes gleamed.

"She has returned to live with us," Yuan explained. "I would place her in your care. Your care, Pearl. Should anything happen to the princess, your head will be removed, following sundry other parts of your body. Remember this. You will guard her at all times, and from herself, as well. But, Pearl," he said, his voice dropping to little more than a whisper, "she is mine. Not yours. Forget this at your peril."

Pearl bowed, straightened, and waited.

Adela glanced at Yuan. Was this some new form of torture?

He smiled at her. "You may go with her, Princess. She will not harm you. And if she attemps to do so, you have but to tell me. Bring her to me again tomorrow, Pearl. After the noon hour, when a man is at his strongest. Bring her to me then, prepared for bed."

Again Pearl bowed. Adela hesitated a last time, and then stepped into the outer chamber. Here the eunuchs were again gathered, and now they were staring at her. But she had survived. She would survive. As the Princess Adela. Certainly she could not afford to be afraid either of Pearl or of the eunuchs.

She listened to Yuan's door close. "Did he take your tongue as well?" she demanded. "Can you not speak?"

"I can speak," Pearl said, her voice low.

"Then tell one of these creatures to find me something to wear. Do you expect me to walk the corridors of this palace naked? My body belongs to the marshal and may be seen by no other *man.*"

Pearl hesitated, then took off her own robe, wrapped it around Adela's shoulders. As usual, she wore nothing underneath, but did not seem embarrassed. Her body had been quite untouched, although it might have filled out a little. Which made the horror of her face the more tragic. But now was not the moment to feel sorry for Pearl. "This way," the woman said, and led Adela from the throne chamber, past a succession of guards, and these were whole men, whose eyes gloomed at them in the flickering candlelight, but whose heads never turned. At the end of the corridor there were four more guards, and now also an officer. "This is the Princess Adela," Pearl said. "Look well on her face, Captain Chen Fu. She will use the Lotus Apartment, and I will remain there with her. You understand, Chen Fu, that the princess is the woman of the marshal himself, at this *moment.*" For just a second her voice seeped into contempt. "She is not to be allowed to leave her apartment for *any* reason, unless accompanied by me. You understand this?"

The captain nodded and saluted. Adela glanced at him, and found him staring at her with an almost physical intensity. His gaze reminded her of Osborne's when they had first met in Hong Kong, or of Lin-tu's—save that there was no *physical* embarrassment involved. So, was he committing her to memory? Or could he appreciate her beauty? But somehow she felt that he was looking beyond the flesh and bones. Looking for what?

And did it matter? She reflected that it well might. She could use all the friends she could obtain, supposing she could obtain any at all. This man—Chen Fu, Pearl had called him—was young and powerfully built, with a strong, broad Chinese face and intelligent eyes. The eyes which would look inside her head? And he was a captain in the palace guard.

As if it mattered. Because he *was* a captain in the palace guard, he was undoubtedly entirely loyal to Yuan. And she was in the care of Pearl, who was holding the door open for her and waiting. She drew a long breath and stepped inside, and listened to the door closing. She was alone with Feng's creature.

Who now also belonged to Yuan.

"You wish to bathe?" Pearl asked.

"Yes," Adela said. "I would like to bathe."

"I will summon a eunuch."

"No," Adela said. "I do not wish a eunuch. You prepare the bath."

Pearl regarded her for several seconds and then opened an inner doorway and descended several steps into the bathing room. Adela took the opportunity to look around. Here was luxury. She stood in a large room filled with brocade-covered divans and draperies over the windows; the windows themselves looked out onto an inner garden—and were barred. As if that mattered, where she was so securely interred, anyway.

Not even Lin-tu would be able to extricate her from this prison—supposing he even knew where to look. Or wanted to look.

But as prisons went, there could be none finer in the land. The room was lit by several lanterns, each hissing as it consumed its own small gas bottle. Presumably the desirability of either laying gas mains throughout the Forbidden City or installing electricity had proved too daunting a concept even for Yuan. In the flickering light she looked at herself in the brass-framed mirrors that dotted the walls, was surprised at the calmness of her face; her hair had now entirely collapsed and drooped past her shoulders. And Pearl being the taller woman, the robe was bunched where she held it at her hips; she was surprised to discover that she still wore her gaiters and boots. The various things that had happened to her today seemed to bear no relationship to the essential fact of her *being.*

She opened another door, went into a bedroom, her ears filled with the sound of running water. The bedroom was on a similar scale to the reception room, save that in place of several divans there was a single huge divan bed in the center of the room. *One* bed, for two women? There was also a desk, with paper and pens, and again windows, opening onto the garden, and several priceless rugs on the floor.

"Your bath is ready." Pearl stood in the doorway.

Adela shrugged the robe from her shoulders, sat on the bed to unlace her gaiters, unbutton her shoes.

"Shall I assist you?" Pearl asked.

"You shall not *touch* me," Adela told her.

Pearl turned away, drew the drapery from in front of the hanging wardrobe in the corner. "Tomorrow I will fill this with gowns for you," she said. "That you may be even more beautiful when the marshal sends for you."

Was she making advances? Because here could be an even more valuable potential friend than the captain of the guard. If she could ever be trusted. Adela stood up, walked into the bathing room, down the steps, and thence into the pool. The water was just hot enough to tingle her flesh. That flesh that should by now have been hanging from her bones in bloodstained tatters. Had she been lucky? Or did she have the gift of survival in her beauty and her courage?

Pearl stood above her, a cake of soap in her hands. "Do you not wish to wash away the marshal?" She also came down the steps into the water. Adela hesitated. The woman repelled her, and she did not doubt her hate. But if she *was* going to survive until Constance could rescue her, she would need all the help she could get.

"Yes," she said. "I wish to be washed."

Pearl stood beside her as she floated on her back, soaped her feet. The tortured eyes gleamed as she stroked the flesh she so longed to possess. "Is it true," she said, "that you have satisfied the marshal? Can that be so?"

Adela had allowed her eyes to close, so that she would not have to look at the ghastly face, and so that she could reveal no hint of pleasure; Pearl's hands were soft and expert, and she knew where to put them, even more than a eunuch. Adela Wynne, she thought, what are you *becoming*? But here was the chance of knowledge. "Should I not?" she asked.

Pearl came to her head, soaped her shoulders and armpits, gradually increasing the movements to stroke over the breasts. "It has been said few women do this, nowadays."

Adela put down her feet and stood up. "Why? Is he ill?"

"Perhaps," Pearl said. "It is said that he passes water more often than most men."

Adela frowned as she searched her memory for whatever scant medical knowledge she had gained from listening to Frank and Constance talking about various acquaintances. Yuan must have a kidney problem. Would that also involve impotence? She didn't know. But she did know that a kidney problem seldom got better without rapid and urgent attention. "Does he see doctors?" she asked.

"Why should he?" Pearl asked. "He is not ill. Merely old."

Adela did some more thinking. The marshal was fifty-three. If *she* thought that was an unimaginable age, she knew it wasn't actually, in terms of health and strength, and sexual vigor. Then he had to be ill, and even more ill than she might suppose. Therefore her time might be even more limited than she supposed. Would his death mean her salvation? Or would he not command her execution before he drew his last breath? That was the more likely. Thoughts, plans . . . Pearl's hands slipped around her buttocks and between her legs; the Chinese woman was kneeling. Instinctively Adela slapped her away, with such force that Pearl fell over into the water, losing her balance and ducking her head. She emerged a moment later, spluttering, her hair soaked. Adela retreated to the edge of the bath, anticipating a physical assault, the woman's eyes were so vicious.

But after a moment Pearl smiled, the most ghastly sight Adela had seen throughout this ghastly day. "The marshal is old," she said. "He can no longer respond as a young man. Thus he has sent all his women away, for fear of shame. Two he has even had beheaded for laughing at his impotence. You were fortunate tonight, Princess. It will not always be so. When you fail him, and he is angry, I will ask him to give you to *me*. That will not be very long now."

Not very long, Adela thought. She was exhausted, and her nerves had been stretched to the breaking point more than once this day. Oh, Constance, she thought. Where *are* you?

"Mr. Wynne." Mr. Glenning shook hands. "Mrs. Wynne. You and I ain't ever met, Mr. Wynne. But I've heard a lot about you from your wife." He grinned at Constance, took out a new cigar, bit the end, spit, and struck a match. "So you've got clout."

"Have you got *news*?" Constance asked.

"Some. None of it all that good. I was asked to call you in by the American minister in Peking. He wrote me this letter, see? Seems he and this friend of yours, Richards, the British consul, went along to see this James Osborne together."

"They saw Osborne? But then surely . . ."

"I'm telling you, Mrs. Wynne. This Osborne is editing this here newspaper, they say. The *China Gazette*. So they asked after the health of his wife, and he said she was fine. So they asked if they could meet with her, and he said she was visiting friends in the country."

"But that was obviously a lie," Constance said.

"Maybe. I reckon they felt so. Here, maybe you'd better read the letter."

He held it out, and Constance seized it, scanned it rapidly, slowing when she reached the relevant part:

I have no doubt at all, and neither does Mr. Richards, that this gentleman was lying. But there was more than that. He gave the impression of a man under an immense strain—physical as well as mental strain. His chair was padded with the softest cushions, and yet he moved constantly, as if he suffered some most painful skin complaint.

He found it difficult to meet our eyes, as well. Now, Mr. Richards informs me that he understands the man is addicted to opium, but I am bound to say that I felt he was even more unstable physically and mentally than could be accounted for by opium use.

"Oh, my God," Constance said, and passed the sheet to Frank.

Both Mr. Richards and I, having concluded that all was not as it appeared when Mr. Osborne landed in Tientsin, although I would hasten to stress that *everyone* who saw her on the occasion, not only Mr. Richards, was convinced she was a very happily married young woman, and having ascertained from eyewitnesses that when the young lady arrived at Hachiapo she was met by an official escort and taken straight into the Forbidden City, this being the last time any reliable witness has laid eyes on her, we determined that Mr. Osborne should be *made* to produce his wife, if necessary by legal process. It was then that we made a most serious discovery. Mr. Richards, acting in his official capacity as representative of the British government, was prepared to bring the heaviest possible pressure to bear on Mr. Osborne, as being subject to British law, and in addition, he anticipated being able to use Mr. Osborne's family connections to influence him. When he attempted to do so, however, he learned that Mr. Osborne *has* no family connections of any importance in England, that he is not related to *any* member of the British artistocracy, and that any wealth he may have displayed during his sojourn in San Francisco was clearly provided by the Chinese government. Mr. Osborne is, in fact, no longer even a British subject, and has not been for some time; he has become a Chinese citizen.

"Oh, my *God*!" Constance cried. Frank took the sheet from her fingers.

This obviously placed him beyond our jurisdiction. Our only hope then lay with the marshal himself, and to this end we sought, and finally obtained, an interview, after a delay, I may say, of several weeks. And achieved nothing, I am sorry to add. Marshal Yuan acknowledged that he knew the young lady, that she was married to the editor of his newspaper, and that he presumed she was living in happy matrimony with her husband. When we intimated that we knew she had entered the Forbidden City on the night of her arrival last year, he agreed that this was so, and told us that he had entertained the happy couple at dinner. Since then, he said, he had not seen Mrs. Osborne, nor had he expected to, because, as he further said, with some suggestion of criticism, in China men do not make inquiries after other men's wives, or attempt in any way to interfere with the domestic arrangements of other men. We were then dismissed. I am terribly afraid that I am bound to suspect, in all the circumstances, that having regard to the fact that we have kept Osborne's house and person under surveillance and have never been able to obtain a single report of Mrs. Osborne being seen by anyone, that after entering the Forbidden City last August, she must have remained there. In what capacity, or even if still alive, we are unable to say, but we are bound to draw the most gloomy conclusions in view of the facts presented to us by Mrs. Wynne. Unfortunately, there is absolutely nothing we can do about it until we can discover some proof as to the young lady's whereabouts, or her fate. I leave it to you to put these sad facts to Mrs. Wynne in the best possible manner. . . .

Constance raised her head, and Glenning shrugged and flicked ash. "Well, Mrs. Wynne, I reckon you're a big girl now. This half-breed of yours sure got herself into one hell of a mess."

Constance had a tremendous urge to slap his face.

"So that's it," Glenning said. "Who knows, maybe she'll turn up one of these days, smiling."

Frank had finished the letter. "Yes," he said. "We won't thank you for your efforts, Glenning, because you didn't make any. Good day to you."

He held Constance's arm and escorted her down the stairs. "That poor child," he said. "I sometimes wonder if she wasn't doomed from birth, just as her mother must have been doomed from birth."

"Oh, Frank," she said. And sighed. "I must write to Charlie."

"What for? Do you think he'll come back? You can't tell him anything he doesn't already fear and suspect. Anyway, you don't even know where he is. You know, I have a damned good mind to go to China as well, and join up with Sun. If I thought he had any hope in hell . . ."

"Frank," she said, holding him tight as they reached the street door, "Adela is gone. Charlie is gone. We don't know if he'll ever come back. You can't leave me too, Frank. You can't."

He looked down at her and smiled. "I know that," he said. "But . . . by God, I hope Sun does succeed in raising an army and beating the hell out of Yuan. God, how I hope that."

* * *

"Mighty Yuan awaits you." Pearl stood behind the chair in which Adela sat enjoying the morning sunshine while she sketched the flowers in her private garden. This garden, her apartment, and Yuan's were her entire world, and had been for six months. But this morning she raised her head in concerned surprise—it was only nine o'clock in the morning.

In many ways it had been a curious six months. She had begun them in full acceptance that her life hung by a thread—or in her case, an erection. Throughout all the succession of mental and physical blows which had been directed at her in those early days, she had known only the determination to survive, and live each moment as it came. Tomorrow could only be considered when the sun actually rose. And the thought that she, a Manchu princess, was daily ministering to the sexual needs of a Chinese soldier of fortune was not to be considered at all, any more than was the growing certainty that Yuan was not sane.

Those early feelings had gradually dissipated. It would not in any event have been possible to sustain such a level of mental preparedness for disaster over so long a time. But in addition she had the evidence of her own eyes that it was not necessary. She did not succeed every time she went to Yuan's bed. He despised the "missionary position" and would too often attempt to take her as a Chinese should, sitting in his lap, or kneeling before him, or even attempting some more exotic means of entry, and rarely could manage any of those. Yet there had been no more terrifying outbursts of despairing rage. He knew that, with her to help him, he *would* succeed, eventually, one way or another; she was always prepared to use her fingers to relieve him, when it became absolutely necessary. And *he* would not leave her body alone. Sometimes he hurt her; she often thought he only with difficulty kept a strongly sadistic streak in his nature under control. But more often he caressed her, although she felt nothing. Nor did she want more. If she was no more than a laborer in the field of his desires, she was content that this should be so. The thought of sinking into contented sexual domesticity with a man like Yuan was horrifying.

Because she sometimes thought that Destiny, having allowed her to dream, had decided merely to laugh at her.

Because she was as truly married to Yuan as if Charlie, her own feelings, Constance, and the revolution had never occurred, as if Constance's acceptance of his proposal had been genuine and they had been married the next day. Certainly she knew that since her arrival in the Forbidden City no other woman had visited his bed. Not only did he tell her this himself, but she knew he could not possibly sustain any other relationship, as he sent for her every day, if, on occasion, only to look at. Thus immediate fear had vanished from her life.

And in its place had come what she had always *most* feared: the deadening dullness of life in the Forbidden City, a gray future which stretched before her into her old age. Six months, and no word from the outside world. She did not suppose she *would* hear a word until the rescuing army burst through the gates, but was it ever going to come? Surely if there was even the slightest storm cloud gathering about her abduction, Yuan would know it by now, and in some way reveal its presence to her. But he only talked about the incompetence and insolence of the various viceroys, all anxious only to feather their own nests, all still opposed to the concept of a revival of the empire. This remained his dream, and it was an end to which he was constantly working, she knew, by persuasion and bribery where possible, but equally by assassination when someone powerful enough to be important proved beyond the reach of venality. Certainly he feared nothing from any Western interference in his affairs, although he occasionally muttered about outrageous Japanese demands.

So she had been forgotten. No doubt Constance had shed a tear. But Adela had always been more a source of trouble and expense to the Wynnes than happiness, so she did not suppose there would be many tears.

And thus she must live, and love, and dwindle. Just as she was reaching adulthood, and reaching, too, more beauty than ever before. She knew this by looking into her mirror. In a few more months she would be nineteen, and her figure was at last filling out, to an American rather than a Chinese ideal. Her breasts had grown, her thighs had widened just a little, her pubic hair had thickened, again in a most un-Oriental fashion —it never ceased to fascinate her master. And had her brain similarly matured? This she could not tell, because she was never allowed to use it, save to devise new means of satisfying Yuan. She could think of no way of escaping this place. And now she knew her first estimate that perhaps Yuan might have a terminal illness had been hopelessly optimistic. She did not think he was totally well. There was an acidity on his breath, an occasional slowness to his movements, as if he suffered internal pain. But he was nowhere near death, that was certain.

And thus she was nowhere near release. Supposing his death would bring her that.

She *did* have ideas, from time to time, about possible salvation. But any ideas she might have depended upon Pearl, because Pearl never left her side for a moment. They even shared the bed. But it was a big enough bed for them not to have to touch, and Pearl never made advances because she was also working to a patient plan, the plan she had outlined that first night. Pearl wanted the beautiful princess for her own, however briefly. This was certainly partly to satisfy her homosexual desires, Adela did not doubt. But she knew it was also a desire to be able to alleviate the sadistic wish for revenge which ran through that tortured brain. In the beginning, having to live in the utmost intimacy with such a depraved creature had seemed the worst of all possible tortures, although she had quickly observed, with interest as well as relief, that Pearl had either abandoned or been forced to abandon the opium habit. Now Adela knew that without Pearl she would have gone mad long ago. Pearl at least kept her senses ever sharp, ever aware, and Pearl was content to wait for Yuan to weary of her.

But recently Pearl had shown signs of becoming confused, and worried, and uncertain, because Yuan was *not* wearying of her. Pearl, Adela thought, was just about there for the taking—when she could think of an adequate reason for doing so. Because Pearl, if the linchpin of any escape plan, would also, if she were ever to be used as an ally, have to be accepted as what she was, in her entirety, and would have to be won in every aspect of her personality. It was a hideous thought, and could only be linked to a positive step toward her own freedom, her own survival. She had not yet been able to discover the possibility of such a step. Because she had not recently had to fear the existence of sufficient danger.

Until now? For Yuan had never before sent for her in the morning.

And he had never sent for her at all before without wishing sex. Yet today he was totally dressed in his khaki uniform and carried sword and revolver. "We are to be separated, Princess," he announced jovially. "For just a little while."

Adela, busily bowing as low as she could—she had persistently refused to kowtow to him—straightened more quickly than usual. "Separated, great Yuan?"

"I have a small matter to attend to in the South," Yuan said. "Do you remember the name Sun Yat-sen?"

"Indeed I do, great Yuan."

"You may recall that I sent him abroad as an ambassador, while retaining some of his people here as hostages for his good behavior. Well, he has betrayed me, as usual. And most of his people have escaped me as well. Lin-tu escaped me first," he added broodingly. "Him I regret. The others . . . I suppose I did not take them, or Sun, for that matter, seriously enough." He smiled. "I still find it difficult to take that absurd figure seriously. But he is back in China, and once again lurking in the Ta Shan with an army. Or what he pleases to call an army. I have ordered the concentration of *my* army on Shao-Kuan, and now to go to join it."

Sun was back, and in arms. There was to be a civil war! Her brain teemed.

"It will not take long to disperse this rabble, I promise you," Yuan said. "But this time I mean to complete what I should have done two years ago. I will stamp this *little* man into the ground, together with all his little followers. Oh, not their heads. I shall keep *them,* to mount on our gates. All except one. Because there is one head in particular I intend to bring back here with me and lay at your feet."

She stared at him, holding her breath. Lin-tu?

"Are you not curious, Princess?" Yuan asked. "Word has come to me that Sun has several Europeans and Americans marching with him. And among them is one Charles Baird."

Adela gasped.

"His head I shall remove with my own sword, Princess," Yuan said. "After I have attended to his genitals and his nose and ears and tongue and eyes. All of these I shall lay before you, Princess. You have my promise."

Oh, my God, she thought. Charlie! But Charlie, fighting with Sun? That could mean only one thing. He wished to rescue *her*, or at least avenge her death. Charlie! Oh, dear, sweet Charlie, But now . . . She discovered that Yuan was still speaking, and was indeed stretching out his hand to hold her chin and raise her face to look into her eyes.

"And then, I think, I will cut off your head as well, sweet Princess, and hang both of you together over my gate."

"My . . ." She panted for breath, from sheer shock at the casual way in which he had condemned her. "Do I not please you, mighty Yuan?"

"Oh, you please me, Princess. But a man cannot live by pleasure alone. Besides, now I know that any woman *can* please me, supposing she is voluptuous enough and wanton enough. Do not presume you are unique as a *woman*, Princess. Once, perhaps . . . once I dreamed that you would give me a son, a son to inherit this great empire from me. Had you done that, I might even have forgiven you your crimes, great though those are. But you have not done so. Because secretly you hate me. Oh, I know this. I can see it in your eyes when you suppose yourself unobserved. So you see, you have failed me, and I have no doubt you would also betray me, given the opportunity. I need you, for my manhood. But can you doubt that somewhere in this vast land I shall find a girl as lovely as you, as voluptuous as you, as willing as you, and more faithful than you, even if she may lack royal blood? *I* do not doubt that, Princess. I have given orders that such a search shall begin immediately, that each viceroy will select the two most beautiful *virgins* in his province and send them to Peking for my inspection. They will be waiting for me when I return from my campaign, and I will make my choice. Who knows . . ." He laughed. "I may keep them all. So look forward to my return, Princess. I will let you help me choose. And then I will put an end to the misery I know you suffer whenever you come to my bed. You will never know misery again." He waved his hand. "Now, go. Enjoy these last few weeks that lie before you. Share them with *Pearl*. She will enjoy that too."

Adela found herself in the private corridor leading to the Lotus Apartment. Pearl no longer wasted the time to accompany her to and from the marshal. There was no way she could escape the guards.

How had she got here? Had she run, or staggered? Or crawled? She was breathless, and her entire body felt weak, as if she had been fed some debilitating drug. After all she had survived, she had just received a sentence of death, delivered with the exquisite mental torture of making her know that she must wait, and wait, with every second of every day bringing the headsman closer. After all, she had never deceived him for a moment with her pretended love. He had used her, because he had needed her. Now he *was* growing tired of her. After all.

She looked left and right, at the walls, at the guards. She felt like a trapped beast in this labyrinth, surrounded by guards. She wanted to throw herself on the floor and wail and tear her hair and *scream* with sheer despair. To have survived so *much*, and yet to have failed at the end of it.

And she could not even give way to her feelings, but

must walk down the corridor as proudly as ever, head held high, to where Captain Chen was opening the door to her apartment for her, as he always did, his eyes fixed on her. They had seen each other every day for six months, and with every day his admiration had surrounded her as she came to her door. Yuan's creature, as yet unaware that his master had condemned this beautiful object to the dung heap.

But these men were Yuan's personal bodyguard. And Yuan was going to war. So there might be others coming to replace them, less loyal, less faithful, less . . . even through her despair and her misery, her brain, as usual in times of danger, was starting to race with crystal clarity, to dream and to plan. She could not just lie in her bed for six weeks counting the hours to her death.

She stopped beside the young captain. "The marshal goes to war," she remarked. "Do you not accompany him?"

It was the first time she had ever addressed him, and for a moment he was too surprised to reply. Then he stood to attention. "I am commanded to remain here," he said. "My lady Princess."

"And what will you do, should the marshal not return?" The question was a shot in the dark, an emanation of another wave of despair at the thought that she would not, after all, have anything to hope for from less loyal soldiers.

Captain Chen gazed at her for several seconds. Then he said, "The marshal will return. The marshal always returns. There is no hand in China that can bring down the *marshal.*"

But she realized there was no admiration in his tone to match his words. Rather she detected contempt. Even anger. Could this man, responsible for security in the very heart of the palace, also hate Yuan, like Pearl, like

herself? Or like Osborne, she thought. But like
Osborne, he continued to serve his master with the
utmost fidelity. Because he feared him more than he
hated him?

But he also admired her. As a princess, or as a
woman? She discovered her heart was pounding almost
painfully, and gazed at him for several more seconds.
"Even the marshal is mortal," she said softly, and
stepped past him into the room.

"Is it true?" Pearl asked. "That the marshal goes to
war?"

"Against rebels in the South, yes," Adela said. She
listened to the door closing behind her. Her brain was
seething so that it seemed about to burst. But now the
despair was being replaced with a bubbling anger, an
almost exhilarated desire to avenge herself, to do anything that could possibly hurt Yuan. She had been condemned to death, at his leisure. For failing to give him a
son. How could a decrepit wreck of a man like that ever
have a son?

She walked across the room, into her bedroom, and
sat at her desk staring at the wall. Survival! She had
made this her watchword, and in that name had been
prepared to undertake any task. To lie down and bewail
her fate now, while waiting for that fate in supine
terror, would be a betrayal of everything she valued in
herself. And having done so much, stooped so low, to
survive in the past, could there be *anything* she would
not now do? She had thought that once before, when
she and Constance and Charlie had begun their escape
from Peking—and thus had shot a man. Well, if she
were given the opportunity to escape this place, would
she not shoot again, as many men as she had to?

"Lady is thoughtful," Pearl observed from the doorway.

So think, Adela told herself. Survival. No matter what the cost. Because there was only one way now that Yuan would ever allow her to live. The thought was horrific, utterly distasteful; when she considered what would be involved, it made her want to vomit. Nor did she even know if it could work. But if she *were* to survive, then it was the only way.

Would she *want* to survive, after Charlie's head had been thrown at her feet? Because that was certainly a possibility. Gallant Charlie, who after all would risk his life in an attempt to avenge her. Yes, she thought; as he would avenge me, so will I avenge him. Because Sun, or Sun's ideas, were obviously never to be eliminated from South China. They were ideas personally abhorrent to her, going against everything she had been educated to believe in, but they would eventually bring Yuan down, as they had brought down the dynasty. She had to live for that day, even after Charlie's death, even after his head had been thrown at her feet, that she might one day watch Yuan also die. That she might twist his love for her, his need for her, and for his son, in his heart for as long as he was alive.

Thus all else was irrelevant, immaterial beside such a goal. Save that there were tools to be used, conquests necessarily to be gained if she were even to begin her journey.

And the first weapon to be shaped and taken for her use had to be Pearl.

"Yes," she said, and turned to look at the woman. "I have much to think about, Pearl. I have maligned you."

Pearl frowned suspiciously.

"I have always considered you the marshal's creature," Adela went on, getting up and shrugging off her gown; like Pearl herself, she had taken up wearing nothing underneath, because she went only to and from the marshal's apartment or into her private garden. Because she saw only the eunuchs and the guards. And Pearl. And Captain Chen Fu. She discovered her heart was throbbing as she stepped out of her slippers and lay down on her bed, one arm under her head, one leg up. It was a pose which never failed to attract Yuan. Because she must now only do what she had to do; she must *want* to do it, so that no suspicion of subterfuge could be aroused.

After six months of nothing but Yuan, would she *not* want that, anyway? With whom was irrelevant.

"Now I know that you are as much his prisoner, his victim, as I," she said carelessly.

Pearl came closer, gazing at her.

"We have both just been condemned to death," Adela said, staring at the ceiling. Yuan had been on the point of leaving the Forbidden City to ride south, and their conversation had been a private one. There was no way Pearl could check her version of what had been said.

Pearl took a sharp breath. "That cannot be," she said. "I have always been faithful to him. No matter what he has done to me, I have been faithful to him."

"He does not think so," Adela told her. "We are to die together, horribly, when he returns from his campaign. We are to be thrown on a dung heap together, after mutilation. He says he will leave us our tongues, so that we may encourage each other as the dogs drink our blood."

She thought she had done that rather well. Certainly Pearl did not doubt her; she clasped both hands around her own throat in horror.

"And do you know why?" Adela asked. "It is because I have not become pregnant. He blames you for that, too. He thinks you have prevented it, by douches or even by witchcraft, out of hatred for him. Oh, I know he is not rational. But he has the power to do what he chooses.''

Pearl inhaled, a rasping sound. "How can *Yuan* be a father?" she asked.

"I agree with you." Adela rolled on her side and rose on her elbow, aware that her breasts were now displayed to their best advantage, that her legs were spread with entrancing lissomeness. "Yet, if we are to live, I must become pregnant."

There was no reply for several seconds, but Pearl's face was so ruined it was difficult to discern changes of expression. At last she said, "You are mad. If Yuan were to find out . . ."

"Can he do worse than what he already intends?" Adela asked.

Slowly Pearl lowered herself to sit on the bed. "You seek to destroy me," she said. "It is a trick."

"How can I destroy you, without destroying myself," Adela asked, "since *I* will be the one actually betraying the marshal? Do you not know that I am aware of the risks we run? Do you think I *wish* to do this thing? Do you not suppose my belly rolls with horror at the thought of it? Do you suppose I wish the embrace of any *man*?" She continued to stare at the woman. "I seek to live. And if I live, so will you. If I die, then you die beside me. Why do you not come and lie here, with your head on my shoulder, so that we may plan?"

Pearl did not move. "And after?"

"I have said, while I live, you will live, Pearl. If I can give the marshal a son, then all things may be possible. For you as well as for me. I bear you no ill will, Pearl. I have grown to love you during these six months. And more than that, I need you, now, and will need you always. You will possess my most intimate secrets. How can *I* ever betray *you*?"

Pearl hesitated a few moments longer; then she stood up, allowed her gown to fall to the floor, knelt on the bed. Slowly she allowed her body to droop forward until she was lying alongside Adela, while her hand reached out, still hesitantly, to touch the breast, expecting to be rebuffed, anxious to possess it for her own.

And so much more. Adela closed her eyes as Pearl came closer. Survival. Only survival.

"And what of the man?" Pearl asked. "Where will you find *him*?"

Adela thought of the man. Because he was more important than ever now. "Outside that door," she said.

13

The Mother

"Come quickly," Pearl said. "The lady princess has fallen and hurt herself."

Captain Chen Fu snapped to attention. "You and you," he called his guards.

"We do not need *them,*" Pearl said contemptuously. "Cannot you alone lift the princess? Do you suppose she wishes these coolies to touch her?"

Chen hesitated. "I will send for the eunuchs."

"You will come with me *now,*" Pearl said.

Chen hesitated for a last second, then ran behind her into the Lotus Apartment, across the outer room, and down the steps into the garden, where Adela lay on her side, twisting and moaning in agony. "My hip," she gasped. "Oh, my hip." Her hair was flailing to and fro across her face.

"Carry her up to her bed," Pearl commanded. "But be careful."

The young man bit his lip as he stooped, and with the greatest of caution attempted to insert his hand under Adela's shoulders, endeavoring without success to avoid her breasts as she rolled to and fro. With his other hand he reached for her knees, and checked when she gave a shriek of agony.

"Fool!" Pearl snapped. "Will you make the injury worse? You must lift from around her thighs. I will hold her ankles to keep her legs straight."

Very carefully, still biting his lip, Chen Fu raised Adela from the ground, while Pearl held her feet. Adela moaned and writhed against him, but he carried her up the stairs and into her bedroom, laid her on the bed. She continued to twist and groan. "I will fetch a surgeon," he said.

"That will not be necessary," Pearl said. "Do you not suppose I understand what to do? It is not serious. There is nothing broken, I do not think. But we must make sure. She will undoubtedly fight me when I touch her, she is in such pain. You hold her legs."

"We should summon a eunuch," Chen said unhappily.

"*Do* it," Pearl said. "If there is a dislocation, it must be pulled out now."

She knelt on the bed beside Adela, waited for Chen also to kneel and hold the flailing ankles, then opened the robe. Adela could hear Chen's sudden inhalation of breath; she was lying on her back and he was gazing the length of her legs at her naked groin. What she was doing was frightening. But it had to be *done*. There could be no hesitation now.

"Do not let go," Pearl shouted. "It is a dislocation, as I thought. Now, pull with all your strength. The left leg. I will press the bone back into place."

Chen obeyed, still staring at the body before him. He pulled so hard indeed that Adela supposed her hip *was* about to be dislocated, and when she screamed in discomfort it was not altogether playacting.

"There," Pearl gasped. "It is done. Do not let go.

Slide your hands up her leg until you can hold her hip while I fetch some cold towels. She may put it out again with a kick. Careful, now."

Adela attempted to roll to and fro, felt herself restrained by Chen's strong hands moving up her calf and thigh, to grasp her hip, pressing it down against her pelvis.

"Keep her like that," Pearl commanded. "I will be as quick as I can."

She left the room. Chen stared at Adela as she slowly stopped writhing, and lay still, allowing her eyes to flop open and then widen in consternation as she looked down at herself and then at the man.

"I . . . I obey the lady Pearl," he stammered.

"You must forget everything you see," she gasped; she was certainly out of breath.

"I would not have had it so, my lady Princess," he said, also panting. "But my lady Pearl . . . I am compromised."

Adela smiled. "Not so, Captain. Your secret is safe with me. And you were assisting me when I was in great pain. I shall never forget how much I owe you. Kiss my hand."

He released her hip, moved closer, raised her fingers, and kissed the knuckles.

"As I shall tell no one, so should you keep our secret, Captain," she said.

He bowed, and glanced at the doorway, but Pearl had not yet returned.

Adela continued to smile. "You may leave me now, Captain. The pain has ceased and I shall lie still. But remember, keep our secret."

"You were alone with him, naked . . . and you sent him *away*?" Pearl was disgusted. "I was not going to return for at least half an hour."

Adela pushed herself into a sitting position. "When one has hooked a fish, does one leap into the sea beside it?" she demanded.

Pearl gazed at her and then sat beside her. "You plan deeply, Princess. You are a remarkable woman. You are a great treasure to me."

Adela looked into her eyes. "As you are to me, Pearl," she said, and held open her arms for an embrace. Perhaps she was not altogether lying. She could not *afford* to lie, because Pearl certainly was shrewd enough, as she was habitually suspicious enough, to penetrate any dishonesty. But to act the part, wholly and without restraint, was not difficult. It had never been difficult. Because Pearl, the poor, shattered woman, so desperately wanted a friend, an intimate, someone to trust . . . and someone to love. As did she? She suspected that might be equally true of herself. She had never possessed an intimate in her life. It had been impossible to seek such a friendship with any of the girls at Miss Evesham's Academy, and she had never had even a passing friendship with anyone her own age in Peking. She had sought such an intimacy with Constance, but of course that could never have worked, and not only because of the difference in their ages, the fact that Constance was her foster mother. She and Constance were too different. They sought different things and reached for different goals.

Thus men. But wherever she had sought to love, she had encountered only disaster. She could tell herself that this was not actually true. She had *sought* to love only one man. He had failed her, but perhaps because, as she had early recognized, he had not yet *been* a man. Now he was prepared to fight, to avenge her death; he would have to suppose her dead.

And now he would die because of that distant love. Because she did not doubt that Yuan would destroy

Sun's rabble. She could pray that Charlie would escape, but even if he did, he would surely then abandon China forever, realizing the hopelessness of his cause. So to her he was already dead.

Lying in Pearl's arms, as now, their naked bodies seeking some mutual haven from the perilous atmosphere with which they were surrounded, she could for the first time truly understand how unhappy her life had been for so long. From the day she had first set foot in Miss Evesham's Academy. Happiness after that had consisted of only fleeting moments. And happiness, true happiness, she doubted she would ever now know. As Lin-tu had once said, she attracted disaster like a steel pole attracts lightning. All because her mother had reached for the stars—and Prince Ksian Fu had stooped to find a diamond in the dust.

Therefore happiness had to be sought on a more mundane scale than she had always hoped. For her it had become the caress of another human being who needed no less than she. That they were both women was irrelevant, just as what Pearl did to her was irrelevant. After Yuan, there could be no feelings of guilt. She needed these moments with Pearl before she could summon the energy again to drive herself onward toward her goal.

Even if her goal amounted to nothing more than survival.

"Tomorrow," she said. "You will bring him to me again."

"I fear I did not have an opportunity properly to thank you yesterday for your assistance, Captain." Adela sat up in bed, her robe discreetly arranged, her hair lying on the pillow behind her shoulders like a shawl.

Captain Chen Fu stood rigidly to attention. "I trust the lady princess is no longer in pain."

"Very little. Thanks to Madam Pearl and yourself."

Chen half-turned his head, as he realized that Pearl had once again left him alone with the princess. "Then I am glad," he said. "As will be Marshal Yuan, no doubt, when he returns. I will leave you now."

"Why?" Adela asked. "Can you not stay awhile and talk with me?"

He frowned. "Talk with you?"

"Even princesses like to talk, Captain," she said. "Please sit down." She patted the bed.

"My lady Princess," he said. "I should not be in your bedchamber at all. Were it ever to become known . . ."

"How can it become known? Do you suppose *I* shall betray your presence? Or the lady Pearl? She is as myself in all things."

"I do not doubt that, my lady Princess. But my men . . ."

"Are they not faithful to you? Besides, do they not know that Pearl is here with us? Do they not know that Pearl is my jailer, that she never leaves my side, and that she hates me? Does not all Peking know these things?"

Chen frowned at her. "That is so," he said thoughtfully. "But you say she is your friend?"

"We have become friends," Adela said. "I would be friends with all of my guards, were it possible. And it is not as if you were with me in the middle of the night, when a man and a woman *might* be suspected of a liaison. You are here when the sun is at its zenith, and with Madam Pearl. Who can suspect you of anything, Captain Chen?"

Chen hesitated, and then sat at the far end of the bed, giving the doorway another quick glance, as if wishing he *were* with Madam Pearl. As an afterthought he removed his cap. "You will forgive me, my lady Princess," he said. "I serve Marshal Yuan . . ."

"And therefore exist on the edge of a knife? Do not we all? But I serve him more than most, Captain. I *know* him more than most. My life is in danger more than most. It is something I must accept, and with which I must live. But do you not suppose I yearn for the company of a man more my own age, more my own spirit?" She drew a long breath. "Even the touch of such a man?"

Perhaps he might not have heard her. "You are a white woman," he stated.

"And thus untouchable?"

"You are also a Manchu princess, an enemy of my people."

"You speak of my family, not of me," she said. "And my family threw me out, from birth, because, as you say, I am white. *I* have never been an enemy of your people. And besides, Captain . . ." Another long breath. "Is not Yuan himself an enemy of your people?"

His head came up.

"I know these things," Adela said. "Does Yuan not seek to create a new empire, a new tyranny? Can you suppose it will be better than the last? Or do you not know it will be far worse? Can you suppose it is what the majority of the Chinese people, *your* people, Chen, really wish? Is this not why Yuan has had to take his army south, to oppose all those who would have done with emperors, for the good of China?" She paused for breath, but also to hold her breath. Now was the moment for him to run from the room and summon guards to bind her and place her in a cell pending the marshal's return, to answer a charge of treason.

But he continued to stare at her. "And I know that you know these things too," she said softly.

Chen stood up. "I must return to my duty."

Adela held out her hand. "Stay, Chen. Stay, and tell me the truth. And know the truth, with me."

He hesitated.

"You accuse me of being an alien, an enemy," she said, still speaking softly. "I am none of those things, Chen. I am a woman who cries out for love. Am I then not to be touched? Why? Because my skin is white, my eyes are blue? Because I am a Manchu? Or because I belong to Yuan? That is the greatest evil that has ever befallen me. And I think it is an evil that has also befallen you."

Still he hesitated, but he had come closer. She could take his hand and squeeze it.

"You dare to utter these things?" he asked. "Do you know what would be done to you, should they reach the marshal's ears?"

"He has told me often enough," she said. "But my desire is greater than my fear." Almost her mind sagged with despair. She had tried everything she knew, save stripping herself naked and wrapping herself around him like a snake. "Am I *that* repulsive to you, Chen?" she whispered.

"Repulsive?" Now he held her hands. "You are the most beautiful woman I have ever seen. The most beautiful woman there can ever have been. But you are as far above me as are the sun and the moon."

"Not so, my dearest Chen," she said, tears of sheer relief welling from her eyes. "Not so. I am flesh and blood, like you, and heart and tears, like a woman. And I would be *beneath* you, in every way. Take me in your arms, sweet Chen, and *love* me as no man has ever done before. For without you, I am nothing. I am dead."

Could it really be her, Adela Wynne, uttering such words? And even meaning them. Because, whether she would or no, they were in the main true. And suddenly here was strength, and power, such as she had never known. Charlie had been almost an accident, unsure of himself, of what he wanted, of what he dared to touch, as if he dared not possess anything. When he had entered her, it had been hesitantly, as if he expected her to cry out and push him away, whether from shame or from pain.

With Yuan there had always been the problem of sustaining an erection long enough for him to be satisfied. Her own feelings had never entered into it.

And Pearl had been only a solace, not a joy.

But here was manhood such as she had never before seen, so huge and towering and dominant she almost cried out *before* he entered her, for fear of injury. And here were other strengths as well. When he sat her on his lap she was entirely sustained by the muscles in his thighs, while his entry was at once gentle and demanding, and he continued into her, farther and farther and farther, all the time working his pelvis to send glowing repercussions through her body, reaching almost to her fingertips. While his hands were the most dominant, the most possessive she had ever known, circling her breasts without holding them, sliding over her hips to grasp her buttocks, and then moving between with the gentlest of fingers, seeking only to heighten *her* pleasure, she realized, even as she also realized she was crying out with joy.

She exploded passion, and clung to him, and was gently laid on her back, and then rolled on her face, and felt herself being pulled up again, by her thighs, until she knelt before him, even if her head remained resting on the pillow. Because he was ready again, and thrusting in, almost before she had caught her breath, and once again he went in and in and in, moving for longer this time, while yet again he drove her through the frontiers of experience.

She lay on her stomach, his lips to her ear. "I worship you, my lady Princess," he said. "To hold you in his arms, a man *would* conquer an empire. Perhaps a world."

She rolled away from him and lay on her back, pulled him toward her, onto her belly, and kissed him, feeling him rising yet again, and entering yet again. "To be loved by *you,*" she whispered, "a woman would risk even the wrath of Yuan."

"He will be on duty by now," Adela said. "It is time."

"Again?" Pearl demanded with disgust. "You are insatiable. Almost, one would suppose you loved this man."

"If I am to become pregnant," Adela explained patiently, "he must enter me every day that I am not actually passing blood, for at least a month."

"They are saying he comes to *me,*" Pearl said, her voice heavy with contempt.

"And is that not what we wish them to say, sweet Pearl?" Adela asked.

Pearl snorted, and went to the door.

Almost, Adela thought, one would suppose I loved this man. That was an absurdity. He was a Chinese, and from even lower on the social scale than Lin-tu, much less Feng or Yuan. He was handsome and strong, and a consummate lover; he gave her more feeling and created more desire within her than she would have thought possible. But she loved Charlie, despite all . . . and because of all, too, as Charlie was prepared to fight for her, and therefore, by definition, die for her as well. As Chen was the most perfect man she had ever encountered, even if she knew nothing about him, about what he believed in or would stand for . . . or would die for.

These things she had to find out, even if finding out was more dangerous than anything else she was risking. "I know that you are aware what Yuan does is wrong," she said. "Yet you serve him. And you must serve him well, or you would not be a captain in the Imperial Guard." She smiled. "Although there is at present no imperium."

He lay on his elbow beside her, passion temporarily spent. In his case, most definitely temporarily. He stroked her hair, and the line of her jaw, and the contour of her neck. Pretenses, these; where his hands always found themselves soon enough, was at her breasts or her groin—which was where she wanted them to be.

"I am a soldier," he said simply. "I have been a soldier since I was fourteen years old."

"And now you are . . . ?"

"I am twenty-two," he said with some pride. Perhaps because he had survived so long as a soldier, she thought.

"And serve Yuan," she said. And when he hesitated, she kissed him. "I wish to know *you,*" she smiled. "How can I know you, unless I know how you think? Of what you think? And why?"

He lay down with his hands beneath his head. "I serve Yuan because there is no one else *to* serve," he said. "He is the greatest warlord in China."

"And you would have him become emperor?"

"The other lords, the great viceroys, will never agree."

"And neither would you?" she persisted.

"I am a soldier. I do not know about these things."

"But you are disturbed by them."

"I am disturbed," he agreed. "There are many dif-

ferent factions at work in Peking. General Chang Hsun
. . . you know of him?''

"I know of him," she said.

"He would restore the Ch'ing," Chen said. And
glanced at her. "But you will approve of that."

Approve, she thought. Chang Hsun, a believer in the
dynasty? And she had never suspected. "I am a believer
in what is best for China," she said. And then knew that
she could not lie to this man. Not more than she had
already lied. "I must wish for the restoration of my
family, Chen. I know that would be better than what
Yuan intends. And I believe the alternative to
Yuan is anarchy. Can you really wish that?''

She was the one on her elbow now, her breasts resting
on his chest. He smiled. "Perhaps I dream, my lady
Princess. Perhaps too many Chinese dream. Because
dreams are all so many Chinese possess, to separate
them from the animals in the field.''

Almost, Adela thought, one would suppose I loved
this man. She lay on his chest and kissed his mouth
while she felt him rise and instinctively enter her as she
spread her legs. Because I *could* love this man. A
Manchu princess and a common soldier.

And she was grossly deceiving him. But then, he
thought he knew her for what she was, a great and noble
lady with too much desire, bored with her elderly master
and lonely now that even that poor solace had been
withdrawn. He was risking a great deal, but no doubt he
had considered the matter and concluded that she dare
not betray him without suffering beside him. He was,
after all, just a man.

But what a man. She had to know, even at risk to
herself. "That day, three weeks ago," she said. "I was
not really hurt. It was a plan devised by Madam Pearl
and myself to bring you in here, to make you fall in love
with me. I wished this," she went on, as he did not

speak, "in order to become pregnant. Because I feared that should I not, Marshal Yuan would weary of me and throw me out." Still not the whole truth. But sufficiently dangerous to confess. She gazed at him. "You understand this?"

Chen's eyes gloomed at her. "No," he said. "It was not necessary to plot to make me fall in love with you. I was already in love with you. I came because I thought you wanted me, whether your accident was true or not."

"I want you now," she said. "More than I have ever wanted anything in the world before."

"But you are not pregnant, so I have failed."

"Who knows," she said, "whether I am pregnant or not? Only time will tell that. But I should be pregnant. You have filled me more than any man, more than I would ever have hoped of any man, had I not known you."

"When Yuan returns, you will wish me no more," he said.

"I will wish you always," she told him. "Will you still come to me when Yuan returns?"

"Would you risk that?"

"To be in your arms, Chen? I would risk that."

He kissed her on the mouth as she had taught him how to kiss. "I came to you," he said, "because to me you were as a goddess, which you are, a princess, which you are—the most marvelous woman I ever saw. I was disappointed at not being able to fight. Because a soldier who does not fight is a nothing. I was angry with the marshal for going to war with Sun Yat-sen instead of dealing with him and trying to build a greater China. I was confused, I think. But most of all, I desired. I had watched you every day for half a year, and I desired you. I dreamed of you every night, and there you were, in my arms. I would die happy, knowing that I had experienced that, knowing that you wanted me, Princess."

A Chinese peasant, who could dream, and think, and hope, and then seek, without fear.

Almost, Adela thought, one would suppose I loved this man.

Captain Chen Fu stood to attention in the doorway of the Lotus Apartment. "The marshal," he announced, "now enters the city. He has sent a messenger ahead, my lady Princess, to command your presence in his private apartment."

He spoke in stilted tones because the door remained open and his guardsmen were waiting outside. Adela and Pearl, surprised at his entry at five in the afternoon, since he had already called upon them before noon, as he usually did, could only stare at him with their mouths open.

"It is reported," Chen went on, "that the marshal has gained a great victory, that the rebels are scattered and destroyed, that he has hung heads over the gates of every city from Canton to Peking. No doubt he seeks your congratulations, my lady Princess."

He gazed at her. Warning her? There was nothing he could warn her against that she was not already braced to encounter, even Charlie's head. But so soon? Yuan had been away barely two months. As he had promised, it had been a brief, triumphant campaign. And now . . . She drew a long breath and nodded. "I thank you, Captain Chen. I will prepare myself."

The doors closed. "Do you think—?" Pearl began.

"I do not know," Adela said. "I cannot think. I can only wait."

"For what? Until the executioner is summoned?"

Pearl asked, her voice brittle. "The plan has failed. You have lain with that mountebank every day for two months, and last month you passed blood as usual. Now . . ."

"Now I am two days late," Adela said.

"Two *days*. That is important?"

"It may be." Adela spoke with a confidence she did not feel as she selected her best gown. She had to be pregnant. She *had* to be. Chen had lain with her, as Pearl had truly said, every possible day. She knew that if she *were* pregnant, she had conceived at least three weeks after the last time Yuan entered her—that is, immediately after her last menstruation. So even that did not necessarily mean her salvation, supposing Yuan ever considered such matters. She would need to twist and turn, to lie and deceive, as much as ever she had in the past. But it was her only hope. No matter what might be waiting for her in Yuan's apartment.

"So you had better hope it *is,*" she told Pearl as the woman brushed her hair. "Or we may both be on the dung heap by dusk."

Chen marched at her side. "I will die for you," he whispered. "Believe this, my lady Princess."

Adela smiled. "I would prefer you lived for me, Captain," she said. "As I shall endeavor to live for *you.*"

The doors opened, and she stepped inside, still smiling, head held high. Even in here she could hear the popping of the firecrackers, the explosions of the rifles, which told of the celebrations in the city. And in this room was not only Yuan himself, beaming and confident, but also Marshal Li Yuan-hung, short and dapper, whom she knew to be his deputy, and also General Chang Hsun, equally smiling. It was the first time she had encountered any of the marshal's aides since first entering the city nearly a year before. Chang

Hsun! she thought. Did he really wish to restore the Manchu?

But now was the time to consider only her own self-preservation. She bowed. "I have heard the most wonderful tidings, great Yuan," she said.

"Of victory," Yuan said.

"We scattered them," Li Yuan-hung said.

"We destroyed them," General Chang said.

"Not sufficiently," Yuan said. "We gained a great victory. We outthought and outfought them. But we did not destroy them. They are still there, in the mountains. These are matters which must be attended to. Which *will* be attended to. But now I must attend to my domestic affairs." He nodded, and the two generals bowed and withdrew. And Yuan sat down. Rather, Adela thought, he fell down on the nearest divan, breathing heavily, face mottled, fingers tugging at his collar.

She hurried to his side. "You are ill, great Yuan."

He pushed her away from him. "Yuan Shih-k'ai is never ill, Princess. I am tired. More tired than I would have thought possible." He sighed, and sat up, rested his chin on his hand, his elbow on his knee, to stare at her. "Your paramour got away. As did Sun himself. There is a poor victory."

Her heart gave a great surge of joy. She had been afraid to ask, afraid even to look around the room too closely in case there had been a ghastly relic waiting for her inspection. "Permit me to be happy for that, great Yuan," she said, deciding to take refuge, as ever, in boldness.

"Happy," he said. "Aye, you would be happy. Can you give me a reason why, having failed to bring his head to you, I should not send your head to him?"

"Because I think that would be a waste, great Yuan," she said quietly.

"You think so?" He got up slowly. "Come." He seized her hand, led her to an inside window that looked down upon a large hallway. "Look there."

Adela gazed at the young women, some thirty of them, whispering and giggling among themselves. She supposed they had to be the thirty loveliest girls in all China.

"Your replacement is there," Yuan said. "Eager and willing. And she will be *pure.*"

Adela lifted her chin at him, looked him in the eyes, and drew a long breath. "But will she also be pregnant, great Yuan?" she asked.

For a moment she thought he had not heard her. Then he turned very slowly. "Pregnant?" he asked. "You? You are *pregnant*?" He frowned at her. "You know this?"

Adela met his gaze. Two days late, she thought. Two days late. She had often been two days late before. But this was, as ever, a matter of survival, if only for a few months longer. "I know this, great Yuan," she said.

He stared at her. "Show me yourself."

Adela stepped out of her robe.

"You do not look pregnant to me," he said.

"I am young, and I have never borne a child before, my lord," she explained. "I will not show for several months as yet. But the child is there. I know it. I can *feel* it." Almost she believed herself. "And I no longer pass blood."

He held her shoulders to stare at her. Then stooped to put his ear against her belly. "A son," he said. "If I could have a son, by a Ch'ing princess . . ."

"I cannot promise a son, great Yuan," Adela said. "It could be a daughter."

"Bah." Yuan straightened. "It will be a son. If it is a

daughter, I will cut off her head. Understand this." He pointed. "I wish a son."

So have I advanced at all? Adela wondered as she bowed. Indeed she had, at least for the immediate future. Suddenly she was no longer quite such a prisoner, was encouraged to seek fresh air—always adequately guarded by eunuchs, of course. But the guards on her door remained men, and were commanded by Chen. And Pearl remained her intimate.

Pearl also remained afraid. Yuan sent physicians to Adela, who examined her, and clucked their tongues, and obviously did not know any more than she did. But they also pampered her. While Yuan could only beam at her. To her very great relief, he no longer summoned her to his bed, he was afraid of hurting the child. To her even greater relief, as well as her gratification, he could not replace her. She knew this, although he would never have confessed it, by his bouts of bad temper, and by the rumors Pearl brought to her that more than one strangled body of a young virgin had been found floating in the canals. No one knew how the girls got there, and Peking was convinced there was a maniac at large.

As indeed there was. Her maniac, she thought, as he sat beside her, fondling her breasts, and professing his love for her. China's maniac. Because his pride, his arrogance, even his intimations of immortality had all grown since his apparently easy victory over Sun's army. Now he conceived all China to be in his hand, and if he was waiting to put forward again the concept of becoming emperor, it was only for the birth of his son.

The thought of his being disappointed in any way made her tremble as much as Pearl. She had certainly missed a period, but it was only one, which had happened before; there was no way they could yet be certain. And now they were alone in their secret, for she also felt it necessary to abandon intercourse, even with Chen. She did not know the truth of the matter, and her body cried out for him . . . but she dared take no risk. And thus their conversations, which she valued even more highly than their passion, had to be suspended. And this brought the greatest of consequences, for whereas each day had been spent in waiting for his arrival, now she waited for nothing, and had to allow her thoughts to roam free, and finally admit that she *was* in love with a Chinese soldier.

And Charlie? She did not know, could only solace herself with the thought that she would never again see him. But at least he lived, and would remember her. While she betrayed him with another man? To survive. He would have to understand that. But then, to love . . .

As the days became a week, and the weeks lengthened into a month, thought of any sort became prohibitive. Now she could only wait, and hope, and pray, and count the hours, while Pearl sat beside her, equally apprehensive, and far more gloomy. "His anger, when he discovers your attempted subterfuge, will be horrifying," she said. "My stomach turns at the thought."

"Do you not think mine does also?" Adela snapped, and moved in discomfort, because her stomach did seem to be rolling at the thought. A moment later she was on her hands and knees and vomiting beside the bed, gazing at Pearl with wide and horrified eyes—she had never vomited before in her life.

But Pearl was laughing and clapping her hands together in relieved delight.

By Christmas Adela's body had noticeably thickened. And Yuan was more pleased than ever. He had never questioned the slight lateness of everything about her pregnancy.

"But he will question the birth," Pearl grumbled, having sunk into her normal pessimism. But she was now suffering a lack of physical love as acute as either Chen or Adela herself. "Sooner or later he will realize that you must have carried the baby for ten months or more."

"Then we must pray for a premature birth," Adela said.

"Ha! How may a birth be premature by wishing for it?" And then frowned as she gazed at the princess, took in the determined mouth and chin. "You would *risk* that? And suppose the baby dies?"

"Then I shall become pregnant again," Adela said. "And this time there will be no doubt, because Yuan will have been here all the time."

Pearl looked from the girl to the door, opened her mouth and closed it again. It occurred to Adela that the woman must occasionally be wondering if she had not virtually committed suicide by becoming involved in such a venture at all. But it was now too late for her to change her mind; any man other than the marshal could have gained access to the princess's bedchamber only by the good offices of her jailer.

And anyway, would *she* not kill her, before she would allow a betrayal? Was she now become a very reincarnation of Tz'u-Hsi, in her determination to survive, and if possible, even conquer? And escape? Because Charlie still lived. She had not actually dared to consider such a possibility, and convinced herself that it could not matter, as he would certainly abandon China and his futile quest, now that Sun's hopes were again trampled in the dust. But even if he returned to America, if she survived long enough and eventually managed to escape . . .

Sometimes she wished she *could* be a second Tz'u-Hsi, at least in ruthlessness and determination.

And then knew that to become like the Dragon Lady would be to reject everything she held dear in life— her personal estimation of herself. And thus what she would have to offer any man, and most of all, Charlie, *should* she ever succeed in escaping this place. How then could she even contemplate risking the life of her baby, merely to convince Yuan it was his? Because that was the only way to save both their lives. And she had almost persuaded herself the child *was* his.

But it was Chen's. And hers. And as such was the most precious thing in the world to her.

Yet she still dreamed of escaping and fleeing to Charlie. Sometimes she thought she was so emotionally confused she was herself going mad. But how could she contemplate a lifetime at Chen's side, however much he loved her and could make her love him? Surely she had to reach for more than that, because it would be a lifetime of flight, and poverty, and banditry, within China. A lifetime of everything she had once dreamed of setting right.

Thoughts of her possible Destiny again coursed through her mind. But was not *this* her Destiny, ordained almost from the moment of her birth, or even before? To be the concubine of a warlord, ruling China. It was hard to doubt, after everything that had happened these last three years, that such had been Destiny's plan, however she had wriggled and fought and stormed against it.

Yet nothing mattered, save survival. But not at the risk of her child. She watched the snow drifting past her window, settling in a white layer over the shrubs in her garden; it had been an unusually cold winter and remained the coldest March within living memory. Now she was big, so big she was ashamed even to be seen by Chen, and seldom left her apartment. And now too Yuan came to see her every day. Perhaps he had at last been calculating, and knew that had he impregnated her the day before he had marched away the previous June, she should be on the point of delivery.

"He will cut open your belly," Pearl said grimly. "And feed your child to the dogs before your eyes."

She would have made a marvelous nursemaid, Adela thought, for terrifying her charges into obedience.

"Why do you not jump up and down, to bring on the birth?" Pearl went on. "Was that not the plan?"

"I have decided that you are right, and it will not work," Adela told her. "Instead, I shall become sick."

"Sick?"

"Then the birth will be delayed, you see, because of my weakness. It will not be difficult. You will give me a purge. Several purges. Now."

She took to her bed, obviously weak, and complained of stomach pains. Yuan and his physicians assumed the birth was imminent and crowded around, but Pearl was able to show them the evidence of some stomach disorder. Yuan naturally suspected poison, and it was with difficulty that Adela dissuaded him from having all the cooks in the kitchen immediately beheaded. "I foolishly ate some pomegranates," she said. "Pomegranates have always made me ill. I shall soon be well again. I only pray the child has not been harmed." A genuine sentiment. Yuan went away in grim pessimism, and Pearl resumed her Cassandric utterances.

But the purges had, Adela realized, been a stroke of unwitting genius. For not only did the physicians accept Pearl's suggestion that this might well involve a delayed birth, but only a few days later she realized that the birth was actually going to be premature, after all: either three weeks late or two weeks early, depending on how one looked at it.

"Is it . . . is he . . . ?" She was afraid to ask, afraid

even to know, aware only of exhaustion after all the pain, and of a thousand anguished possibilities which ranged through her mind.

Yet she should have been able to tell from Yuan's smiling face. "Our son is well," he said. "Not as big as I had hoped, but then, you are a small woman. And he is strong, and has a loud voice. I shall call him Yuan Hsu, and one day he will sacrifice to heaven and be the greatest emperor since Shih Hwang Ti."

The immortal. The man who had first united China, who had conquered all the Far East; had sent his ambassadors to India and even to make contact with the distant Romans; who had built the Great Wall and the Grand Canal. And who, like Caesar, had given his name to all succeeding emperors: Hwang Ti.

That was Destiny. But *I* shall call him Peter, Adela thought. And trusted that Yuan would not trouble to consult a Western calendar as to his son's birthday, and thus discover that it was April 1, 1914.

"This is a great and unhoped-for event," Yuan announced, standing beside her bed and gazing around the room, suddenly crowded with men where none but himself had ever been allowed, to his knowledge. Li Yuan-hung was there, sycophantic as ever, and Chang Hsun, beaming with borrowed pride, because was not the new prince at least partly a Ch'ing? There were also other generals and state officials she had never seen before. And even Captain Chen Fu, the faithful captain of her guard, standing at the very back, allowed to visit his mistress on this most special occasion. Your son, she tried to convey with her eyes, your son, who will one day perhaps be emperor of China. But he would not meet her gaze.

"It can therefore be regarded as a sign from the gods, of their pleasure with my triumph, and my plans for the future," Yuan was saying. "My plans for the refoundation of the empire will be put to an assembly of the viceroys as soon as they can be gathered." He gazed around their faces, willing anyone to show dissent. Nobody did, although Adela could see several unhappy glances being exchanged. "But that is for the future," Yuan went on. "What I mean to do today is a more personal, a domestic, and a happy act." He smiled down at Adela and rested his hand on her shoulder. "It was long, as many of you may know, my wish to marry Princess Adela. This plan was thwarted by the machinations of the devil woman who called herself mother to the princess, and through circumstances beyond my control, the princess was wed to another man, and thus placed forever beyond the reach of my husbandly love. Indeed, as a married woman, she could not even, she *cannot* even now, be considered as a concubine. But she is the mother of my son. And am I not Yuan Shih-k'ai, ruler of all China? Are not the laws, are not even the customs of this land, mine to change as I think fit?" Once again he dared a dissent, his eyes moving from face to face. "This I now decree," he announced. "That whatever her past, Princess Adela is now the chief concubine of Marshal Yuan Shih-k'ai, and will be granted those honors and those rights as of this moment. So now, bow to Princess Adela, ruler of Yuan Shih-k'ai's domesticity."

Suddenly, here was life as it had always been intended to be lived. She was not free, of course, in the sense that she was not permitted to leave the confines of the Forbidden City. But the Forbidden City was large enough to provide the semblance of freedom, at least for a while, and certainly after the long confinement in her prison apartment. Nor was she permitted to mix freely with others. Yuan gave her an entourage of several women and two eunuchs. This was actually a distasteful aspect of her elevation; it meant that she and Pearl had less time alone together, and it meant that bringing Chen to her chamber was out of the question.

And then, suddenly, to her consternation, the question no longer arose. One day Chen was not there. Adela nearly betrayed herslf with fear that he had been discovered and executed. Pearl was able to reassure her —Chen had simply been promoted for his good work in guarding the princess so ably for so long, and had already left for his new command with the field army.

"Without saying good-bye?" Adela wailed.

"There was no time for him to do so," Pearl explained. "He was ordered to leave immediately. Besides, how could he impose upon Yuan Shih-k'ai's chief concubine?"

Adela wept herself to sleep that night, even as she tried to make herself understand the workings of the Chinese mind, and regard for law and tradition which commanded its every desire. Chen would sleep with her when she was the marshal's prisoner, out of love for her and hatred for the marshal. Yet he would no longer approach her once she ceased to be a prisoner and became instead another man's concubine, just as he continued to serve without question a man he loathed and distrusted, simply because he was a soldier.

But even understanding brought her no solace. He was gone. As Charlie was gone. What was then left to her? What pleasure could there be in the walks on the islands which studded the Ornamental Water—shuddering at the memory of her escape from this place three years before—of taking tea in the Mississippi steamboat, of painting, or gardening, and even of caring for Peter. Life was nothing without Chen.

But even had he stayed, he would no longer have come to her. She would have had to endure the misery of seeing him every day, without ever being able to feel his touch. He would even have rejected his son, as indeed he *had* rejected his son; as Yuan's concubine, her child was Yuan's, and thus *he* possessed no rights. In every way she was Yuan's, now and always, as she was even again summoned to his bed.

Yuan was now happy. "Circumstances are at last falling out exactly as I have always hoped they might," he said. "Next year I shall become emperor. It is all arranged."

"The viceroys have agreed, my lord?" She lay on her stomach beside him and ate sweetmeats, while he played with her hair, or her bottom, or her toes, as the mood took him.

"They *will* agree," he said grimly. "I will have the head of any man who objects. No, no, sweet Princess, I have never feared the viceroys. I have had to hurry slowly because of the barbarians. Do you know that they have refused to recognize my government as being more than a caretaker for the Ch'ing? That is an insult, eh? But now . . ." He chuckled. "Now they have problems of their own. I have heard on the telegraph from Europe—Osborne has told me, as it is his business —that all Europe prepares for war because of the assassination of some Austrian archduke. He prophesies that it will be a great and bloody contest during which they will have no time for my affairs. Indeed, the French and British and Russians will no doubt now wish to recognize me, Osborne considers, in exchange for my support against the Germans, such is their anxiety."

Adela was not interested in what might be happening in Europe, compared with what was happening in Peking. "*Osborne?*" she cried. "Is that creature still alive? Did you not have him executed?"

"You know I did not," Yuan said. "Execute my dear friend James? I had the skin removed from his back, and from his chest as well. Oh, for a long time he *felt* the anger of Yuan Shih-k'ai. But he is a useful man. He can do things for me that are beyond the reach of any of my Chinese agents. Such as obtaining you for me. Would you have returned to China with a Chinese?''

Adela rolled on her back, eyes closed. Osborne! Did she really hate him even more than Yuan himself? ''I do not see how you can trust such a man, great Yuan,'' she said. ''He hates you. Do you not know this? He has said it to me.''

''I know he hates me, sweet Princess,'' Yuan said. ''But do you not also hate me?''

Adela opened her eyes, but he was smiling. ''It is not the lot of a ruler to be loved, if he would *rule*. A ruler maintains himself in two ways only. By making people fear him, and by making them need him. China needs me, thus I have nothing to fear. And those who serve me, fear me, too much to betray me. Osborne is useful to me, and thus he lives. And do not forget that he is your husband, still, in the eyes of the world. Do you not know that he has been approached more than once by the American minister here in Peking, asking for news of you? Inspired by Constance, undoubtedly. Oh, I should like to have her here, so that I could show her the error of her ways. But James has always been able to allay their suspicions with reassurances that you are alive and well, and happy, and now, even a mother. Will that not make Constance happy, to know that she is a grandmother, even if not by blood?''

''I can see that the man is a treasure to you, my lord,'' she murmured. Her brain was suddenly teeming. She had disappeared almost two years ago. And thus had been supposed dead, and forgotten, she had presumed. But if Osborne was still her husband ''in the eyes of the world,'' and if Constance was still inquiring after her, then all was not yet lost. Certainly if the American

minister could be acquainted with her true situation . . .
Because that might be possible now. Not for her. But
Pearl was no longer confined strictly to the Forbidden
City, nor to her side all the time, when there were others
to relieve her.

"So we may regard the future with equanimity,"
Yuan was saying. "Only the Japanese stand in our way.
They are an ambitious, grasping people who hope to
carve an empire out of China. Thus it is in their interest
to keep our country in a state of continuous anarchy. I
negotiate with them, and they make outrageous
demands. They already have Korea, which has for so
long been under Chinese suzerainty. Now they seek
Manchuria. *Your* Manchuria, Princess. It is the price of
their support for my aims. And they feel that now is the
time to act, while the English and the French, the
Russians and the Germans, are so embroiled; they know
the Americans will never use force to stop them, on their
own. Well, Princess, I have decided to grant them their
wish."

"You will give them Manchuria?" Adela was aghast.

"Why not? At least for the time being. Then they will
support my claim to be emperor, and I will be able to
strengthen my position, to unite all China behind me.
Then . . ." He smiled. "It may be possible to re-
negotiate the situation with the Japanese. We owe them
a great deal, in *re*negotiation, do you not think? Formosa, Korea, the Ryukyus, and now Manchuria, not to
mention the defeats they inflicted upon us, upon *me,* in
1894. Your father and I fought shoulder to shoulder in
that war, Princess. We were both defeated, because the
dowager empress would not send us the men and the
supplies we needed. Your father chose to die. That was
noble of him. I chose the ignoble but perhaps more
useful path. I chose to live and prosper. And even, one
day, to be avenged. It shall happen. If necessary, I shall

conquer all Asia for my son. For all my sons, Adela. Because will you not again soon be pregnant?''

As he had told his generals, he considered himself the blessed of the gods, because the gods had restored his virility. Thus, she realized, her position had not improved at all. How could she give him other sons, when Chen could no longer come to her? How could she *exist,* when Chen could no longer come to her? And even if she existed, how could she condemn her son to a lifetime of intrigue and warfare, which must end in his death in battle or his assassination by rebelling warlords? How easy it had all seemed, to create a life, that she might preserve her own. But that life was now *her* responsibility.

There could be no time to lose. Constance must be informed not only that she was still alive, of her exact situation, but also of what Yuan intended, to set all Asia ablaze, if need be, in the pursuit of his ambitions. Constance could take the knowledge to the State Department and begin the process of limiting and perhaps even removing the marshal. Adela did not know how she and Peter would fare in such a process, but it had to be better than waiting here for an assassin to burst into her chamber, or an executioner to drag her to the block.

''The message is written in English,'' she told Pearl. ''So there is no risk of anyone's understanding it even if you lose it. But you must not lose it. You must deliver it to the American legation in the Tartar City, to the minister himself, and make sure he understands who it is from.''

Pearl gazed at the paper in terror. ''This will mean our deaths,'' she said.

''It will mean our *lives,* can you but deliver it,'' Adela insisted. ''And can you believe the alternative is *not* our deaths, when I fail again to become pregnant?''

"There are other men," Pearl said.

Adela shook her head. "There are no other men for me. And the risk would be too great, anyway. Deliver that letter for me, Pearl. For us. It is our only hope."

Because she had to hope, even if she knew there was at least a chance that the American minister would tear up the letter, dismissing its contents as nonsense. Yet he would not. Because he had been to see Osborne, probably at Constance's request, and asked after her, and been told a lie. This letter would establish that lie. And once Constance knew that . . . Constance had sought her and sought her. And would be seeking her still. Once she *knew* that Adela was still alive, and knew, too, where to look for her . . . The minister would at least have to tell her that.

She almost felt she could face the future with confidence, slept heavily that night, and awoke to find Yuan standing at her bedside, the letter in his hand.

Adela sat up, gasping for breath. She knew it was the letter she had written even before he dropped it on her chest. Now he looked from her to the baby, sleeping beside her. Then he said, "Come. Do not disturb the boy."

She eased herself out of bed, gazing at him, waiting for the sudden blow or the explosion of anger. Her brain seemed filled with cotton, her stomach with lead. But he said nothing, himself waved the hastily gathering terrified maids away and held out a robe for her to wear, before escorting her through the outer room, past equally terrified eunuchs and then guards, along the corridor and down a flight of steps to an inner court. Here the door was held for her by a eunuch; the only other people present were eunuchs, she realized—and Pearl.

She blinked in the sudden daylight, for it was just past

dawn, and gasped in horror, and nearly knelt as her
knees threatened to give way. The woman was spread-
eagled over an erect stone slab built in a slight curve
from base to top, so that Pearl's body arched toward
them, her naked flesh gleaming sweat. She was secured
by ropes passed around her thighs, just above the knees,
and her upper arms, just above the elbows, and thence,
very tightly, to steel hoops set into the stone, pinning
her in the desired position, but allowing her to kick if
she wished, and to move her wrists and hands. The rest
of her could only gasp and heave, as she did, constantly,
to indicate that she had already suffered the bamboo
rods.

And now she stared at Adela, and Adela felt her
blood turn to water. Pearl knew she was going to die in
the most horrible manner possible. And she was a
woman who *hated*. And possessed too many secrets.
Would she not wish to know that the princess would
follow her on the slab, and feel the knife?

Because *she* had put her there. By believing that
because she wished something to happen, it would
happen. She had murdered Pearl as surely as if she held
a pistol to her ear, simply by giving her the letter.

"The poor foolish creature does not understand,"
Yuan explained, "that whenever she goes abroad, she is
followed. And as soon as it was discovered that her
destination was the American legation, she was
arrested."

Oh, my God, Adela thought. It simply had not
occurred to her to tell Pearl that she could not simply
walk straight from the Gate of the Zenith to the
legation, but must make her visit there part of the whole
day's shopping, and after she had been sure she was not
under surveillance. She had assumed Pearl would know
these things. She had *assumed*.

"Of course," Yuan went on, "you were similarly

foolish in presuming it could be done without my knowledge. She has confessed, of course. Not that it was necessary, as no one else in this city but you, save for myself, *could* have written this letter. I am very angry with her. I expected little better of you, but Pearl was sworn to serve me, and to watch you and guard you, in my name. Not be suborned by you."

Adela was trying to control her breathing. But her breathing was at the mercy of the pounding of her heart, and that was entirely out of control.

"So I am going to make her *feel,* as she dies," Yuan said. "This is an old form of execution that has not been used for years. It was felt, even by your great ancestors, that it might upset the barbarians, you see. Because of course it should be performed in public, so that her screams and her agony and her body may be made the subject of jokes as she dies. Alas, we cannot have everything, as I too, coward that I am, do not wish to *upset* the barbarians. But we will do the best we can, here, in private. Because at least *you* will watch her die."

Adela closed her eyes. Oh, God, she thought. Oh, God!

"You will *watch,* Princess," Yuan said. "Every time you close your eyes, the execution will cease and wait for you to open them again. Thus you will but prolong her agony. So keep your eyes open, Princess." He nodded to the eunuchs. "Commence."

Adela gasped, and did sink to her knees as the execution began. The eunuchs were very efficient. Two stood by with constantly replenished buckets of water to throw upon their victim. Others began to caress her, slowly lifting her breasts away from her body. Pearl uttered a huge scream, followed by curses, calling upon Adela for aid, upon heaven and hell to end her misery, while her breasts were slowly cut away, then each ear, her nose, her lips, before axes were used to remove her hands and feet. Adela found herself vomiting, and feeling sure she would die herself, even before Yuan could get to her, from the surges of her heart which threatened to tear *her* chest apart.

But at last the eunuchs sliced away Pearl's tongue, and the shattered carcass could only *heave* feebly.

"Throw her on the dung heap," Yuan commanded. "Be sure the dogs are loosed." His fingers seized Adela's shoulder and raised her. "Shall I now replace her there with you, Adela?"

Adela stared at him. She could not even discover the solace of anger.

Yuan smiled. "But you are my announced concubine. The mother of my son. Your life is precious to me, my sweet Princess. I shall not take it from you yet. But remember what you have seen here today. Remember it, my sweet Princess. Remember *Pearl*."

Remember Pearl. Was there any chance of her ever forgetting?

It was not merely the horror of the execution itself. Not even the memory that she had once threatened Pearl with just such a fate, to begin the process of winning her confidence. It was because she had grown almost to love the woman over the past two years. Easy to say there had been no one else, the fondness for Pearl had been a necessary part of her survival plan. Easy to say that one could not remain on such intimate terms with anyone for so long without at least reaching some rapport with him or her. These things were true. But her feelings for Pearl had, as time had gone by, become deeper than those forced on her by necessity. If Pearl had been a vicious, angry, twisted soul, such a collapse of her personality had been forced upon her, Adela knew, by the events of her life. Orphaned—like herself —by the Boxers, she had been brought up by an uncle who had prostituted her from the earliest possible age, and taught her to smoke opium in order to make her more of his slave than ever. "Rescued" by Feng, then one of Yuan's lieutenants, and made a personal concubine because of her beauty, she had also degenerated into a life of sexually oriented hate, which had turned her entirely against the male sex. Fleeing Feng's encampment after her protector's execution, and after she had been the plaything of the young men for several hours, she had made her way to Yuan, expecting justice against Lin-tu, unaware that the girl she had chained to the wall of the opium den was the marshal's own chosen wife. Then had followed the terrible destruction of her beauty, the almost equal torture of being deprived of the opium on which she had for so long depended, and a fresh life of servitude and misery—until the two years when she had become almost human, perhaps for the first time in her life. Only to meet the most terrible of all deaths, because she had tried to help the girl who had been the only friend she had ever known. And even her death had been in many ways noble, as she had refused to betray the ultimate secret, when it might have saved her life.

A life like Pearl's, which was, Adela knew, repeated in its essentials if not always in its horrific detail, a thousand, perhaps a million times in each generation all over China, was the strongest of all arguments in favor of Destiny.

And also, perhaps, of some reformation of the misgovernment and injustice and misery that held this huge land in its unrelenting grasp?

But not by her. Never by her, now. Because her Destiny had been written in huge letters, she now knew, ever since she could remember. Ever since she had first understood her identity. She was a Ch'ing princess, and it had been her fate to be the concubine of a warlord,

from the day of her birth. No matter how Constance
had planned, and endeavored to make things happen,
no matter how she had herself endeavored to alter the
preordained course of events, nothing had availed. She
was here in the Forbidden City, where she belonged,
surrounded by eunuchs and handmaidens, not one of
whom felt anything more than hatred for her, however
they might all be anxious to obey her every whim. And
here she would remain for the rest of her life, entirely
cut off from the outside world, from anyone she could
love or even converse with. Without word, even
Constance and Charlie would eventually have to decide
she was dead. And no doubt soon enough they would be
right. Even if Yuan did not execute her for her failure to
become pregnant again, she could not see herself
existing in this *non*existence for very long. If only Chen
could come back. But Chen's return would be the
greatest disaster of all. She would not be able to resist
summoning him to her side, and how could she, without
involving his destruction? The thought of Chen bound
to that bloodstained slab of stone to be cut into pieces
before his own eyes made her wish to faint.

Then what was left to her? To be a concubine and
make her lord happy, which she did to the best of her
ability, however much *she* hated *him,* but with increasing difficulty as his health now very visibly began
to deteriorate. To be a mother to her son. Here was her
only joy, as the baby became a sturdy toddler. But the
boy himself would be removed from her care at the age
of six. Yuan told her this, indicating that she had best
make haste and produce another, if she would continue
to enjoy the privileges as well as the pleasures of
motherhood. Six! But this was not only because Yuan
intended his son to be a warrior, and unweakened by the
harem and eunuch influences which had caused the
decay of so many dynasties in the past. It was also,

again as he told her, because he had no intention of allowing the boy to become too dependent on his mother, or even to know her, save as a shadowy background figure. "Mothers intrigue with their sons against their fathers," he said with a smile. "History tells us that. It is better to prevent temptation."

So by Peter's second birthday she was already within four years of utter loneliness. Because by now it was obvious even to Yuan that he would not again be a father. To Adela's enormous relief, this no longer seemed important to him. In fact, his continuing physical collapse—the ever-present exhaustion that often left him prostrate and unable to conduct any business for hours and sometimes days on end, made it impossible for her to relieve him no matter how hard she tried—was now the most worrying thing she had to fear. However much she loathed him, and knew him for the bloodthirsty monster he was, he was yet her protector. While her life after his death . . . Even if she were privileged *to* live, and privileged to retain her position as the mother of his successor, what would be left to her? To degenerate into a monster herself, using her eunuchs for stimulation, her maids for amusement, having them whipped for the slightest transgression, executed at whim? She could understand, in such circumstances, why many empresses *had* undergone just such degeneration, as they stifled beneath the unending boredom of their existence. The thought of becoming like them was terrifying.

But would she even be allowed to live, once Yuan died?

"The marshal spent a bad night," remarked General Chang Hsun.

Adela raised her head. She sat, as she sat on most fine mornings, even in the early spring, on a chair placed for her on one of the little islands that dotted the Orna-

mental Water—no longer a source of terror—and
sketched. As this was about her only amusement nowadays, she had become quite proficient. Her ladies and
eunuchs were gathered some distance away, and Peter
charged about her easel—he had just celebrated his
second birthday—amusing himself with trying to catch
butterflies. An idyllic scene, she thought, could she
suppose a single soul or heart on this island was at
peace, either with itself or with its fellows. While she . . .
Eight months before, she had celebrated her twenty-first
birthday. It was a year and a half since Pearl's death,
nearly two years since Chen's departure . . . and three
and a half years since Osborne had so successfully kidnapped her.

All of her life, it seemed.

For companionship now she depended on General
Chang. He was commander of the entire Imperial
Guard, as Yuan insisted upon calling his own personal
troops, just as he insisted upon calling himself emperor,
even if it was a title still not recognized by any of the
provincial viceroys—his insistence upon an imperial
restoration, in his person, indeed kept the entire country
in a state of simmering civil war. Chang was not a
personality Adela felt she could ever actually like, but
he had always been amiable enough, at least to her,
because of course, as Chen had told her, she was a
Ch'ing, and Chang regretted the passing of the dynasty.
As commander of the Imperial Guard there was
nowhere in the Forbidden City barred to him, and he
often sought her out to pass the time of day; this also he
could do as he chose, for he was Yuan's best friend, and
thus utterly trusted by the marshal. And of course he
never approached her except when she was surrounded
by her people, watching every movement, to make sure
he did not even touch the princess's hand, even if they
remained out of earshot of what he might be saying.

He was valuable as her only source of knowledge of what was happening in the outside world, even if his information was scanty enough. But she did know, for instance, that the European war continued and even intensified, with enormous casualties, apparently convulsing the entire continent, and that the United States, while remaining aloof from that contest, was deeply embroiled with Mexico, and might even go to war with that country once again. The entire world seemed to be caught up in crisis, crisis which left it entirely uninterested in what might be happening with the moribund Chinese colossus—save for the Japanese, officially taking part in the Great War as an ally of the British, but still far more concerned with carving for themselves an Eastern empire.

So today, perhaps, he would have some fresh news to bring her. He invariably began every conversation with a reference to his master.

"I believe he did," Adela agreed, "spend a bad night. He often does."

"It is not thought that he will *ever* regain his health and strength," Chang said softly.

Adela turned his head. Whatever her, or anyone's, private feelings, such a thought was not utterable within the Forbidden City. Except by General Chang?

"I have taken it upon myself, privately," Chang went on, watching her closely, "to relate the marshal's symptoms to an American physician in the Tartar City."

"What symptoms?"

"His skin is scaly, like that of a reptile," Chang said. "His breath is foul. You lie with him. Have you not noticed these things?"

Adela gazed at him; she could only wait to discover what he was leading up to.

"He can retain little in his bladder," Chang went on.

"He vomits from time to time, without reason. He has lost much of his energy and is now losing the clarity of his mind. Have you not noticed *these* things, Princess?" He smiled, as again she did not reply. "He is all but entirely impotent. Have you not noticed *that*, my lady Princess? This physician with whom I spoke says that without immediate treatment, the marshal does not have long to live. Even with treatment, he does not believe the marshal can be saved, if things are as far advanced as I have described. He says the marshal is suffering from something called uremia; that is, his kidneys no longer perform their proper function of filtering his water and sending the waste into the bladder as urine. They are instead permitting the impurities and waste matter to penetrate his entire body. He is dying of poison, self-created."

"Why do you say this to me?" Adela asked. "Do you not suppose the marshal would have your head, even *your* head, Chang, were I to repeat this conversation to him?"

Chang bowed. "That will not now save his life, Princess. I should have thought you would be more interested in what happens after his death."

Again she gazed at him, and he smiled. "He is my friend, and I have served him faithfully and well. But there are things which I know, Princess, and it would be well for you to know them too. The marshal is hated throughout the land. He is hated by the generals and the viceroys because of the way he calls himself emperor and seeks to make them worship him as the Son of Heaven, and because of the way he has allowed the Japanese to penetrate Manchuria, and does not go to war with them. He is hated by the people because his tax gatherers are everywhere, and are not to be avoided. And he is hated by the republicans. Oh, they are still there in their mountains, watching and waiting. They have no generals to match his skill, and they have no armies to set against his. The army remains loyal. Or at least . . ." His eyes gloomed at her. "It remains loyal to *me*. But who can say what will happen when the marshal dies? He dreams that he will be succeeded by his son, by *your* son, Princess. But it is far more likely that the lords will seek to extirpate every last remnant of his reign and his dynasty. They will seek to murder your son, Princess, and you also. These things surely must be considered by you."

His gaze shrouded her. Because he was a man. And she was the most beautiful woman in China. Her nostrils dilated with distaste. But was he not offering salvation? For what price? As if she did not know.

"But you would save me from such a fate, *faithful* Chang," she said. "And perhaps see me to the safety of the coast, and an American ship?"

He frowned at her but clearly did not comprehend that she was being sarcastic. "Is that all you seek, Princess? To turn your back on your Destiny? It cannot be. There can be only one hope for you, and for me, and for all those who have linked their fortunes to Yuan. But more, it is the only hope for China. Was not this country great and strong as long as your mighty ancestors were on the throne?"

Her head jerked in sheer surprise. "You would restore the emperor?"

His eyes were hooded. "That must be the intention of every loyal servant of the Ch'ing, my lady Princess. But you are of course aware that the emperor is at present living in Japan, and is in the hands of the Japanese government, as are his father and uncle, Prince Ch'un. Clearly I wish to see him once again sacrificing to heaven, but equally do I know that the Japanese would impose even more demands upon us, as the price of his restoration. On the other hand, we have at least a regent, ready to hand, able to conduct affairs until his majesty can be returned to us."

"A three-year-old boy?"

Chang smiled. "Who has a mother. A mother who has a powerful friend, commander of the Imperial Guard."

"And a prince who also has a father, whom you tell me is the most hated man in China."

"His father will not be relevant, once that father is dead," Chang reminded her. "He will be presented to the people, the world, not as the son of Yuan Shih-k'ai, but as the last of the Ch'ing, and more, as the acting emperor for his cousin. I think after the anarchy that has prevailed in China these last four years and more, that the people will welcome the return of the Ch'ing. I think your feet would be set on the path of greatness, my lady Princess. I think *that* is your Destiny."

Her Destiny. To be dowager empress. Well, virtually. After all, a reincarnation of Tz'u-Hsi. It was incredible. It was impossible. And it would happen. What had Yuan once said? "The Western powers only regard me as a caretaker for the Ch'ing."

Chang continued to smile. "Because what is the alternative, my lady Princess? A shameful death?"

If it could happen. If she had the power, not to be a Tz'u-Hsi, but to be a Victoria, or an Elizabeth, or a Maria Theresa. To correct all the ills that beset this land. To end the abuses that had created unfortunates like Pearl. To bring China back from the dead and into the forefront of world affairs. She was dreaming. She was twenty-one years old . . . and this was her Destiny.

"What of Li Yuan-hung?" she asked, hardly believing it was herself speaking so calmly.

Chang shrugged. "He is an obstacle, certainly. He

also anticipates Yuan's death, but *he* then wishes to open negotiations with Sun Yat-sen for a republic. He is no friend to you, my lady Princess. He will have to be—''

''No,'' she said. ''He is an honest man, and a good one. I may believe that you are right in what you see as best for China, General Chang, but we will not begin our reign with murder. Nor would I have my son rule, my family restored, by decree. Li Yuan-hung is right to wish to consult with Sun Yat-sen. If the country is, as you say, tired of anarchy, then it will wish the Ch'ing to resume our rule. If not, then I will not be *imposed* upon my people.''

Chang considered, and then bowed. ''In which case, my lady Princess, it may well be necessary for us both to dissemble for a while, until we see how the wind blows. I would know this: should I decide to act for the restoration of the Ch'ing in the person of Prince Yuan Hsu, will you support me and lend me your authority?''

Adela hesitated. ''If you can convince me it is what China wishes, General Chang, then I will support you.''

Again Chang bowed, and straightened, and looked into her eyes. ''In which case, my lady Princess, the sooner we set our plans into motion, the better. Only one fact is certain: Yuan is dying. Can you not believe it would be an act of kindness, as well as policy, to . . . terminate that suffering?''

Adela stared at him. This was Yuan's best friend speaking.

''There is no one else with your advantageous position, my lady Princess,'' he went on. ''You spend hours alone with him, hours when he is often asleep or too weak to move. A pillow . . .''

''Never,'' Adela declared.

''Do you not also hate him?''

''I will not murder him, Chang. Or anyone.''

Chang regarded her for a few moments, and then bowed again. "Then we must pray for a speedy deliverance, my lady Princess."

Was she not being a fool? Was not Chang offering her everything of which she had ever dreamed, on a plate? Or at least a safe exile back to the United States and Charlie. But Charlie was hers either way, because as dowager empress, she could bring Charlie to her. She wondered what Constance would say to that.

But then, as dowager empress, she could also bring Constance and Frank back, and set them up again, and end their poverty.

Dreams. All of which remained at risk for every moment that Yuan remained alive. Because at any moment he could regain sufficient angry strength and vicious power to command her execution, or commit some other hideous crime. He deserved to die; his life no longer served any purpose whatsoever. She wondered what he would say were he to know that his faithful Chang had proposed his murder? Surely Yuan, who had practiced deception and treachery all his life, would have to smile at that complete turn of the wheel. As she sat beside him, and watched him, half-asleep, breathing stertorously, smelled the rank odor of his breath and his body, she found herself gazing at the pillow he had thrown to one side in his discomfort. He was indeed helpless, should she but decide . . .

And then she would be a murderess. Now and forever. Tz'u-Hsi had not been afraid of murder for her own ends.

But she was not Tz'u-Hsi.

"Where is my son?" Yuan asked.

"He sleeps, my lord," she said.

"Fetch him to me, Princess. Fetch him."

"I will do so, my lord." She got up, went to the door.

"Do not leave me," Yuan cried. "Do not leave me. Without you, sweet Princess, I am nothing."

She hesitated, biting her lip, took a step back toward him; she did not really want Peter to come into this death chamber.

"Sweet Princess," Yuan said. "Why have you always hated me, always fought against me, who desired only your love?"

She stood by the bed, looking down at him. There was nothing she could say.

"Sweet Princess," he said. "I adore you." And sighed. And then spoke and breathed no more.

IV

The Princess

14

The Opportunity

A beaten army is a depressing sight. An army that stays beaten over any length of time degenerates into a rabble. After three years it becomes little more than an outlaw band.

Charles Baird actually supposed it was a miracle there was an army in existence at all, after yet another winter in the mountains. When he remembered the aftermath of their defeat . . . They had hoped so much, expected so much—and known so little. When their spies had informed them that the marshal was concentrating immediately south of Shao-Kuan, *his* reaction, without any experience of warfare, had been that this was to their advantage; Yuan obviously intended to come and find them in these mountains, which they knew better than he and where the disparity in numbers and equipment between the opposing sides would have been less obvious. Sun had thought differently. "The cities," he had said. "These are where we gain our true victory. And Yuan has made the mistake of underestimating us. He has abandoned his cities. We will take the valley of the Yangtze, and march on Shanghai. When we hold

Shanghai as well as Canton, Yuan's days are numbered."

So they had abandoned their mountain fastnesses, and their loyal Cantonese base, and marched for Shanghai. No doubt the political strategy had been sound. Shanghai was the most international city in China, and Sun still desperately sought, as he still desperately needed, the support of Britain and France, at least in money and arms; how better to gain that support than by demonstrating that he was no mere guerrilla leader, but possessed the men and the will to conquer China before their very eyes?

Such a move would also, he hoped, by its boldness, and especially if attended by success, sway those northern viceroys and warlords, each commanding considerable armies, and most at least covertly opposed to Yuan's policies and ambitions, who continued to pay lip service to Peking but who certainly hoped for a considerable change in the direction their country seemed to be taking.

But as military strategy it had been ludicrous. They had turned away from their enemies, deliberately; soon Yuan had discerned their intention, and followed, and they had discovered themselves to be running away from him. Morale had sagged. And when they had at last turned to fight, still far from their goal, they had simply fallen apart. It had been less a battle than a series of probes by Yuan's men, each probe sending one of Sun's battalions fleeing in terror before the well-controlled artillery and machine-gun fire of the government troops, the disciplined rifle volleys and the fierce bayonet charges of the well-equipped khaki-clad soldiers.

Those of them who could, had regained the mountains. And here they had stayed, save for occasional forays down into the valleys. Now they were become guerrillas. There had been only one difference to all the previous abortive risings inspired by Dr. Sun: such past fiascos had been followed by the deliberate disbandment of the army and the departure of the doctor for Europe in search of more support; this time he had stayed. "Here we fight, and from here we shall eventually conquer," he declared. "And here we shall die, if need be."

So Charles Baird had stayed too—only he, out of all the European and American volunteers who had first elected to follow Sun's banner. But then, those others had had lives to live, businesses or inheritances to return to, even wives and sweethearts waiting for them. They had of course promised to do all they could to encourage governmental or private support for the republican cause. But then Fate had stepped in, and Europe had become embroiled in a war of its own. There had been no money, and no guns, and no bullets, to spare for Sun Yat-sen and his Kuomintang.

Charles Baird had stayed because he had nowhere to go. Letters found him occasionally, brought out by their supporters from Canton. But letters from Constance and Frank held no attraction for him. They represented a world that had no existence here in the Ta Shan, a world that he knew could never again have any existence for him. Adela had disappeared from the face of that world. According to Constance, Osborne continued to claim that she was alive and well, but no one had seen her since the day she had set foot in China, and even Constance had finally accepted the worst. So whose arms was *he* to return to? This was at least an acceptable way of committing suicide.

What a fool he had been, he thought as he sat by his rough tent and cleaned his rifle and revolver carefully, as he did every day on rising, regardless of whether or not he might be using them in the foreseeable future.

There was nothing else for him to do. He wore a roughly made sheepskin coat, sheepskin breeches, sheepskin boots; even in early May the wind in the Ta Shan was cold. He made himself think of Robinson Crusoe. Save that he was not alone, or even restricted to only a man Friday. There were several hundred other men in this camp with him, similarly dressed and armed. And there was also a considerable number of women, and even, after three years, children. Any one of these women could have been his, would have been happy to go to the white man. But he kept himself in lonely mental and sexual seclusion, and dreamed.

Because he had been such a fool. She had been his, all his, with that single-minded determination which was her greatest asset. And he had been afraid to take what he so badly wanted. Afraid of . . . That determination? That smile? That beauty? Or the certainty that she would *drive* him, in which direction he did not know, but always upward? Adela could think of nothing but the top of each mountain peak she came to; her valleys were but pathways to the next peak. How he wished he could climb a peak now, with her at his side; four years ago each peak had seemed dizzily terrifying in its unknown grandeur.

As she had recognized, that day in her bedroom in San Francisco, when she had said, "You are afraid, Charlie."

What would she see in him now?

He watched Lin-tu, walking beside the doctor, the gaunt figure of Captain Chiang Cheng as ever immediately behind them. Lin-tu had not been with them in the valley of the Yangtze. He had joined them afterward, when they had been retreating in fear and disorder, like beetles, each man anxious to clamber on the back of the one in front, to save *his* head from being hung over a city gateway. Lin-tu, as ever, had been contemptuous of what he had found. Even of Sun. Lin-tu would never have risked his army on the plain.

He had been even more contemptuous to find Charles Baird marching with the doctor. He remembered Charlie Baird too well, from the escape out of Peking. He also remembered that Charles Baird had possessed what should have been his. "With creatures like this," he had asked, "you wish to overthrow Yuan Shih-k'ai?"

Charlie had not taken offense. He could not afford to. He could only attempt to prove himself. He thought he had managed that, over the past couple of years. Whereas Sun still dreamed, and had even set up a sort of Kuomintang government-in-exile here in the mountains, and corresponded with viceroys and provincial nobles who at least offered tacit support for his dreams, and who kept inviting him to meetings—at which, as his rebellion had failed, they would undoubtedly arrest him and send him, or his head, to the warlord—Lin-tu acted. He was a born bandit, a born guerrilla leader. He had made himself responsible for the active arm of the movement, led forays down into the valleys, attacking government outposts, holding summary trials of those who would not offer their support to the doctor, shooting, looting, raping, and murdering. This was his life. Charles Baird had ridden at his side. Sun, who was well aware of the situation between them, had advised against it. "He has no cause to love you, Mr. Baird," he had said. "And should he consider you have at any time failed him, he would be within his rights, as field commander, to have you executed without trial. And *as* field commander, only he can be the judge of what is a failure."

Well, Charlie thought with a certain grim pride, he was still alive. Because he had been able to shoot and loot, and even rape and murder, with the best of them. Because he had ridden and fought with the reckless courage of a man who did not care whether he lived or died. Only Adela had ever made a coward of him, because he had known he would never be as much of a man as she wanted him to be. He could be all the man required by Lin-tu. He thought that over the years there had even grown up a certain rapport between them; Lin-tu now regarded him as a worthwhile lieutenant. He was approaching now, accompanied by Sun, and smiling. "There is news," he said.

Charles scrambled to his feet.

"My scouts have sent ahead to say they are bringing in a horseman," Lin said. "A white man." He grinned. "Shall we not go and see who this white man is?"

But he already knew, that was obvious. Charlie frowned as he followed Lin out of the encampment toward the open land sloping down into the valley, watched the group of horsemen approaching, squinting into the morning sunlight, hardly able to believe his eyes.

He was looking at James Osborne.

Charlie ran forward, reached the renegade before Osborne had properly recognized the big bearded figure, seized the man, and tumbled him from the saddle. "Fetch a rope," he shouted. "Fetch a rope, Dr. Sun, and let us hang this scoundrel from the highest tree we can find."

"For God's sake!" Osborne cried. "Get him off me. I came in peace. I have news, great tidings."

"James Osborne," Sun said, coming to stand above him. "Let him up, Mr. Baird. Let us look upon him."

Reluctantly Charles released Osborne's shoulder, and the Englishman got to his feet, brushing dust from his jacket. He carried a revolver hanging from his belt, under his coat, but he had more sense than to attempt to draw it, surrounded as he was by republican officers.

"Nevertheless," Lin said, reaching for the gun butt, "we will relieve you of this, Mr. Osborne."

"And you had best tell us what you are doing here," Dr. Sun said. "Or we may well indeed hang you. For spying as well as for kidnapping Princess Adela."

"Spying? Kidnapping?" Osborne looked from face to face, attempting to meet their gazes, then hurriedly passing on to the next. 'She is my wife, before God and man."

"Let me have him," Charlie growled. "For five minutes. Let me have him. His wife. His widow, he means. I want to hear him scream, as she must have done."

"I came under a flag of truce," Osborne cried. "I came in peace. I came to bring you momentous tidings. My *widow*? I come *from* my wife the princess."

They stared at him, even Charlie, with his mouth open, unable to believe the tumultuous beating of his heart.

"*From* the princess?" Lin inquired softly. "You are claiming that Princess Adela is still alive? That Yuan Shih-k'ai did *not* execute her?" He glanced at Charlie.

Osborne was getting his breathing under control. "I have credentials," he said. "In my pocket."

Sun nodded to Chiang Chung-cheng, and the young captain pulled open Osborne's jacket and took out a sealed envelope. This he gave to Sun, who slit it open, read the first few lines of the enclosed letter, and raised his head. "This is from Marshal Li Yuan-hung."

"Who writes to you on behalf of Princess Adela and her son—"

"Her *son*?" Charlie cried.

Osborne smiled. "Did you not know? Marshal Yuan was not *that* decrepit when she first returned to China."

"And Li is writing to me on her behalf?" Sun asked. "Then what has happened to Yuan Shih-k'ai?"

Osborne smiled at them all. "Marshal Li writes to you as temporary head of state, and as regent for Yuan Shih-k'ai's son, Prince Yuan Hsu, who is also the son of the princess, who was Yuan's chief concubine before his death."

"Before his death?" Lin whispered. "Yuan Shih-k'ai is dead?"

"This last month," Osborne told him. "Some say he was poisoned, Others that he did indeed die of disease. But he is most certainly dead."

"Yuan Shih-k'ai is dead," Lin-tu said. "Yuan Shih-k'ai is dead," he shouted. "Yuan Shih-k'ai is dead," he shrieked. His cry of triumph and relief was taken up by the entire encampment, and accompanied by the firing of rifles and revolvers.

"Dead," Sun said. "The devil is dead, at last. And Li . . . ?"

"Invites you to Peking for a conference on the future government of China," Osborne said. "In Peking."

"A conference," Sun said, and looked at Lin-tu. "We must prepare to leave immediately."

"It is a trap," Lin growled.

"Not necessarily," Sun said. "I know Li for an honest man."

Lin-tu snorted. "Did you not know Yuan Shih-k'ai for an honest man, before he betrayed you?"

Sun hesitated, then squared his shoulders. "I have not told you this before," he said. "But I have been in correspondence with Marshal Li for some time. Clandestinely. He has kept me informed of Yuan's declining health. Why else do you suppose I have never lost faith in our eventual triumph? Now what we have all wanted and waited for has come to pass. Yuan is dead, and Li would choose the best possible government for China. We must take part in such a process, whatever the risks. It is our Destiny."

"Destiny!" Lin-tu sneered.

"You have nothing to fear from Marshal Li, gentlemen," Osborne said. "He is a man of his word. Besides . . ." He smiled at Charlie. "The princess will be there. No doubt she waits for *you*."

Franklin Wynne took the steps of the apartment building four at a time, gasping for breath, but smiling his anticipated pleasure as he reached the landing, pulled open the door, burst inside. "Connie!" he shouted. "Connie!" And checked, as he always did, when he came upon his wife unexpectedly.

She sat by the window and looked out at the sea. As he had promised, with their children gone, and with no Osborne loan to pay back either, he had been able to find them a place halfway up the hill, with a distant sea view. They had become genteel once again. But miserably so.

There was now too much gray amid the yellow of Constance's hair. Perhaps in the last few years there had been more than he had been prepared to notice; it had always been too well disguised in the pompadours, the chignons she had worn. Even when loose, her hair had always seemed to be a reflection of the vivacious confidence which dominated her face and her personality. But the vivacity and the confidence had both gone. Constance looked older than her forty-five years, far older. And for the first time he could ever recall in this woman he had loved almost from the moment of their first meeting, she was uninterested. Except in the ocean, which separated her from China and Adela. Even now, as she turned to look at him, vaguely surprised that he should be home at this odd hour, attempting hastily to arrange her features into that famous smile, her expression suggested a faint resentment that he should have dragged her back into the real world so abruptly.

But now she would smile genuinely. "Connie!" he cried again, and held her arms to lift her to her feet. "I have the most stupendous news."

She gazed at him, lips parted. "Dela?"

"Is alive and well."

"How do you know?"

"A letter from Charlie."

"From Charlie?" She had not heard from her son in months.

"Nobody else. *He* knows. It is a long letter. You will have to read it. But, Connie, the main thing is, Yuan Shih-k'ai is dead."

"Yuan? He's dead? Oh, Frank, if I could believe that . . ."

"Believe it, Connie. Because it's true. Yuan is dead, and his successor, some fellow called Li Yuan-hung, is arranging a get-together between himself and Sun to decide upon a constitution and a properly elected government for China. Isn't that marvelous? Charlie is going to Peking with Sun, and, you won't credit this, with Lin-tu as well. Seems they're all friends now. And he's going to see Adela."

Constance sat down again. "And she is well, Frank? Really and truly well?"

Frank sat beside her. "Not only well, my dearest girl. She is a mother."

"A . . . ?" Constance's jaw sagged. "By *Yuan*?"

"One must presume so. Charlie describes him as a prince named Yuan Hsu, so I would say Yuan is the father. My God, I suppose that makes him our grandson—legally, at any rate. Anyway . . . But all of that doesn't matter anymore. Nothing that has happened matters anymore. It is what is *going* to happen that's important. Dela is well, and Charlie is going to see her, and—"

"What about Osborne?" Constance asked. "Is he dead too?"

"Osborne?" Frank glanced at the letter. "As a matter of fact, Mr. Osborne seems very much alive. It seems that Osborne is the fellow who took the news of Yuan's death from Peking to Canton. Who acted as this Marshal Li's agent. So he would certainly appear to be thriving."

"And Charlie did nothing about him?"

"Well . . . he says, 'I can tell you that I nearly scragged the fellow on sight. But when I heard what he had to say . . . He'll divorce Dela, of course, and then, well . . . I suppose I will have to ask her to marry me all over again.' Isn't that marvelous, Connie? Isn't it marvelous the way everything has turned out? Provided Osborne doesn't now start asking for his money back, of course."

"Everything," Constance muttered, gazing out of the window at the sea. Everything was always turning out all right, in Frank's eyes. Until they came to grasp the substance of their fortune, and discovered it was not really there at all, that they were merely the pawns in someone else's game. She was being pessimistic, she knew. But that Frank should airily dismiss everything that had happened to Adela as no longer mattering, after she had been a prisoner inside the Forbidden City for nearly four years, and assume that now, as with a snap of the fingers, she was free, and powerful . . . and at the same time the innocent young girl they all remembered—that was asking *too* much of fortune.

But did that truly matter? Did it even matter that Charlie, afraid of the girl, might find the woman, the *survivor*, who was also now a mother and the widowed concubine of China's greatest figure of the past ten years, even more fearsome? The only important thing was that Adela *was* alive. After everything that had happened, she was alive.

Constance smiled at Frank through a mist of tears. "I'm sorry, Frank. I suppose I find it all a little difficult to take in. As you say, it really is the most wonderful news. I must write—"

"Write?" Frank shouted, getting up again in his exuberance. "*We* can get there quicker than any letter."

"We, Frank?"

"I've resigned from my job," Frank declared. "I've booked us passages on the next ship sailing for Tientsin. We're going to China, my darling girl. Back to China. Back to Adela. And Charlie."

"You may tell the marshals to enter," Adela said. She stood in the center of the reception room of her apartment, the Lotus Apartment, where she had spent four very long years, her son at her side. *He* had spent all his life in these two rooms and that small garden. It was time for that to change. And she would have it so.

Li Yuan-hung entered the room, followed by Chang Hsun. Both wore uniforms, both bowed deeply before the princess.

"My lady Princess," Li said. "How my heart grieves for you in your bereavement. If I have delayed visiting you to present my condolences before now, it is because I wished to respect your grief, your desire for solitude."

"For six weeks, Marshal Li?" she asked. And looked at Chang. He also had remained away ever since Yuan's death. So they were Chinese, and reverence for the dead took a high place in their thinking—the princess had been in mourning, surely, for her lord and master. But she would have expected Chang at the least to try to communicate with her. Now he did not meet her gaze.

"There have also been considerable affairs of state to

be attended to, great Princess," Li pointed out, as softly as ever. Now that he had raised his head and *was* looking at her, she wondered that she had never before noticed how shifty his eyes were.

"You have not yet greeted Prince Yuan Hsu," she said coldly.

The generals bowed again; the little boy merely goggled at them.

"May he live forever," Li said.

Getting angry was a waste of time with men like these. But it was certainly very necessary now to be forceful. Polite, she reminded herself, but forceful. "Please sit down," she said, and clapped her hands. "Tea," she commanded her waiting women. She sat herself on one of the divans, patted the cushion beside her for Peter to join her. Together they looked across the room at the two Chinese, carefully seating themselves, also together. "I am of course most anxious to discover the situation in the country," she said.

Li and Chang exchanged glances.

"I would like also to know why I am still being treated as a prisoner," Adela went on. "Wherever I go, I am still surrounded by guards. And when last week I intimated that I wished to leave the Forbidden City to shop in the market, I was told this was impossible. That is why I sent for you. Last week," she reminded him.

Li smiled deprecatingly. "The guard officer was but attempting to do his duty, great Princess," he explained. "How may a Ch'ing princess go shopping in the market like some provincial housewife? How may you go abroad without a suitable escort? And how may you go abroad at all, until the mourning period is finished?"

"I have now mourned six weeks," she said.

"Six weeks," he commented. "Who can say if that is adequate for such a man, such a giant, as Yuan

Shih-k'ai? Should it not be six months? Or even, perhaps, six *years*?''

Adela's head came up as she glared at him.

"Besides," Li went on hastily, "it is for your own safety that you remain within these walls. You will have been aware that Marshal Yuan was not overloved by many people."

Adela gazed at him, still fighting back a desire to lose her temper. Or even to despair. She had supposed, with Yuan dead . . . Once again she looked at Chang, and this time he returned her gaze, but without expression. Or was his very lack of expression a message telling her to be patient?

"But you will be pleased to learn," Li was saying, "that events are progressing exactly as we all have hoped they would. I have sent emissaries to the South to the encampment of Dr. Sun Yat-sen, and the doctor is on his way to Peking now for a conference at which we will decide a suitable future for this great country of ours. You will be pleased to see Dr. Sun again, great Princess. He comes with his entourage. Old friends of yours. Lin-tu is with him. You remember Lin-tu?" He smiled at Adela's sharp intake of breath. "And Charles Baird."

"Charles?" Adela bit her lip in an attempt to conceal the sudden explosion of joy which filled her mind.

"So you will see that you have a great deal to anticipate, great Princess," Li said. "As to what the future may hold for you, or for me, or for any of us, that I cannot yet discern. We must wait for events."

"I understand that, Marshal Li," Adela said, feeling her tension beginning to dissipate in a rush which almost threatened her with tears. Charlie was coming. With Dr. Sun. To her rescue. And Lin-tu? But Lin-tu could be nothing more than an embarrassment when standing beside Sun and Charlie. Everything was going to work out, as she had dreamed but never dared hope, at last. But . . . She dared not ask about Chen, dared not even think of him. Yet how could she even think of leaving China without seeing him once more? And how could she *dare* do that?

But there was somebody else even more important to her future than Chen, because *he* lay across it like a dark cloud. "I would like to know the whereabouts of James Osborne," she said. "Is he in Peking?"

"Ah . . . " Li's eyes became even more liquid. "He has left Peking, great Princess."

"Then I wish him found and brought back."

"That you may be avenged for the wrong he had done you?"

"That our marriage may be annulled, Marshal Li. Not that I consider he should escape a *certain* punishment for his crimes against me."

Li bowed. "He will be found, great Princess. Be assured that the matter of your marriage will be taken care of. But have you not more important things to consider? For yourself, and for your son?"

She flushed at the rebuke. "I intend to do what is best for my son, Marshal Li," she said. "But I would have you know, and believe, that neither Prince Yuan Hsu nor I have any desire to act except as we may believe, or be convinced, is best for China. If it is desired that we should remain here, and even continue some of the prerogatives of the marshal, pending a more permanent arrangement, I shall be happy to do so. If, indeed, such a permanent arrangement"—she glanced at Chang— "equally requires our remaining in Peking and retaining the reins of government, then again I shall be prepared to carry out such duties to the best of my ability. If, on the other hand, it is thought best for my son and me to leave China forever, then be sure that we will also do that, with contented hearts."

"I did not doubt it," Li said, and gazed at her. "I have never doubted that a princess of the Ch'ing would be prepared to accept whatever role her Destiny might thrust upon her, or whatever *sacrifice* that Destiny may call upon her to make, for the good of her country."

Adela's slowly relaxing mind gave a sudden enormous lurch. Because there was yet a third alternative, clearly passing through his mind, and one which might be thought entirely suitable for the chief concubine of Yuan Shih-k'ai, who was also a Ch'ing princess, and who above all else was the mother of Yuan's son. After everything, she realized, she was still a prisoner, and even condemned? That would surely depend on Dr. Sun, a gentle and courteous man . . . but she had not seen the doctor for five years, and much blood had been spilled in the intervening time.

And when Dr. Sun rode into Peking, if Charlie were at one side, Lin-tu would be at the other.

For the third time she looked at Chang, who at last spoke.

"All things, even the hand of Destiny, will be revealed in the fullness of time, my lady Princess," he said. "That is the only truth of which any man can be certain."

15

The Coup d'Etat

Adela heard the drums and the bugles, the tambourines and the cymbals, the rifle shots and the exploding firecrackers, long before the entourage of Dr. Sun was even near the Gate of the Zenith. Each decibel seemed to chime with the pounding of her heart. Charles was approaching. But also her final joust with Destiny?

The entire population of the Forbidden City had turned out for this auspicious occasion. But then, Marshal Li had assured her that all of Peking itself was lining the road to welcome the man who for so many of them represented their dream of a better life. Li said these things openly. Adela understood that he genuinely believed, insofar as he believed in anything, that Sun might be the man to hold the future of China in his mind. He only mistrusted Sun's control over his lieutenants, and sought an honorable future for himself. That was understandable, and acceptable. It was almost noble.

It was not so noble for her to realize that he meant to use her as a bargaining counter to obtain what he wanted, from Sun's chivalry and known friendship for her, or to sacrifice her to Sun's necessities, should he be *too* much at the mercy of his extremist lieutenants.

That Charlie was accompanying Sun promised, at this moment, nothing more than a deepening of the tragedy which threatened to hang about her neck like a shroud. *Were* she to be sacrificed, then Charlie would be sacrificed too.

But these were almost pleasurably agonizing reflections compared with the sheer excitement of meeting him again. She had not seen him for more than four years. Then she had walked away from a boy, hoping he would run behind her and thus prove himself a man. But then she had been a girl herself, convinced that life owed her something, that Destiny had a place for her in its vast scheme of things. Now she was a woman who had looked on many horrible things, who had experienced many horrible things, and who understood that only survival mattered. Charlie had lived and fought in the most desperate circumstances for most of those four years. What had *he* learned in his progress toward manhood?

Because it was not enough for him to be just Charlie. Unknown to him, he had a rival, whom he must equal and surpass, to seize and hold her entire love. It was unfair that this should be. But she had long since understood that life was not a matter of fairness. It was a matter of Destiny. That she had been born at once beautiful and with royal blood had set her feet, even before she had been aware they were moving, upon a devious and often terrifying path. That she had survived had been because of those strengths born in her, transmitted from her parents and her great ancestors, even from Nurhachi himself. That she had met Chen Fu had preserved at once her life and her sanity. That she should ask the man to whom she was prepared to devote that life at least to match her savior was an aspect of *his* Destiny, whether he would or no.

But it was still a fearful thought, when it could involve his life as well.

And when she had to receive him as Princess Adela, chief concubine of the great warlord. Li had been very insistent upon this; he knew the value of proper ceremonial. The meeting was a matter for men, and thus the avenue before the Dragon Staircase was filled only with men, with the soldiers of General Chang's Imperial Guard—why had he made no sign as yet? or was his heart, his mind, too little to *dare*?—and the general himself, with Marshal Li, cocked hats a mass of plumes, and the mandarins of the *tsung li yamen,* and the other state offices. No eunuchs were to be seen at all, but to either side, gathered on the verandas of the temples, were the women, white-robed and excited. In only five short years Yuan Shih-k'ai had taught these cloistered creatures the pleasures not only of seeing but also of being seen. There were undoubtedly even Ch'ing princesses still among them, ancient aunts and cousins passed by in the tumult of successive revolutions, reluctant ever to enter the outside world even if they had possessed the means, content to shelter beneath the anonymous umbrella of life in the Forbidden City. Only the direct line of succession mattered, and *they* were all in Japan.

Save for the princess, far removed from any direct line, but the most important person here today, as the mother of Yuan Shih-k'ai's son. She stood on the Dragon Staircase itself, and although she was surrounded by guards as well as women, they remained at a distance, using the side stairs, for only royalty could tread the image of the Dragon. Thus only Peter stood at her side. For this greatest occasion of his brief life, Li had had created for him a magnificent uniform, blue jacket and white trousers, toy sword and cocked hat with plumes. Peter had been absolutely delighted, had shrieked his pleasure when he had been dressed. Now he was hot and bored, yawned and pulled at her hand. He wanted to draw his toy sword and brandish it, and cut at trees and shrubs, and even people, and prove himself a warlord. It was one of the few words he knew. Warlord.

She gazed down the avenue, herself feeling hot and sticky in her heavy brocade robe, her hair piled on the top of her head in a Chinese chignon rather than a pompadour, secured with heavy wooden pins. The robe itself was in imperial yellow, and she wore imperial-yellow slippers. Her fingers were so heavily laden with jeweled rings she could hardly raise her hand, her face so heavily caked with makeup she could not feel the rays of the sun, although their heat penetrated everything.

But at least the end was in sight. Dr. Sun was riding his horse through the gate, and there dismounting, gesturing his lieutenants to do the same. As usual he and his people, in their workmanlike khaki, their absence of braid and plume, made a considerable contrast to the brilliance of the troops awaiting them, the almost incandescence which seemed to surround Li and Chang and their officers. Adela squinted in the glare, wished to crane her neck, even to wave, to see if she received a wave back. But there was more than one tall figure dressed in khaki to be seen.

She wondered if Sun remembered the last time he had come to Peking in his search for power, and been rudely rebuffed? Did he anticipate, and fear, a similar act of treachery today? Had he prepared against it? But there was no suggestion of apprehension or mistrust as the short figure advanced toward Marshal Li, shook hands and then embraced, and was introduced to General Chang. These men had fought against each other most bitterly in the Yangtze valley only three years ago, at the behest of Marshal Yuan. But that was the past; today they were concerned with the future.

Her heart was pounding as she began to identify faces. Lin-tu! Unmistakably. A tall young Chinese with granite-hard features, whom she had never seen before. And then a man with sun-browned white skin and a beard, certainly tall, and broad-shouldered, also wearing khaki uniform, but too much *beard*, and too pale-skinned to be Chinese. Could it be? It had to be! Her knees touched each other in anxiety.

The introductions were over, but others were now necessary. Li walked to the foot of the Dragon Staircase and beckoned her. She descended toward him, Peter at her side, faced Sun Yat-sen. "You are already acquainted with Princess Adela," Li said.

Sun bowed and then held out his hand. "I have heard rumors of your death, great Princess," he said. "You will know how happy I am they were . . . exaggerated? And how delightful I am to look again upon your beautiful face. And this is your son?"

She had been carefully coached by Li. "This is Prince Yuan Hsu," she said. "Last of the house of Ch'ing."

"A famous name," Sun said enigmatically. "Permit me to introduce my officers. Marshal Lin-tu you have already met." His eyes twinkled. Did he know of that infamous bargain so long ago?

Adela held out her hand. "I am honored to meet you again, Marshal Lin," she said. "And in such felicitous circumstances."

Lin bent but did not take or kiss her fingers. "As I must be honored," he said, "to stand in the presence of so much beauty." He straightened, and their eyes met. You betrayed me, his eyes said, after I had risked my life for you. And you betrayed my love for you. But I will have you yet, one day, Princess. Prepare yourself against that day.

She tilted her chin at him and looked past him at the gaunt-faced young man.

"My aide-de-camp, Colonel Chiang Chung-cheng," Sun said.

The colonel shook hands gravely.

"And my American adviser," Sun said, now openly smiling. "Colonel Charles Baird."

He stood before her, gazing at her, taking her in, only slowly bowing from the waist as she raised her hand. She felt she should say something, but she could think of nothing to say. This young giant *was* Charlie. This man with the firm grasp and the battle-hardened eyes, with the well-worn sword and revolver belts, the aplomb of the professional soldier.

Then what did he see in her?

Sun came to their rescue. "There is much talking to be done," he said. "Talking that will bore you, great Princess. But I am forgetting; Colonel Baird is your brother, is he not? You will entertain the princess, Colonel Baird, while Marshal Li and I consult about the future."

Adela walked down the corridor to the Lotus Apartment, slippers silent on the marble floor. Yet there was noise enough, from the heels of Peter's boots, and Charlie's, just behind her.

Guards saluted and eunuchs bowed, maids whispered. She smiled and nodded to them, because if she relaxed for a moment her face would have collapsed into tears. Of anticipation or apprehension? But that Yuan Shih-k'ai's favorite concubine should be leading a man to her private apartment was sufficiently disconcerting for these ancient upholders of Chinese custom. That she *was* doing so, however, was equally sufficiently indicative of Marshal Li's approval. His bribery, his removal of her from the affairs of state, she thought. As if she cared a fig for affairs of state, when Charlie was immediately behind her.

And but twenty-four hours ago she had dreamed only of escaping this apartment. Now it had suddenly become the most precious place on earth.

The doors were opened for her and she walked through, and stopped, and turned, and gazed at them, Charlie, with three maids and three eunuchs to either side, and Peter standing between them, all looking totally bemused.

"Leave me," she said. "I would be alone with my *brother*. Aisha, you may take the prince with you. Take him into the garden and let him use his sword."

"My sword," Peter shouted, immediately drawing the weapon and brandishing it, to the great alarm of the eunuchs. "I can use my sword."

"Be careful he does not injure himself," Adela said. "Or anyone else. Peter, say good-bye to your Uncle Charles."

Peter stared at Charlie suspiciously.

"Thank you, Aisha," Adela said.

The maid bowed and took Peter's hand to lead him outside.

"And you others, go," Adela said.

One of the eunuchs stepped forward as if he would protest.

"Go!" Adela snapped. "And close the doors. No one is to enter this apartment until I ring."

A last hesitation, and then they filed from the room. The doors clanged shut with a dull thud. Adela walked to the table, her back to Charlie, and pulled ring after ring from her fingers, depositing them in a pile on the lacquered wood. "I do not know how I stand state occasions," she remarked.

She was being utterly artificial, she knew. But how else could she be, after four years? Four *such* years.

"Greatness becomes you," Charlie said. "You were born to it."

She turned to face him. "It is a burden I would most happily shed."

They stared at each other, and the cheeks above the beard flushed. But he did not speak.

"Please be seated," she smiled. "Would you like tea, sake?" She smiled. "I imagine I can even discover Scotch whiskey, if you desire it."

"Nothing," he said. "It would mean an interruption."

"That is true," she agreed. "Would you mind terribly if I changed my gown? It is quite unbearably heavy and hot."

"Of course not," he said.

She went into the bedroom, left the door open. She walked to her wardrobe, released the gown, stepped out of it, stood for a moment allowing the cool breeze entering the window to play over her naked body while she pulled the pins from her hair, allowed it to fall past her shoulders. She wondered if he would come to the door. Was she seducing him as deliberately as she had seduced Chen? But that had *been* seduction. She had not known then that she could love him, or any man. This was an attempt at restoration.

"I knew three years ago," she said, "that you were with Dr. Sun. I prayed for you every night."

He would certainly be able to hear her, even in the outer room, with the adjoining door open.

"I thought you were dead," he said. "I prayed for your soul every night."

She turned, because he *was* standing in the doorway.

He flushed. "I'm sorry," he said. "I didn't mean . . ." He was staring at her. He did remember a girl. Now he was looking at the most beautiful woman in all China. As well as the most notorious.

"Now are our prayers answered," she said. And was in his arms.

* * *

Adela kissed his mouth, kissed his eyes and his cheeks and his forehead, having to pull his head down to her, while she waited for him to possess her. Certainly his hands found her body, but then fell away again. She was asking too much, that four years could be so quickly dismissed.

She released him, turned her back on him, walked to her wardrobe and selected a loose gown in cool linen, which she put on but did not fasten. "Do I shock you?" she asked.

"You amaze me," he said. "That you should be here at all, and more beautiful and confident than ever, that you should . . . well . . ."

"Have survived?" she asked. "It was a matter of will. Of determination, to wait for you." She walked to the bed and sat down; the robe fell back from her legs as she kicked off her slippers.

"And now to see you here, so obviously in command of the situation, in such surroundings . . ."

He had not, then, sufficiently grown up, even now. He could still be awed by appearances. But she was not prepared to indulge in subtlety and seduction here. She did not know how much time they had.

Nor, at this moment, and for the same reason, was she prepared to correct his false impression that she was controlling events, to tell him just how precarious was their very existence. Perhaps he too had lived precariously for four years, but his had been the peril of failing to respond to a given situation with adequate force or confidence. He would know nothing of the agonizing courage required to sit and wait, knowing that one's fate was beyond one's control, as she was doing now.

Almost beyond one's control.

She sat up. "To survive, Charlie," she said, "I have

had to do many terrible things. And suffer many terrible things."

"I know." He came closer, stood at the foot of the bed, gazing at her, taking her in. There was no man in the world who could do that and not want her. "Osborne," he said. "And Yuan. Oh, I do know, Dela. When Osborne came to Dr. Sun's camp, I wanted to kill him. Sun would not let me. But the thought . . ."

She decided not to correct him about Osborne, either. Right this minute. She could never tell him about Chen, and if he were able to accept that there had been more than Yuan, that at least was a sop to her conscience. "And this dismays you?" she asked.

"Of course not. Dela . . . how I have dreamed, how I have hated myself for permitting these things to happen to you."

"Was it not Destiny?" she asked. "And are not those belts you wear, those weapons you carry, unbearably hot? Is not your uniform too warm for comfort?"

He hesitated, then removed his belts, sat on the side of the bed. "Do you mean you really wish . . . ?" He bit his lip.

"I survived for four years on the dream of you, Charlie," she said. And if that too had not always been true, she was prepared to believe it was true now. "Without that dream I would have gone mad. I did not bring you in here to make love to you, and nothing else. I brought you in here to talk, and plan, and . . . to tell you that I love you. But, Charlie, hold me in your arms just once. Hold me and tell me that you love me, despite all, that you will stay at my side, now and always, no matter what may lie ahead of us."

"Oh, Dela," he cried. "How willingly will I swear to that." He held her close, and now he kissed her eyes and cheeks, while his hands slipped inside her robe to stroke the velvet of her skin. "I did not know . . . I dared not suppose, my darling," he said. "I could only dream. Oh, Dela . . ."

"Such dreams are behind us now," she said. "We are awake, but we are still dreaming about reality." She unbuttoned his tunic. Because she *had* brought him in here to make love. Her body cried out for it, but her mind cried out for it even more. To estimate a man's true worth on his performance in bed was grotesquely unfair and primitive. Yet for her there could be no other way. For four years she had existed by virtue of her sexuality, had lived, breathed, slept, and eaten nothing but her ability to arouse and consummate Yuan's desires. And then there had been Chen, to restore her belief in herself as a woman, rather than a machine. But that was all gone now, and she was simply a princess, a diplomatic plaything. Only this man could again make her a woman, and more than that, make her real, make her know that she lived and breathed and *felt,* and was not merely a symbol. Only this man.

Her nails scraped across his chest and around to his back. "Awake," she said. "But still dreaming."

"Will you marry me, Dela?" Charlie asked.

Adela raised her head in surprise, and then realized that he had never actually asked her before. She had done the assuming, incorrectly.

"If you are sure that is what you wish," she said.

He propped himself on his elbow beside her. Amazingly, after Chen and Yuan, she had been almost afraid of him. He was so much bigger than any man she had ever remembered, because she had not remembered *him* at all clearly; she had never had the opportunity to commit him to memory. He had also known only one way of making love, and his weight had alarmed her, as well, even if he had most skillfully held himself above her. But weight and size were only to be enjoyed, where the man was confident. Other positions undoubtedly greatly heightened the sensation of lovemaking. But none was quite so comforting as to feel a strong man's body entirely covering hers, and oddly, none was quite so dominating, for her—to sit on a man's lap, even to kneel before him, had always meant she was at the mercy of *his* muscles, his desire, his strength to sustain her. When Charlie lay on her, and entered her, she knew he was there to stay, until she wished him to move. And he did not lack confidence. That much had he certainly matured.

Now he smiled. "Can you doubt that I wish it?" he asked.

She lay back and gazed at him. "I am what I am," she said. "What I was born to be. What Destiny created me. That is what you are asking for, Charlie."

He was serious, although no trace of a frown crossed his forehead. "Meaning that you wish to remain in China and be a princess or even perhaps a regent for your son?"

"No," she said. "No, I do not wish that." And for the first time she knew she was telling him the absolute truth. "I have known that it might be necessary, and I know that it may still be necessary, at least for a while. But it is not what I wish. I wish to go with you, Charlie, to the ends of the earth. What I meant was, I cannot turn my back upon anything that has happened, to me or about me. Nor can I turn my back upon my son. If we are able to leave China together, you and I, I can promise you not to bring Peter up as a Ch'ing prince, never to remind him that he is Yuan Shih-k'ai's son . . ." And thus tell him he was Chen Fu's son? But she could deal with only one situation at a time. Charlie was here and now. "Yet he will know these things," she went on. "And I will not deny them." She smiled. "I caused your parents sufficient grief, Charlie. You must be prepared for the problems Peter will cause us. And I am his *mother*. I did not adopt him.''

"But you will abandon all of this wealth and power to come with me?" he asked. "And be with me wherever I go?"

"Willingly, Charlie," she said. "Oh, willingly."

"Then have I got to be the most fortunate man on earth," he said, and covered her again.

There was so much she wanted to say and do. But nothing so much as to lie in his arms. And if she was deceiving him, there was nothing else she could do in the little time that was available to them. Not to tell him of Chen was criminal. Not to tell him that all their plans were meaningless, in the context of who and what she was, and her Destiny, or rather, of what Li Yuan-hung and Sun Yat-sen, Chang Hsun and Lin-tu might even now be deciding, was worse than criminal. Yet she had had these few brief moments with him, to hold and to savor, and to dream together, no matter what the future might now bring.

She could only pray he would feel the same. For the moment had arrived. She listened to the outer door of her apartment opening, then closing, pushed him off her and threw a coverlet over him, dragged it over herself as she sat up, facing the maid who stood in the inner doorway, bowing. "I said I was not to be disturbed," she said, simulating anger where she knew only fear.

The maid bowed again, gazed at the man for several seconds, and then bowed a third time. "I am commanded to summon you, my lady Princess," she said. "Your presence is required in the council chamber."

There was no time to bathe, even if there were several maids waiting to attend her. They had to do what they could manage with cloth and basin. And then dress her in her imperial-yellow gown and let her gaze at herself in

the mirror in an attempt to repair the damage done to
her makeup. There was no time to arrange her hair,
either; it lay in raven tresses down her back.

In China, she wondered, before decapitation, do they
cut away the hair? She thought not. Rather does one
executioner hold the hair high, while the other slices
through the neck. She shuddered.

"I shall come with you." Charlie looked ridiculous,
sitting up in bed with the covers around his waist.

Adela looked at the maid-messenger. Who bowed.
"It is *your* presence that is requested, my lady
Princess," she said.

"Will you forgive me?" Adela asked. "I shall not be
long. They but wish my agreement to whatever they
have formulated."

"If you are not back in half an hour," he said, "I will
come and fetch you. Dela . . ."

She hesitated, and then, before them all, crossed the
room and kissed him. She was in a mood to defy the
world. Because the next fifteen minutes would bring her
either all the power in the world or all the freedom in the
world—or all the death in the world. And for him and
Peter as well. Was there so much difference between
those three aspects of life?

"I will return to you in half an hour," she said. "Do
not move from there."

She followed the maids and eunuchs down the
corridors, past armed guards, and into the great council
chamber. She had never been in here before, although
she knew of it well enough. To her surprise, only the
four principals were present, Chang and Li, Lin and
Sun, seated at a table, getting up to bow to her as she
entered. She stood just within the doors, listened to
them closing behind her. She was, at last, face to face
with her Destiny. But approaching her in a strange
form, she thought. Sun and Lin looked angry—Lin

much more so than his master. Li looked as bland as ever. Chang looked noncommittal as ever. Her heart lurched. Could it be . . . ?

"My lady Princess," Li said. "Please to come forward. Will you not be seated?"

There was a vacant chair between the opposing sides. Chang held it for her, and she slowly sat down, looking at Sun and then at Li.

"I have invited you to join us, great Princess," Li said, "because I know how anxious you must be to learn the results of our discussions, the future path that China will take under our leadership."

Adela inclined her head. She could only wait.

"First," Li said, allowing his gaze to take in her undressed hair, "we are truly sorry to have disturbed your rest. We had no idea the hour was so late or that you retired so early."

"With your *brother,*" Lin commented, and refused to be abashed when the others, even Sun, glared at him.

"It is no matter," Adela said, returning his stare and refusing even to blush. "I must apologize to all of *you* for having retired. I did not know you would complete your discussions tonight."

"Where the fate of a nation hangs upon men's thoughts, those thoughts are likely to be accelerated," Li said. "Well, then, great Princess, you will perhaps be sorry to learn that it is the decision, and the wish, of Dr. Sun and myself that the concept of China as an empire, ruled by a dynasty of princes"—he smiled—"or even princesses, is out of keeping with the needs of a modern society. It is therefore our decision that China should become a republic as rapidly as this can be arranged."

He paused, awaiting her reaction. She kept her face still; she did not even look at Chang Hsun; in any event, he was unlikely to reveal his opinion of the decision. "I have long known and understood Dr. Sun's mind," she said. Was she relieved? She thought so. But she dared not admit relief until she knew what her own fate was to be.

"It has therefore been decided, and Dr. Sun has magnanimously agreed to this, that it would be best for me to retain the outward show of power and perform the tiresome executive duties that attend a head of state," Li said, his expression never changing. "Pending the holding of elections for a constituent assembly."

Adela's head turned before she could stop it, to gaze at Sun. Yuan Shih-k'ai might have used those very words. He *had* used words very like them five years ago. Sun's face was grim rather than sad today; his expression also betrayed no opinion.

"Not that Dr. Sun will leave the country," Li hastily added. "He has a part to play in the coming elections. He even has some considerable hopes of himself becoming first president of the republic of China. Thus he has much to do in the coming months."

So Li was not quite as ruthless as Yuan had been. But how had he gotten Sun to agree? And even more, Lin-tu? Naked force? She gazed at Lin-tu, and he met her gaze, his eyes hostile.

"But you will be more interested in our deliberations concerning you and your family, Princess," Li said. "As I have warned you in the past, there are those"— his gaze also drifted to Lin-tu—"who believe that the Ch'ing should be extirpated from the face of the earth forever, who regret that all the main members of the dynasty are beyond the reach of vengeance in Japan, who rejoice that at least two such members are present here in Peking. I would have you know at once, my lady Princess, that Dr. Sun and I reject such barbaric considerations. That you and your son can be with us on so famous an occasion will always fill our hearts with joy."

Adela found she was holding her breath. Like all Chinese, he masked his intentions with so much double talk that it was still impossible for her to discern whether or not she had yet been condemned to death.

"However," Li went on, "it is apparent to us all that every moment you remain in China, your life is in danger, as is that of your son. It is therefore decided that at the earliest possible moment you and the prince will be taken to Tientsin, and there placed on a ship for the United States."

Very slowly Adela released her breath. She had not believed this moment could ever actually arrive.

"It is further decided," Li continued, "that you will be paid a pension for as long as you live, great Princess, as a Ch'ing, and indeed as the last and perhaps the greatest of the Ch'ing, who brought such solace to the warlord in his declining years. Thus you will never want. This pension is to be the responsibility of the government of the republic."

Adela raised her head. She could feel tears starting from her eyes.

"And it is finally decided," Li said, "that Colonel Baird will be instructed to accompany you, as your permanent aide-de-camp and bodyguard."

She *was* going to weep. That, after so many fears and suspicions, these men *were* going to act honorably by her and Peter, and even Charlie . . . Then why were Sun and Lin looking so angry?

"I thank you, Marshal Li," she said. "I thank you all. Now I know that the future of China is truly in safe hands. May I ask how soon my son and I, and Colonel Baird, may leave for Tientsin?"

Li's eyes were hooded. "As soon as it can be arranged," he said. "That will be, great Princess, as soon as Dr. Sun returns to Canton and disbands his army."

Again Adela's head turned sharply to look at Sun. Because now she understood. And yet, did not, sufficiently.

Li rose. "So our conference has been terminated to the satisfaction of us all," he said. "It is at last possible to look forward to a future for China, a future of greatness and perhaps even prosperity. A future with which perhaps all our names will be linked, as men, and a woman"—he smiled at Adela—"who saved their country from anarchy and barbarian interference. My lady Princess, my felicitations."

He bowed and left the room. After a moment's hesitation, almost as if he expected Adela to accompany him, Chang followed his leader. But she had no wish to find herself alone with Chang Hsun at this moment. Everything had turned out exactly as she had most wished, and he would no doubt want to whisper plots. But plots were behind her forever.

Besides, she was curious to discover just *how* everything had turned out so well. And the doors remained open, while outside her guards and women waited and watched. She could be in no danger here, not even from Lin-tu.

"I have much to thank you for, Dr. Sun," she said. "Be sure of my eternal gratitude."

Sun said nothing, as he too slowly rose to his feet.

"You are an evil succubus hung around our necks," Lin-tu growled. And looked at his leader. "And he would not cast you off."

Adela looked from one to the other. "I would know the truth of the matter," she said.

"It is of no importance," Sun said. "As Marshal Li

has told us, all has worked out, no doubt for the best. We must simply be patient.''

"Patient," Lin-tu snapped. "Patience is your besetting weakness, Sun Yat-sen. Patience! Do you not know, Princess, that Li gave Sun a simple choice of acquiescing in his plans or of standing beside him and therefore sharing in the responsibilities as your head and that of your son were publicly struck from your shoulders. For crimes against the state, he said. Oh, you are guilty of crimes against the state, Princess. The sight of your head rolling in the dust would not only be the most beautiful any man could see, it would also be the most just.''

Adela stood up in turn, staring at Sun. "Li offered you this?''

"It was a form of negotiation," Sun told her, in some embarrassment. "He knew I would never agree to such an act.''

"And thus he has surrendered everything," Lin snapped at her. "Everything he has worked for all of his life, to save your worthless skin, *great* Princess.''

"Have you, Dr. Sun?" Adela asked. "Have you really done that?''

Sun smiled, and shrugged. "I do not believe so," he said. "Li wished my agreement to his proposals, thus he used every means that came to his hand. But behind it all, he is an honest man, and a patriotic Chinese, as well. I am neither exiled nor under house arrest. Indeed, he *wishes* me to return to my people in the South and make sure of their support. He fears only a continuing anarchy, to the ruination of our land. And he is quite right when he says that he controls the army, and that the army will need to be persuaded that I represent the will of China, as indeed will the great viceroys need to be so persuaded, before they will fully accept my authority. You must remember, great Princess, that I come from no noble house, but am simply a man with a dream. To many Chinese warlords I am an upstart peasant." He sighed. "These are sound reasons for Li remaining in control pending elections. I but wish he had put them to me honestly, as man to man, confident that I am no less a patriot than himself. But then, a man's methods of doing business are often irrelevant. It is the outcome of his deeds which matters."

Adela bit her lip.

"An honest man." Lin-tu sneered. "Who commands you to disband your army."

"To prevent a clash with *his* army, Lin," Sun said gently.

"You are a fool, Sun Yat-sen," Lin-tu declared. "A trusting fool. Li is treating you with more contempt even than did Yuan. Yuan at least considered it necessary to exile you for his own safety. Li does not care what you do, provided you disband your army. I will serve you no longer. I have given my life to your cause. I have *wasted* my life in your cause. I shall waste no more of it." He went to the door, paused, and turned, to point at Adela. "You are fortunate, Princess, in that this *honest* man believes you are an innocent pawn in these affairs, and therefore feels that to rid the world of your presence would be a crime. Flee while you have the opportunity. There are few others in China so convinced of your innocence." He marched down the corridor, while the guards and women stared after him.

"I am so sorry," Adela said. "Oh, Dr. Sun, I am so terribly sorry."

Sun shrugged, and took her hand. "I do not believe he is right in his estimation of Li, or I would not have agreed to the marshal's proposals."

"But Lin . . . to have him quarrel with *you* . . ."

"We have quarreled before. He is an uneducated

man, and therefore a suspicious one. He regards you, from all the circumstances—your birth, the remarkable way you survived the Boxers, your upbringing, even your beauty, and more recently your . . . relationship with Yuan Shih-k'ai—as being dangerous, more dangerous, perhaps, than all the rest of the Ch'ing put together. He sees you as some kind of evil spirit, sent especially by the gods to bring havoc in your wake. He cannot understand that you are but a girl seeking happiness." He gazed into her eyes. "Are you *not* such a girl, Princess?"

"Yes," she said. "Oh, yes. But have I the right to claim happiness at your expense?"

"You have cost me nothing," Sun said. "I am sure of the South. With that support I shall have sufficient votes to win any election that may be held, whereas northern support is splintered among the various warlords. I regard the future as established."

"But suppose Lin-tu is right, and Li Yuan-hung *does* plan treachery?"

"I do not think he does," Sun said. "But even should he, I am no longer so easy a man to bedevil as I was in 1911. Even Yuan Shih-k'ai found that out. I am served by the most loyal of aides." He glanced through the door to where Chiang Chung-cheng waited, towering above the guardsmen to either side. "And your own Charles Baird. I understand something of the differences between you, in the past, great Princess. But it is the future that must concern you. He is a good man, and a trustworthy one. He has served me truly for three years. Now I willingly release him to serve *you.*"

"But can you spare him?"

"I think so. I have, too, the love of my people. It is nothing for me to disband my army. My people will return to their homes, but they will sleep with their rifles at their sides, and should I again have need of them, they will come swarming to my help. No, no, Princess. Do not fear for me. Or for yourself, anymore. Those days are behind you. Go home to America, and live, and be happy. You are entitled to something of that.''

"And Lin-tu?" she asked.

Sun smiled. "He will rejoin me when he has overcome his pique. He always has before.''

"He really is an incredibly *noble* man," Adela said. "I hope things do work out for him. I am almost coming to believe that they may then even work out for China. And he has the highest opinion of you, Charlie.''

"Yet you would now have me abandon him," Charlie said.

She glanced at him. She had dreaded this mood of reaction, even as she had known it had to come. "You must do as you think best, Charlie," she said. "I have been given no choice.''

The three of them sat around the low table in her apartment and ate their dinner, Peter as usual staring at his uncle suspiciously. He was utterly confused, poor little mite, she thought. But would he not be even more confused when his uncle suddenly turned out to be his father?

Charlie smiled and ruffled Peter's hair. "As you say, you have been given no choice, my darling. Therefore I have no choice either. And again as you say, I hope things work out for the gallant doctor. But what of the dynasty? Can you really come to terms with its demise? This is forever, you know.''

"I know," she said. "But these last four years I have seen too much, and learned too much. I have discovered just how thoroughly my family has neglected China. And I have discovered even more just what a crime it is, what a crime it must *become* for one man . . ." She smiled. "Or presumably, one woman, to hold total power. From all they say of her, Tz'u-Hsi was even more of a vicious tyrant than Yuan Shih-k'ai."

He smiled in turn. "Yet I have always had a feeling that you once dreamed of what *you* might be able to accomplish, given such power."

She glanced at him in surprise. She had not suspected such discernment in Charlie. "Why, yes," she agreed. "I think I did. More recently than you may suppose. But I think I have learned my lesson. I do not have the ruthlessness to rule. Nor do I have the deception to divide and thus conquer. I am, after all, only half a princess."

"You are all the woman in the world, to me," he said. "And I suspect to a whole lot of others."

Words she longed to hear, even if they brought tears to her eyes. To a whole lot of others. Well, she hoped, to one other, at any rate. But he was gone, and her only course was to hurry away from even his memory, from everything that had frightened and fascinated her at the same time, and try to pretend it had never been.

Her life had immediately changed beyond comprehension. She was still confined to the Forbidden City, but this, she was assured, by both Li and Chang, was for her own protection; there were still too many radicals and Yuan-haters about. She knew they were lying, of course; they did not wish her either rushing to the American legation to betray their secrets, or just disappearing—they wished her to remain firmly their prisoner until they were satisfied with Sun's compliance with their ultimatum, when they could transport her secretly to the coast and place her on a ship in the Gulf of Chihli, and hopefully have done with her forever.

But within the Forbidden City her life was her own.

She was still surrounded, when she wished to be, by maids and eunuchs and guards. But only when she wished. No one questioned her decision that her brother should live with her in the Lotus Apartment; to provide Charlie and her with increased privacy, a separate but closely neighboring apartment was provided for Peter's use, while one of the senior maids was deputed as his nurse. Adela herself spent every possible moment with the boy during the day, Charlie always at her side, talking about America and the new life they were going to; to her relief and pleasure, Peter seemed to be over-coming his innate suspicion of the big bearded white man who was his uncle.

For the rest, everything she wanted that could be obtained was immediately provided. For these last few weeks of her existence as a princess, she was to be treated, apparently, in every way *as* a princess.

There were, of course, things she wanted which could *not* be provided—or so it was said. News was one. As Sun's departure faded, she began to fret; surely he must have regained Canton and fulfilled his part of the bargain by now? Even more did she seek news of Osborne. Had theirs been a Chinese marriage, she could have had it ended with a snap of her fingers. But it had been an American marriage and could be ended only in an American court. She wanted Osborne, less to punish him now—that was behind her in her newfound happi-ness—than to make him subscribe his name to the neces-sary documentation to procure her an annulment in San Francisco. But Osborne was not to be had. "Alas," Li explained on one of his rare visits to her, "the scoundrel seems to have disappeared. From his meeting with Dr. Sun in the Shan, we know he went on to Canton. And thence to Hong Kong. But from Hong Kong, although we know that he is no longer there, we have no idea what has happened to him. But we are looking, great Princess. We are looking. He will be found eventually, and made to bend his knee before you."

"He does know where Osborne is," she grumbled to Charlie. "I am sure of it. The man is so deceitful . . . and it doesn't seem to occur to him that we need him *now*."

Charlie was prepared to be more relaxed about it. "Does it really matter?" he asked. "You have not lived with Osborne since August 1912. It doesn't matter what he's been telling the American minister and Mr. Richards. Surely Li will provide you with an affidavit that since your arrival here you have been Yuan Shih-k'ai's mistress and nobody else's. By the time we get home it is going to be Christmas, the way things are going. Then we can sue for divorce on the grounds of abandonment. We'll win, Dela. We'll win. If you can stand a little scandal."

"I can stand anything," she said. "To be rid of that man." Christmas, she thought. An American Christmas, without fear, and without want, as well. Oh, if only they could get home for Christmas. Lying in Charlie's arms was no longer enough. If she was to be rid of China, then she wanted to *be* rid of China. But was she ever to be rid of China? She awoke from a deep sleep, to discover her room already becoming light with the early dawn, to listen to the sound of the outer door of the Lotus Apartment opening. She sat up, gently squeezing Charlie's shoulder as she did so, to alert him. An assassin? After all these years, all these escapes, all this *survival,* an assassin?

The bedroom door opened, and she gazed at men in uniform, and General Chang Hsun.

"What is the meaning of this?" Adela demanded, drawing the sheet to her throat. "General Chang?"

The general stood to attention and saluted. "It is time to arise, my lady Princess," he said. "And join Prince Yuan Hsu in the throne room, to receive the homage of your officers and people. The homage of all China, to the princess regent of the Ch'ing. Long may she reign over us!"

16

The Ruler

"Are you mad?" Adela shouted, throwing back the covers and leaping out of bed, careless of her nudity.

Chang gazed at her for several seconds, as did his men. Then he said mildly, "Cover yourself, great Princess."

"Oh . . ." Adela snatched a robe from her wardrobe, drew it around her shoulders, glanced at Charlie, who as so often in moments of crisis seemed unable to move. "Or is this your idea of a joke, General Chang?" she demanded in a lower tone.

"A joke, great Princess? About such a subject? And would I dare interrupt the princess's"—he too glanced at Charlie—"*slumber* to make a joke? I am here to tell you that all your troubles are behind you, that the moment you have so long awaited is finally here."

"The moment . . ." She glared at him, could hear herself inhaling. "You would not dare!"

Chang nodded. "Now *is* the time to dare, my lady Princess. But come, we must hasten."

"Hasten? To attempt a coup d'etat? I absolutely refuse."

"To complete the coup d'etat I have already carried

out, my lady Princess," Chang told her. "In your
name, or at least that of your son. If you do not act
now, in my support, and quickly, then all of our heads
will jostle together in the same gutter. She is confused,"
he said to the captain at his side. "No doubt it is the
presence of the man. Shoot him!"

The captain leveled his revolver while Charlie at last
came to life and looked for his own weapons—but they
were on the other side of the room.

"No!" Adela screamed, throwing herself across the
bed and across Charlie as well, having the strangest
recollection of attempting to save Osborne from Feng's
soldiers.

"I felt you might wish to save his life, great
Princess," Chang observed. "If you would save all of
our lives as well, you must come with me now and play
your part. Five of my men will remain with Colonel
Baird to see he comes to no *harm.*"

Adela knelt on the bed, panting. Indeed, she felt like
a trapped animal. All had been going so perfectly. But
had she not known, deep in her heart, that everything
had been going *too* perfectly?

"Haste, my lady Princess," Chang said.

Adela hesitated, then got out of bed.

"Dela," Charlie said. "Dela . . ." He bit his lip.
What was he to say? Let them shoot me? Because would
they not then immediately shoot her as well? And Peter?

"Come," Chang said. "Your Destiny awaits you,
great Princess."

She was hurried down corridors and through a
succession of hallways, all filled with soldiers of the
Imperial Guard, eager to salute her, but obviously in a
state of high tension, until she found herself in the great
throne room where she had first confronted Yuan, how

many centuries ago. This room was also crowded, with soldiers, certainly, but also mandarins, generals, women, and eunuchs. And a group of men obviously under guard, among them Li Yuan-hung, eager to face Chang as he went ahead of Adela into the room. "Are you mad, General Chang?" Li demanded in turn. "Have you entirely lost your senses?"

Chang ignored him, advanced by himself to stand before the throne. "You are gathered here this morning," he announced, "by order of Princess Adela, princess of the royal house of Ch'ing, in the name of her son, Prince Yuan Hsu. Kneel to the prince of the Ch'ing, and to his mother."

Most of the crowd hesitated, but several, those who were already in the plot, no doubt, and schooled by Chang, immediately performed the kowtow, and slowly their example was followed by the remainder, save for Li and the other men under arrest, until the room was filled with kneeling figures. Chang also remained standing. While Adela gave a gasp and ran forward. Hitherto she had been standing in the shadows at the back of the chamber, surrounded by soldiers, and had been happy to remain there; apart from her confusion, she was in utter dishabille, wearing but a single garment, with her hair clouding down her back, and not a trace of makeup on her face. But Peter . . .

He sat on the throne, wearing his uniform, and gave a cry of relief at seeing her. "Mother! Men came and . . ." He began to climb down from the chair—his legs did not reach the floor—and Chang gently lifted him back into place.

"Keep him quiet," he hissed.

Adela rested her hand on Yuan Hsu's arm. "Ssssh, my darling," she said. "It is a surprise party. Will you not enjoy a surprise party?"

"Rise," Chang commanded. "Rise and listen to the words of the princess regent." He held out a sheet of paper.

Adela took it, but did not immediately look at it. She was too concerned with returning the stares directed at her as the men in the room for the first time took in her presence. It was easy to tell who were Chang's men and who were not. And Chang's men were in a considerable minority, save for the soldiers lining the walls. But no one present was *her* man.

"The notables await your words, great Princess," Chang said.

Adela glanced at him, then looked at the paper. She drew a long breath. She had to humor him, at least for a while, until she could think, and understand, and decide what to do. " 'Be it known,' " she read, " 'that after long and painful deliberation, I, Adela, princess of the Ch'ing, mother of Prince Yuan Hsu, have decided that I must act to save China from disruption and anarchy, and with the support and confidence of my loyal Imperial Guard, and their great commander, Marshal Chang Hsu, have decided to take control of the government.' "

There were gasps all around the room, but none louder than her own. She looked at Chang, who gave a brief bow in recognition of his sudden promotion. But when she hesitated to continue, he frowned, and leaned toward her. "Read it, great Princess," he whispered. "Read it loud and clear, that all may hear you. Should I snap my fingers, your paramour is immediately shot."

Adela drew another long breath, tried to control the tendency of her voice to shake. " 'For when I look around me, what do I see? A continuing state of anarchy in this great country of ours. And more, my appointed head of state, designated by me to supervise the return of my family the Ch'ing to their proper position and authority, has negotiated a settlement with the so-called republicans, the rabble of bandits and traitors that follow the archtraitor Sun Yat-sen. Now this false man, this Li Yuan-hung, would seek to exile me and my son, and send us forever from China, and grind the name of Ch'ing forever in the dust. Great nobles, ministers of state, who have for so long upheld the banners of the Ch'ing, how could I stand by and watch these things happen?' "

"That is a lie," Li shouted. "She did not *appoint* me. She is a false princess. She is—"

"Silence that traitor," Chang commanded, "who dares to question the words of Princess Adela."

Li gasped as his guards struck him in the stomach.

"Read on," Chang again commanded in a low voice. "Read on, loudly."

Adela tried to concentrate. " 'I seek no power for myself,' " she said. " 'More than is necessary for the restoration of the greatness of China. Nor do I seek to return to the old ways, where Manchu and Han were separated by law and custom. I do not seek to restore the pigtail, my ministers. I seek a partnership between the two great peoples who inhabit this great land, for the restoration of China to her proper place as supreme in this world of ours. For more than fifty years, since the dynasty weakened, since the British and French barbarians first stormed the Taku forts and marched on Peking, has the glory of China lain in the dust. They have been fifty bitter years, my lords, for us all. They are too well remembered. But let us not forget the two centuries that happened before them. Let us not forget the true greatness bestowed upon this land by the house of Ch'ing. Let us not forget that Ch'ien Lung, mightiest of my ancestors, who reigned for sixty years before his voluntary abdication, was in his day the greatest ruler in the world, that beside him those petty princelings of

Europe were as dust beneath his feet, or that his day, my ministers, was barely a hundred years ago. And let us not forget, either, that Ch'ien Lung himself was only four generations separated from T'ien Ming himself, the immortal Nurhachi, ruler of Manchuria, who led his eight banners to the conquest of the four quarters of the globe. *This* is the greatness I would restore. I seek it not for myself, nor even for my son. I seek it for his majesty the emperor, Hsuan Tung, now exiled in Japan. Lend me your support, great lords, that I may reestablish order in this land of ours, that I may reestablish *strength,* and that I may then demand of the Japanese not only the return of our lawful emperor and his family but also their immediate evacuation of those of our lands they have alienated, not only my own native Manchuria, but Formosa and Korea and the Ryukyu Islands as well.' "

There was an outburst of clapping, which took her by surprise. It was instigated by Chang's men, but taken up by the entire room. Chang beamed.

" 'Help me to achieve these things,' " Adela said. " 'And once they are done, I will be happy to step aside, with my son, and depart into exile, sure again that China is set upon the path of prosperity and greatness.' "

The paper was finished. Slowly Adela raised her head to gaze at them and listen to the tumult, the cries of acclamation, the clapping of hands, and to look, too, at Li Yuan-hung, head bowed and arms secured behind his back, being marched from the room.

"That was dishonest and deceitful," Adela stormed. At last they were alone together, in Yuan's old office, which Chang had appropriated for his own use, and she could give vent to her feelings.

"How so, great Princess?" Chang asked, holding a

chair for her. "Did you not agree to support any action I might take in favor of the Ch'ing?"

Adela sat down without quite meaning to. But actually she was exhausted, quite drained of strength by the emotional discharge of the previous two hours. "But it was not *necessary*," she insisted. "Had we not gotten everything we wanted already?"

Chang sat behind the great desk, opposite her. "We got nothing, great Princess. Your family was deposed and sentenced to perpetual exile, and China was threatened with a republican government. Oh, it may have been what *you* personally desired, having regained your paramour . . ."

Her head came up, but he did not even blink. "But the situation for China is exactly as I, as *you*, great Princess, outlined it in your speech."

"*My* speech," she said contemptuously. "And that is another thing. Dragging me from my bed, forcing me into an absurd situation, giving me a tissue of lies to read . . ."

"Forgive me, great Princess," Chang said patiently. "But every word you spoke was a profound truth. And they were the manifestation of your Destiny. I may have written them out for you, but they were words you *should* have spoken, unprompted. What, yield China to republican theorists? Yield China to Sun Yat-sen?"

"I should have been consulted," she grumbled. But she was on the defensive. Because had not everything he had written down for her to say represented a thought, a feeling of her own, at least in the past? She had determined to put such considerations behind her, but she had not entirely suppressed them.

"Would that not have been a mistake? Would you not have tried to resist me?"

"And do you imagine I will support you now?"

"Indeed you will, great Princess. Simply because you

have no other choice. To the world, and more especially to *China,* you have stood beside me and declared *your* intention and *your* decision.'' She glared at him, and he smiled. ''Besides, is it not what you have always wanted to have happen, truly? You are become the most powerful woman in China. In the absence of the rest of the Ch'ing, you are far more powerful than Tz'u-Hsi ever was. Indeed, it is possible to consider you the most powerful woman who has ever sat upon the Dragon throne. Or stood beside it. And you will be there for some time. It will undoubtedly be a lengthy and tiresome task, regaining the emperor from the Japanese. It may take forever.''

The suggestion implicit in his remark was too immense for her to take up at that moment. She had to concentrate on the present, until she could spare the time to consider the future. ''Save that I have no power at all,'' she remarked. ''Except as you think fit.''

Chang inclined his head reverently. ''It is always wise for a young woman to accept the advice of an older man, great Princess. Fear not, I seek nothing from you, save your acquiescence in my plans to perpetuate your fame and your race. I have no desire to usurp your bed. That is to say, I would not be a man did I not *desire* to possess the most beautiful woman I have ever looked upon, but it shall remain, I promise you, only a desire.'' He gave another of his quick smiles. ''For I have observed that those who seek to love you too well, great Princess, suffer for it. Besides, you have a lover, have you not? Enjoy him, great Princess. I shall not take him from you.''

''Unless I refuse to do as you demand.''

Chang shrugged. ''As I alone know what is best for China, great Princess, what needs to be done, and when, should you fail to do as I suggest, now and always, then no doubt we are all bound for the block.

Colonel Baird may well discover himself to be the fortunate one, should *I* execute him before someone like Lin-tu can get to him."

Angry breath hissed through her nostrils. "And if I tell you that I hate and despise everything you have done, everything you will do?"

Chang bowed. "That is invariably the lot of those who would serve, great Princess."

"And that I will laugh when the warlords come here to cut off your head, even if mine must roll beside it?"

"I do not doubt your courage, great Princess. No man dare do that, having studied the vicissitudes of your life. But the warlords will never break into the Forbidden City to destroy us while we *govern*. And while we possess the army. And those things I intend to do. Beginning immediately. You will excuse me."

He thought he could dismiss her from his presence like some schoolgirl? "I have not yet finished this discussion," she pointed out. "I wish to know what is to happen to Li Yuan-hung."

"He awaits your pleasure, great Princess. I have two orders here awaiting your signature. One commands his instance decapitation. This is the one I would recommend, that the country may understand that you can be harsh. The other, in view of the high position he briefly occupied, and his position at the side of Yuan Shih-k'ai, offers him the use of the silken cord."

"I would have you prepare a third," Adela said. "He is *not* to be harmed."

Chang raised his eyebrows.

"Let him . . . let him be sent into exile or some such thing."

"That is impossible."

"It is what *I* wish," Adela said.

They stared at each other for several seconds; then Chang's eyelids flickered. He was clearly deciding that she would have to be humored in *some* directions. "If that is what you wish, great Princess. But he cannot be exiled. He has too great a following. I will place him under permanent house arrest on his estate. Will that satisfy you?"

"If I am assured no harm will befall him, even by *accident.*"

Chang sighed. "Upon the souls of my ancestors, great Princess."

Which was an oath no Chinese would ever dare break. She had won her first victory. On a minor subject, perhaps. But still a victory. It was time to build on her advantage. "And Dr. Sun?"

"He, alas, is beyond our jurisdiction at the moment. And will no doubt take care to remain so."

"I meant, will we not reopen negotiations with him?"

"How may the house of Ch'ing negotiate with a sworn enemy?" Chang inquired. "In the course of time, when we have attended to more pressing matters, we will dispatch a military force to Canton to destroy the republicans once and for all."

"And if I forbid it? If I *would* negotiate with him?"

Chang bowed. "I must beg the great princess to permit herself to be guided by the experience of her councilors in these matters. She will have enough to do here in Peking. Much of it of a most pleasurable nature. What, do you not wish to welcome your mother and father?"

"My . . . ?" She stared at him in amazement. If he had been saving this trump just in case she became difficult, he had certainly played it with maximum effect. Her brain seemed to have gone blank. Constance, here, in China?

"They landed in Tientsin yesterday, great Princess. As soon as the countryside has been made safe, they will be coming up to Peking. They wish only to kneel at your feet."

She did not know what to say or do; certainly she was sure she wanted, she needed, Charlie at her side.

"That will not be possible, on so public an occasion, great Princess," Chang explained. "*I* may understand that, like all human beings, you suffer the weaknesses of the flesh. But to the world of common folk you are, and must remain, above such things as human desire, as you must be above human weakness and human error. You are the great princess, and must be known only as such."

"And do you not suppose Mr. and Mrs. Wynne have returned to China at least as much to see their son as to see me?" she demanded. Charlie had told her he had written to his parents, although he had had no idea when the letter would reach them, if indeed it ever would. But apparently it had.

"Mrs. Wynne will have ample time for spending with her son, great Princess," Chang said. "But she will wish to see *you* first."

Adela understood; here was a chance for propaganda. She still did not know what to do for the best, how to combat this enormous albatross that had been hung around her neck, to direct herself from this terrible treadmill on which her feet had found themselves. Charlie, when at last she managed to regain her bedchamber, could offer no help—indeed, she was reluctant to seek it from him. She had at least lived in these surroundings, and at this risk, for more than four years, during which, she now knew, her nerves had been forced to accumulate the strength of steel wire, even as she had developed an almost deadly patience, to wait and to watch, to be prepared to accept catastrophe should it envelop her, but equally always to be prepared to recognize and seize any small opportunity for her advancement that might be presented to her.

Charlie knew nothing of such an existence, just as he had no experience of the utterly subservient luxury with which he was surrounded. As she had not explained their true situation to him, as indeed *she* had supposed such traumas were behind her following the agreement between Sun and Li, the events of this morning had been like a thunderclap on his senses. When she tried, belatedly, to give him the true picture, he was unable to grasp the immensity of what had happened, kept saying, "But that is quite incredible. It just can't be happening."

Feelings such as she had had on the train with Osborne four years ago. He would have to learn, as she had done, that all things were possible in the tangled web of Chinese politics and Chinese ambition. As he would, she was sure. But for the moment she was on her own. She needed the time to think, to analyze just what *had* happened, to decide what was likely to happen next, and she was being given no time, but was whirled from one council meeting to another, at which decisions had invariably been made before she arrived, just as she spent her days reviewing one battalion after another, watching the soldiers march past Peter and herself, then presenting them with new colors and entertaining the officers to tea, to dazzle them with her smile and her beauty, make them wish to serve only *her*. She knew only that to attempt to go against Chang in any way would be to endanger Charlie, as well as Peter himself. She could only wait, and pray, and dream, and dread the thought that in the parade she might encounter the face of Chen Fu—but she never did. Nor would she risk betraying either of them by asking after this other colonel in her life. Because were Chang even to suspect that she had another follower, and especially one who commanded a regiment in the army, he would undoubtedly have Chen assassinated.

And now, Constance!

"Remember," Chang told her, "I shall be there watching you and listening to you, great Princess. Act your part, and attempt no subterfuge or pleas for help. A snap of my fingers . . ."

"I understand your meaning, Chang," she said. For the occasion she wore one of her imperial-yellow robes, with her raven hair forming an enormous ruby-and-emerald-studded natural crown rising eighteen inches above her head, and stood beside the throne on which Prince Yuan sat, surrounded by ladies and eunuchs, officers and mandarins, people she had hastily been introduced to during the last week but whose names and faces she hardly recognized, all of whom were watching her. While Chang, as he had promised, stood immediately beside her. In public he never left her side for a moment.

She watched the doors, scarcely daring to breathe, as they were thrown open and Constance and Frank entered. Constance wore pink, with an enormous hat, clearly a new outfit bought especially for this occasion. She looked quite lovely, but totally bemused. As did Frank.

Adela went toward them, arms outstretched. "Mother!" she said. "Father!"

"Dela!" Constance spoke in a whisper as she took in the magnificent creature she had once dandled on her knee. "Can it be you?"

"I am like a bad penny," Adela said with a smile. "I always turn up. Have you no kiss for me, Father?"

Frank Wynne glanced right and left, almost guiltily, as he embraced the princess of the Ch'ing.

"Kneel," Chang commanded the assembly. "Kneel to the parents of the great princess."

Without a moment's hesitation the assembly performed the kowtow.

"Oh, Dela," Constance said. "Oh, my dear, dear child." There were tears in her eyes.

"Come, Mother," Adela said. "And meet your grandson."

"I am truly sorry, Mrs. Wynne," said General Chang Hsun, "that it has not been possible for you to see more of your daughter. But you understand, affairs of state . . . You are comfortable in your house? It has been restored to your satisfaction?"

"Very much so," Constance said. "Although we would have preferred to live here in the Forbidden City, closer to our children."

Chang gave one of his quick bows. "Alas, dear lady, that too is impossible. Protocol, you understand. The great princess must not only rule, she must be seen to rule, to be as far above us ordinary mortals as are the heavens themselves. Therefore she cannot be seen to possess an earthly mother, who is not even Chinese or Manchu—not even when that mother comes to us in so beautiful a guise."

Constance glared at him. She had lived long enough in China herself to be fully acquainted with Chinese double talk. But now was not the time to be angry, as she looked around the glittering assembly, the princess's reception. It could not, presumably, be described as a Christmas party, in a non-Christian land, for all that Christmas was but a week away.

Yet the concept of such a reception was an even more Western idea than any entertained by Yuan. For here was everybody who was anybody in Peking, even the legation officials and their wives, even Mr. Maltby, the

American minister, and Mr. Richards. All were clearly overwhelmed at being allowed into the Forbidden City at all, gazed in wonder at the eunuchs who guarded the doorways, at the magnificent splendor of the cloth-of-gold draperies, the gold and silver cutlery and crockery, at the glittering uniforms of the Chinese marshals, the robes of their women. But most of all, at the princess herself, tonight dressed not in imperial yellow, but in a scarlet robe, close-fitting at neck and breast and thigh, slit to the knee to permit her to move freely, smiling graciously as she circulated among her guests. Unutterably lovely, unutterably scintillating, as much in her personality as in the jewels which sparkled in her hair, at her ears and neck, and on her fingers. Unutterably confident.

And yet, unutterably sad? Or was that something only a mother could see?

Certainly she was lonely. Because Charlie was not at her side? Charlie was never at Adela's side. Charlie was something *she* had to follow up.

"I understand these things, Marshal Chang," she said. "And have no wish to disrupt the princess's arrangements. I but wish I could see more of my son. Or *anything* of my son."

She had been allowed but a single interview, and then with Chang and several others as well as Adela herself present. Charlie had certainly looked well, and he had equally certainly looked at Adela with adoring, if watchful eyes. But just as certainly he had not been happy. She supposed "watchful" was as good a word to describe him as any. He had expressed nothing but joy at seeing her again, and a wish to see more of her in the near future. That had been five weeks ago.

Chang gave another bow. "It is a pity he could not attend this evening's reception," he said. "But again, it was the princess's wish, and for the same reason as I just told you. She cannot afford to reveal the slightest human weakness. How can you not admire the courage and the *will* shown by so young a woman in seizing and using so much power, because she feels it is for the good of her country and her people? I tell you, Mrs. Baird, I, and all my officers, are overwhelmed with joy that we have been given the opportunity to serve so great a lady. And I know Colonel Baird feels the same. Should you not be happy about that?''

Constance stared at him, and then at Adela. Again she thought: The princess's wish. Could she really believe that? Everything she knew about China, everything she thought she knew about Adela, told her that was a lie, had to be a lie—in which case the poor girl was trapped in the center of a more gigantic spider's web than ever. As was Charlie. On the other hand, watching her, taking in that supreme mixture of confidence and condescension, remembering how the girl, then only seventeen, had taken charge of their escape from this city . . . was she not making the same mistake as Frank had made in San Francisco? The girl she remembered had disappeared more than four years previously. Out of what that girl had experienced, this woman had emerged, beautiful, assured, dominating, powerful . . . and ruthless? Chang claimed so. Could he not just be telling the truth?

Christmas, Adela thought. She and Charlie and Peter had planned to be home by now, their adventures behind them. Now their adventures had only just begun. The biggest adventure of all. The adventure she knew in her bones could only end on the scaffold. Unless she managed to do something about it.

But there was almost nothing she *could* do about it. She had been totally outwitted, as had Li and Sun, by Chang. He had planned and schemed, gotten her to agree to act, should it become necessary to save her life, and then had seemed to forget all about it, while he had been waiting with a deadly patience that had deceived them all. He had appeared to support Li in his demands on Sun, had appeared to agree that the dynasty should never be allowed to regain power and that the princess and her son should be exiled. And had been but waiting for Sun to return to Peking and disband his army before revealing his hand. And it was *his* hand, no one else's. In the few months since the coup d'etat this had come home to her with ever-increasing force. His officers and the mandarins in the government regarded what had happened with incredulous apprehension, but like her, considered themselves as helpless, so long as Chang controlled the army, and more especially, the Imperial Guard here in Peking. Those viceroys and warlords who had visited the city to see for themselves had also bowed low before her, and listened to Chang expounding his plans, and gone away to think, and wait, and see.

They waited, no doubt, for many things. For her recognition by the Western powers, although with the war in Europe approaching a critical stage, with both sides apparently exhausted, that was less important than it would have been five years ago. But they also waited for the Japanese reaction to events, for what attitude the Empire of the Rising Sun would take to the proposed restoration of the Ch'ing, their traditional enemies, no less than to the words spoken by the Ch'ing princess regent, who had seemed almost to threaten them. And perhaps they waited too for Dr. Sun. No word had been heard from Canton, despite the messages Chang had sent south, inviting the doctor to subscribe to the new regime or be declared an outlaw. Dr. Sun had said his army could be disbanded and reformed whenever he chose. Was he now reforming that army? Or was he again, as usual, about to be proved over-

optimistic? But whatever he was doing, he would have
to feel that Lin-tu had always been right and that
Princess Adela was indeed the evil genius of China.

If only there were some way she could correct that
impression without endangering them all. She was well
aware that Chang kept her under surveillance at all
times. But tonight she was surrounded by such a
hubbub of conversation that although her maids—
Chang's spies—were ever at her shoulder, even they
were not always within earshot. Had Charlie been
present, it would have been simple. But Chang would
never let Charlie appear in public. He pretended it was
to preserve her image to the public, which was absurd,
as everyone knew she kept a man in her private apartment. But she also knew the marshal was not even concerned about her using Charlie to convey messages to
her European or American friends. Charlie was kept
behind the scenes simply so that he could immediately
be beheaded should she attempt to betray Chang.

A danger she had to remember at all times. But
Charlie knew what she had in mind, and agreed with her
that she surely had at least one friend in this throng,
who could safely be approached. Apart from the
Wynnes. She dared not attempt to convey the truth of
her situation to *them,* because Chang would be instantly
suspicious of a tête-à-tête with her mother at such a
gathering, when she could summon Constance to see
her, in front of him, at any time, were there something
legitimate to be discussed.

Besides, Constance was so obviously overawed by
everything she had encountered since returning to
Peking, Adela found it difficult to believe she could
possibly be of any help.

But Richards . . .

And here at last he was. She had been slowly working
her way toward him, while attempting to appear to be

doing so entirely by accident. But now he was bowing before her. "Mr. Richards," she said, and held out her hand for him to kiss. "How goes the situation in Europe?"

"As well as can be expected, your Highness." His lips brushed her flesh. "How goes the situation here in Peking?"

"As well as can be expected." Her maids had drifted back, bored with the repetitious conversation. "I will need your help," she said in a low voice, "if I am to reverse events."

He frowned at her. "Have you not achieved everything you have always desired, your Highness?" His smile was sad. "I will admit you led us all a merry dance. We thought you were in danger."

"Do you not suppose I was? Do you not realize I still am?"

"Dear, beautiful lady," he said, "I once risked my career to save you from what I supposed was a fate worse than death. It was pointed out to me by my superiors that while I had undoubtedly acted as a gentleman should, I was also guilty of interfering in events that did not concern me. If, I was told, the girl was a Ch'ing princess, then she must be considered as a possible danger to the stability of China. It would have been better to let her marry Yuan, they said, whatever the personal consequences to her of such an act, and let her be forgotten as soon as possible. Knowing you, I disagreed with them then. Now I know that it is never wise to disagree with one's superiors. They know so much more than oneself."

She stared at him, eyebrows raised.

"That mistake," Richards said, "has cost me dear, in that I continue to be British consul in Tientsin, instead of perhaps his majesty's ambassador to . . . Who can say? Perhaps it has even cost me a knighthood. These are, after all, the accepted goals of a diplomatic career. And yet, you know, your Highness, I regard myself as privileged to have witnessed at close hand your quite remarkable career. I thought you were an innocent, hard-done-by, entrancingly beautiful young woman. Now I know that you are truly a Ch'ing, in your ability to manipulate, to grasp, and to hold. I congratulate you, Princess Adela. I do not envy you. And I can no longer afford to fear for you. You have reached out and grasped the greatest prize there is in all Asia. Whether your fingers are strong enough to retain the prize, your Highness, is a matter for yourself alone. And if they are not, may God have mercy on your soul."

He bowed and walked away.

Alone. So alone. And she could not even be angry. She knew it must appear to everyone, from Richards to Sun.

And to Lin-tu?

But . . .

"If even Richards thinks *you* engineered the whole thing," Charlie said, "Dela . . . what *are* we to do?"

Despite her elevation to princess regent, she had preferred not to move from the Lotus Apartment. This had become home to her. As it would remain home to her, now, for as long.as she lived. She did not doubt that the moment she *had* to leave these walls would be her last. "I don't know," she said. "I just don't know, Charlie. I am so terribly sorry to have gotten you into this mess. . . ."

But he was all she had. They had not discussed the slowness of his reactions the day Chang had burst into her bedchamber—in retrospect she was grateful for them, as otherwise they might all now be dead. The important thing was that he was here, sharing her captivity, with courage and even humor, although he must know by now, as well as she, the most likely outcome of Chang's adventure. Saving him from such a terrible fate was looming at least as large in her mind as saving herself and Peter. Because Charlie was surely innocent in his part in this, even by birth or Destiny. He was here only for love.

"Stuff and nonsense," he said. "Dela . . ." Although they were alone, he yet lowered his voice to a whisper. "Our only hope is Dr. Sun. Somehow we have got to get a message to him."

"Do you not suppose he thinks as Richards does? You know, even when we spoke together the day before he left Peking, after Lin-tu had had his outburst, Sun sort of asked me to tell him that what Lin said wasn't true. He *needed* to be told, to be reassured."

"And you reassured him," Charlie said.

"Yes. But now he will be thinking it is all a lie. Everyone thinks I'm a liar, and a deceiver, and a schemer." A reincarnation of Tz'u-Hsi, she thought. That was ironic. Whereas she, after dreaming for so long, had rejected the concept as too horrible, now everyone thought it. She wondered if, somewhere along the line, she had inadvertently sold her soul to the devil. "There is no *reason* for him to believe me anymore, Charlie." She sighed. "Or even you."

"Maybe." He pulled his beard. And then snapped his fingers. "There is *someone* who will believe us, no matter what. Mother!"

"Do you really think so? If you were to see the way she looks at me . . . I don't know what to do about them, either. I've given orders that Wynne and Company offices are to be reopened in accordance with any instructions issued by Frank, but so far as I know, nothing has happened. They're just living there in that house, with everything provided for them by the government, as if wondering if they've done the right thing in coming back at all. Thinking that I have somehow bewitched you and everyone else, and seized all the power for myself."

He smiled and kissed her on the nose. "You *have* bewitched me, my darling. But you did that years ago. I don't want ever to stop being bewitched. But Mother will certainly believe what *I* have to tell her. If I could only get a few moments alone with her . . ."

"Do you think so, Charlie? Do you really think you could convince her that we are, actually, prisoners?"

"I know I can."

"Because if you could do that, and she could persuade Richards, or even Mr. Maltby . . . or are we just dreaming? Is there anything anyone can do?"

"Mother can make a fuss," he said. "She's good at doing that. She'll make such a fuss the State Department will *have* to sit up and take notice."

"Then you shall see her," Adela said. "Alone. I will insist upon it."

Even if I have to sacrifice myself, she thought. Because surely she can get *you* out of here, my dearest Charlie.

"I doubt it is wise," Chang Hsun said. "I cannot permit it."

"Because you are afraid he will tell his mother that he and I are prisoners here?" Adela asked.

"Will he not do that?"

"Will she not form that conclusion anyway, if she is not allowed to see him alone? She can *see* that he is a prisoner."

Chang paced his office, hands clasped behind his back. "It is true that she has been clamoring to see him this past week," he said. "I had presumed it was because of the new developments . . . Their being here at all is a great nuisance. I had forgot that they know Chinese ways too well."

"What new developments?" Adela asked.

"Have you not heard? The United States means to declare war on Germany. No doubt it has already been done."

"War?" she cried. "With Germany?"

"It is no concern of yours, great Princess. Indeed, it is all to our advantage. Let the entire world become consumed with war, that they may leave us alone until we are ready again to be noticed."

War, she thought, spreading across the face of the entire globe like some horrible fungus. What would Charlie wish to do? What *could* he wish to do, save get home as quickly as possible to play his part? She gazed at Chang. "Were you not going to tell me of this? I am an American citizen. Did you not suppose I might be interested?"

"You are a Manchu princess," he reminded her severely. "Any other blood that you may possess is nothing more than a misfortune."

"And Colonel Baird? He is a soldier. Can you not suppose he might wish to go and fight for his country?"

Chang raised his eyebrows. He had not thought of that possibility, clearly. "You would permit this, great Princess?"

"Could I in honor prevent him if he wished to go?"

"Honor." He sneered. But she could see the conflicting thoughts taking shape in his mind. He would dearly like to be rid of Charlie; in his absence he was sure the princess would be more pliable. On the other hand, Charlie was his principal hold on her.

And what did *she* feel? She had dreamed of getting Charlie to safety—and here was a way it could be done. To the safety of a war? But anywhere had to be safer for Charles Baird than confinement in the Forbidden City.

Then would her isolation be complete. Could she exist without Charlie?

Yet would she be released from at least one ever-present nightmare. "You will still have Prince Yuan Hsu," she pointed out.

Chang glanced at her, face still a picture of indecision. "You think Mrs. Wynne may wish to persuade her son to return to America?"

"I am sure of it. And, Chang, I will give you my word, if you will let Colonel Baird go, I will remain always at your side, and I will more actively promote your cause. *Our* cause," she added hastily.

Her heart pounded. When it came to deceiving, to double dealing, she was not quite the tyro she had feared herself. Had she not once even outsmarted Lin-tu?

"I will give Mrs. Wynne permission to see her son," Chang said. "Alone."

"Charlie!" Constance said. "Oh, Charlie."

"Mother!" He was receiving her in the Lotus Apartment, and tea had been prepared but left unserved.

"I never thought . . ." Constance shrugged. "I didn't know what to think, I guess. Only that you were being kept a prisoner here by that girl. . . . I suppose you never really do know someone until something like this happens."

He held her hands, sat beside her on a divan. "Mother, whatever are you talking about? I am not a prisoner. Oh, well, I suppose I am, in a sort of way. But both Dela and I are prisoners, and little Peter, too."

"Peter?"

"That's what we call the prince. Yuan Hsu. Your grandson, Mother."

"He is no grandson of *mine,*" Constance declared.

"Mother!" Charlie bit his lip. "You must try to understand, and you must try to help us. Let me explain the true situation to you. Chang has pulled off a coup d'etat. It had all been arranged, between Li Yuan-hung and Dr. Sun, that China was to become a republic and that Adela was to be exiled to the States. With a pension and everything. Well, you can imagine how pleased we were with that. And with the idea that Sun was going to succeed at last, because there really wasn't any doubt about that. As this fellow Chang realized. He is an ardent monarchist, but more than that, he is a disciple of Yuan Shih-k'ai's and believes in a military dictatorship, with him as dictator. So he took over the government. He's imprisoned Li, virtually declared war on Sun all over again, and claims to be ruling in the name of the Ch'ing."

"Is he not, as he has the backing of a Ch'ing princess?"

"Adela does *not* support him, Mother. Believe me. She hates what he has done. What he is making her do."

"*Making* her do? She is enjoying every moment of it. You haven't seen her in public."

"She is acting," Charlie insisted. "Doing what Chang tells her to do. If she does not, he would execute me. Or even Peter."

"You mean you *believe* that?" Constance cried. "Nobody else does. I tried, at first. I wanted to believe it, Charlie. But there can be no doubt about the truth now. I've talked with Mr. Richards and Mr. Maltby, the American minister, and well, everybody. Everybody knows Adela engineered the whole thing. Can you deny it's what she's always wanted? Always dreamed of? You know how she has always talked of her Destiny. This is what she thinks her Destiny is, and has always been. To rule China. I hate to say it, Charlie, but she is *evil*. Every bit as evil as Yuan ever was."

"Mother, that is simply not true." He sighed. "Then you won't help us?"

"I'll help *you*. I've thought it out. Have you heard

that President Wilson has declared war on Germany?"

"I've heard there was a possibility of it."

"Well, he has. So Frank and I are returning to the States. Oh, we have hated it ever since we came back here. Seeing Adela . . . it gives me the shudders. Anyway, Frank is a reserve officer, and he's only forty-nine, you know. And very fit. He feels he must go back and join up. And I agree with him. You must come with us."

"Me?"

"We can force Dela to let you go, Charlie. You are an experienced soldier. Your country needs you. Now they are having something called selective service back home. It's a sort of conscription, but it's also the luck of the draw, as of course they don't want *everyone* in uniform. All the names go into a hat, and the lucky ones get conscripted."

"The *lucky* ones?"

"Don't you want to fight for your country?"

"Well, sure. But as you say, I'm already a soldier. I wouldn't be all that keen on being sent off to Europe if I was happily married or starting up in business or something like that."

"Oh, really, Charlie. The important thing is that Mr. Maltby will provide us with a letter saying that you have been drafted. It won't be true, but no one will know that. Then Adela will have to let you go, or she'll be sheltering a draft dodger, a fugitive from justice. She won't dare risk a confrontation with the United States government."

Charlie shook his head.

Constance frowned at him. "What's the matter? Don't you *want* to get out of here?"

"Sure I do. *With* Dela."

"And she won't leave."

"She *can't* leave, without help."

"That is nonsense," Constance declared, "and you know it. What you are saying is, you'd prefer to stay here than fight for your country. As a kept man? That's what they are saying of you, you know. That you are Princess Adela's lapdog and paid lover." She paused, cheeks pink, aghast at what she had said.

Charlie refused to lose his temper. "Mother," he explained, with great patience, "you, and Richards, and the whole wide world can believe whatever you like. I know the truth. And even if I didn't, I happen to be in love with Dela. I let her go, once, very stupidly, and I damned near lost her altogether. I don't ever intend to let that happen again. *And* I regard myself as married to her, because we are going to *be* married, just as soon as we can find Osborne and have that marriage annulled. So, from this moment on, where she goes, I go. Where she stays, I stay. If you can help us both to get out of Peking, out of China, with Peter, I'll jump for joy, and so will she. And I'll join the United States Army the very next day. If you can't or won't help us to do that, then I stay here with Dela. For the next thirty years, if I have to."

Constance stared at him. "For the next thirty years? Do you suppose you are ever going to *see* thirty yourself, you silly boy? Richards tells me there is no doubt that there is going to be a counterrevolution against this Chang and Adela in the very near future. When that happens, they are both going to be put against a wall and shot, Charlie. And you'll be standing there beside them if you don't get out while you can."

He smiled at her. "Then that's Destiny. It would be better than trying to live without Dela."

"You fool," Adela said. "Oh, you magnificent fool." She lay in his arms and rolled to and fro in her ecstasy. "How I love you."

It was the first time she had ever said that, in quite those terms, to any man. Because it was the first time any man had ever done anything so magnificent. Going off to fight with Dr. Sun when he had imagined her dead had been entirely masculine, the sort of gallant gesture one would expect from any gentleman, under the circumstances. Electing to remain within the Forbidden City with her, to share her fate no matter what, had to be love.

"So I guess now we're on our own," he said, and kissed her on the mouth.

On their own. Which meant, however splendidly he had behaved, or would, she now knew, behave in the future, that she was on *her* own.

Chang was amused. "Colonel Baird wishes to remain with the great princess," he said. "You should have had more trust in him. But now, perhaps, the great princess will be happy. And do not forget that we have a bargain, you and I, great Princess. Colonel Baird is *free* to leave, should he wish. Still."

"Indeed I understand that, Chang," she agreed. "And I feel I have been remiss in abandoning so much of the executive power into your hands." Because now it was necessary to stop hurling herself against the bars like a terrified child. She would extricate Charlie and Peter and herself from this mess only by careful and meticulous planning, and first on the agenda would have to be reestablishing her personal credit. If the world was convinced that she had planned and executed the coup, then she would have to convince the world that it had, after all, been the best thing for China.

Chang's eyes narrowed suspiciously. "There is nothing for you to concern yourself with, great Princess," he said. "Everything is going according to plan."

"I would say that *nothing* is going according to

plan," she argued. "Has my government yet been recognized by the Western powers or the United States?"

"It has not yet been recognized, great Princess. But I had anticipated a delay while they are at war."

"Indeed? And what of the Japanese?"

His eyes shifted. "They are a deceitful people."

"You mean they also have refused to recognize us. Why have I not been told of this?"

"There is naught to concern yourself with, great Princess," Chang said again. "They have issued an insulting statement to the effect that they will recognize no relict of Yuan Shih-k'ai, as they call you, nor will they recognize his son. They are attempting to ignore altogether the fact that you are also a princess of the Ch'ing, the only available princess of the Ch'ing, just as your son is the only available prince of the Ch'ing."

"You mean that they are opposing us," she said. "As Dr. Sun opposes us. What of the viceroys and warlords?"

"They are contumacious people," Chang said hotly. "They—"

"You mean we are opposed by the entire country, as well as the Japanese, and probably by the United States and Europe when they get around to remembering that we exist."

"We are here," he argued. "In Peking. We hold the center of government. We *are* the government. We have but to remain—"

"Until they come to destroy us," she said. "It will not do, Chang. We ride a tiger. I know that we cannot simply dismount. Our only hope of survival is to earn that recognition we presently lack."

"It will come," he growled.

"Only by our making it come," she said. "Fortunately, it can be done, very simply."

He frowned at her, suspicious as ever.

"Is it not true," she asked, "that the United States, in declaring war upon Germany, has called upon all the neutral nations in the world also to declare war on Germany, in order to end this hideous conflict? Has China responded to this call?"

"Do you think me mad?" he asked. "Our only hope is the continuing enmity of Germany against Britain and France and Russia. It would suit us best were this European war to last forever."

"It is not going to last forever, Chang," she told him. "It is going to end very soon."

"And if it is won by the Germans—"

"Do not be a fool," she snapped. "How can the Germans defeat the British and the French and the Russians *and* the Americans? Let me tell you, Chang, that when this war ends, as it will, in an Allied victory, those Allies will remember who were their friends and who their enemies. And who did not support them. But those that did support them, why, they will be supported in turn. Even against the Japanese. This government, our government, Chang, *must* declare war on Germany, and quickly."

He pulled his lip. "There is some merit in what you suggest, to be sure."

"What I *wish* is the only hope for us all, Chang. It must be done."

"I will put it to the council," he said. "I will recommend it, you have my assurance."

"Thank you," she said. "That will go far toward ensuring the recognition of our government. Now we must do something positive for our people here in China. We must entirely outlaw the smoking of opium."

He frowned at her. "Opium smoking was outlawed more than ten years ago, great Princess. It was one of the last decrees promulgated by the dowager empress, your predecessor, Tz'u-Hsi."

"And it remains a dead letter," Adela pointed out. "Because the people do not *wish* to stop smoking opium."

"The people do not *know* what they wish," she declared. "Opium is an evil thing. It robs men of the will to think. To *be* men. I will have the law of 1906 made effective."

"The people will hate you for it," Chang said doubtfully.

"The people will *love* me for it, Chang. See that it is done. And finally, there is the matter of James Osborne. I want him found and brought back to Peking."

Chang sighed. "Alas, great Princess, the man Osborne is in Japan."

"Japan?"

"He is, as ever, intriguing against us. He represents himself as Yuan Shih-k'ai's right-hand man and attempts to turn the Japanese even more against you. They supported Yuan, you may remember, in exchange for trading rights in Manchuria. In your name I have demanded the abrogation of that treaty, because I knew it would please the warlords. This is the real issue between us and the Japanese. But I doubt we will ever reach agreement with them while Osborne is there to stir up enmity between our governments."

"I see," Adela said thoughtfully. "That is something I shall have to study, Chang. But what you have just told me makes it all the more imperative for us to gain the support of Britain and France and the United States, so that once they have settled with Germany, they will support us against the Japanese."

"If the Japanese will wait that long," he said lugubriously, then bowed and withdrew. With some relief, she thought. Because he was realizing that she was a more forceful personality even than himself. But it remained difficult for her to capitalize on this first success by keeping control of the day-to-day business of government, because there were so many departments, so many officials, all of whom seemed to have been in office for years, through the reigns of Yuan, and Prince Ch'un, and even Tz'u-Hsi herself, who existed surrounded by their lists and their books, their customs and their privileges. And were encouraged by Chang to keep their secrets from her and to refer their decisions to him alone. Perhaps, she thought with a certain pride, he is realizing that he has erected no puppet here, but a woman to be feared.

Yet, slowly, it seemed to her that a government, and a policy, directed entirely to the good of China, was taking shape. There was much that remained to be done, and there was much that was still being badly done. And under the circumstances, Osborne had to be considered no more than a nuisance; he could be dealt with when the time was ripe. Thus they waited throughout the summer of 1917 for Western recognition of the regime, but it came only in an equivocal form: the Allied nations conveyed, through their representatives in Peking, that they were grateful to have China on their side in the Great War, but there remained many things to be settled once that war was ended—if that war was ever to be ended, she thought, as revolution now swept across Russia in turn to lessen the odds against the Germans. But the Japanese seemed willing to wait for that end, at least. They negotiated, but the return of Prince Ch'un and his son seemed no nearer. This certainly pleased Chang. "Prince Ch'un does not wish to return to Peking," he said. "Until his safety can be guaranteed. He waits for full recognition of the restoration of the Ch'ing. He does not understand that when that is obtained, we will have no need of him.''

An idea that did not please Adela at all. The return of Ch'ung was her only hope of getting Charlie and herself out of here.

She was equally disturbed by the failure of Dr. Sun to respond to any of their overtures. He had, apparently, set up what he called the true government of China, under the auspices of the Kuomintang, in Canton, and persisted in describing Chang and her as usurpers and traitors. This concerned her on purely personal grounds, while it enraged Chang. But she was reluctant to send troops against the doctor, with whom she still hoped one day to negotiate, and resume her friendship, and Chang was equally concerned to keep his army available in the North until the Japanese question was settled.

Thus she lived as much on a knife edge as she had ever done, but sustained by the apparent tranquillity of North China under her rule, and by the unfailing support of Charlie. She supposed, if this was to be her existence for the rest of her life, and that might be a long time, as in the August of 1917 she celebrated her twenty-third birthday, she could have suffered many worse fates. Charlie undoubtedly fretted that he had not been able to join the United States Army, and he continued to make dramatic plans for their escape, but none of these had any hope of success while Chang kept them so closely guarded. "We *shall* escape," she promised him. "In the fullness of time. Either when Prince Ch'un returns or when my rule is sufficiently accepted to make it possible for me to dismiss Chang and summon Dr. Sun to Peking, and then abdicate for Peter and myself. This is what we must work for, and only this will truly succeed, and at the same time restore our reputation in the eyes of the world.''

But as the weeks passed, and the rains set in once more, and the war in Europe showed no signs of ending, even her mind began to turn to force. Now indeed, she almost wished that Chen Fu would return to Peking, with loyal troops at his back. But she still had no idea where he was, and she still knew that to inquire after him and thus arouse the slightest suspicion in Chang's mind would be suicidal. Enough to feel that he *would* return one day. And then . . . ?

She did not know herself what she would do. She could only resolve to practice that patience which was her most valuable asset, and watch and listen, and try to be happy in Charlie's arms and in watching Peter growing into a strong and handsome boy, and awake on a fall morning, as she had done a year before, to find her bedchamber filled with armed men.

"Dress yourself, great Princess," Chang commanded. "We must flee this place."

17

The Republic

Adela sat up in total incomprehension, even as her heart seemed to thud all the way down into the pit of her stomach. Had she not always known, deep down there, that this moment had to come?

"Haste," Chang said, himself going to her wardrobe to fetch her a robe. "I have already roused the prince, and there are horses waiting."

"But . . . what has *happened*?"

He snorted. "The warlords have decided against us. It is your fault, great Princess. They have always relied upon the profits from the sale of opium for large parts of their income, and you would now take that away from them. They are also against even appearing to side with the barbarians in their senseless war. So they are in arms, and are marching on Peking. I had hoped to negotiate with them, but they have executed my messengers. They will be here in six hours. They are demanding your head, great Princess. And that of your son. And mine."

"But . . . the army?"

"They have suborned the army," he snapped. "Only the Imperial Guard remains loyal, and how long even

467

that . . . These men I have with me *are* loyal. So come, haste."

She got out of bed, pulled on the robe. "Where are we to go?" She was for the moment concerned only with Peter's safety.

"We shall go where the Manchu have always gone in time of defeat. We will ride to the Imperial Hunting Park in Jehol, on the border of Manchuria itself. There we will find support. There we will raise a new army."

"That is madness, Chang," she said. "That idea is finished, nor will I plunge all China into a civil war in pursuit of your ambitions. We must try to gain the coast. First, we must take refuge in the legations and negotiate our departure from there."

"We are going to Jehol," he told her. "Not you," he said to Charlie, who was also busily dressing.

Charlie gazed at Adela.

"Do you suppose I will leave this room without Colonel Baird?" she demanded.

"You will do as you are *told*," he said. "I have been too indulgent toward you, and this is the true cause of our misfortune. But you will not be abandoning Colonel Baird. Take him outside and shoot him," he commanded his men.

"No," Adela shouted.

Chang grinned at her. "You have nothing to offer me now, great Princess, in exchange for his life."

"You think not?" She drew a long breath. But she had never doubted that if it came to such a decision, Charlie at least must be saved. "I, and my son, remain your only hope, Chang. Kill Colonel Baird and I swear I will denounce you to the world, and more, will end my own life, and that of my son, at the earliest possible moment. Permit Colonel Baird to live, and I . . ." She bit her lip. "I will do anything you may require."

"No, Dela," Charlie said. "I am not worth that."

"Indeed you are not," Chang agreed. "I will not take him with us, great Princess. He will but complicate matters."

Adela sighed, and shrugged. "Then leave him here."

Chang's smile widened. "Why not?" he said. "Bind him on the bed," he told his men. "The soldiers of the warlords will undoubtedly hang him when they find him here."

"Bastard!" Against all of her principles, Adela lost her temper in a fit of mingled anger and fear. She struck at Chang, attempted to reach his revolver, and was thrown to the floor with a force that knocked all the breath from her body. Dimly she heard the sounds of Charlie also fighting, cursing and swearing, but equally to no avail in the face of so many opponents. She was dragged to her feet, her arms carried behind her back, her wrists pinioned; she had not been so manhandled since the day of 1911 the mob had broken into Constance's house. Her robe was disarrayed, her body was bruised, and her hair clouded across her face; angrily she blew it away, saw that Charlie was also being bound, hand and foot, and thrown on the bed.

"Chang," she said. "Bring him as well, or leave me. Chang . . ."

"He has served his purpose," Chang said. "He has warmed your bed sufficiently. We will find you another bed warmer, great Princess. When it is possible to find you another *bed.*"

"Dela," he shouted. "I'll come after you, Dela. Just wait for me. I'll come after you!"

"Charlie!" she screamed as she was pulled from the room. Her last memory, as the door slammed shut, was of him straining desperately against his bonds.

Fighting herself, regardless now of the dignity demanded of a Ch'ing princess, of her resolve always to preserve her aura of calm confidence, she was forced along corridors and down a flight of stairs, and, in the cold gray of the dawn, into a courtyard, where another score of horsemen and perhaps an equal number of women and eunuchs waited, already mounted, with a sleepy Peter in their midst.

"Peter!" she shouted. "If you have harmed him, Chang . . ." she panted.

"I would not even harm you, great Princess," he pointed out, lifting her into the saddle. "For all your hysteria, I am attempting to save your life. These men who march on Peking, they *seek* your life. Do you not understand that?"

She was seated astride, her legs exposed, and he was mounting beside her and taking her reins to lead her horse from the courtyard and through the deserted streets until they came to the North Gate, the Gate of Spiritual Values, and the bridge across the canal. Ahead of them lay Prospect Hill and the private park of the Ch'ings, where recently she had walked, Peter often at her side. But this they skirted today, to ride north toward the Great Wall, urged on always by Chang's exhortations. Perhaps fifty people Adela counted, out of all the imperial splendor which had represented the dynasty and which had so recently been *hers* to command.

"Chang," she said, having got her brain working again, "to flee is an admission of guilt. Take me back, Chang, and stand at my side. Let us face these warlords together. If we have failed to govern China as they think fit, then let us abdicate together, with dignity." This is 1917, she wanted to tell him. Where people *behave* with dignity.

"Are you then impatient to kneel before the headsman?" he asked. "Do not suppose those men will allow you that privilege, after they have first heard you scream in contrition, watched you writhe before them in agony, great Princess. You are the most hated woman in all China."

"But why?" she wailed. "I have never harmed a living soul, save in self-defense."

"You think not? Those men are composed of all the disaffected, all the ambitious, all the rebellious elements in China, great Princess," he told her. "Republicans and monarchists, and sheer power-hungry barons, they are all marching together. And do you know who is marching with them, and will call loudest for your blood? Lin-tu. He has foresworn Sun Yat-sen and now declares himself to be a believer of autocracy. His autocracy, great Princess. Not yours. He is sworn to kick your head across the floor. Is this the man to whom you will offer to surrender?"

"Colonel Baird," remarked Marshal Tuan Ch'i-jui, reclining on the imperial throne, legs thrust in front of him, peaked cap resting on the back of his head, mustache drooping to either side of his thin lips. His generals and officers stood around him, and, as had been the case when Yuan had first seized power, there was not a woman or a eunuch to be seen. "The imperial concubine." He waved his hand. "Oh, release him."

Charlie rubbed his hands together to aid in restoring his circulation, reminded himself that getting angry with these men would not help Adela, and that was all that mattered now. "The princess—"

"Has fled, leaving you behind," Tuan observed. "That is in keeping with her known character. She is certainly the most vicious creature who ever walked this earth. My heart bleeds for you, Colonel Baird. Believe me, you have nothing to fear from me or my associates; we are well aware how the princess has kept you imprisoned here this last year. I will make arrangements for your safe journey to the coast and for your passage back to the United States. You are dismissed."

"I would know what you propose to do about the princess," Charlie said, not moving. "If you will provide me with an escort, I will go and fetch her back."

"What happens to the princess is entirely up to her," Tuan told him. "I have already dispatched a force behind her. I have sent an old friend of hers to find her. Lin-tu. You remember Marshal Lin-tu, Colonel Baird? If anyone can find the princess, he will do it. Besides, I understand that she and Chang have left an easy-enough trail to follow. But as to whether Lin-tu will actually bring her back . . . He has orders to do so, certainly, that she may be dragged at a horse's tail to a place of public execution. But he hates her more than any other man in China, and may be unable to restrain himself . . . and then, she is a Ch'ing. Might she not prefer to take her own life in preference to facing such an unpleasant and humiliating end to her career?"

"But she is innocent," Charlie shouted. "It has all been the doing of Chang—"

"I have heard," Tuan observed, "that she is capable of bewitching men with her beauty. I am sorry for you, Colonel Baird. Take him out," he commanded. "Put him back in the Lotus Apartment until transport to the coast can be arranged for him. You will enjoy those memories you must have of that apartment and the princess, Colonel Baird."

"The princess is innocent," Charlie shouted again. "Marshal Tuan, listen to me . . ." Hands seized his arms and dragged him from the room, returned him to the Lotus Apartment, where the door clanged shut. He looked around himself in futile anger, but Chang's men had removed his sword and revolver. He could do nothing but try to prevent himself from going mad. He had lain on that bed in the most complete mental agony he had ever known, for seven hours after Chang's departure. The thought of being separated from Adela at all had been bad enough, but then he had supposed her in danger, at least of rape, from Chang and his people. Then he had supposed that once the warlords' army reached the Forbidden City, he would be able to organize a rescue party. He had fought his bonds in desperate anxiety, and had at last gotten free, but only just in time to face the soldiers who had burst into the apartment, to bind him again and drag him before Tuan Ch'i-jui, and learn the worst. Now . . .

He paced the floor. His only hope was, first, to believe that Adela would never contemplate suicide. That was too Oriental for her Occidental mind. But could he be sure of that? Had she not been forced to think like an Oriental, merely to survive, these past five years?

But she *had* survived—that was the point—when there must have been several occasions suicide would have appeared as the only acceptable answer to her torment. Thus she would survive again . . . to be returned here by Lin-tu. He dared not allow himself to consider what she might have to suffer at the hands of the man she had betrayed, not once, but twice, even if Lin-tu had himself prophesied that second betrayal. But she would survive that as well, and be returned here as a prisoner to be executed. That was the earliest moment he could now hope to assist her. He had to escape this place, gain the American legation, and *force* Maltby to interfere. Whatever had happened, whatever she had been forced into, Adela yet remained an American citizen, and could legitimately claim the protection of her country's representative. Maltby would have to see that.

If she did survive to come back. And if she were not immediately executed on entering the city. He threw himself across the bed in despair, raised his head as there came a sound at the door, rolled and reached his feet in the same instant, gazed at the Chinese officer who stood in the doorway. He was not a tall man, but was strongly built, and with equally strong, determined features. Nor was he old; Charlie estimated him to be about the same age as himself—yet he also wore the insignia of a colonel.

"You are Charles Baird?" he demanded.

"Yes," Charlie said. "But I am not going to the coast, now or at anytime. I demand to be taken to the United States legation."

"You lived here," Chen Fu remarked. "With the princess."

Charlie frowned. "We are betrothed."

Chen almost smiled. "I came here to see her too," he said.

"*You?*"

"I am the father of her son," Chen said. "I am Chen Fu."

Charlie sat down again, with a thump.

"This disturbs you?" Chen asked. "She belonged to another, when I came to her. She belonged to Yuan Shih-k'ai when I came to her and loved her. Do you love her, Charles Baird?"

Charlie raised his head. He wanted time to think. But what did he have to think about? Only that Dela had never told him. But did that matter now? "Yes," he said. "I love her."

Chen studied him for several moments. Then he said, "You know she has been condemned to death?"

"Yes," Charlie said. "And I would save her. If I can get to the American legation . . . if you take me there now . . ."

"The legation," Chen said contemptuously. "They cannot save her. They will not even try. Do you love the princess, Baird, sufficiently to risk your life for her?"

Charlie flushed. "Of course. I have already done so."

"Then will you ride with me to her rescue?"

"You and I?"

"There are men who will ride with me. Faithful men, who, like me, wish no part of this clique from Pei Yang who seek to rule this country. They are no better than Chang or Yuan Shih-k'ai himself. This country must be ruled by its people, not its warlords."

"You are a supporter of Dr. Sun?"

"I am a supporter of the Chinese people," Chen said enigmatically. "I have a dozen men who will ride with me to the ends of the earth. Will you come with us?"

Charlie gazed at him.

And Chen smiled. "You think I will murder you, for love of the princess? I will not do that, Baird. I also love the princess, and she is the mother of my son. But the Ch'ing have no place in China anymore. She must understand this. You must make her understand this, and then take her away from China forever."

"That is all she wishes to do," Charlie said.

"Then we will at least save her life. Or die attempting to do so. For she rules our hearts, even if we would not have her rule our lives. But once we desert this army and ride after her, it is us against the whole world, Charles Baird." He went to the door. "Will you risk all, to save the princess? From Lin-tu?"

The rain was cold, and driven into their faces by an even colder wind surging out of the Siberian tundra. Late September was no time to be making north; all the birds had already left for warmer climes.

Progress was slow, even without the eunuchs and the women. Chang had abandoned *them* soon after passing the Great Wall, disgusted with their moans and their grumblings. "Then go back to Peking," he had commanded. "Go and make your peace with the warlords, if you can."

That had caused them to wail even more, but he had refused to allow them to rejoin the group, and when one of the eunuchs had run behind their horses, begging for mercy, Chang had shot the unfortunate creature himself.

Here *was* nightmare. Partly because of the rain, which never ceased, and of the leaden skies which permitted no glimpse of the sun; partly because of their soaked clothing, which there was no means of drying or changing, even at night, and which made the cold seem greater than it actually was. But most of all because it was difficult any longer to hope. Suddenly even the insecurity of Peking seemed like a pleasant dream. Peking had at least been warm, and there had been good food to eat and hot tea to drink . . . and there had been Charlie. Was Charlie still there? Or had he been put against a wall and shot? Of only one thing had Adela ever felt certain during this last summer, since Charlie had refused to return to the States with his mother, and that had been that they would at least die together, and would live together until that moment. Now even that dream was scattered to the wind.

She could find no single aspect of her situation on which to concentrate, around which to build those plans which had always been so important a part of her life. She could not even concentrate on death, because that was unthinkable while she had Peter to care for. The little prince was the most confused of them all. Only a few days ago he had appeared to be lord of all he surveyed. Now his toys and his maidservants were gone, as were the guards and mandarins who had gravely kowtowed whenever they were in his presence. Now he was cold and wet and hungry, and surrounded by men whose faces were familiar enough but who scowled at him and muttered among themselves. He was only three and a half years old, and it was all too incomprehensible. Only his mother remained constant, and therefore, to him, she had to *be* constant, and smile, and tell him stories, and remind him that they were merely engaged upon a picnic. The longest and most miserable picnic there could ever have been.

Such was their early haste that they reached the Great Wall two days after leaving the city. But even that had not been fast enough, for by now scouts sent back by Chang had ascertained that they were already being pursued. Thus there had been no time to admire the architectural wonder of the Chinese world, which, Adela realized with faint surprise, she was seeing for the first time, and, no doubt, the last. The following day had come the dismissal of the maids and eunuchs, as Chang had urged them to still greater speed. "You can manage your own toilette, great Princess," he said. "There is no state occasion to prepare for."

She wondered she was not afraid of immediate rape. She was alone in the midst of a score of men, all of whom eyed her with undoubted physical desire. Yet she obviously remained, to these simple soldiers, the great princess, the sole reason for their being in this dank netherworld at all. Even Chang obviously felt this, and she had in fact early feared that, away from all the requirements of protocol and power, with little for either of them to hope for, he might well seek to relieve that desire *he* certainly felt for her—there was nothing to stop him now. But he too merely gazed at her with deep, brooding eyes, no doubt, she thought bitterly, like so many others, attributing all his misfortunes to her mere presence.

The degeneration of Chang was in fact the most alarming aspect of the entire situation. However Adela

disliked and distrusted the man, she had never doubted
his energy. He had created this entire scenario by that
energy, allied to his ambition. He had never lacked
confidence. Until now, when he rode in an angry, despairing silence, leading his small party north, as if he
realized he was but going nowwhere, save to their death.

She thought that she would prefer to ride away on her
own, with Peter, if death truly were inevitable, and live
her last few hours in comparative peace. But that was
impossible, since she was entirely surrounded by armed
guards. Then one morning she awoke shivering beside
Peter in her makeshift tent and became aware that
something was different. There was no sound of
stamping, snorting horses to be heard. Or of muttering,
cursing men. Only the wind soughing across the steppes,
driving occasional rain flurries before it.

Peter continued to sleep; it was still very early. Adela
gently disengaged herself from him, opened the tent
flap, and looked out at the gray dawn, the empty land-
scape. She stepped outside, heart pounding in sheer
horror. How she had wanted to be alone. But now . . .
there were no horses, no men. They had stolen away,
without even folding their tents. But surely someone . . .
She stumbled across the soggy ground to the tent used
by Chang himself, pulled open the flap, gazed at the
marshal, nostrils dilating. She had once before seen a
man with his head blown away. But Feng had been
executed; Chang had undoubtedly killed himself—the
revolver still lay in his lifeless hand.

She gasped, and closed the flap, and found herself on
her knees, looking around her like a frightened animal,
while the wind scattered her hair across her face and
pushed raindrops into her eyes. Chang was dead. He
had at last lost faith even in himself. Now she and Peter
were alone. The escort had taken even their food and
drinking water. There was nothing for them to do

except die themselves. Adela gazed at the murky southern horizon. Or wait for their pursuers to arrive.

Adela stood by where Chang's men had lit the fire the previous night; it still glowed. She searched the earth, but they had left her not even a morsel of food. She had to suppose she should be grateful that they had even left her her life, at least temporarily.

"Mother?" Peter stood in the doorway of their tent. "Where men? Where horses? Where Chang?"

Poor little mite, she thought; his entire life had been dominated by Chang. "Chang has gone away," she said. "With his men."

"I'm hungry, Mother," Peter confided, losing interest in the missing men.

Adela sighed, and once again gazed around the unending steppe, undulating gently in every direction, soggy and rainswept. Presumably there were many pools of recently gathered water which they could safely drink. But food . . . They had seen no living creature for several days. She chewed her lip. But that had been surely because Chang had taken care to avoid meeting anyone. Only the previous day, as she remembered, they had abruptly altered their direction to the northwest, when they had been pressing northeast for the previous week. There must have been a reason for that. So if she and Peter were to walk east or just south of east . . . just south of the rising sun, she thought, gazing at the glowing orb just clearing the horizon, and realizing with a spasm of comfort that the clouds had cleared, at least in the east, and that the rain had finally stopped. Was that not a hopeful sign? There had to be people cloes at hand.

It was better to go looking for them than to sit here waiting for death.

"Then we shall go and find some food, my darling,"

she said. And swept him into her arms. "That way."

She carried him for perhaps a mile, and then had to stop, her legs as weary as her arms, the one from splashing through the soft ground, the other from carrying the boy. They sat together on a slight hillock, while she panted.

"Where is the food, Mother?" Peter asked.

"Not far," she promised, and stood up again, gazed to the south, and then to the north . . . and saw a horseman, standing his mount on a hillock very like theirs, and looking toward them. He was perhaps half a mile away, she estimated, and surely he could see them, if they could see him. One of Chang's men come back for her? With food? Oh, how she hoped someone had done that, no matter what it involved.

"Hello," she shouted, waving both her hands. "Hello!"

The horseman continued to stare at her, and now there was a flash of light as the sun reflected from something he was holding in front of his face. Field glasses! He was looking at her through binoculars.

"Hello!" she shouted again, gathered Peter into her arms, and ran down the slope, stumbling toward the man, and stopped again as he wheeled his mount and cantered off to the north. "Oh, my God," she said. "Oh, my God!"

She sank to her knees and stayed there, sobbing in sheer despair, her whole body trembling.

"Mother?" Peter asked. "Didn't the man like us?"

Adela dried her eyes on her sleeve. "No," she said. "He didn't like us, Peter. Come on." Once again she gathered him into her arms. Whoever could the man have been? Out of the North. She was sure he had been wearing a uniform, but it had been no uniform she had ever seen before. She couldn't understand it at all, couldn't understand why he hadn't come for a closer look. They, a woman and a child, could have posed no threat to him. And yet, with his glasses, he would have had to be able to make out that her robe, however crushed and soiled, was of the richest materials. Had he even been an itinerant bandit, he would have come closer to discover what she possessed that might be worth plundering. It was almost as if he had known who she was, and that knowledge had been sufficient to drive him away.

Memory of the horseman dissipated into pain, and she stumbled through the morning toward the still-rising sun, arms and legs, back and shoulders, all a mass of aches, stomach rumbling with hunger, throat now parched with thirst, but afraid to stop even when she splashed through puddles, afraid that if she were to kneel to drink, she would never rise again, until suddenly she heard the stamping of hooves, and raised her head to find herself surrounded by armed horsemen. She gazed at their commander. Lin-tu!

Lin-tu dismounted, to stand before her. "Well, great Princess," he said. "Now does the wheel turn full circle. Or has your wheel turned at all, since the Shan?"

His eyes seemed to coat her with ice. He wanted her to beg, as she had done in Feng's encampment. To offer herself, perhaps, as she had done then. He did not realize that those days were gone forever.

She set Peter on the ground and scooped hair from her face as she stood straight, to return his gaze. "Wheels do not turn for princesses, Lin," she said. "For them, all aspects of life, all changes in fortune, are but as different sides of the same coin."

He gave a brief, almost mocking bow. "Courage to the end, great Princess," he said. "I have no doubt you would sadly disappoint those who hope to hear you scream, should it come to that. Tell me, where is Chang?''

She pointed over her shoulder. "There is an encampment a few miles away. The marshal is there. His men deserted us, and so he killed himself.'' She wondered if she should tell Lin-tu about the mounted man, and decided against it. If he had been alone, he was irrelevant. If he had been the scout for some large body of either bandits or other revolutionaries, then that would be Lin-tu's problem, and possibly even to her advantage; she could gain *no* advantage by alerting him to either possibility.

Lin turned to his second in command. "There is a village marked on the map, not far from here," he said.

"A mile, perhaps, Marshal," the captain said. "To the east.''

"I will go there and camp for the night. You will take half the men, Captain, and visit their encampment of which the princess speaks, and bring me Chang's head. But act with caution; it may be a trap. We will wait for you in that village until tomorrow morning.''

The captain saluted, and rode off, followed by twenty of the forty men who accompanied Lin.

"Now, you, Sergeant," Lin said, "provide a horse for the princess and the boy. She is capable of riding astride.''

One of the soldiers dismounted, to double up with a comrade, and Adela in turn mounted, Peter seated in front of her. She dared not think, dared not even attempt to hope. "Should it come to that," he had said. What had he meant? But what else could his presence mean to her? Was she but waiting until they reached the village? Yet for the moment even apprehensions for the future had to take their places behind needs of the present. "My son is both hungry and thirsty," she said.

"There will be food in the village," Lin-tu told her, but handed Peter his own water bottle. "And are you not thirsty, great Princess?"

"I will drink, if there is sufficient," she said.

"Then drink." He waited while she in turn slaked her thirst, and then signaled his men to resume riding, now also turned toward the sunrise. Actually, it was nearly noon, and almost warm, after all the dampness of the preceding week. The ground steamed, and they rode through a white mist. But not for very long before they saw houses, and then people, staring at the woman and the boy, clearly without knowing who they were, as they were even more thunderstruck by the soldiers and the rifles.

Lin-tu dismounted and faced the village headman. "You have a house?" he demanded.

"Indeed, great lord," the headman said.

"I shall require it for twenty-four hours," Lin told him. "My men will camp here on the street. And we shall need food, and tea, and water. Your people will prepare these things. But first, show me this house." He assisted Peter and then Adela from the saddle.

The headman bowed and hurried before them toward the largest house, or rather, hut, in the village; there were only perhaps a score of buildings all told, while beyond, the cattle were already corraled for the winter, shaggy beasts that stared at the strangers and mooed at each other in concern.

The headman opened his door. "My wife and children," he said, gesturing at the half-dozen people within the house.

"Get them outside," Lin said.

The headman spoke abruptly, and the woman gave

Lin a terrified glance, repeated at Adela, before she gathered her babies in her arms and chivvied the older children in front of her and into the street. Lin stood with his hands on his hips, surveying the one room, the huge double bed which indicated the headman's comparative affluence, the table and chairs. "Hardly fit for a princess," he remarked.

Adela sat at the table; she felt her legs would not support her anymore. "There was no need to force them from their home," she said. "I would have slept in a tent."

"There are things one cannot do in a tent," Lin said, and her head came up in consternation. She had not doubted, from the moment of their meeting, that sooner or later he would seek to make her atone for her betrayal of him. But if he were to take her now, when her nerves no less than her muscles were stretched to the breaking point . . . She gasped with relief as the village women hurried in with plates of rice and pots of tea, great dishes of yogurt.

"There is no meat, great lord," the headman explained anxiously, hovering in the doorway. "Had we but known you were coming, we would have killed an animal."

"It is of no matter," Lin said. "Leave us."

The headman gazed at Adela a last time, and then bowed and withdrew.

"There is food and drink," Lin said. "You will be comfortable here."

Adela stared at him, trying to grasp that he did not, after all, mean to sleep with her. Instead, he seemed about to leave her and Peter alone. Almost she could breathe again. But she still did not understand. "I . . . I thank you," she said.

His eyes gloomed at her. "You have been condemned to death," he said. "There will be no trial. My orders are to return you to Peking, where you and the boy are to be dragged through the streets and publicly beheaded.''

She might have been kicked in the stomach, found herself on her feet, fingers clasped around her throat. ''I have committed no crime,'' she whispered.

''You have committed treason by usurping the throne,'' he told her. ''But even had you not, you are a Ch'ing. That is sufficiently criminal.''

She bit her lip. Once again she simply could not think. But her instincts told her he was not yet finished.

Now he came closer, put out his hand to take her chin and raise her face. ''Such beauty,'' he said. ''I looked upon it once and sought it for my own. And lost it. Perhaps fortunately. Now I think, as you are anyway to die, why not possess you, and possess you, and possess you. Because *you* no longer possess life.''

She could hear herself breathing, such was the anxious rush of air from her lungs. Peter, still seated, looked from one to the other in terror, even if he did not understand what was happening.

''And then I think,'' Lin-tu went on, ''that to possess you even now, great Princess, would be to lose my own soul. But you are too beautiful, and I wanted you too badly, once, to wish to see that beauty exposed to the jeers of the multitude, that head kicked through the dust by laughing boys.'' He released her, went to the door, and there paused. From the wallet he wore on his waist belt he took a long length of silken yellow cord. ''There are rafters.'' He pointed. ''And this is an imperial cord. I give you twenty-four hours to make your peace with your ancestors, great Princess, and end your life. And that of the boy. I will come for you at noon tomorrow. If you are not dangling from that beam by then, I shall spare you nothing, Princess. Remember my words. I shall spare you *nothing.*''

* * *

"May I eat, Mother?" Peter asked. "I am so hungry."

She ladled food onto the plate before him, poured tea.

"Are you not hungry, Mother?" he asked.

"I will eat later," Adela said. And waited while he filled his mouth and chomped happily.

It was warm in the hut; she could feel her clothes beginning to dry. She would, as Lin-tu had said, be comfortable here.

She walked across the room and looked down on the silken cord. Strange, she thought, that I should have lived almost my entire life in this land, with these customs and these requirements, and never seen the cord before. Because, after all, I am only half a princess.

But now she must die like a princess, or suffer like the commonest malefactor, Peter screaming at her side. She sat on the bed, idly watched the fleas jumping as she disturbed them, wondered why she felt no desire to scream, no desire to throw herself on the floor in a paroxysm of despair, no desire even to vomit. Those desires were there, lurking on the edge of her consciousness, but they were kept in check for the moment by an immense tiredness, and exhaustion of the spirit which rapidly overtook and absorbed her physical exhaustion. To have traveled so far, and at such cost, to yet come to this at the end. Tears rolled silently down her cheeks.

"Mother is sad," Peter said, belching. "You are sad for Chang?"

Her head jerked, but Peter did not know that Chang was dead; she did not think he had taken in her conversation with Lin-tu—he had been too frightened. And perhaps he was more accurate than he knew. If his life had been dominated by Chang for the past year, hers had been equally so. Chang had appeared as her evil genius, and if she had known that everything he had done, everything he had *thought* of doing, was horribly wrong, yet had he appealed to her instincts, her belief in her Destiny. So what right did she have to rail against that Destiny now? Following Chang, this ending had always been inevitable.

"Yes," she said. "I am sad for Chang."

"Chang will come back for us," Peter said. "I am so tired, Mother." He gave a yawn and fell asleep, mouth open, breath faintly whistling.

He was the lucky one, she thought. But was it not a stroke of luck for her as well? He was asleep.

She bit her lip and gazed at the cord. She felt that as long as she did not actually pick it up, it could not harm her. Then was she not going to pick it up? Was she going to pin her faith in that oldest and best of American sayings, that while there was life there was hope? And thus be dragged naked through the streets while the crowds jeered and laughed and threw mud and filth at her, and at the end, as Lin had said, the boys kicked her head to and fro like a football? She had even heard of public executions where the victim had never reached the headsman at all. The mob had seen to that, had secured its grisly trophies from a still-breathing corpse.

She was on her feet, heart pounding, sweat rolling down her still-chilled shoulders. If she did not use the cord, and on Peter, she would be a coward, and thus she would die like a coward. But they still had some twenty hours to go. Hours in which he would sleep again, surely. But hours, she knew, in which every second would make it harder than ever to find the courage to end their misery. If she were going to die like a princess, then it had to be now. Peter's death had to be now, at any rate, while he slept and would not even know what was happening to him. Then to kill herself would be simple; she would have absolutely no reason for living.

She stooped and picked up the cord, was faintly surprised to discover that it *was* silk, soft and slippery. It
would scarcely bruise her neck at all as it squeezed the
breath from her lungs. She gasped, as if it were already
doing so, took a step toward the bed and the sleeping
boy, and thought of her father, who had also chosen to
take his own life rather than face humiliation. She wept,
and knelt beside her son, and raised his head to gently
pass the cord around his neck, and checked, as from
outside there came a sudden flurry of hooves and rifle
fire. She turned, panting, while Peter woke and rose to
his knees. "Mother!"

"Sssh," she said, pulling the cord away. "Oh, sssh!"
She listened to shouts and barked commands, but could
not understand what was being said. Yet she knew it was
her Destiny, resolved not yet to let her die. Her lucky
star! She did not care who it was, even as the wildest
hopes raced through her mind: Charlie? Dr. Sun? Even,
in some miraculous fashion, Frank Wynne? Or Chang,
risen from the dead. At this moment she would even be
grateful to see Chang come through that doorway.

She faced the door as it opened, gazed in horror at the
man who stepped inside, smiling at her.

James Osborne!

Lin-tu was at his shoulder, a disarmed and angry Lin-
tu, guarded by . . . Japanese soldiers? She had never
seen a Japanese soldier before in her life, but she knew
these had to be, just as she suddenly knew that the
horseman she had seen that very morning had also been
Japanese.

And now, Osborne? She sat on the bed, waves of
exhaustion sweeping over her.

"This is an act of war," Lin-tu was expostulating.
"You have invaded Chinese territory."

Osborne was still smiling. "How can I invade Chinese territory, Marshal Lin, when I am Chinese myself? I but seek to regain possession of my lawful wife." He stood beside Adela. "The princess *is* my wife, you know, Marshal."

Lin glared at him, while Adela held her breath. "She is a condemned traitor," Lin said.

"By certain warlords known as the Pei Yang clique," Osborne pointed out, "not necessarily by the people of China. And even if she had been condemned by the entire country, could I stand by and see my wife executed?" He took Adela's hand and squeezed it. "As soon as my agents informed me by the telegraph that Tuan Ch'i-jui had finally made up his mind to march on Peking, I knew I would regain her. You may be sure, Marshal Lin, that I yet had a difficult decision to make. Tientsin, or the steppes? But I felt sure that Chang—I knew him well—would flee to the steppes, to retain possession of the princess, rather than to Tientsin, and leave her to gain the safety of an American ship. I gambled, you might say, and moved with my men to the border, and sent my scout to seek, and find. As they did."

"Your men," Lin grumbled. "Japanese soldiers."

"Not entirely," Osborne said. "I have my own people as well. The Japanese were simply to reinforce me, as they still consider the government of Yuan Shih-k'ai to be the rightful one for China. And when I saw you divide your force, Lin, I knew my task was simple."

"You are committing treason," Lin said. "You will die beside your . . . wife."

"I am behaving as a loyal follower of Marshal Yuan," Osborne said with dignity. "As well as a faithful husband and father, in rescuing the marshal's son, who is also my son, and his chief concubine, who is also my wife. We shall take our leave of you now, Marshal

Lin. Find your way back to Peking. Am I not generous? I could have you shot. I *should* have you shot. Instead, I give you a message. Tell Tuan Ch'i-jui and his clique to beware. Tell them that they fight against forces beyond their control. Tell them that when Yuan Shih-k'ai's armies reassemble in the name of his son, they will be supported by the might of the Japanese empire. Tell them these things, that they may shake in their bones and anticipate the hour of their destruction." He pulled Adela to her feet. "Shall we go, my dearest Dela?"

The villagers stared at them as they rode away into the gathering gloom of the evening. Perhaps, Adela thought, they are as bemused as I. Or even Peter. "Mother?" he kept asking. "Where are we going?"

"To safety, little Prince," Osborne said, smiling and slapping him on the shoulder. "But it is a long and arduous journey."

Osborne, in the guise of a knight-errant? Or even a rescuing hero? She could not believe it. If only she could put her head down for twelve hours and sleep, and awaken refreshed and able to comprehend what was going on. "I . . . we owe you our lives," she said.

"As I told Lin, could I stand by and watch my *wife* executed?" he asked.

She bit her lip, but she did not suppose now was the time to remind him that she was not his wife, and could never be his wife—or to demand an annulment. "Where are you taking us?" she asked.

"Far, far away," he said.

"But . . . to Seoul?"

"Why should I wish to return to Seoul? I'm not sure the Japanese would be all that pleased to have me back right now. Oh, they *will* support me, us—when they are absolutely sure we are worth supporting. But they will require proof. No, no, we will leave these good fellows tomorrow morning. They will retire over the Korean border, and we will turn west. For Sinkiang.''

"Sinkiang?'' She just could not comprehend. Sinkiang was the westernmost part of China, the most remote place on earth, which still housed the scattered nomadic tribes of Tartars from which her own ancestors had arisen centuries before. But to get there, she knew, was an immense journey. It meant traversing the length of Mongolia, and *that* meant crossing the infamous Gobi Desert.

"No one will ever find us in Sinkiang," Osborne asserted. "And I have been there before, on missions for Yuan. I happen to know that out there they are still faithful to his memory." He grinned. "Indeed, I doubt they realize he is dead. In Sinkiang we shall raise an army in Prince Yuan Hsu's name. These warlords, this Tuan Ch'i-jui, wishes a civil war? Well, by God, he will have one.''

"Oh, my God," Adela said. "Oh, my *God!*" She reached for his arm. "Mr. Osborne! James!" she begged. "Can't you see, cannot any of you blind, ambitious fools see, that it is all over? Tuan will fall of his own weight. Whoever replaces him will also fall. The Chinese people will have their republic. There is nothing you or I or anyone can do to prevent that. Except die. James, you cannot condemn this little boy to a lifetime of banditry. James, take us to Seoul. Let us get on a ship for the States. Just let us sail away and out of your life. Out of the lives of the Chinese. We shall never trouble any of you again. Please, James.''

He grinned at her. "You would spend the rest of your life in poverty as an ex-princess?" The smile died. "And you would condemn me to a lifetime as a fugitive? That was never meant to be, dearest Dela. Tomorrow we ride for Sinkiang, and so help me God, if you try to escape, I shall have you tied to your horse on your belly.'' He reached across in turn to chuck her under the chin. "There are so many things I want to do to you, and with you, my dearest wife. Isn't it strange how things turn out, that we shall have had to wait more than five years properly to begin our honeymoon?"

"Halt, there," came the cry. "Or we fire into you."

Lin-tu raised his head. Since leaving the village he had been riding in deep thought; his men had been afraid to disturb him, even as the dusk had started to draw in and they might have hoped to make camp.

He was uncertain of his own emotions. He had certainly made a tactical error, born of overconfidence, in dividing his already small force; had he kept his forty men together, Osborne would never have dared risk attacking him. But did he honestly regret that? Had not the sight he had been dreading more than anything else in the world been that of the princess's body dangling from a wooden beam? He had given her that choice only because there *was* another sight he had dreaded even more, that of her kneeling before the headsman.

He loved the girl. Or the woman, as she had become, he had to suppose. He loved her for a variety of reasons, of which her beauty and her sexual emanations were only a part. He loved her for being a part of Constance and for being the girl whose life he had saved eighteen years before. He loved her, he was realizing, almost as a daughter.

Yet he had never doubted that she had to die for the good of China. Because as long as she lived, with her beauty and her royal blood and now her royal son, who was also the son of Yuan Shih-k'ai, she would remain a rallying flag for all those who sought to make China a personal domain. He even had his doubts, had he returned her to Peking, whether Tuan *would* have executed her, or would not have become another Chang, or even another Yuan Shih-k'ai.

Now she was gone. Where? To do what? Only to suffer at the hands of a man like Osborne. A thought that made him angry. And to reappear again one day, the consort of an ambitious general?

Yet he had turned away from her because he had been outnumbered. Now he had been rejoined by his other men, and still he was riding south. And now . . . His men had reined in and were gazing to left and right, aware that they had been ambushed, but unable in the gloom, and surrounded as they were by uneven ground, to ascertain the size of the opposing force. But there *were* no other soldiers this far north.

It was time to throw off his doubts and become once again Lin-tu, the immortal revolutionary, the man who had survived a thousand deaths. He kicked his horse and rode clear of his squadron. "Show yourselves, if you are men," he shouted. "And if you are bandits, beware the wrath of Lin-tu."

Rifle bolts clicked as the men stood up. There were only some twenty of them, he estimated at a quick count. And two officers. But they were well placed to either side, and undoubtedly had his people well covered.

Then he smiled, as even in the semidarkness he recognized the white man. "Charles Baird," he said. "You are a surprising fellow, Colonel Baird. I would have supposed you had fled to the coast by now. Who is this?"

"I am Colonel Chen Fu," Chen told him.

"And what are you doing here?" Lin inquired. "Ah, I am being thoughtless. You seek the princess? You, Colonel Baird, I can understand, even if I do not understand how you come to be permitted this quest. But even less can I understand how you persuaded this foolish fellow to accompany you."

"Because he also seeks the princess," Charlie told him, and pointed, scarce daring to breathe. "What is in that sack?"

Lin grinned, reached into the saddlebag, and pulled out Chang's head, holding it by the hair. "Our mutual enemy."

Charlie gasped with relief.

"And the princess?" Chen asked.

Lin-tu told them what had happened.

"Osborne," Charlie growled. "By Christ, the thought of that rat with his hands on Adela . . ."

"They are not more than twelve hours in front of us," Chen said. "And will undoubtedly stop for the night. If we do *not* stop, we can overtake them by morning."

"You, will pursue Osborne and the Japanese?" Lin demanded.

"Right into Seoul, if we have to," Charlie told him.

"With twenty men?"

"If we have to," Charlie said again. And looked at Lin's troop. "Do not try to stop us, Lin. Through your own incompetence you lost her. Now we will ride behind her."

Lin gazed at him for several seconds, and then grinned again. "You will stand more chance of regaining the princess with sixty men," he remarked.

Charlie frowned at him. "You mean . . ."

"Why not? The thought had already crossed my mind. I do not like being outmaneuvered by the Japanese, any more than by Mr. Osborne. We will ride together, Colonel Baird. What a woman is this princess, to be sure, to have three such men all riding behind her. I wonder if we all seek the same thing of her?" He held up his hand as Charlie would have spoken. "There is an old Chinese saying, Colonel Baird. One must catch one's fish before one can commence to prepare it for the table.'' He signaled his captain. ''Let us see if we cannot turn the tables on those Japanese.''

Another village, another headman, another hut. And another bed. Adela was so exhausted she threw herself across it, eyes flopping shut, Peter at her side. Although they had both slept soundly for several hours the previous night in the Japanese encampment, they had been forced to spend another very long day in the saddle. When she had suggested to Osborne that they make camp earlier, he had shaken his head. ''We have a very long journey in front of us,'' he had reminded her. ''And I am tired of sleeping in tents. I know of a village where we will be welcomed.''

So the three of them, and Osborne's six Chinese, had ridden all day. The Japanese had by now no doubt already crossed the Korean border and were in snug billets, Adela thought regretfully. While she was embarked upon another desperate, exhausting adventure with a man she hated even more than Yuan Shih-k'ai. And feared? She did not think so, physically. She had the measure of James Osborne. She even felt sure she could outthink and outwit him. But only when she had slept and slept and slept, and rested her exhausted muscles, and given herself a chance to think what came next, what could possibly come next, for Peter and herself. Only gaining a friendly seacoast seemed to hold out even the slightest hope of survival— and every step they took into the interior of China made *that* more difficult.

But for the moment, only sleep mattered. And here at last was the village, although the welcome did not seem to be quite as enthusiastic as Osborne had predicted.

''This will do,'' he told the headman. ''Now, I wish a

woman to sleep with the prince, in her house, and care for him. Your wife will do, if she has somewhere other than here to go.''

Adela rolled on her back and sat up. "Peter sleeps with me."

"*I* sleep with you, my dear Dela," Osborne pointed out. "As I am your husband."

She opened her mouth in angry protest. Last night, in the Japanese camp, he had been the perfect gentleman, and had not attempted to enter her tent, even if he had placed a guard on her door. If he was now going to . . .

But he was ignoring her. "You will see to these matters," he was telling the headman. "And to food and drink for my men, fodder for my horses. Or I will tell my people to take your women."

The headman bowed. But he was a bolder headman than the last Adela had encountered—or he was able to count; Osborne had only six men, whereas Lin-tu had commanded twenty. "You will pay for these things, great lord?"

"Pay?" Osborne demanded. "Be thankful I do not burn your village. Feed my men. And care for the boy. Remember that he is a Ch'ing prince and will one day be your emperor. And send in food and sake. No tea, now, sake. Do not shake your head at me. I know you keep the stuff hidden away. Send it in or send me your daughter and I will mount her after I have satisfied my wife, the princess."

The headman bowed and left. His wife scooped the unprotesting Peter from the bed and followed him—the little boy was fast asleep. Adela was too tired to attempt to stop her. And if there was going to be a scene, she did not really want him to be present. That there was going to be a scene, despite her exhaustion, was certain; she had no intention of sharing a bed with James Osborne. "You," she said, sitting down again and then lying down, her eyes closing of their own accord, "are unspeakable. And also a liar. Or do you just *dream*?"

He stood above her, looking down at her, smiling. "What makes you think that?"

Her eyes opened as she frowned in alarmed consternation.

Osborne sat beside her. "It is six years since Yuan had me . . . what shall I say? . . . diminished? Six years is a long time."

Adela rolled away from him, and he caught her arm and rolled her back again. "And for the last three years, as I have felt my powers returning, I have certainly dreamed of you, my dearest Dela."

She was about to be raped by a monster. Suddenly her exhausted mind snapped and she lost her temper, pulled her arm free in an explosion of angry strength, and swung her other hand at him, fingers curled to open his cheek with her nails. He gave a cry of pain and fell away from her, and she rose to her knees, desperately seeking a weapon, and spotting his rifle where he had placed it by the door. She scrambled off the bed as he regained his feet, blood rolling down his cheek. She was ahead of him, running for the gun, when the door opened to admit the headman and four women, carrying food and rice beer, and between her and the weapon. They stared at the two white people in amazement.

"Help me," Adela said. "Please."

"Get out," Osborne snapped. "And stay out."

The headman waved at the door, and the women ran outside.

"Help me," Adela shouted. "Don't leave me . . ." She turned as Osborne seized her shoulder. She tried to hit him again, but his hands had slid down to grasp her arms, and now, as she tried to kick him instead, he lifted her bodily from the floor and threw her on the bed. She hit, lost her breath, gasped and turned, and found him kneeling above her. She swung her fist and he struck her across the face with the flat of his hand. Her head rocked to and fro, and pain tears mingled with those of anger to spurt from her eyes and join the blood dribbling from her cut lips. Osborne dug his fingers into the neck of her robe and ripped; he was an immensely strong man. She tried to bring up her knees, and he slapped her again, and then stood away from her, still ripping her gown, to leave her naked on the bed.

"My wife," he said. "The most beautiful woman in China. How I have waited for *this* moment, my dearest Dela."

She inhaled, tensed her muscles, watched him drop his breeches, and gasped in horror. What had been merely sickening the first time she had looked at it had become unthinkable in its aroused state. She dug her heels into the mattress to push herself up the bed, had her ankles seized and her body jerked flat again. She rolled away from him, but he was on top of her, hands pinning her shoulders to the bed, while he squatted on her thighs. "Why not?" He smiled. "I like it better this way."

She heaved, and attempted to roll, and was thrust so hard into the mattress she thought she would choke, only dimly heard the door opening and Osborne's roar of rage.

"But the scout has come in, General," the man cried. "There are people following us."

The hands slipped from Adela's neck, the weight was lifted from her buttocks. "People?"

"Three score men, it is thought, General," the soldier said, trying not to look at Adela as she rolled on her back and struggled for her breath. "Not two hours away, and commanded by Lin-tu."

"Lin-tu?" Osborne was incredulous.

"A white man also rides with him."

"Charlie," Adela breathed. "Oh, Charlie! It has to be Charlie." She sat up.

Osborne glared at her, and then pointed. "Take this woman," he said. "Take her and tie her to her horse. Prepare to ride." He dug his fingers into Adela's hair, pulled her to her feet. "Baird," he snarled. "And Lin-tu. I promise you this. If they overtake us, I will throw them your *head.*"

This should have been agony, and the most utter humiliation Adela had ever known. She was dragged naked from the hut and placed in the saddle of her horse; her ankles were secured by a rope passed under the animal's belly and pulled tight to keep her in place; her wrists were tied to her reins, which were then led by a soldier. The sun had set and the evening was already very cold; she shivered and her teeth chattered. But those around her were so obviously terrified that they had no time to enjoy their mistreatment of her. Her only fear was for Peter, who screamed in alarm when he saw her and when he also was tied to the saddle of a separate horse. Osborne gave him two resounding slaps. "Shut up, God damn you," he shouted. "Mount. Mount, and ride."

He took her reins from the soldier, himself led her horse. "Lin-tu," he muttered. "How in God's name . . . ? And Baird. By Christ," he shouted, "I shall *crucify* you."

As on the train, his terror was itself terrifying. And as on the train, she was at his mercy. Far more so now than then, because he knew he had no hope of surviving if his pursuers caught up. She could not herself understand what was happening, how Lin-tu and Charlie should be riding together to her rescue, how Charlie had escaped

from Peking at all. But he was coming. Thus she had to
fight to survive, as she had always had to fight to
survive, until he could reach her.

Survive the cold, first. Yet that was less difficult than
she had feared, for every so often Osborne, in another
paroxysm of terrified anger, leaned across and dealt her
a blow across the shoulders with his whip, which was
agonizing but sent the blood coursing through her
arteries. Her principal problem was the exhaustion
which, despite the acute discomfort of her position,
kept sending her into deep sleeps from which she was
afraid she would never awaken, only to be stirred back
to consciousness either by another blow or by Osborne's
repeated exhortations to his men to hurry up.

Yet progress remained slow; if the men themselves
were tired, their horses were even more so.

"Lin-tu," Osborne growled. "By God . . . Hasten,
there. Hasten!" And he hit her again. Yet even he ran
out of energy in time, and she did fall into a deep
slumber during the last two hours before dawn, awoke
with a start at first light, as her horse was brought to a
halt. They had ascended a small hill, and behind them
the rising sun was playing across the plain. She raised
her head, pins and needles hurtling through her hands
and feet, saw Osborne studying through his binoculars
the way they had come, twisted her neck in a desperate
search for Peter, saw him, also still tied to his saddle,
but fast asleep, drooping over the reins, which were held
by one of Osborne's men. She sighed with relief, and
became aware of her thirst, and her discomfort, and the
insects that had attacked her during the night. . . .

"Too close," Osborne said. "Too close," he
moaned. "They are devils from hell. They never *stop.*"
His voice almost broke. "We must fight them here.
Dismount. Take cover. Load your rifles . . ."

"We cannot fight sixty men, General," said one of the soldiers.

"If you run, they will still catch you."

"They will not even follow us," the man said. "Because they do not seek us. They seek you. And the woman. We will leave you now." He smiled. "Give them the woman, and they might let you live."

"You cannot leave me," Osborne shouted. "I am your general. I am the representative of Yuan Shih-k'ai. I am—"

"Yuan Shih-k'ai is dead," the man reminded him. "And you will be also, if you try to prevent us leaving."

You cannot leave *me,* Adela wanted to shout; not alone with this madman. But the men never looked at her, merely mounted and rode away.

"Bastards," Osborne shouted. "Treacherous bastards," he sobbed. His hands suddenly reached for her and she felt her bonds slip away, and he held her thighs and pulled her from the horse. She was so cold and stiff and aching that she could not stand, but fell to her knees.

"Get up," he snarled, pulling her hair to raise her. She moaned with pain and reached her feet, leaning against him. "I'll ride straight through them," Osborne said. "By God I will. With you in front of me, they'll not dare stop me. Come on, get up." He lifted her onto his horse, swung into the saddle behind her.

"Mother!" Peter wailed, waking up.

"You can't leave him," she gasped.

"Goddamned brat," Osborne said. "We'll settle *his* ambitions." He pulled the revolver from his belt.

"No!" Adela screamed, and dug backward with her elbows. The revolver exploded harmlessly, and she twisted her body to strike at him again, summoning energy from the very depths of her exhausted soul. He gasped as he lost his balance and fell from the horse, the revolver flying from his hand. Adela jumped down behind him, missed her footing, and went sprawling, but landed next to the gun. She rose to her knees, holding it in both hands, as she had on that never-to-be forgotten evening on the sampan outside Tientsin.

Osborne was also on his knees, about twelve feet away from her. He looked left and right, and only then realized that she had the weapon. "Dela," he cried. "No, Dela, you are my *wife*!"

Adela squeezed the trigger five times.

A coat was thrown over her, the revolver was gently taken from her grasp. "Peter . . ." she whispered.

"The boy is all right," Chen Fu told her.

"Chen? But . . ." She blinked at Charlie.

"What you might call a band of brothers," he said with a wry smile.

She licked her lips. "Osborne . . ."

"You hit him four times, great Princess," Lin-tu said. "And each one would have killed him."

Tears rolled down her cheeks. "*You* came back," she said. "To help *me*?"

"I came back," Lin-tu said, "because I have a duty to perform."

Her head jerked, as Chen and Charlie both tensed, and looked right and left. But they were outnumbered two to one by Lin's men.

Lin smiled. "Did you suppose I came with you out of love for the princess, Colonel Baird? Am I not Lin-tu, destroyer of kings? And queens? And even princes and princesses?"

"Oh, my God," Adela whispered. "Oh, my God!" She looked from one to the other of the two men in her life, who were staring at each other, trying to decide, by mental telepathy, what they were going to do. She grasped both their hands. She did not want them to die attempting to save her. But *she* did not want to die, either.

Lin-tu holstered his revolver, signaled to his men. "You *were* right, Colonel Baird. I did come with you, out of love for the princess. If I did have a duty, in that I was sent to secure her, I have decided my greater duty is to let such courage free. Once I thought you were too beautiful to live, great Princess. Now I have realized that you are too beautiful to die before your time. I can offer you nothing better than flight. Should you go south, never approaching the coast, you will eventually come to the Ta Shan, and thence Canton. And thence even our old friend Dr. Sun, if he is still there. It is a long and arduous journey, and within a few weeks winter will be upon us. Who knows, perhaps I am again condemning you to death, great Princess. But if you have courage, and if these lovers of yours have courage, you will succeed."

He turned away.

"Lin," she said. "Thank you."

He half-turned his head. "I shall not look upon your face again, great Princess," he said. "For both of our sakes, see that it is so." He mounted, led his men into the morning.

"In a few weeks," Lin had said, "winter will be upon you."

There was already cold such as Adela had never known; she rode huddled in a borrowed uniform, Peter often clutched in her arms for mutual warmth, while her horse picked its way through the snow, and her breath turned to ice before her nostrils. At night all twenty-four of them huddled around their campfire, and during

the days they were often less concerned with following a
direction than the occasional spoor of living creatures
they found, in their search for food.

Yet it was a happy time. A happier time than Adela
could ever recall. She never doubted their survival.
Apart from the presence of Chen and Charlie, both
experienced guerrilla soldiers, adept at living off the
most empty land, she had never seen twenty such men as
followed Chen. They were young, tough, hard-bitten,
utterly devoted to their equally young sergeant, a
stocky, grim man no older than herself, named Mao
Tse-tung. But Mao in turn was utterly devoted to Chen.
It was amazing to think that these men were her natural
enemies. They abhorred the Ch'ing and everything to do
with either monarchy or warlord dictatorship. They
were not even for Dr. Sun and the Kuomintang. They
dreamed of some abstract form of government that
would bring justice and prosperity to all Chinese.
Amazing, but no longer disturbing. Because she had
sought the same, and still possessed the ideal. Even if
she knew for certain it was not the Destiny of Adela
Wynne to bring it about. It had never been the Destiny
of Adela Wynne. By her birth and her beauty she had
become caught up in an almost primeval upheaval of
hatred and ambition; by her courage and her beauty and
the love they inspired in men, she was going to survive
even her mad adventure. She would be content simply
with that.

But who could tell, she thought to herself, during
their interminable campfire discussions, that such an
achievement might not well be the Destiny of Chen Fu.
Or even so lowly a person as Sergeant Mao, in this
topsy-turvy world.

It was a happy time, too, because there were no
traumas. They risked death every day as they traversed
icy slopes or faced off starving bandits, and they risked

death in a general way from cold and starvation. But these were incidental. For the first time in her life she had become a human being, pure and simple. She slept each night huddled for warmth between Charlie and Chen, and neither attempted to touch her. Common sense told her she could thank the cold for this; it was simply not practical to remove a single article of clothing. But she also believed, because she wished to believe, that there was an unspoken bond between the two men, which by mutual agreement left the question of possession of her to some future time, and therefore left her own personal decision to that future time as well.

And it was a happy time *because* of the lurking sadness, for the choice would *have* to be made. Between the father of her son, the most dynamic lover she had ever known, but a man already engaged in following a personal star to which she would also have to become attached, whatever the hardships and dangers that would necessarily lie ahead, for the rest of her life—and a man she had known *all* of her life, whose love for her had been constant, she now knew, all of her life, and who for all his faults possessed depths of courage and stamina and determination such as she had seen in few men.

It was a decision that came upon her sooner than she had expected it, early in 1918, when she awoke one morning to find the stream by which they had camped for the night thawed and sparkling as it rushed down the hillside. She got up, stood beside it, and felt that she could breathe, for the first time in six months, without hurting her lungs.

"Spring," Chen Fu said behind her. "It is the most glorious time of the year." He was fully equipped, early as it was, and his men were saddling their horses. Now he pointed. "Beyond those hills is the valley that contains the headwaters of the Pearl River. It leads into Canton.''

"Have we arrived there already, Chen? Really and truly?"

"You have arrived there, great Princess," he said. "You and Baird and the boy. My men and I will leave you here and ride north. We have much to do."

"But . . . you only came with us, all this way, to protect us?"

"Should I not wish to protect my son?" he asked. "And his mother?"

"But, Chen . . . he is *your* son."

Chen shook his head. "He is *your* son, great Princess. I can offer him nothing but hardship and violence and probable death. I can offer you nothing better than that, either. Thus I offer you nothing. Your future lies in the United States, with Baird. And that is my son's future, also."

"And you will just ride away?"

He smiled and kissed her on the forehead. "I am bold enough to think that, before I die, I also have a future, here in China. And for China." He walked to his horse, where Mao Tse-tung and his men were already waiting.

"An epic tale," Sun Yat-sen observed, pouring tea. "To cross the breadth of China in winter . . . and then you say the spring floods held you up another two months, after Colonel Chen left you? I truly wonder you survived."

Charles Baird smiled grimly. "It was country I had learned to know well under your command, Dr. Sun. And that of Lin-tu."

"Ah," Sun said. "I had forgotten." He gazed at Adela. "There are still those among my people who would execute you, great Princess. They are unable to differentiate between you and Chang, and you and

Yuan. Perhaps even between you and this Tuan Ch'i-jui. They know that although I have set up a republican government here in Canton, and attempt to rule South China according to the laws of democracy, Tuan is every day securing his hold upon the North. China has been divided before, but never for very long, history tells us. Soon the warlords must rule the entire country, or the Kuomintang must do so. It will be a great and bloody conflict, which may last for years. For the rest of my life perhaps. But I do not shrink from the prospect, because I am sure of eventual victory."

"But . . ." Adela was suddenly breathless. "Will the Japanese not support Tuan, if he concedes Manchuria?"

"Very probably they will," Sun agreed. "But we have been promised the support of this new government in Russia, this Lenin. And . . ." He glanced at Chiang Chung-cheng, silent as always at his side. "We do not lack resources here at home. Not you, Charles Baird," he said, as Charlie would have spoken. "You have played your part, and you now have a greater task, that of caring for the princess. Because you also have played your part, great Princess, and unlike my people, I believe that you know that. I once offered you a pension to retire from China. This offer I make to you again, together with safe conduct to Hong Kong, and a passage thence to San Francisco. I make these offers freely, Miss Wynne, but I make them to you *as* Miss Wynne, not as the great princess. I make them on condition that you never return to China."

"I will give you my word on that," Adela said.

"Can I believe your word?"

"Yes," she said, "because you do me wrong to call me Miss Wynne. As soon as we reach Hong Kong I shall become Mrs. Baird. But I am that already, before God. I bear Charlie's child." Sun raised his eyebrows, and she smiled. "Well," she said, "as we told you, we were delayed by floods for two months after Chen had left us."

Never return to China. Adela stood between Charlie and Peter at the rail of the ship, and watched the hills of Hong Kong sink into the distance. Tomorrow they would sight the hills of Formosa, still in Japanese hands. A symbol of the thought and ambitions that had disturbed her when she had first seen these hills seven years ago. Because it was seven years ago that her adventure had really begun, as she had stepped off the ship in Hong Kong, beside Constance, and come face to face with James Osborne. Seven years that seemed an eternity when looked back upon.

Never return to China. She had given her word, and she meant to keep it. Her future lay with Charlie, and Constance and Frank, in America, free, thanks to Sun's generosity, from fear and free from want. But what of the little boy standing beside her and also staring at the distant hills; what would he think of never seeing his father, following a dream in the hills beyond Peking? Even her unborn child, as American by conception as it was possible to be, might hold an opinion of never visiting the land from which he would certainly draw his instincts and his character.

Never return to China, she thought as she nestled into Charlie's arms. She was only twenty-three years old.

Never is a very long time.

Passionate Historical Romances from SIGNET

(0451)

- ☐ **JOURNEY TO DESIRE** by Helene Thornton. (130480—$2.95)*
- ☐ **PASSIONATE EXILE** by Helene Thornton. (127560—$2.95)*
- ☐ **CHEYENNE STAR** by Susannah Lehigh. (128591—$2.95)*
- ☐ **WINTER MASQUERADE** by Kathleen Maxwell. (129547—$2.95)*
- ☐ **THE DEVIL'S HEART** by Kathleen Maxwell. (124723—$2.95)*
- ☐ **DRAGON FLOWER** by Alyssa Welks. (128044—$2.95)*
- ☐ **CHANDRA** by Catherine Coulter. (126726—$2.95)*
- ☐ **RAGE TO LOVE** by Maggie Osborne. (126033—$2.95)*
- ☐ **ENCHANTED NIGHTS** by Julia Grice. (128974—$2.95)*
- ☐ **SEASON OF DESIRE** by Julia Grice. (125495—$2.95)*
- ☐ **KIMBERLEY FLAME** by Julia Grice. (124375—$3.50)*
- ☐ **PASSION'S REBEL** by Kay Cameron. (125037—$2.95)*

*Prices slightly higher in Canada

**Buy them at your local
bookstore or use coupon
on next page for ordering.**

Sensational Reading from SIGNET

Romantic Fiction from SIGNET

*Prices slightly higher in Canada
†Not available in Canada

**Buy them at your local
bookstore or use coupon
on next page for ordering.**

Fabulous Fiction by June Lund Shiplett from SIGNET